BREAKING CONVICTION

Conviction Series Book Three

GREER RIVERS

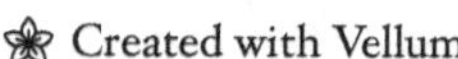 Created with Vellum

BREAKING CONVICTION

Snake

The enemy is two steps ahead.
Every time we think we have answers,
We're left with only more questions.
I've made mistakes,
Hunted the wrong villains,
And now innocents are paying the price.
Naomi's found herself in the middle of it all.
She can't know how broken I am,
The rage that I keep buried inside,
Or that my past has become her nightmare.
Naomi fears she's a damsel trapped by her villain,
But she's my queen.
And it's time she breaks free.

Naomi

The villain has me trapped.
Every time I think I can escape,
The chains strengthen and my hope fades.
I've made mistakes,
Trusted the wrong man,
And now I'm paying the price.
Snake wants me to run away from it all.
He doesn't know how caged I am,
The fears that keep me frozen in place.
Or that my dream has become my nightmare.
Snake worries he's a monster ruined by his past,
But he's my knight.
And it's time I break free.

A NOTE FROM THE AUTHOR

Breaking Conviction is a small town, protective hero romantic suspense with legal, military, and mature themes. It is the third in the Conviction series of interconnected standalones, all of which contribute to an overarching plot, but no cliffhanger for the couple in their respective story. Please consider reading this series in order for best enjoyment. HEA guaranteed.

This series takes place in Ashland County, a small, fictional, southern county somewhere in the mountains of the Carolinas. Ashland County is full of steam and legal intrigue, so some characters may appear in other stories written in the same universe.

The Conviction series should only be read by mature readers (18+) and contains sexually explicit scenes, along with descriptions of human trafficking, drugs, strong language, and physical, sexual, and domestic violence.

Protect your heart, friends. Reader discretion is advised.

To survivors who are able to leave:
Carve your line in stone.

To those who have to stay:
You are brave.
You are strong.
You are unbreakable.

PROLOGUE

"Mommy, is he still followin' us?"

Thea's timid whisper battered into Naomi's heart, the pain in her chest somehow worse than the wounds swelling on her face. She glanced in the rearview mirror to see her four-year-old daughter trying her damnedest to see out her window and the back windshield.

Naomi searched the road behind them, but her fiancé's white Corolla was nowhere in sight. She'd been circling the women's shelter for what felt like hours, but it couldn't have been more than thirty minutes and she hadn't seen him in the past few turns. She'd called the shelter to tell them she was coming, but she needed to throw him off the scent first. She knew all the back alleys and shortcuts in Ashland County's small city center. It wasn't the first time she'd sought out Sasha Saves.

Naomi found a covert flyer in a diner bathroom on her lunch break a few days ago. She'd checked out the center's website afterward, but got spooked when her fiancé made one of his impromptu visits at work. Thankfully, the site had instructed her to press the "Escape" button twice to quickly change the screen, but she'd been too scared to research on the computer again after that. Ever since then, she'd used her lunch hour to scout

out the thrift store that was supposedly a front for the crisis center. She'd been trying to muster up the courage to go inside, to convince herself that it was time, that she was finally done with him.

It'd been months since his last blowup, but last week Dean slammed her into the driver's side of his Corolla hard enough to cause a dent. She'd pretended to shake it off at the time, even though she could tell something inside him was brewing. Of course, he'd been nicer after that, but for once, instead of basking in his overcompensating kindness, she'd used his leniency to her advantage to scope out possible means of escape.

Dean had been a security supervisor for a global tech company for a while, but was more stressed than usual at work lately, more liable to fly off the handle. The way he'd shoved her days earlier was an escalation they hadn't had in months, and Naomi had known it was only a matter of time before his mood took another nosedive. Unfortunately, that morning had proved her right.

Naomi glanced to the back seat again. She wasn't sure how Thea even knew her father was following them, but kids were perceptive like that sometimes.

After a painful swallow, Naomi answered despite her sore throat. "I-I think your daddy's gone to work, now, baby. You don't need to worry 'bout him, 'kay? Everything's gonna be just fine, T."

Her words came out as a hoarse whisper and hazel-green eyes brimming with tears and childlike understanding met hers. One leaked down her sweet baby girl's round alabaster cheek as she blinked back at Naomi and nodded.

Naomi tore her focus away from the droplet of emotion, afraid of what she'd do if she kept witnessing the emotional toil her relationship was having on Thea. She couldn't go back on her resolve. Not this time. Whenever Dean took his stress out on her, her usual course of action meant hiding in shame in her bedroom and licking her wounds. After that morning, she didn't know how long she was gonna last if she kept that up.

Naomi wished she could explain the situation to Thea. But what could she possibly say? How did she explain that the man who was supposed to be the shining knight in her daughter's fairy tales was the monster in her own?

She'd already called out of work for the day, and judging by the way her swollen eyes burned every time she tried to blink, Naomi would probably have to call out the rest of the week too.

Her boss would understand, or at least she wouldn't question it. Gail Haynesworth had enough to deal with as CEO of Charitable Technologies International, the same company Dean worked security for. As her assistant, as long as Naomi was connected to her laptop and phone at all times, Gail didn't pry. Mediating two company employees in a relationship would be messy and well beneath her pay grade.

A honk brought Naomi's focus back to the road and she slammed on the brakes. She'd almost run into the car in front of her, totally missing that the light was red. At least, Naomi assumed from all the stopped cars that the light must be red. Her eyelids were so swollen behind her sunglasses that she could hardly see.

No more playin'. It's time to finally get help.

Deciding to suck it up once and for all and bare the secrets that scarred her inside and out, Naomi searched the street for an open parking space, miraculously finding one just behind the pale nondescript building.

Perfect.

As soon as she pulled into the available spot, between a light purple Chevy Spark and a black Ford truck, Naomi leaned her forehead against the steering wheel, inhaling and exhaling to center herself.

She was going to do it. *Really* do it this time. Come clean with someone about what went on behind closed doors. The attacks had no rhyme or reason now and she needed to get out.

Just that morning, they'd both been getting ready to leave for work, Thea for preschool, and it'd only taken one sassy comment and he'd been spittin' mad.

The first punch had taken her by surprise. He'd never hit her in the face before and she'd been so disoriented she hadn't even registered what happened afterward until he started choking her. Something about that, in particular, set off alarm bells in her head that narrowed her focus to the moment and she'd been able to scramble away.

But the most terrifying part of the argument was the look of horror on Dean's face. His lightly tanned skin had turned a sickly pale as he stared at his own hands, as if what he'd done to her was their fault instead of his. As if in that moment he'd had no agency over his emotions or decisions.

The apologies he'd laid at her feet had sounded sincere, but fuckall to apologies. At this point, she'd just filed it away with all his others. His shock and remorse over his own actions had given her no comfort. It meant he'd lose control again and now neither of them knew what he was capable of. The thought made her feel dizzy. Or maybe that was the pounding in her head.

Dean was the man she'd said yes to marrying. At the time, she'd convinced herself that the father of her child was supposed to be the love of her life. That's what she'd been taught by her parents, at least.

Too bad it'd never been that way with Dean. Their relationship was more about the life she yearned for, rather than the life she was living. It was devastating to think she'd been suffering for a dream. But it'd be soul-crushing—and judging from that morning, life-threatening—to stay in a relationship that barely survived on false apologies and broken promises.

Her phone vibrated in her pocket for the hundredth time and Naomi took it out to finally check the messages there. Twenty-seven calls and voice messages, and forty-three text messages, all from Dean Jones in the couple of hours since she'd lost him while driving.

She thumbed through them all, opting not to listen to the voice messages and barely registering the text messages until the last.

Dean: I have to go to work. Please be there when I come home. I'll go to therapy this time, I promise. I'm so sorry sweets. Please forgive me. Know I love you.

She cringed at the apology and the god-awful nickname that came with it, but even still, hope slithered its way into Naomi's soul.

Therapy. This was a good thing. He'd never offered that before. Maybe... maybe that would help.

Naomi lifted her head to see the pale brick building. Inside was the Sasha Saves crisis center, her safe haven. But her heart lodged in her throat at the thought of opening the doors to her defenses and spilling her secrets for everyone to see. Once she did, the path would be set for her and she'd have to see it through, ending life as she knew it. Ending the dream of a happy family, just like the one she grew up in and craved again. Ending any possibility of a fairy tale of her own.

She was about to break free, so why did she feel more trapped than ever?

CHAPTER ONE

Getting treated in the Sasha Saves clinic went by in a blur, both literally and the time she spent there. When Naomi finally gathered the courage to go inside, her eyes were so swollen she could barely see. Thankfully, she'd been escorted through the thrift store to the medical room by the nonprofit's manager, Nora, a chatterbox who talked like Twitter and was even smaller than Naomi's five feet, two inches.

Each moment that passed, Naomi couldn't shake the feeling that her body was acting on autopilot. It was the oddest sensation, watching from outside her body, and she wondered briefly whether she'd been concussed. But no... this felt emotional, maybe even mental, not physical. A break from the present. She didn't hate the numbness.

Nora asked questions. The clinic medic, a giant named *Devil* of all things, gave her ice and cleansed her wounds with surprising gentleness for a man with his size and name. Thea screeched at the top of her lungs. It was chaos, but she barely registered it.

On the outside, she was doing just fine answering questions and going through the motions. Inside, she was still in shock that she was in a fucking domestic violence clinic.

How did I let this happen? What am I doing here?

Thea's little body clutching against Naomi's legs finally broke down the courage she'd shored up in the car.

Maybe that's why she lied.

"Can you tell me what happened? Who did this to you?"

The pretty blonde who'd taken Nora's place, Ellie, snapped Naomi back into a conscious state of awareness. She was only a few hours into her attempt to get help for the first time and already she hated *everything*. That stupid question, the kind young woman asking the stupid question, her disaster of a fiancé for putting her into this situation.

At least Thea had finally calmed down and sat on a beanbag in the corner of the room, eyes glued to an iPad. Unfortunately, her screeches still played on repeat in Naomi's head, drowning out reason.

"Bike accident."

Lie... Lie. Lie. Lie. Please see that I'm lying.

Damn it all, she might've hated everything at that moment, but what she hated most was herself. She had this chance to finally regain control over her life and here she was, *wasting* it.

Why the hell can't I tell her the truth?

In absolutely no world would anyone believe that her obvious black eyes and fingerprint bruises on her neck were due to a fucking *bike accident*. Like... what the actual fuck was she think-ing? The main character in the horror movie she was watching was making a grave mistake, and the only thing Naomi could do was internally shout at the screen.

At this point, she just wanted to get the extra-strength ibuprofen and leave. Her head was pounding so hard she seri-ously considered skipping the medicine and instead taking Devil's pen and stabbing it into her temple to relieve the pres-sure inside.

Ellie was obviously trying her best to convince her to open up, and honest to God if she was going to share her fears and burdens with anyone it'd be this angel in front of her, but Devil didn't seem to want to let it go.

"Numerous contusions... petechial hemorrhaging... lacerations... closed fist... swelling... orbital areas..."

Each word another punch right to her chest. She desperately wanted to scream the truth, but whoever was in control had apparently decided to waste everyone's time, and once again, the words bubbled up without her permission.

"It was an *accident*."

Ellie tried to reason with her, but Naomi was on a self-destructive roll and she argued back again, coming up with even more nonsense for the bullshit story.

"Thea and I were ridin' our bikes and... uh... hers swerved into mine. I crashed onto the ground." She hated the way her voice lilted up at the end, like she was questioning herself. But the more they pushed, the more she instinctively felt the need to shove back.

An indecipherable look flashed over the giant's face before he spoke, his large hand scrubbing his short strawberry blond beard. "You have the opportunity to get help for you and your daughter, don't you want to take it?"

There wasn't any judgment in his tone, only concern, but the words set off a boiling hot rage. It burned underneath her skin, as if every emotion she kept hidden from Dean finally had a chance to explode in this controlled environment, despite the fact these people didn't deserve it.

Even knowing on some level he was just doing his job, just trying to do what's best for everyone, fear of the consequences, lack of control, and instinct to protect her life as she knew it, took over.

"Are you sayin' I'm a bad mother?"

"Absolutely not, Naomi. We don't think that." Ellie's eyes were wide and earnest as she answered, but only a Band-Aid over the wounds these people weren't responsible for. "If your injuries need to come from a bike accident, then that's where they're from."

If my injuries need to come from a bike accident...

With one simple sentence, Ellie told Naomi they knew she was full of shit, but that they were trusting her to make her own decisions. The weight of her situation was lifted by the gravity of that freedom and for the first time in years, the tightness in her chest loosened and she didn't feel like she was suffocating.

They weren't going to force her to come clean. According to Ellie, they weren't even going to report it as long as Thea was safe.

For once, in a twisted way, Naomi had power over the situation. This clinic was giving her the opportunity to save herself with their assistance when she was ready, and the freedom of choice to decide all on her own when that would be.

Because what if this was Dean's wake-up call? It was certainly hers and that alarm was motivating her to seek options. Would that morning be the last time he put his hands on her? Maybe they could finally be the family they were supposed to be for Thea.

Sure, Naomi wouldn't have the love for Dean that her parents showed for one another before her daddy died. That ship had long since sailed on the stormy seas that had been their relationship. But if he fixed himself, she could make do. Especially for Thea. T deserved to have her father. No matter what Dean had done to Naomi, he'd still been good to Thea. Not great, but... good.

A crash at the medical room door zapped every nerve ending, setting fire to Naomi's flight response until it registered that the others in the room had relaxed.

She swiveled her head and even in her half-blurred vision, she could tell the intruder was handsome—no, freaking *gorgeous*. He had navy blue hair and silver streaks, dyed so naturally that it looked like he'd been born with it, and carried boxes—of wires, maybe?—in front of him like it was nothing. His tight black

Henley shirt accentuated the corded muscles in his arms and the black ink of his tatted fingers and neck.

I wonder what else is tatted...

Moisture pooled in her mouth and Naomi cursed herself for honest to God drooling over a man. In a domestic violence shelter, for crying out loud. But truly, who could blame her? She'd take any distraction she could get to avoid thinking about the pain still radiating through her body and why she sat on a patient's examination table.

Plus, she'd always been a total sucker for tattoos. Dean's were half the reason she'd fallen into his bed just before her junior year of college. The other half had been equal parts sophomore recklessness and cheap bar tequila. She'd *thought* she'd learned her lesson in both. Good Lord knows she'd never had a lick of that devil water since, but here she was pining over another man pretty much solely on his ink.

Naomi blinked back her stare and moved her gaze up to take in more than just the man's muscular body to see his pale face blushing beet red all the way from his neck to his black rectangular glasses. He sure knew how to rock the whole tatted Clark Kent vibe, but from his kind eyes, she wondered if he even knew how much his presence commanded the room. Naomi was drawn to those piercing baby blues... until she realized he was consciously *refusing* to look at her.

Devil huffed. "Snake, I know you're not used to coming to Sasha Saves, but you can't barge in like that."

Snake? His name is literally Snake? For the love of God, who is naming these people?

He had yet to look at her and she didn't understand the mix of feelings roiling in her belly at that realization. Was it frustration? Disappointment? Maybe Dean had hit her harder than she thought, because her emotions were either nonexistent or all over the damn place and she was sick of the roller coaster.

"I, uh, I know. I'm sorry." Snake's baritone soothed her irritation... which the realization, of course, made her irritated all over again. She was about to open her mouth to interrupt, but her breath hitched the moment his bright blue eyes met hers. "I'm here to upgrade the security for the pla—*shit*."

The twisted look of disgust on Snake's face concentrated all her contradictory and confusing emotions into one unmistakable feeling.

Shame.

CHAPTER TWO

Shit. Shit. Shit. Shit.

The words shouted much louder in Wes's mind than the whispered curse that had just escaped his mouth. A dark auburn-haired woman sat on the examination table, and Wes couldn't peel his eyes away. Her face may have been shadowed in swelling and black and blue bruises, but the disheartened—no *ashamed*—look there was clear as day.

Why the fuck did I open my damn mouth?

Every neuron fired off synapses in his brain, searching for a solution for making this poor woman feel shitty with just a single word. A rewind button to prevent the horror he knew was written all over his face, or hell, even a control+alt+delete sequence, erasing him from the room altogether would be better than standing there like an idiot while she suffered internally.

"Hey, look what I got."

Bright red curls entered the bottom of his vision just before an iPad was shoved into his stomach. Wes caught the tablet and after somehow managing to balance the boxes with his other hand, he looked down to see the world's cutest kid. She had the toothiest grin on her round pale face, hazel-green eyes, and what had to be a princess dress to match.

With the red tint in the woman's hair, he figured she must be the girl's mother, and found himself wondering whether they looked alike before he realized the child was staring at him expectantly.

Wes examined the iPad to see a paused animated movie of a young woman with fire red hair, just like the little girl. "Oh, wow." He set his boxes to the side of the room and turned back to crouch to her level. The corners of his lips lifted and matched hers as she pointed to the screen.

"It's Merida, from *Brave*. You hafta come watch." She pulled the long sleeve of his Henley before her mother interrupted.

"Thea, baby, don't be rude." The woman's voice came out as a rasp and Wes swallowed to make the phantom pain in his throat go away. But he couldn't cool the electric hot anger filling his veins. He knew what caused that type of vocal injury all too well. Whatever son of a bitch strangled her better fucking pay. "What if he doesn't wanna watch the show? He has things to do."

She was right, he did have things to do. He was the glorified IT guy for the nonprofit, granted, one who could kill a man in under six seconds with his keyboard wielding hands... maybe even with said keyboard. His current task was nothing pressing, just a little tune-up on the already well-oiled machine that was Sasha Saves security system. And when a child invited you to watch a movie, you watched the damn movie.

"Sorry," the girl mumbled obediently. "You hafta come watch... if you wanna."

There officially had never been a cuter kid.

New mission: 1. Make this kid smile more. 2. Make her mom worry less.

He had a feeling accomplishing one goal would achieve the other, and it was the least he could do after making the woman feel embarrassed.

"I think I have some time," he answered. "As long as it's okay with your mom. Um..." He looked to the woman for her approval, resisting the urge to outwardly cringe again at her injuries. Instead, he channeled the rage he'd harbored since childhood into his tightened fists and tipped his head in Thea's direction with the iPad in his hand. "Is this alright?"

At her slow nod, the kid shined a toothy grin at them both and tugged him to a beanbag in the corner, instructing him to sit down beside her while the little queen took her throne.

"We're gonna watch Merida now."

"Sounds good." He chuckled. Wes had every intention of looking like he was going to watch the movie, while also eavesdropping on the grown-up conversation around him. He didn't know why it was so important for him to know the woman's story, only that the need to help in some way was overwhelming.

"That's so strange," the mom's whisper grated against his ears. "She's never taken to anyone like that. Not even her—" She cut off her words with what sounded to him like a feigned cough, as if she was preventing herself from finishing the sentence. But with her injured throat, it turned very real quickly and the painful hacking made him see red.

"You sit by me? 'Kay?" Thea stole his attention as she patted the floor beside the small beanbag. "Closer, else you can't see the movie." Her command had him grinning as he did what he was told. She had all the authority of a CEO tempered by her adorable high-pitched voice.

"You're a bossy little thing, aren't you?"

She whipped her head at him and scrunched her nose while pursing her lips. "Mommy says I ain't bossy, I'm a boss."

Wes worked his mouth to keep from laughing at the sass rolling off her, since she was obviously very serious on the subject.

"A boss, huh?"

She nodded once with conviction, as if it was information he should already know. "Yup, I'm a boss *and* a princess. Just like Merida."

"Fair enough. Well, what should I call you, then? Your name's Thea, right?"

She nodded. "Mommy calls me all kinds of things, Thea... T... Theresa Jane Ward." She lowered her voice to a whisper, "but that one's only when she's mad."

"Hm..." He rubbed his chin to make it seem like he was choosing. "That's a lot to pick from. What about 'Boss Lady?'" She wrinkled her nose and he decided to try again. "Princess?" he asked, and her lips pursed in thought.

"Which one is better?" she finally asked with a furrowed brow.

He chuckled and draped his arms over his bent knees. "Now that, I don't know. But officially, you're the boss *and* the princess. The way I see it, you can be anything you want."

She seemed to seriously think over his words before finally nodding with a small smile. "I like princess best. Merida's a princess, too, and she can shoot a bow and arrow."

He chuckled back and held out his hand. "I like that reasoning. Well, people call me by lots of names, but you can call me Wes."

She tilted her head at the gesture, analyzing it before gripping to shake, just barely able to wrap around two of his fingers.

"Nice to meet you, Wes. I am Thea and I am four." She dropped her hand and held up the other with four fingers. Her deliberate delivery was laced with a touch of excitement, as if she'd practiced all her life to introduce herself and now that she'd finally gotten the chance, she didn't want to screw it up. Hell, she was only four, maybe that's exactly what she was doing.

"Good job, *Princess* Thea." There was a flash of surprise in her widened eyes right before she preened as Wes continued on. "It is very nice to meet you. Now... what're we watching?"

She giggled and began to chirp away about her "favoritest movie ever," even though she "only liked the parts without the bear." Wes made sure to listen to every word, but he also aimed his hearing to her mother as well.

Years of being in charge of communications and intelligence made it easy to pick out different conversations and acquire necessary information from multiple sources simultaneously. First it'd been with the Night Stalkers in the Army, then the clandestine paramilitary group MF7, and now at the private security firm, BlackStone Securities. He'd never gotten the opportunity to listen to an overview of a Pixar film, though.

There was a knock on the door before a lyrical voice called out. "It's Nora! And I brought backup." A whirlwind of dyed gray hair on the woman the size of Tinkerbell entered the room, followed by Jules, the victims' rights attorney for Sasha Saves. Despite having a noticeable baby bump, the tall woman was still sharply dressed, all the way down to red sky-high heels.

Wes wasn't there often, but he knew the drill. Jules would speak to the woman about her options—both legal and otherwise—and hopefully, the woman would decide to use Sasha Saves's services. After all, the nonprofit had a stellar attorney backing her, and she'd be protected by the full force of Black-Stone Securities.

His team was heavily involved with Sasha Saves as a pro bono security service. Not only did Wes help out, but one of Wes's team members, Jason Stone, or Jaybird, as they called him, was Jules's fiancé and Ellie's big brother. Hell, Devil volunteered his services as a medic and he was a member of the BlackStone Crew as well.

So yeah, she'd be protected by the best, to the best of their ability. Once Jules explained that to her and judging by the woman's injuries, surely she'd use the clinic's resources. Especially since she had a little one to think about.

"I wanna go home now." The woman—he thought he'd heard Nora call her 'Naomi'—sighed, sounding depleted. "There's nothin' to talk about—"

The words entered Wes's mind, rustling up memories he'd tamped down for decades and he resisted the urge to groan in frustration.

"Yeah, yeah. I hear ya." Nora shrugged before seemingly looking at Devil's clipboard of notes. "Bike accident, hm?"

Fuck. She's going back to the bastard.

Wes refused to listen to any more. Paying attention to a woman throwing her life away for *'love'* would just piss him off.

After a moment of focusing on Thea's chatter, the room grew quieter and he perked up at the mention of his call sign in Naomi's hoarse voice.

"...Snake, right? He can stay. So long as we whisper. Thea looks so... carefree, right now. I want her to keep that feelin' for a little while longer."

Why did the way Naomi said that, as if she was both grateful and heartbroken, make his own chest squeeze with tightness?

Devil, Ellie, and Nora agreed to leave the room, and while in the back of his mind, Wes had heard Naomi mention attorney-client privilege, he also wondered if she just wanted privacy. Something told him it was probably both, but hell, he couldn't resist listening in.

"I can't leave him," Naomi blurted in her rough voice and the words fell like boulders at her feet, rolling toward him until they pinned him to the floor. He wondered if they had the same effect on her. Surely the admission made her feel trapped in her nightmare.

Wes closed his eyes and tightened his lips to keep from yelling. Shouting. Doing anything to prevent her from making such a colossal mistake.

Now see, this is why I never come here. It's none of my business.

On the side of his brain where he could remain logical, neutral, and detached, he knew he was right. On the other, emotionally charged side of his brain, he didn't give a fuck.

"M-my daddy was a captain in the Ashland County Sheriff's Office before he was... before he passed. He'd skin me alive hearin' me say this right now, but I can't leave yet. I need to try everything I can first."

"Naomi," Jules began with gentle authority. "If your dad was a cop, then you should know how dangerous these situations can get. You've been *strangled*. Do you know how serious that is?"

"I-I know it looks bad. I mean, it *is* bad—"

"It really is. Strangulation is bad on its own, but your injuries are some of the worse I've seen. Petechial hemorrhaging—that redness in and around your eyes—is fuckin' scary. I'm surprised you can see anything at all."

There was a soft sigh. "I can't leave just yet and it's never gotten this bad before. He said he's gonna try therapy and honestly, it was all just a—"

"—huge—"

—misunderstanding. Wes's inner thoughts finished in time with Jules's and Naomi's. *Tale as old as fucking time, that one.*

There was a huff and Wes wished he could look at Naomi, try to assess what she was thinking. Even if he could turn to read her facial expressions, he probably wouldn't be able to tell from the swelling.

"Naomi, I'm sorry, but the way this has escalated. It's not a 'misunderstanding' anymore. Strangulation is serious." Jules's voice had dropped some of its gentleness to match the harsh truth. "A woman who's been strangled by her significant other is seven *hundred* and fifty percent more likely to be murdered by the same person—"

"But I'm never lettin' him lay a hand on me—"

"—with a *gun*... Now tell me, Naomi. Does whoever did this to you have a gun at home?"

There was a pause, and Wes's stomach dropped along with his hope for her.

Goddamnit.

"I-I... I hear you. I want all the information, but I need time. I have to try... at least once more. It's not always this bad and my baby needs her father. Growing up without one..."

Wes's heart pulsed in his chest at Naomi's vulnerability and everything left unsaid in her reasoning. She'd said her father had died. When was that? Was it when she was a kid? He knew better than anyone the impact a parent's death had on a child. That shit twists your soul up until you're wrung dry.

The need to comfort her was nearly overwhelming. At this point, he'd say anything she needed to hear to prevent her from going back to her abuser. But his words had never worked before. Instead, he waited patiently for Jules to take the reins.

"Listen, I was raised by an addict—"

"He's not an addict—"

"—I get it, I'm not presuming to know your circumstances, but at least the way *I* grew up, I had to realize something."

"What's that?"

"In some ways, loving an addict isn't so different than loving an abuser. Your boundaries are stripped down, over and over again, until you feel like you don't have the right—nor the energy—to keep building those walls back up. They'll just get torn down again."

"It's just... I don't know what to do. I don't even *want* to be with him. But leaving what I know... it's terrifying."

Jules lowered her voice and Wes strained to hear her. "You have to figure out your line, girl. How far are you gonna let this go? You need to decide that *today*. Define your line for yourself, then screw markin' that shit in the sand. You carve your line in fuckin' stone, got it?"

"I-I hear you. But you make it sound so easy."

"*None* of this is easy. I can tell you all the legal stuff you need to know, give you all the brochures to look over. But your most important decision before you leave today should be what your final straw will be. What will he have to do to get you to leave? In the meantime, pray, send good vibes, or whatever the hell you do that he doesn't cross your line, but if he does, you *have* to love yourself enough to escape and take your baby girl with you, alright? We'll help you every step of the way."

"But if y'all help me, he'll get in trouble." There was a hitch in Naomi's breath as she muttered. "I don't love him... and I know I should hate him. But I don't for some reason, and I can't send Thea's father to jail. I-I'm not there yet."

"I get it, I swear I do. It's okay. First off, know he'll be getting himself behind bars all by his lonesome. And we have plenty of different resources here. No one likes to hear it, but prosecution honestly isn't best for every case. Help doesn't always mean justice. Sometimes it means escape."

Wes kept his eyes on the screen as Thea skipped to the last third of the movie. In his periphery, Jules left the room to join the others in the office, leaving Naomi to think with the pamphlets she'd been given.

Thea squirmed in the beanbag beside him and he lifted his gaze to see she wasn't watching the screen anymore. Wes followed her worried eyes to see Naomi covering her face with a towel Devil had given her. Normally, kids might not notice Naomi's shoulders shaking silently, or register that she was trying her best not to sob. But he knew for a fact a child who'd grown up in trauma would no doubt understand the signs.

He made to stand up, pausing midway to whisper to Thea. "Hey, keep on watching the movie for me? Your mom's fine, I promise. I'm just gonna go check on her."

Her red brows furrowed. "And you will come back?"

Wes grinned before whispering, "Yeah, princess. I'll be right back. Just make sure to let me know what happens, okay?"

At her nod and small smile, he stood and took deliberately noticeable steps toward Naomi. Her head was bent and he didn't want to sneak up on her, so he waved his hand low so she could see it. Still, Naomi jolted and groaned, her hand shooting up to her neck, obviously in extreme pain.

"Shit, Naomi, I'm so sorry. I tried not to sneak up on you."

"Huh, *sorry*," Naomi whispered to herself in what sounded like a mocking tone. "Hate that word."

Wes felt his brow furrow and almost asked her to elaborate, but she took a breath and met his eyes. Her face was damp with tears and Wes stood directly in Thea's line of sight to prevent her from seeing her mother so upset. She'd probably seen much, much worse that morning alone, but shielding someone from trauma was never a bad thing, especially not a child.

"Thanks for tryin'. I'm just not… I wasn't expecting you, is all." An indecipherable look passed over Naomi's swollen face. "Not to be rude, but I'm kind of busy." She waved the brochures in the space between them and Wes took a step back.

Her "not to be rude" tone was very much so a rude one, and although he got the picture loud and clear, he didn't want to sit back down with Thea until Naomi had collected herself fully.

"I didn't want to interrupt, it's just Princess T over there was getting worried." Again with that face. He was usually so good at telling people's thoughts from their body language, but Naomi's injuries made it impossible. Jules was right. They were some of the worst he'd seen, too. Her eyes were swollen to slits, but when she peeked out of them, the whites of her eyes were filled with an inhuman blood-red that was painful to see. He couldn't imagine how she felt.

"Princess T?" she finally asked in her scratchy voice.

He laughed and rubbed the back of his head. "Yeah, fits doesn't it? Anyway, I think she likes it." He pointed his thumb over his shoulder. "I told her I'd check on you, but she had to tell me what happened with Merida while I was gone."

"She'll be able to do that, no problem," Naomi muttered with a huff. She wiped her face, wincing every time she dried more tears from her cheeks. The muscles in Wes's arms twitched to take the towel from her and do it himself. It looked like she was being way too rough, as if she was punishing herself for feeling something.

Just before Wes gave in and took control, she finished and sat up straighter on a ragged exhale with her eyes closed. "Okay," she whispered, whether to himself or her, he didn't know, but he decided to take it as a cue.

"You okay now?"

Her eyes opened again, but only barely, as she nodded.

"Yeah… I'm fine." There was a lilt in her voice, like she was unsure of her answer, but he decided to listen to what she was saying rather than look into it.

Because, honestly, it was a stupid-ass question. Of course, she wasn't fine. Who could be in her situation? If she wanted to pretend to be fine at that moment, then he'd let her. She wasn't letting them help, so he'd at least give that to her.

"Good. I gotta get back to Her Majesty, but Naomi?"

"Yeah?"

She lifted her face more and it took everything in his power to keep his face neutral at her wince. Instead, he took a steadying breath and told her the words he'd heard years ago, hoping she'd listen better than his mother had.

"Trust your instincts and make sure to put *your* oxygen mask on first."

CHAPTER THREE

What the hell does that mean?

He watched her as if he was waiting for her to respond in some way, but how do you respond to a cryptic message like that?

Trust my instincts... I don't even know what they are anymore.

So, what could she say? Everything about Snake's presence confused the shit out of her when she already felt out of control, irritating nerves that were already shot to hell. Butterflies she'd thought were long dead and gone were going haywire in her stomach, and his concern for her and Thea took her breath away.

Yeah. Definitely can't tell him any of that.

He still stood in front of her, preventing Thea from seeing her cry. For a moment, Naomi's heart squeezed at his thoughtfulness, right before it twisted painfully.

Why was he being so nice? It didn't feel like he had any ulterior motive. But what stranger was that concerned about another stranger's feelings? And how did he know that shielding T from her momma's pain was exactly what they both had needed?

His body was close to hers and even though he had to be a

foot taller and towered over her, she felt an overwhelming sense of... security.

And *that* was dangerous.

The last thing Naomi needed was someone to set Dean's jealousy off. If he knew she was even talking to another man, he'd go fucking ballistic. He never gave a crap about the circumstances. It frustrated the hell out of her, especially since she'd never once in the entirety of their five-year on-again, mostly off-again relationship given him any reason to think she'd stray.

Naomi looked away and thankfully, he got the hint and cleared his throat before turning to walk back toward T and plopping down beside her. Thea's face lit up like a sparkler, setting Naomi's spent nerves alight with panic.

Thea had never looked at her father that way. *Ever.*

The level of danger a man like this *Snake* brought was damn near biblical; a temptation that promised her knowledge while threatening her downfall.

The door opened wide, revealing Jules's questioning eyes. Naomi waved the brochures at her, too embarrassed to admit that she was too injured to freaking read the dadgum things.

"I-uh. I'm finished. Y'all can come out now..."

Everyone filed in and began talking at her again. She mostly tuned them out, entering that bizarre space again where she could answer when spoken to, while not paying a lick of attention. Instead, all she could hear were Snake's words reverberating around in her head as she tried to solve his stupid little riddle.

Thea giggled at something on the iPad, drawing Naomi's gaze. Her breath hitched when Thea squealed and Snake's grin widened, almost as if he were transfixed just on how happy T was.

Dean had *definitely* never looked at Thea like that, or Naomi, for that matter. Not even when things were 'good'. Hell, when they'd only decided to try for a relationship after figuring out that yes, there are consequences from one-night stands.

Like when a guy swears up and down he used a condom when

you were too tipsy to notice and the inevitable surprise bundle of joy that comes afterward.

Finally, Ellie stopped talking and must've sensed that Naomi was just ready to *go*. It had to have been obvious, because good Lord, was she tired. As she slid off the examination table, Devil and Ellie had to even assist her to prevent her from collapsing.

"Hey, kiddo." Nora's lyrical voice broke through the exhausted haze in her mind. "Come with me and your mommy and we can go shopping in the store. You can get anything you want."

Well, that shit definitely woke Naomi up. Her pulse skyrocketed as Thea began to screech with excitement. She hated to let her down, but they couldn't accept this.

"No, Nora, we can't possibly—"

"It's on the house," Ellie's soft voice and smile interrupted her, like that was the answer to the problem they were causing. Thea alternated between laughter and shrieks as she jumped up and down on the beanbag, barely keeping her balance.

The insistence stabbed at her pride and she almost opened her mouth to object with, 'We don't need your freakin' charity.' But just as soon as the self-righteous, misplaced anger flitted across her mind, Naomi stopped, almost laughing out loud at her ridiculousness. She was quite literally using the services of their nonprofit, aka charity.

Resisting the urge to roll her eyes at herself and her Santa-sized mixed bag of emotions, she still objected, because they obviously didn't understand where she was actually coming from.

"No, Ellie, that's not the issue—"

Thea's cut-off scream interrupted them, and Naomi locked her gaze on her daughter. Snake was crouched over, groaning like he'd been somehow kneed in the crotch and T was scrambling across the play area on her hands and knees, her eyes wide and lips trembling as she cowered away from Snake. Her terror had Naomi instantly in momma-bear mode against the man, even though he hadn't done anything to deserve it. *Yet.*

"Sorry." Thea's voice came out uncertain, like it did every time Dean was about to blow up about something.

Naomi took a step to protect her daughter from whatever wrath this man was about to bring. He was doubled over as if in pain, but God help him if he snapped at her little girl. Getting kneed in the balls would be the least of his problems.

A low rumbling escaped him, halting her mid-step at the odd reaction.

"Oof, you got me good, princess." The pained chuckles continued, and when Naomi met T's eyes, she had no doubt that Thea's expression was a mirror image to her own confused look. Naomi tried to smile to ease Thea's mind, and it must've worked because soon, giggles tinged with nervousness bubbled from her before she stood back up.

"Okay, but Wes has to come!"

Wes? Wow, I like that much better... She cringed. *No, better stick with Snake. It's... easier.*

The thought tickled her mind and she locked it down before letting her shoulders rise and fall with frustration. It didn't matter *what* she thought of his name. She shouldn't think anything about him at all. If she allowed a man with his charm into her life, there was no telling what she would do or the repercussions that came with it.

She wanted to object more, but hell, she hadn't seen Thea that excited in a while. Even at the tender age of four, the girl was a certified shopaholic, and would be inconsolable if Naomi told her no. There was no way Naomi could handle seeing a look like that on her baby's face again today.

Maybe I can hide the stuff in the trunk... would he check there?

She had to figure something out because Dean couldn't know where they'd been. She'd said she just needed a drive to clear her head. The shopping cover might work for other people, but her injuries looked so bad, he'd know something was up if she told him they went shopping. Nora had to understand, right? So why had she suggested it? Was there some other motive?

Thea's squeal snapped Naomi from her mental spiral. Not everyone was out to get her, for chrissakes.

When did I stop trusting everyone? This is ridiculous.

Thea launched herself at Wes again and took him by the hand, totally ignoring that the man was still slightly hunched over in pain. But Wes's smile was wide and Naomi felt her lips attempt to mirror his before she schooled her expression. The extra-strength Advil that Devil had left her before they went into the office was thankfully kicking in. The emotion on her face only hurt slightly rather than unbearably, but still, she couldn't let him—or Thea, for that matter—know the effect Wes had on her.

"All right, let's go, Babs." *Babs? I thought her name was Jules...* "I gotta get my favorite boss ass bitch back to the office before your fiancé decides to unalive me for keeping you from him."

Thea led the parade quickly down the back halls, leaving Naomi to blindly stumble on as she navigated her way with her hand against the wall. She followed T's spirited chatter until she finally reached the thrift store.

It was nicely laid out, brightly lit, with tons of options for clothes and household items. She absentmindedly ran her hand along a sleeve of a soft sweater and if her blurry vision was correct, found what looked to be a brand-new tag.

"What do ya think?"

Naomi jumped and clapped her hand against her chest. Nora was in no way intimidating—at least not size-wise—but she'd rounded a clothing rack without Naomi realizing it and being snuck up on, even unintentionally, always set her on edge.

"You got this, Nora?" Jules asked cryptically before walking away like she already had the answer. "I've gotta check something real quick before we go."

"Yeah, Babs, I got this. So... what do ya think?" Nora asked again, but Naomi was still confused.

"Uh, what do I think about what? The store?"

Naomi's pain might have lessened, but her sight was still

poor. She tried to analyze the look on Nora's blurry face, but thankfully, Nora shared her thoughts.

"Yeah… sorry about getting Thea all riled up, but I wanted a chance to chat with you more privately. I didn't realize she loved shopping so damn much."

"The girl's got an addiction. She'd live in the mall if she could." Naomi's chuckle was strained as she tried not to dwell on the fact that there had indeed been an ulterior motive. Although, ulterior didn't always mean a *bad* motive.

"We're always lookin' for volunteers, ya know. Sometimes I have to twilight as a sales associate on the floor, so I'm tryin' to recruit all the talent I can get to help a sister out."

"Twilight?" Naomi couldn't help the question in her voice. She'd gotten knocked around, but following this woman's train of thought and vocabulary was exhausting.

"You know, it's like moonlighting. But since I already daylight as Jules's assistant at her law firm, and I moonlight as the manager for the crisis center, the thrift store is my third job, so… twilighting."

Naomi frowned as much as her injuries would allow. "No offense, but I'm pretty sure that's not a thing."

Nora's laugh was almost like music. "You sound like Jason, Jules's fiancé. No offense taken. Stick around, though, babe, and you'll eventually learn my language."

Naomi shook her head with a soft laugh of her own. "As fun as that sounds, I'm not sure how often I can swing by and 'stick around' just to shop."

The pixie woman's shoulder lifted. "Well, it's like I said… the thrift store always needs vols. Especially since proceeds go to kids with cancer. Can't stop someone from wanting to volunteer for cancer kids, amiright?"

Naomi's head tilted and once again she was silently grateful that the pain was easing. "Cancer kids? I thought the money went to the clinic."

Out of the side of her eye, Naomi followed Ellie and Devil as they left the store. She scanned the room out of habit and found the front exit was a straight shot from the aisle she was on. There was also the door to the clinic right behind her. She wasn't sure how to exit that way, but there had to be some way out.

Part of her mind told her she was safe and could relax. But the other, the part that had probably kept her alive for so long, made her continue to catalog the room. Jules had mentioned needing to speak with the volunteer behind the checkout counter before they left and a quick glance confirmed that. Wes and T were over in the kids' section. The giggles and easy laughs coming from that corner cracked the fragile glass surrounding her heart.

"The money does go to the clinic." Nora nodded, bringing Naomi back to their conversation. As she talked, Nora sifted through the racks on the clothes in front of them, straightening each shirt on its hanger. "But no one knows that but us, and no one else needs to know that. As far as anyone outside of Sasha Saves is concerned, the money goes to cancer kids. Well, except the government, but they know errbody's business, the bastards."

Naomi bristled. "So y'all lie? That's pretty messed up."

Nora's sigh was exaggerated and Naomi imagined she was rolling her eyes. "Girl, stahp and chill out. We do both, *capisce?* We just don't tell people about the women's clinic part, or that everything inside is free for survivors, and a portion of the thrift store proceeds does, in fact, go to wee babes with cancer." She led Naomi by the hand closer to the cash registers and pulled some brochures from a slot on the desk. "Here." She handed the brochures to Naomi but except for the large font of the store name, they were too blurry.

"I-I'm sorry, I don't know what these say. I-um, I can't see them."

Nora's breath hitched and she muttered something under her breath before she started to type and talk at the same time. "Well, I know you've got yourself a mean *bicycle* at home... but even if you can't read them, they can at least be your alibi. They include info on the cancer proceeds, so if you put them in your purse, you've got yourself some evidence to back up your story. Volunteer with the store. Help those cancer kids. Not even a *bike* can complain about that shiz without lookin' shitty AF."

Naomi tried to work around what Nora was saying, but she was so exhausted she just wanted her to get to the point. "Why would I volunteer here? I mean, why do you want *me* to volunteer here? I'm not lettin' y'all help me more than you already have. I have a job and I can't just leave T alone all the time."

"Look, doll, we're super flexible with our volunteer hours, you set them completely. And obvi Lil' T can come hang. We need someone who's good with kiddos like you to help out with the ones that come in here with their moms. Shoot, Lil' T can even play with them. It'd be a major relief to the moms to see their kids happy, as you know. So... volunteer at the thrift store."

Naomi twisted the information around in her mind, trying to look for gaps, holes, or excuses. It was a nice offer. Her boss, Gail, had mentioned before that the company needed to get more involved with pro bono and nonprofit work. Working at the store would definitely qualify.

"Plus," Nora continued, probably sensing her logic was working. "If you... I dunno, have had your last straw and need to just like *not* go home after your shift here, you could take what you need from here and jet, with our help... ya know? That guy over there..." Nora tilted her head to indicate Wes, who was bowing to Thea as if he were her humble servant. "He and five—" Nora gulped. "I mean, *four* other dudes are a team from BlackStone Securities, a security firm that works very closely with us. They're some bad mamma jammas in the private security world, but good to have on your side."

Naomi felt her eyes widen. Had Dean heard of them before? He came from the same security 'world' as Nora put it. Did they know *him*? Fuck, what if they take his side—

"And they'll protect *you* from anything, Naomi. I swear it.

You just gotta give 'em a chance. They have literally fought battles to help survivors."

The words took the edge off her anxiety. Not everyone was her enemy. Her father had shown her good men existed.

She went to massage her temple, barely remembering in time that it would hurt like hell. She closed her eyes in thought instead, letting Nora's offer and logic piece together like a puzzle in her mind. And the picture... was freakin' perfect, actually.

Nora was right, Dean couldn't get mad—or at least, not *too* mad—especially if she told him Gail wanted her to volunteer.

Define your line.

Jules's advice whispered across her mind. What *would* it take for her to leave Dean? The racing thought jacked up her pulse and drew her attention straight to the kids' section. From what she could tell with her blurry sight, T held green heels and was putting a crown on Wes.

A memory of Naomi's daddy and his huge belly laugh as he played dress-up with her flashed in her vision, fitting over the picture in front of her like an outline, and a hot knife of grief twisted in her heart for the parent she'd lost.

What would happen to Thea if Naomi weren't around anymore? Naomi knew all too well what it was like to not have two parents at home, and up until that moment, she'd been worried over the effect kicking Dean out of their lives would have on her daughter.

But what if things got so bad that she... never got the chance?

"Okay..." Naomi made her decision just as she opened her mouth. "Alright, yeah, I'll volunteer. I can just um... come with T after work or something?"

Nora waved her hand. "Whenever works for you, babe. We have a skeleton crew of paid thrift store employees, so our volunteers can come and go whenever they please."

Naomi huffed some cleansing air from her chest, feeling lighter with her choice. There was no way to know if Dean going to therapy would work, or whether he would escalate even further. She'd promised herself one more shot at their relationship, but now she was making a different promise entirely, defining her line, and allowing him to even touch her in anger again was too far. If he ever made a fist toward her again, she and T were gone.

And now she had the perfect escape plan.

CHAPTER FOUR

"Wes, look at all them toys! Now you can be king and my mommy can be queen and I'll be Princess T."

Thea curtseyed her adorable yellow and green dress as she bowed to him, and Wes couldn't help but smile. Hearing his real name for a change, and in her high-pitched voice no less, felt better than he'd realized it would. It helped that she was so damn charming it was impossible not to fall in love with the kid in two seconds.

"Why thank you, milady." Wes bowed, keeping his hand on his shiny crown and trying to adopt his most regal voice. It'd been a while since he'd played with his sister's kids, and he hoped he wasn't too out of practice.

Thea's giggle reassured him that whatever he was doing, at least he wasn't doing it terribly. She kept up her chatter while taking out every single toy from the large store bin, setting them up around a small pink table for sale. As she worked dutifully to make sure her stuffed animal royal subjects were taken care of, Wes tilted his head, trying his hardest to hear what Naomi and Nora were saying.

He ventured a look behind him to see Naomi nod, and for

the first time, she had what might've been a genuine smile on her face.

"Ugh," Jules groaned long and low as she walked to the store entrance. "Y'all, I don't wanna be *that* pregnant lady, but my feet are about to revolt. And I hate to say it—"

"Come on... say it, *say it*, you know you want to." Nora smiled and steepled her hands like a villain.

"These damn shoes are killin' me."

"Yes! Jason owes me five bucks!" Nora shot her fist up in the air and Naomi's jolt made Wes's lips tighten. "Jason thought you'd wear those damn stilts up until your due date, but I knew you'd cave. Since I'm your lovely chauffeur, I'll make a detour on the way to the office so you can change." Nora grinned while Jules rolled her eyes.

Ever since Jules's car was blown up last year, she'd refused to drive anywhere. Thankfully, being seven months pregnant, her fiancé had absolutely no problem being glued to her hip and when he couldn't, Nora, her assistant and best friend, was attached to the other side.

"Yeah, yeah, yeah, you win. Anyway, I'll see you in the car." Jules waved to them as she walked out.

"Sounds good, Babs... oh, Sn-a-ke! We need your help!" His name was drawn out in Nora's pretty singsong voice, but he cringed anyway as he got up. Hopefully, Princess T kept using his real name instead of his *cool* nickname. His nephew had heard it once and never turned back.

"Come on, Wes, let's go." Thea grabbed a pair of too big, green high heel shoes before snatching his hand. His smile returned, thankful she didn't use his call sign.

Feeling a little ridiculous with the crown on, he removed it from his head and placed it on Thea's. She beamed up at him and tugged him forward while carrying her loot in her other hand.

When they got closer, he tried to go slowly, unsure how much Naomi could see from her wounds. Her eyes had to be a dime's width away from being shut altogether, and he didn't want to frighten her *again* by surprising her with his six-foot-two frame.

Thea dropped his hand and collapsed against her mom, wrapping her arms around her jean-clad legs. The hitch in Naomi's breath told him that his instincts were right. She hadn't been able to see her daughter flying at her. One hand clutched the back of Thea's dress, while the other searched for balance.

Wes threw an arm behind her back to catch her. Not knowing the extent of her injuries under her bulky sweater, he was careful not to squeeze her too tightly. He tensed against the wild impulse to pull her into an embrace and instead turned to Thea to give her a stern, but gentle, look.

"Careful, Princess."

Thea's pale cheeks blushed bright red as she toed the ground with a worried frown. "Sorry, Mommy. Are you okay?"

"I'm fine, baby. It's okay. You didn't do anything wrong." Naomi shrugged out of his hold and if he was reading her swollen face correctly, she was trying to scowl at him.

Yeesh. Don't scold the kid. Got it.

"Sorry, just trying to help," he mumbled and wasn't sure she heard him. Her stiffening body language could easily have been from pain or from being pissed off.

"Snake," Nora interrupted, using her *up-to-something* voice. He didn't like that shit one bit. "Our dear Naomi needs you to drive her home."

Wes's and Naomi's exclamation erupted simultaneously. "*What?*"

He stepped back to take both women in. "Is this something that Naomi wants?" he asked, only to have the woman in question *definitely* scowl at him.

"No, *Naomi* does not want that." She turned her distorted glare on Nora. "Nora—wait, what're you doing?"

Nora held a brochure about a foot away from Naomi's face. "If you can read this, babe, I'll drop it and let you go on your merry way."

"Mommy, I can read it! I can! She showed me how!"

Naomi squinched her face and attempted to widen her blood-filled eyes before sighing in defeat.

"Thought so." Nora tucked the extra brochure back in its holder on the counter. "Okay, here's how it's gonna go. I gotta take Momma Babs home. We can't in good conscience let you drive your daughter's sweet precious baby angel face around. You can't even see a foot in front of your beautiful face. My car's so full of junk that I can't fit a booster seat back there. So my deal is... either we leave your car here and coordinate an Uber for you, or Superman drives your car and we have another one of the BlackStone Security men come pick him up."

Thea wrinkled her nose. "Superman?" She glanced at Wes and he winked at her before she turned back to Nora and shook her head. "Wes isn't Superman. He's the king and Mommy's the queen and I'm their Princess T."

Wes's smile returned fully while his heart tripled a beat. But the naïve organ slowed to a halt at Naomi's gasp. Her mouth opened in horror before bending to Thea's level.

"Theresa Jane Ward, never, *ever* say that again, do you hear me? Especially not when we get home."

"Yes, ma'am." Thea's lip puckered out and Wes crossed his arms to prevent himself from reaching out to comfort the little girl. Naomi probably didn't want Thea to accidentally say something in front of the asshole at home. She had to be terrified of the guy. Wes could almost make out where each blow was struck. The thought threatened to short-circuit his brain and unleash the control he always held so close to his chest. The reason behind reprimanding Thea made sense, but it still made him grind his teeth to keep from arguing and making the woman even more annoyed at him.

Naomi stood back up, and thanks to her short stature, her hands rested comfortably on Thea's shoulders.

"I hear what you're sayin', Nora, about gettin' a ride. I-I can't

get an Uber though because I can't leave my car here. That...
that just won't work out."

Wes cleared his throat. "I'm fine driving your car, Naomi."

"And I've already texted Hawk to come pick Snake up," Nora
admitted with a smile.

Wes tilted his head and narrowed his eyes at her just as she
schooled her face. "You have?"

"Yep. I had a feeling she'd need it."

"Mommy, it's okay. I like him." Thea turned in her mother's
grip and used that stage whisper only children could pull off.
"Wes was real nice and he even played with me."

Naomi's hand drifted to her temple, only to make a detour
through her dark auburn hair, like she was resisting a habit
because of her bruises. Finally, she sighed with a slight nod.
"Okay, fine, I guess I don't really have another choice."

"Yay!" Thea jumped from her mom's grip and went to the
cash register, placing the crown and green high heels onto the
counter. "Mommy, we're gettin' these first though, 'kay?"

"Oh, it's on the hou—"

"No, it's not." Naomi waved her hand at Nora, cutting her
off. "I'm payin' for the dang things."

Nora threw up her hands and backed away. "Alrighty, it's all
you, boo."

The volunteer took Naomi's cash and gave her a paper bag
with the crown and heels inside, which Naomi promptly turned
to give to Thea.

"Here ya go, T. You know the rules. You wanted it, you
carry it."

Thea squealed and ripped the heels out of the bag and held
them up. "Mommy, I got a surprise."

"Oh, you did, did you?"

"Yup, I got these for you!"

"Is that right?" Naomi chuckled out a strained huff before
propping her hands on her hips. "But I thought Mommy paid for
them?"

Thea scoffed. "Yeah, but *I* told you to buy 'em. Try 'em on." She shoved the items into her mother's stomach and Naomi's body sank against the counter with a measured breath, as if she was trying to be nice even though her nerves were shot. Seeing her try to hold everything in was too much for him to bear.

"Princess T, let's go, your mom can try those on when you get home."

A swollen scowl formed on Naomi's face as she spoke through gritted teeth. "I've got this. I don't need your help, thank you."

Shit, why can't I just shut the fuck up?

But he knew why. That inherent need to step into a situation and help, sometimes even overstepping, was a learned behavior. Or at least that's what the therapist said.

Naomi took off her boots and stuffed them in the remnants of the paper bag before stepping into her new green heels. She twisted her feet to look at them. "Shoot, these actually fit pretty good."

"Don't forget!" Thea stretched on her toes and Naomi bent low so that Thea could place the rose gold crown with green gems on top of her mother's dark auburn hair. She clapped her hands against her cheeks before exclaiming what was obviously something she'd picked up. "Gorgeous!"

God, this kid is adorable.

Naomi held the crown to keep it from falling and her bruised lips lifted in a small smile. "I love it, Thea. Thank you, baby."

That pleased Thea to no end and she giggled before looking at Wes. "See, Wes? I toldya Mommy would look even more beautifuler."

"You're right Princess T, the queen is more beautifuler than I could've imagined."

CHAPTER FIVE

He felt Naomi's eyes appraise him, but he refused to look at her. She'd already gotten mad enough at him during the short time they were together and he still had to drive them home.

"Alright, kid, let's move out. Nora, can you just shove that box of electronics in the office?"

"Got ya covered." Nora waved them away with her eyes on her phone. "Hawk said he just finished a client meeting so he'll be able to pick you up. Just shoot him the addy."

Wes nodded and began to walk out the front door until a small hand slid into his. He schooled his face so Thea couldn't see his surprise at her sudden show of trust. When he looked down though, he noticed that Thea had her mom's hand in her other, and damn, did that jump-start his heart for some reason.

He cleared his throat and led the way around the building, where he assumed the gray Nissan Murano was Naomi's vehicle. When they got to the car, Naomi fiddled around in her purse and gave him the keys. Before she could stop him, he opened the door for Thea and helped buckle her into her car seat. When he held the door open for her, he tried not to laugh at her jaw, literally hanging open.

When he got in the driver's side, Naomi was still staring at him through her narrowed eyes. He started the car and raised his eyebrows.

"Where to, queen?"

"Don't call me that." Her rasp came out forcefully before giving him the address, and he imagined there'd be a bite to it if she had her full voice.

He texted the address to Hawk before plugging the route into his phone GPS. After lodging it into the phone holder, he headed to the growing part of town where neighborhoods were being built on top of each other. He got lost in thought, trying to block out Thea's fucking shark song that his niece and nephew couldn't get enough of. At least this one sounded like it had a cool remix in it.

"You got a kid?"

Her words startled him, and he frowned before taking a turn. "Uh, no. Can't say I've had the honor yet."

"Really? You're good with them. At least Thea. She isn't usually so... free."

Wes propped his elbow on the door window and scrubbed his shaven chin with his hand, trying to think of what to say. Her leg bounced in the seat next to him as she fiddled with the strap of her purse lying in her lap.

"My sister's got two—a boy and a girl—and they're the coolest kids I've ever met." He turned around briefly to wink at Thea. "But Princess T is right up there."

Thea grinned around a sour apple sucker that must've been in the back seat. Her dimple winked back at him before she retrieved an iPad from the hanging car seat organizer in front of her.

They were silent again and Wes bit his tongue to keep from asking Naomi the question he'd been begging to know the answer to for years. He tasted copper before finally giving in.

"Why don't you leave?" It came out in a hushed whisper, but her fidgeting stilled and at the way she tensed up, he knew he should've kept his goddamn mouth shut.

But hell, he'd never understood why women in her situation didn't see what everyone else could. He'd met her less than an hour ago and already he could tell she was smart, protective, and fuck, he felt like a skeeze to admit it, but he'd noticed her curves more than once. Why the fuck did she stay with someone who treated her like anything less than the queen she was?

He'd asked that question plenty of times before, with another woman in what felt like another life, and he'd never been satisfied with the answer.

"I don't see how any of that is your business, *Snake*."

The way she hissed his nickname made him bristle. He'd never been a fan of his call sign, but he especially didn't like it when she said it like *that*.

"It's Wes," he gritted out, before relaxing his jaw. "Please... call me Wes."

She was refusing to look at him again, and he noticed her hand scrunching up the bottom of her thick sweatshirt.

"It's just... you have options, Naomi. I can—I mean, *we* can help." Her light ivory knuckles reddened at the top of her fisted hand. "Sorry, I know I overstepped. I'm just worried. I've seen this before—"

"Yeah, working at the clinic, I'm sure you've seen it a hundred times—"

"Not at the clinic."

The words must've surprised her because she clammed up and retreated to look out the window.

After a few more silent moments, they were close to her house and he was afraid they'd end on a sour note. Wes didn't know why it was so important that she knew where he was coming from, he just couldn't stop himself. His fingers tightened on the steering wheel to keep from reaching over to rescue the hem of her sweater from her fidgeting.

He turned into a pop-up neighborhood, one of those that sprang up in six months with dozens of nice, cookie-cutter craftsman houses and small yards. A car appeared in the rearview mirror and he glanced up to see Hawk's sedan following behind. He must've been close to town already because the BlackStone Securities Facility was twenty minutes outside of Ashland.

Naomi's eyes darted to the rearview, her back straight until whatever she saw made her relax back into the seat. Wes ground his molars together.

Fuck, this bastard has her terrified.

His tongue was raw from biting back every thought, but he refused to frustrate her any more. It took them a few more turns before she said anything.

"House is second on the right."

Wes nodded. "Pull into the driveway?"

"Yeah, in front of the left garage door, but not too close and make sure not to get in the way of the right side."

Wes felt his brow furrow at how precise she was in her instruction. "You don't want me to pull inside?"

"No, that's... that's where Thea's father... my fiancé's workshop is."

There hadn't been one single pleasant interaction with this woman, so why the fuck did that word pierce something inside him? It was like he was compelled to get through that hard shield she insisted on hitting him with. Maybe it wasn't her at all. Maybe she was just another woman in his life who needed saving.

Despite trying to minimize his reaction, his knuckles ached to give back tenfold what her fiancé had done to her. More copper seeped from his silent tongue. Fuck, at this rate he wouldn't be able to eat without searing pain reminding him of her and all the things he couldn't say.

Wes pulled into her driveway and parked exactly as she'd asked. Before he could get out and open her door, she was already escaping, stumbling out and immediately going to her daughter's door. While she was helping Thea out of her car seat, Hawk's car pulled up in front of the house.

"Naomi, I—"

"Say thank you and goodbye to Snake, T." Naomi lifted Thea onto her hip with a wince. It was almost comical since she was nearly half her mom's size already.

Thea popped the sucker out of her mouth. "He's leavin'?" Her lip poked out and Wes's heart ached to make those lips widen into a toothy grin again.

"Yeah, baby, he's leavin' and we need to go inside. Your daddy will be home in a bit."

Thea nodded and smiled slightly at Wes, waving her small hand. "Bye Wes, thank you for playin' with me."

Wes mustered up a smile back. "It was nice to meet you Princess T." He bowed and even though he felt like a fool, her giggle made it worth it, until he straightened back up and saw the anger written on Naomi's face again.

She mumbled a thanks and goodbye before heading to the garage, entering a code and opening the right door, revealing a pristine, empty parking space.

Bet that fucker parks there while he makes her park outside.

The thought made his legs tense with the urge to go after them, but he backed away, afraid he'd do just that if he didn't distance himself. He watched them take the short steps inside the garage and enter the house without another glance.

When the door slammed, something inside Wes jolted and panic seized the quickening pulse in his veins. He couldn't shake the feeling that he was making the biggest mistake of his life, letting Naomi walk back into that house. But she was an adult. Not only that, but a soon-to-be-*married* adult, to her child's father. Wes needed to back the hell off and let this relative stranger live her own fucking life.

Wes pivoted and marched to Hawk's sedan, refusing to look back before he opened the passenger side and collapsed into the seat.

Hawk's left elbow rested on top of the door panel, with his other hand on the top of the steering wheel. His left index finger rubbed his lips back and forth while he slowly shook his head, his dark eyes staring in thought at the house.

Ellie called him a younger, military version of Idris Elba, and Wes had never thought of it before. Hawk was just his team lead and friend, a brother in arms. But right then, with his determined scowl and singular focus, Wes saw it.

Wes took a moment to collect his thoughts, resisting a sigh of frustration. Hawk pulled the car out of the driveway, pausing in front of the house before setting off back to Sasha Saves.

Hawk's deep voice filled the space, emphasizing the commanding presence the BlackStone Securities leader had earned over their years together in MF7 and then BlackStone.

"You good?"

Wes released a rough exhale as he studied the forest green craftsman home. In one of the windows on the top floor, the blinds in a window shuttered closed.

"No, I'm not good. And I don't know why."

CHAPTER SIX

It took two freakin' uneventful weeks of excuses to her boss, working from home, icing her wounds on and off, and a shit ton of makeup, but Naomi finally felt confident enough in her own skin to leave the house.

It'd been her first day back to work in person and she'd ambitiously decided it should also be her first official day volunteering at Sasha Saves. Unfortunately, Gail had run her ragged with plans for this stupid party the company was helping to host. It was only an hour and a half into Naomi's volunteering shift, and already she was rubbing her back, regretting her eagerness to take on everything at once.

"How're ya likin' it, sweets? Bet it's a nice change from sittin' on your ass behind that reception desk all day long." Dean's voice oozed over the phone, totally unaware that he'd just been rude as hell. *Hopefully,* he was unaware. Maybe he was just a jerk.

Naomi grimaced, trying to think of how to answer. It worked her nerves to talk to him about Sasha Saves. She'd hidden the crown and shoes in Thea's dress-up clothes, so she'd been able to play off that awful day as one where she'd driven off to think. But ever since she'd told him *Gail* wanted her to volunteer, Naomi had been on edge that he'd somehow figure out her backup plan.

Dean had been sweet as saccharine since his little outburst—as he'd taken to calling it—and he'd even booked a therapist. He'd said that the only one that could take on a new patient was still booked solid for two whole months. She'd heard that mental health options sucked across the country, but hell, apparently small towns were downright *shitty*.

"I like it so far," Naomi finally answered. "Nothin' too excitin'. I'm glad Thea's preschool has a night program. Poor thing'd be bored as hell right now since I'm just unloadin' inventory." Of course, she could've just stayed home, but that hadn't been an option. "How's your night out with the boys?"

"It's good. Had to stop watchin' the basketball game to talk to you. They're rivals, so it's a nail-biter and I'll probably miss some great plays..."

"Dean, you don't *have* to call me every fifteen minutes."

"Shit, sweets, you'd think you'd be more grateful. This might be *the* game of the season. And I'm missin' it for *you*."

Oh, God. spare me. Or take me. Either's fine as long as I don't have to hear this BS.

She would've given anything to give him a taste of that sass, but his voice had an edge she hadn't heard in weeks. Best to play it safe.

"You're right. I'm sorry. Thank you for takin' the time to check up on me." *Gag. Change the subject.* "It's neat they get donations from people that live in town, but the manager has been able to secure donations of 'oops' items from department stores, too. There's actually some pretty nice stuff in here."

She dug around the large box and searched the item pictures until she found the right ones for the window display, a pair of periwinkle heels. She placed them in the front window, remembering the green ones Thea had so graciously 'bought' for her.

"Yeah, yeah, yeah. That's, uh... interesting. I'm sure y'all are probably raisin' a ton for those cancer kids. How much did you say they raised last year again?"

Naomi's heart stuttered. Had his tone gotten even sharper, or was her paranoia kicking in?

"Uh, from my online orientation, I think they've only been open for like half a year? But they've managed to donate twenty-five thousand dollars so far."

Dean whistled on the other side. "Hot damn, maybe I need to get in on the thrift store game."

Of course, he'd see the dollar signs behind the *not*-for-profit. It was one of the reasons he'd left the Ashland County Sheriff's Office. AIE Securities and Charitable Technologies International scouted him for the supervisory security role and he jumped ship like a fish off a hook.

"Yeah, I think we're doin' pretty good for ourselves, though. Money-wise, I mean."

"Speaking of doin' someone good..." His sensual chuckle at what he believed constituted a *joke* made her grimace at the phone. "I want you to be ready for me when I get home tonight, sweets. It's been too long since I've had you underneath me."

The entirety of his sentence made bile rise in her throat, especially hearing the name her daddy had used for her momma with such affection. Knowingly or not, Dean had learned to use the endearment as a weapon, slicing through her every time he spoke it. Her revulsion was so strong she'd almost forgotten what he said.

"That sounds great... But oh, dadgummit." She lowered her voice. Not that anyone else was in there. "I just started today..."

"What? Shit, *again*? That fuckin' blows."

"Yeah... that's kind of how periods work, unfortunately." *Not.*

Thank God for ignorant men. Sometimes it almost seemed like Dean enjoyed making her bleed, but if her body did it on its own, he avoided her like the damn plague. Since she'd gotten an IUD after having Thea, her period had been every twenty-eight days on the dot. She'd had it last week, but fortunately, Dean had still been too apologetic from his "outburst" to touch her. Before their argument, she'd managed to put off sex for a while. She'd always found an excuse: stress, work... Shoot, her period was now coming around practically every other week.

But now she had to be more cautious. Her fibs were one of the reasons why he'd snapped two weeks ago.

She was banking on milking his guilt for all he was worth, and for as long as she could, at least until she could imagine him on top of her without nearly having a panic attack. Even though he'd been better than ever, she wasn't ready to be that vulnerable with him again. She was starting to wonder if she ever would be.

"Naomi?"

At hearing the new male voice, panic knifed down Naomi's spine and she spun around to see Wes standing inside the front door. He was a few feet away, but close enough that his body heat warmed her despite the winter chill coming through the open door. His mouth opened, and it took her a second to figure out what to do.

"Wow, you look—"

She slapped her hand over his mouth before he could say anything else.

"Who is that?" The tone on the other end of the phone was gruff and fear twisted to stab through her back and into her heart.

"Uh, he's no one." Naomi dropped her hand slowly and gave Wes a pointed look, hoping he'd get the message. "Just the tech guy."

His blue eyes bore into hers, sparking with an emotion she didn't fully understand, but felt deep in her core. He kept watching her and pulled his phone from his back pocket before breaking eye contact to type and walk back to the checkout counter.

"—believe you." *Shit.* She hadn't been listening, but Wes had only caught her in his trap for half a second, right? Dean couldn't have said too much. "Is this so-called tech guy the only other person there?"

"What? No, that's crazy." She scanned the empty store. Nora

had stepped out for a minute and, *of course,* that was the time the hot guy with a heart of gold walked through the door. "God no, there're tons of people here." Her voice lilted up at the end and she almost cursed into the phone.

God, do I always have to sound like I'm questioning my own lie?

"Men *and* women?" Dean's voice was lower, more menacing, and she could imagine him tugging at his dark blond hair. She laughed, sounding like a lunatic to her own ears, but hopefully Dean didn't notice.

"Both, but there're no customers." At least she wasn't lying there, and she added to her story to further throw him off the scent. "They're smart enough not to leave me all alone on my first—"

The Sasha Saves phone on the checkout counter rang, making Naomi jump a mile high before she relaxed and silently thanked God.

"Oh, hey. Sorry, I gotta go. I-I'm about to answer my first call for the store." She fled through the aisles to the ringing phone. "Isn't that so exciting?"

"Naomi, how many—"

"Sorry, sweets." The words slithered out of her and she hoped he took the bait. Unlike her, he didn't have the same hang-ups she did. It'd be different if he'd heard empty apologies as many times as she had, and if he could use the term of endearment as a weapon, she'd wield it like a shield.

The shrill phone snapped her out of her thoughts.

"Shit, really gotta go."

"Fine, love y—"

Naomi hung up before he could finish his sentence and clutched her phone against her pounding chest, hoping she hadn't just kicked the hornet's nest. She'd tell him the connection cut off or a customer came in, so it seemed like an accident. Anything to convince him she hadn't hung up on him to avoid saying those three words. He'd burned her too many times and she just couldn't bring herself to say it anymore.

Neither of them had ever truly meant the words, but "I love you" is what people said after they'd been together long enough. Lately, though, keeping up with the lie felt like ash on her tongue.

She took a deep, relaxing breath, composing herself to answer the store phone.

"Sasha Saves Thrift Store, how can I help you?"

"Yes, I was wondering if you could help me find someone." Wes's calm baritone flowed over, soothing her nerves like aloe. She darted her eyes up and around to find him casually standing behind the checkout counter, his phone to his ear, and his piercing baby blues analyzing her. "I was hoping to speak to a woman I met a couple of weeks ago. Is she in?" His voice came over the phone speaker as well as in person, and Naomi rolled her eyes but couldn't hold back her smirk, nor resist the urge to play along, even if only for a second.

Relax. It's just a silly prank. Playing along won't make me fall in love with him, Jesus.

"I'm sorry, sir. I don't know to whom you are referrin'."

"Really? You couldn't miss her. She's a great mom, sweet Southern accent even when she's annoyed, and the cutest kid..."

Is this jackass really gonna try to use my daughter to flirt with me when he knows good and well I just got off the phone with another man?

It was official. All men are pigs.

Naomi rolled her eyes again with a sigh and gave him her most unimpressed look as she answered. "Sorry. I checked. She doesn't want to speak with you. She doesn't have time for BS." Then, for good measure, she tilted her head and twisted her mouth. "Can I take a message?"

Wes's brow furrowed and he shoved his hand into his pocket. "Can you just let her know I've been thinking about her and that I hope she's doing okay? I've been worried, but I didn't want to overstep."

Naomi's breath hitched and she hung up the store's phone, as if it would cut off the very real conversation that was happening in person. How could he make her feel more with just one question than Dean had the entire time they'd been together? When was the last time Dean asked *anything* about her well-being? Like *really* asked her without being an ass about it? Let alone cared?

Wes was dangerous. If she didn't get ahead of her feelings, he was liable to ruin what she had. It wasn't the best relationship, sure, but she'd promised herself to try again with the father of her child. Thea deserved both parents in her life.

A sliver of doubt snuck into her mind, threatening her with the nightmares she'd had ever since Dean had looked her straight in the eyes as he choked her. In her dreams, a demon took over, ready to suck the life out of her and steal her soul.

She shook her head, reminding herself once again of her goal. It'd be the performance of a lifetime, but if 'fake it 'til she made it' benefited Thea, then the least she could do was try one last time. She'd taken Jules's advice, defined her line, and written it in stone. Her nightmares would never come to life. She wouldn't let reality get to that point again. This time, if he so much as raised his hand to her, she'd be out, utilizing everything Sasha Saves had to offer.

Phone back in his pocket, Wes stepped forward and placed his hands wide on the opposite side of the counter. He wasn't leaning over her, at least not crowding her in the way Dean did, but her skin tingled at Wes's nearness as she imagined his body caging her in.

She wondered if it would feel like freedom.

"No." The word whispered out of her, as she tried to deny the vision in her head.

She crossed her arms and tried to step farther away until a hanger poked her back, making her jump. This man was a threat to life as she knew it. She didn't know how to feel about that.

"No, what?" Wes asked, his icy blue eyes freezing her into place.

"Nothing." She gave him a pointed look. "You're a trouble-maker, Snake, you know that? What're you doin' here, anyhow?"

"Troublemaker, huh?" There was a twinkle in his eye that made her stomach flip. "I kinda like that. But please, call me Wes."

"I think I'll stick with Snake. Or Trouble. Both are fitting."

He sucked his teeth before pointing below the counter. "Well, to answer your question: I came to check the security again. Apparently it's been acting up."

"Well, why don't you go do that then?"

He lifted a shoulder with a snort and dipped his head toward whatever he'd been tinkering on behind the counter. "Already did. Seems Nora didn't think to just press a damn button."

Naomi walked around to join him behind the counter and looked down at a black box. The light that had been annoyingly flashing red earlier was now a constant green glow.

She straightened again and tightened her crossed arms. "Fine, does that mean you're done? I'm obviously very busy." Realizing too late how empty the store was, she instead grabbed a random piece of paper to wave at him and tried to ignore the lilt in her voice. "So I'd like it if we both went on about our business. Nora just left to run a quick errand, leaving me all by myself on my first day and I have inventory I need to set out. So go on and do whatever you need to do and I'll do the same."

Snatching the closest pen, she tapped it against her lips as she studied the prop piece of paper, hoping he'd just go away. But she couldn't get her mind off how her body thrummed under his gaze, how close he was, how his body trembled with desire just like hers did... until she realized his body wasn't trembling at all. It was shaking with laughter.

She tossed the pen to the counter with a growl and threw up her hand. "What?"

His smile made her belly flip. Good Lord, she was being so rude to him and he was taking everything she threw at him. Why was he even putting up with her shit?

"It's just—" He muffled another chuckle with his hand.

"What, Snake? What on God's green earth is so damn funny?"

His face sobered slightly and his eyes heated. His voice dropped low, and desire made her panties damp as he took a step toward her. "It's Wes."

Each inch closer to her made her chest tighten until she was afraid she was going to pass out. His smile widened as he got closer and reached for—

—*the piece of paper?*

He snatched it from under the pen and waved it back at her. "It seems you happen to be 'very busy'… with the back of a flyer." He placed the flyer right-side-up on the counter, proving his point.

The smug jerk crossed his arms before leaning against the counter like only men who were supremely confident in literally *everything* could do. It was downright infuriating, but he'd caught her fair and square.

She looked down her nose at the paper. "So it is."

Deciding playing it cool with him wasn't getting her anywhere, she tightened her lips before marching around the counter and back to the window display. Maybe if she ignored him, she wouldn't be so tempted to flirt back. She'd wanted to make sure she finished her task before Dean called her for the fourth dadgum time.

"I really do need to shelve inventory and finish this display, so if you insist on bein' on me like white on rice, at least help."

Naomi was studiously *not* looking at him, but she could feel his gaze warm her back. She imagined him rolling his infuriating —*heart-stopping*—eyes at her with that stupid—*sexy*—grin and she tried her best to hide the upturned corners of her own lips.

"You might think your attitude is scary, but I don't think it's having the effect you're looking for."

She opened her mouth to snap at him again, but she kind of liked that he really did seem impervious to her sass. Her parents had taught her to stick up for herself at an early age, and her cheekiness was one of her favorite parts of herself. Why didn't she use it more often if it made her feel this good?

Because Dean doesn't like this side of me.

"Trouble, trouble, trouble," she muttered under her breath. The thought had sobered her, though, and she cleared her throat before resuming her task. She'd just finished setting up the window display when Wes arrived at the store, so she bent to grab the large box of shoeboxes. Before she could, two big hands landed on the sides and picked it up.

"What're you doin'?" The words rushed out of her.

"You said if I wanted to be around you, I needed to help. So..." He lifted a broad shoulder and smirked. "Where should I put this, love?"

CHAPTER SEVEN

"Don't call me that, either," she hissed, but she had been feeling lonely in the store's silence... and the box *was* heavy... and her back had already started to ache.

Still, he couldn't know how much she appreciated him being there helping her. A woman in a committed relationship needed to keep a man like Wes at arms' length. But, like a whale's arm, which was real freakin' long, according to Thea's children's encyclopedia.

She meant to glare at him, but her eyes had a mind of their own as they traveled up his strong, muscular arms, thick chest, and all the way up to that masculine jawline, until she met his gaze. Her mouth went dry, all the moisture pooling down to one *specific* spot on her body as his icy blue stare grew heated with promise. Like he'd literally kneel at her feet and use those sinful lips to worship her pus—

"In the back!" she blurted out before clearing her throat, hoping it cleared her wanton thoughts too.

"What?" His eyes narrowed before she nodded toward the box and pointed toward the shoe area. "Oh, right. Yes, ma'am. Will do."

Naomi massaged her temple. *What the hell am I supposed to do with him?*

"So how was work?"

The tension in her shoulders relaxed at the change of subject. *Dear sweet baby Jesus, praise the Lord for small talk.*

Mundane conversation was safe. She could do that, had actually perfected it with friends and strangers alike for years. It's easy to hide secrets behind boring, meaningless words.

"Uh, i-it was good. My first day back since... since you last saw me."

There was a pause and she was afraid he was going to come up with the same questions they'd ended on two weeks ago, but he surprised her, yet again.

"Congrats! That had to be a relief. You seem like the type who's unable to sit still for too long. But I'm sure it was exhausting, too."

"Um, yeah..." Not entirely comfortable with how good it felt that his reaction had been completely different from Dean's. Him knowing exactly how she felt, no matter how ordinary the feelings, was refreshing.

No. Not refreshing. Unsettling. It's unsettling. Hell, I can't go swooning over any guy that's nice to me, damnit. Especially not if he looks like that.

"It was and... I am. Exhausted, I mean." She lifted a box of shoes and waved generally over the wall, studiously ignoring the impressive tattoos peeking out from his shirt. "We, um... need to unload these and shelve them."

"Can do." Wes nodded and grabbed a box. She waited to see which one he would get before reaching in. No fingers touching, electricity-sharing clichés for her, thank you very much.

"What do you do again?" Hell, he genuinely sounded interested. "Your daughter said something that sounded an awful lot like 'sexy assistant,' but I feel like that might not be the whole story." He winked at her and Naomi snorted before shelving her box.

"Good *night*, that girl's gonna kill me someday. I'm an *executive* assistant to Gail Haynesworth, CEO of Charitable Technologies International."

Wes paused before grabbing another box and tilted his head with a grin. "No shit?"

Pride at his response filled her chest. Dean liked to remind her how he'd gotten her foot in the door at CTI, but Naomi was the one who'd fought tooth and nail to be Gail's EA, despite her lack of a bachelor's degree.

It was a big opportunity in a rural county like Ashland, or anywhere, really. Most of CTI's work was digital and overseas, so even though the main office was small, Gail's reach wasn't. The nonprofit had distribution centers all over and shared life-changing tech to non-industrialized countries across the globe. Naomi was proud as hell that she was the right-hand woman to one of the most influential nonprofit execs in the world.

"Yeah, I've been with CTI for a while. It's a great job. I'm learning from the best on how to be the best." Was that braggy? Sure as shit, she was bragging, but she didn't get to flaunt herself often, and getting the wide smile on Wes's face felt fucking fantastic.

His smile fell as he seemed to be thinking. "CTI... CTI... CTI, CTI, CTI... I heard something about them a while back, I think. Weren't they in a big lawsuit or something?"

Naomi huffed. "Yes. It was a nightmare. We make, sell, and donate computer systems and tech around the world and we were caught up in some bullshit patent suit between several other companies. Anyway, everyone was prepped and ready to go for a trial and then BOOM, the next day we settled with the defending party for pennies on the dollar of what the suit was worth. There was a huge turnover in the company, tons of my friends were fired. Thankfully, the board kept Gail and she kept me. That was all a couple of years ago. But things have been... tense ever since."

Wes nodded. "Shit, that sucks. At least you kept your job, I guess?"

"Yeah." She shrugged. "That was a plus. Although now I've been roped into some stupid party planning committee. It's turned into one of my main job duties and I did *not* work my ass off to plan parties for a bunch of old sexist white men. Nothing wrong with being an event coordinator, but *I* didn't sign up for it, ya know? I hate parties and—what?"

It'd taken her a few boxes of shelving until she realized it, but Wes was stock-still and staring at her.

"What? Do I have somethin' on me?" She patted herself and looked down briefly before returning to his face when he spoke.

"No, no. You're fine." His gaze left hers as he fidgeted with the shoebox in his hands. "A party planner, huh? Is that um... is that the Ashland Elite Scholarship Party?"

"Oh, pfft." She waved her hand. "Yes. It's supposed to be some charity event with all the bigwigs in Ashland County. The date and time and event list are stupidly secretive, blah, blah, *blah*. Gail and I both think the theatrics and dramatics are stupid as hell, but what can ya do?"

There was another pause as Wes slowly shelved one of the final boxes.

"Ellie actually went last year."

"No way?" Naomi propped her hand on her hip. "That's wild. What a small world. I don't remember her name on the list, but there were plenty on it. I was only there for a few minutes to make sure it was runnin' smoothly, but then I had to leave—" She cut herself off, not wanting to admit that she'd had to leave because her Dean was too jealous to allow her to stay. For once, he didn't seem to notice her caginess.

"A list? For what? Of attendees?"

She barely knew this man, so it could've been her imagination, but his voice sounded stilted as he talked. For what reason, she had no clue. They were just talking about a freakin' party, for goodness' sakes.

"Yeah, the party planners, aka mostly me" —she rolled her eyes— "get a guest list each year."

"Oh, um…" There was a hitch in his voice, like he was excited but cautious. "I know Ellie met someone there last year… maybe a… scholarship donor, or something. I'm not sure, but I know she's been trying to figure out who it was."

"That shouldn't be too hard to figure out. I can give her the list and she can see if she recognizes their name or something."

Wes's hand paused over the last box. "That would… that would be amazing." He was choosing his words carefully, and she narrowed her eyes at him. She didn't understand why he was being so odd, but she shrugged it off. Wes could be as weird as he wanted, but if she could help Ellie out, even in the slightest, she'd do it. Giving her a stupid guest list after Ellie had been so kind on one of the worst days of her life was the least she could do. It kind of actually felt good to break the rules for once, even if it was a ridiculous one.

"I've got my laptop in my car. I'll just go get it right now. I think I might have a flash drive or something."

"Wow, yeah, that'd be great." He huffed out a laugh, like he couldn't believe his luck—*weirdo*—and threaded his fingers through his blue-black hair before holding out his hand. "I can go get it for you, though. You don't need to be walking out there alone at night and that way you can hold down the fort."

Naomi eyed him warily, wondering what his game was. He was chivalrous and thoughtful… and had to be up to something.

Or maybe he's actually one of the good ones.

She resisted a groan and bit the inside of her lip. It was exhausting trying to find things wrong with him. It would be so much easier to stay away if he was just another jerk.

"Sure, thanks. That'd be nice." She retrieved her keys from her purse behind the counter and tossed them to him. "It's on the floorboard of the front passenger seat."

He nodded and set off, in no time coming back with her laptop bag.

"Kinda unsafe to leave it just out in the open like that, you know." He gave her a pointed look and she almost wanted to laugh. She'd take some fool out on the street with her pepper spray any day over an angry, volatile Dean.

"Thank you for your concern." She unloaded the laptop and fired it up.

"Here, I've got a flash drive." He pulled his keys from his pocket and unhooked what had looked like a normal key. He pulled it apart, revealing a USB port.

"Well that's nifty." She took it from him, again making sure not to touch him, before examining it. "Thanks." She uploaded the document onto Wes's flash drive before ejecting the USB.

"That was easy enough." He took the fake key and returned it to his key ring before stuffing them into his pocket again. "Sure you won't get in trouble with this?"

Naomi waved her hand and trilled her lips. "If it'll help Ellie with whatever she needs, I'm down. That's got this year's list, and prior lists too, by the way. And, like I said, the whole secrecy thing is stupid as all get out. I couldn't care less whether their little party was 'outed.' Maybe then they'd take me off the freakin' party plannin' committee."

"Fair…" Wes laughed but scrubbed the back of his midnight hair. "Thank you for your help, Naomi."

The fine strands looked so soft and she almost got lost in imagining running her fingers through them. Her eyes panned back to his face and her cheeks warmed at the seductive curl of his lips.

Seriously? A simple 'thank you' is all I need to get hot and bothered these days? Damn.

She snapped her attention back to her computer. "Well, I guess you'll be leavin' then. See ya." Mad at herself that she even cared about where he was going, she stuffed her laptop in her bag, maybe a little too roughly.

"What?" The obvious question in his voice made her pause before tucking her laptop under the counter.

"I figured you were leavin'? You got what you came for, didn't you?"

Wes jolted back as if she'd slapped him. The genuine confusion and hurt in his eyes made her second-guess herself and all her preconceived notions about him.

He stepped forward and got *so close* that comforting citrus and cedar flowed over her. She barely resisted inhaling on a deep breath, but when he stroked his hand down the outside of her arm, she couldn't hold back her gasp. The thin material of her sweater did nothing to stop the warmth of his fingertips and good God, did she wish she was wearing short sleeves instead.

"Naomi, I came here because Nora called me to help with the security. I stayed for *you*, not some list. I didn't even know you had it."

Oh... right. I'm an idiot. But what's his play, then?

Now she was the confused one, and no matter how badly she wanted to explore whatever *this* was, she didn't have the time, nor the relationship status, to play games.

She stepped back, out of the orbit of his citrus-cedar scent and away from his gentle touch. The space should've made her feel better, but it felt like ripping a Band-Aid from a wound that wasn't ready for fresh air.

"I-I really should be gettin' back to it. Nora should be here at any—"

The Sasha Saves cell phone dinged and Naomi checked the text.

HEAD BIC: Hay, girl, hayyy. Can't come back tonight. Got a thing. But Superman should be good company

"Who... BIC? I swear this girl speaks a different language sometimes."

Wes came up behind her and read over her shoulder. She fought the instinct to cover the phone but remembered that this was the Sasha Saves phone, not hers, and this was Wes, not

Dean. There was no need to brace herself for a needless jealousy blowup or interrogation.

"Ah, that's Nora. She definitely does and somehow I'm fluent. Lucky me. Do you want me to translate?"

"Ugh, yes, please."

Wes laughed and took the phone from her hand. "BIC stands for 'Bitch In Charge,' I believe. She's saying that she won't be able to come back to Sasha Saves tonight but... she made sure I'm here." His eyes narrowed at the screen before he typed. "Okay, I told her we'll keep the place afloat."

Naomi snorted before she realized what he meant. "Wait, you're stayin' with me until my shift is over?"

Wes's brows furrowed. "Yeah, I mean, you've only got, what, like..." —he checked his digital watch— "less than an hour before you gotta close up?"

"Yes, but it's my first night here! Shouldn't I be, I don't know, supervised? I don't know what the hell I'm doin'."

Wes laughed. "Look, I don't come around here a lot, but I know a little bit about the store. I can help unload boxes from the back, I'm great at math if you need it, and I can make sure you're safe. You shouldn't be here all alone at night."

Her emotions were warring inside her, unable to decide whether she was flattered by his chivalry or offended by his assumption that she was incapable of taking care of herself. She chose offended. Getting caught up in his manners was going to tear her to pieces inside if she let it.

"Thank you, but I'm not interested. I'd rather just be by myself."

Her voice ticked up at the end of her insistence and she silently cursed. Thankfully, Wes didn't seem to notice and only rolled his eyes.

She felt a pang of remorse at finally getting beneath that layer of kindness. But she *had* to keep her distance with him and letting in even an inch of his charm was going to screw her up and potentially the life she was trying to lead.

Besides, almost everyone had a breaking point. It was best to find it out ASAP rather than be slapped in the face with it when it was too late. Literally, in her case.

"If you don't want me around, fine. But I'm not leaving you here alone. I'll just sit behind the counter while you work, is that fair?"

Naomi narrowed her eyes at him, still not totally understanding his game. She wanted—no—*needed* him to go home. If Dean found out she'd been alone this long with another man, he'd go apeshit. Let alone the fact that every minute with Wes made her want an hour more.

She was also seriously considering that something was wrong with her in the head. The way her chest filled with warmth made her have to admit to herself that she was secretly glad he was putting up a fight against leaving. It was refreshing to be fought for, instead of fought with.

"Fine," she finally agreed. "But don't bother me and let me deal with any customers that come in. Got it?"

He lifted his arms in a hands-off position before miming zipping his lips closed.

The last forty-five minutes of the shift went by slowly. Dean called two more times, just 'checkin' in to make sure she was okay.' Each conversation was an eternity, but thankfully Wes pulled his phone trick every time, giving her a legitimate out.

Unfortunately, absolutely no customers came in, so it was just her and Wes, all alone.

There'd only been a few shoppers since she'd started working. Nora warned her that Friday nights in a college town were slow, but it was a straight-up ghost town. And the only company she had was the man who was beginning to feel like he was studying her.

Every time she got near him, her body knew instinctively. Her stomach tightened and her core grew heavy with desire. When he wasn't merely a few feet away, all she had to do was look up and there he was. And she looked up *a lot*. By the end of the shift, her nerves were shot and she was ready to hightail it the hell outta there.

They closed down the shop together in silence, following the list of instructions for each volunteer and putting the store money in the safe to be counted the following morning, turning off the lights, and locking up.

Wes led her around to the back of the building with his hand lightly on the middle of her back. She should've shrugged it off. She'd definitely intended to, but she found herself leaning into him instead.

Trouble, trouble, trouble. I'm gonna get myself into so much fucking trouble.

They walked in tandem, despite the fact that he was a foot taller. There was no way his strides were as short as hers, and yet, it was almost as if they'd practiced being in sync. She analyzed him until she realized he'd actually slowed down to match her steps. His head was on a swivel, too, looking out for them.

Her heart kicked up. It felt *good* to be protected. After her daddy passed, Naomi had to watch out for herself, and frankly, she'd been failing miserably at it since she and Dean crashed into each other.

As they rounded the back of the building to her car, Wes's warm hand on her back held her closer, and she let him. His touch made her feel more secure than she had in... years. When they got to her Nissan, brightly lit in the streetlight, she used the fob to unlock the car and reached to open the driver's side, but Wes got to the handle first and opened it with a damn smirk.

"After you, *milady*."

Naomi scowled to keep from giggling like a simp at his dramatic bow and hand flourish. She climbed into the car, considering saying something snarky, because damn him for making her belly flip. But he hadn't done anything to deserve her derision. He'd been a complete gentleman all night, keeping his word at not bothering her—which, coincidentally, had bothered the hell outta her, but no way was she telling him *that*.

"Thanks for, you know, seein' me to my car. You're still a troublemaker, though."

Oh God, am I flirting? Shit.

"Is that so? I prefer gentleman, but tomato, tomahto." His sincere grin widened in the streetlight before his brow wrinkled with an emotion she wasn't sure of in the dim light.

"Okay... well. Bye." She awkwardly reached for her door, but Wes held his hand out against the door to stop her.

"Wait—"

Her breath caught in her lungs as soon as he slapped his hand against the window, lodging his body between the car door and her, closing her in.

"Shit, sorry, but... please, Naomi, before you go again... tell me why you won't leave him."

His words came out in a whisper, but it felt like he'd shouted them into her soul. The concern on his face was clear and she could tell he was begging her to answer him, almost as if the need to know the answer was driving him crazy. But his hand was on the inside of the door and she couldn't close it and with his pointed question, she felt *trapped*.

"That's none of your damn business, Snake, now get the hell away from my car."

To her surprise, he snatched his hand and backed up, lifting his hands and lacing them behind his head, exposing a peek at his Adonis belt. Instead of allowing herself the second to enjoy the view, Naomi slammed the door and started her car, barely giving herself even enough time to check the mirrors before she backed out. A warm tear joined the heat his question had brought to her cheeks and she swiped angrily at her eyes, refusing to believe she was crying over leaving a veritable stranger. Over the path she'd been trying to convince herself was the right decision.

It wasn't until she was turning onto the main street that she finally looked in the rearview mirror.

Wes was still standing under the light, watching her, worry etched in his face, his hands on his hips in a superhero pose.

Superman, that's what Nora called him and Thea liked to pretend he was a king. But Naomi's life wasn't a stupid comic movie, or a silly fairy tale, and Wes sure as hell was no damn hero.

He was the villain in this story, plain and simple. He *had* to be. If she didn't pull her shit together, lock these frivolous feelings down in a deep, dark cave and throw away the key, he'd get her killed in a heartbeat.

CHAPTER EIGHT

Dean Jones stumbled into the laundry room from the garage and pressed the key fob to his white Corolla to lock it. Once the horn beeped, he jammed his keys back in his pocket and let the door slam behind him. The loud shake throughout the house made him wince as he realized it was late enough that Thea was likely asleep.

Shit.

He propped himself against the washing machine to gain his bearings before swiping his face to try to see past the spins. The sickly sweet smell of booze and another woman's perfume stained his palm and he held his breath, eyeing the sink from the laundry room's open door before glaring at the open door itself.

She never closes that shit, even though I've told her a million times she's lettin' the hot air in. Goddamn disrespectful. Dad woulda tanned my hide if I'd been so careless.

Dean shook his head and immediately regretted it as the very air around him seemed to wobble. Trying his best to ignore his disorientation, he staggered to the kitchen sink, pinballing against the counter, the refrigerator, and the breakfast table along the way.

He set the water temperature to scalding to clean off the

evidence of his night out with the boys. Tonight, he'd let things go a little too far with the floozie near the pool table. They'd only gotten a little handsy with each other, though, so at least he hadn't been unfaithful. She'd been hot as hell, too. He deserved a goddamn medal after turning down her offer for a quickie in the bar bathroom.

There was a time when he wouldn't have even thought twice about giving a woman like her the fuck of her life. But, ever since he proposed to Naomi he'd been on his best behavior. As far as he was concerned, screwing around pre-proposal didn't count and what she didn't know wouldn't hurt her.

It'd definitely been tempting though, especially since he'd taken the time out of his boys' night to call his ungrateful *fiancée*, and she'd blown him off repeatedly. On the other hand, the woman at the bar had been making eyes at him all night. When was the last time Naomi had ever looked at him like that? Had she ever?

He couldn't remember, and what sucked even more was that he was no doubt going to have to put up with Naomi's prudish bullshit for a little while longer. Not too much, though. A man had needs, and he wasn't sure how much longer he could put up with his blue balls.

The last time he'd flirted with Naomi, she'd curled up into a ball and laid there like roadkill, insisting she wasn't in the mood. His own woman had told him no *again*, but then she'd had the audacity to act like the victim and make him out to be some kind of goddamn villain. It'd pissed him the hell off. The woman had grown up too soft. She wouldn't know a villain from a hero if it could save her life.

He brought his hands up to see if he could still smell the woman on him, but his senses were too dull from the alcohol. There was a full bottle of hand dish soap, the fucking fancy kind she always bought like they were made of money. The shit went down the drain, for chrissakes. Why did she always insist on spending money on brand-name soap, of all things? The thought made him irritated with her all over again, so he squirted enough on his hands to coat him from finger to forearm.

The light turned on, making him realize he was washing his hands in the dark like a crazy person.

"Dean?"

The object of his frustration was leaning against the hallway doorjamb as she rubbed her eyes. Half the time, she annoyed him nearly as much as he loved her, but fuck was she sexy all the goddamn time. Even after obviously just waking up with yellowed bruises still fading around her cheek.

He wished she'd stop washing her makeup off at night. It made him sick to his stomach to see the evidence of their last disagreement all over her face. She probably did it just to make him feel guilty.

Mission accomplished.

Still, the rest of her was smoking, with her thin cotton shirt showing off her peaked nipples. It was only barely long enough to conceal her cunt. His dick managed to twitch to life despite the beer in his system.

"Yeah, sweets, it's me." He turned back to the sink, mad at himself all over again for being too faithful to cheat and too picky to just take what was his. But he'd learned real quick that fucking Naomi when she wasn't in the mood wasn't much better than going at it solo. The latter always ended up being less of a hassle, too.

"You been drinkin'?"

He paused, washing his hands before answering her. "Yes. You know I went out with the guys. I ain't a choirboy. I'mma have a drink or two."

"Right, sure. Sorry. Did you, um... did y'all have liquor or beer?"

"Beer. What's with the twenty questions, Naomi? I'm a goddamn adult."

"Sorry, sorry. I was just a... just wonderin' is all."

Placated by her answer, he nodded before shutting off the water and drying his hands.

"Sorry if I woke you up. You finished watchin' that show with Thea?"

Her eyes widened and she crossed her arms, making her hunch over and hiding her tiny tits. Whenever he got his cut from this recent job, the first thing he was going to do was get a boob job for his girl. She'd never mentioned it, but that'd make it an even better gift. There was no way she didn't want one. A curvy ass was nice and all, but nothing beat going face-first into a pair of double Ds. Hers were barely B cups.

"Um, yeah. The movie's done, but, uh... Thea's still not sleepin' well at night. Is it alright if I sleep with her again?"

He resisted rolling his eyes. There was only so much celibacy a man could take from his woman. She had to know he was getting tempted to look outside their relationship. How did she stand it? Was she getting it from someone else?

Maybe it's one of those guys Mr. Dickins talked about a couple of weeks ago.

The accusation raced through his mind, but he forced himself to think of the other options. Mr. Dickins was a crazy, nosy asshole and the story seemed far-fetched as hell, but that was usually where the truth was found.

He couldn't think that way, though. For now, he had to believe that Naomi wouldn't betray him like that.

Naomi had been too beat up that day to risk being seen by anyone else. Just in case, Dean had even followed her all around town, making sure she was only taking that drive she'd said she'd needed. The fact that she left during their argument still burned him up, but after his outburst, he'd felt obligated to let her go. Besides, why the fuck would someone else drive her home? Her eyes had been swollen, sure, but she'd been able to see just fine when she'd left the house. He hadn't overreacted *that* badly.

The excuses soothed his conscience. He wasn't sure if he fully believed all of them, but right now he had to convince himself until he found out otherwise. If not, he'd be liable to bring it up with her and, of course, she'd make that shit an argument too.

He had to be on his best behavior, at least for a little while. Pretending to grovel sucked ass, but he was man enough to admit that during their last disagreement, he'd gone at least a little overboard.

She wanted him to go to therapy for his temper. He'd even caved and called some places, but when he finally reached a therapist who had an opening, he'd come to his senses and hung up. If anyone found out he was going to *therapy,* he'd be a laughingstock in this small town. Only weak ass pussies go to therapy.

"Dean?"

Her prompting brought him back to the conversation. How long had he been in his own head?

Shit, maybe I had more than I thought.

He blinked back to present. "Yeah?"

"Can I sleep with Thea tonight?"

The question made his already hazy vision cloud further, but he had to keep it together a little while longer, just until he was back in her good graces.

"If you think she needs it, then that's fine, sweets. But I miss you in bed. It's been a long-ass time. I don't know how much more I can take. I've said sorry over and over. Why can't you just forgive me already?"

A look he couldn't decipher crossed her face before she cleared her throat. "I'm sorry. I-it's not that. She's just been havin' nightmares lately."

Poor kid. He knew how shitty nightmares could be, but hell, she had to get over them at some point. The kid needed to grow up eventually.

Not to mention, Naomi was always with Thea. *Always.* And now that she was doing that damn volunteering job, Naomi was going to have even less time for him. Just as soon as he thought it, he remembered his game plan for getting her to forgive him faster.

"Hey, what're you doin' tomorrow?"

His question obviously caught her off guard as she played with the hem of her shirt.

"Um, nothing planned yet, I don't think."

"Great. I made reservations at that new place in town."

Her face brightened beautifully before confusion and wariness marred it. "Wait, Julep? For tomorrow night? I saw on social media that they're booked up for months."

He forced a grin, unsure about the swirling emotions in his chest. It was always a great feeling to impress her, but he also hated that she'd question him. He decided on the first.

"AIE Securities has a bigwig behind it who got me the res for two. You interested?"

"For two? What about Thea?"

He bit back a groan. Always with the kid. He loved his daughter, absolutely, but he wasn't fucking obsessed like she was, damn.

"We'll drop her off at the church."

"Dean, she's been kinda goin' there an awful lot lately—"

"And whose fault is that, Naomi?" He huffed out a breath to try to calm himself. But the fucking nerve of her to bring it up now that she's decided to spend her time away from home. "I work all the damn time right now, tryin' to provide for this family. If you don't want her bein' away from home, then stay at home."

She snapped her mouth shut and nodded once. He was almost grateful she'd listened to him for once until it registered in the back of his mind that his chest was heaving from raising his voice at her. The damn woman was more skittish than a rat. She used to have a fucking backbone, for crying out loud.

After a few calming breaths, he put on his best show to apologize, once again refraining from pointing out that she'd been the one to irritate him in the first place.

"Fuck, I'm sorry, sweets. I didn't mean to light into you like that. It's just like I said. I miss you. I feel like you're never home and now I'm tryin' to do somethin' nice for you and it's like you don't even want it."

Understanding finally washed over her face, although it was tainted with something else he couldn't quite figure out. Damn booze. He read this woman like a book when he was sober.

"You're right. And I do appreciate it. I-I'm excited. It should be fun. Thea will be fine at the church."

He felt his lips lift at the corners in a smile and watched in awe as her whole body relaxed.

"Come 'ere, sweets." He held out his arms and waited for her to slowly make her way to him. When she did, he wrapped her up in an embrace and felt a sharp stab in his chest when he realized he couldn't remember the last time they'd hugged like this. It was surprising how fucking good she felt in his arms, even when they weren't having sex. The thought immediately made his dick jump against her belly and he felt her tense against him.

Goddamn prude.

He sighed against her soft auburn hair, frustrated she was still on the fence about him. His apology tour was taking a while this time, but she was worth it. At least she had been. If she put him off for too much longer, she might be too much of a hassle to put up with.

But he couldn't stand the thought of letting her go. She was his and he was going to do everything in his power to keep her.

CHAPTER NINE

"Can you believe those Neanderthals? I don't know how you can sit through meetings with all that BDE swinging around."

Nora scoffed and perched her combat boot heels on top of Wes's computer desk in the BlackStone facility war room. For the third time. He casually pushed them off and she dramatically allowed them to land hard onto the ground, as if they weighed a thousand pounds, but she never ceased texting.

"BDE... big dick energy?" Wes kept his eyes on the screen but raised an eyebrow.

Nora snorted. "Usually, but your crew is full of Big Dumbass Energy."

He could tell she was determined to get on his nerves today, but he grew up with a little sister and Nora's brand of torture was actually kind of fun. He'd be able to handle whatever the little pixie threw at him with ease and a smile. But first he needed to figure out how the fucking *hell* she bypassed his security... *again*.

"It was just Jaybird and Devil acting like cavemen," he replied. "The rest of us were just innocent bystanders. Did you hack my phone or something? How'd you use the temp code without me giving it to you?"

She raised a freshly dyed black eyebrow. "Do you really want me to tell ya, Superman? You know if I do, we'll be 1-0."

Wes grumbled and settled back into his chair before scanning over his wall of computer screens, his mecca. There was nowhere else he felt more at peace.

Except when Naomi smiled at me.

Fuck, he was such a sap. He was starting to sound like the romance novels his BlackStone Security teammate, Phoenix, was obsessed with.

Ever since Wes had seen Naomi again a week ago, he'd been hooked. Naomi's healthy, unbruised light ivory skin was flawless and highlighted by her striking eyes and dark auburn hair. When his willpower had broken and he'd stroked down her sleeved arm, it'd taken everything inside him not to continue on down to trace her curves. He'd finally been able to see the depth of her chestnut eyes, with warm orange undertones that seemed to spark every time she got sassy with him. Which was a lot. Fortunately, he liked to see her fire.

"Anywho, weren't they the absolute worst? When Hawk asked me to come to this meeting, I didn't know Assistant District Attorney Marco Aguilar and Officer Henry Brown were going to be invited too. That's damn near errbody. Gods, if Ellie ever finds out she's the only one left out because Jason and Devil don't want her to know anything about the party, she's gonna flip her lid."

Stifling a smile, he responded in a bored tone. "Yeah, man. I don't know what their problem is."

He had an idea actually, and it had something to do with the steamy self-defense training videos he'd been deleting from the BlackStone server right and left.

The first time he'd seen Devil and Ellie in a... *compromising*... position, much closer than any training session Devil had ever given *him*, Wes had nearly spit out all of his coffee. Hawk had come in at just the wrong time, smiled, said 'Good for Devil' and then ordered Wes to delete all evidence. But hell, if they didn't start using a damn bedroom, he was going to have to intervene.

"I know they're worried about her," he continued, keeping the gossip to himself. "But at some point, you gotta trust people to know what's best for themselves. Taking away that agency is only gonna perpetuate the problem." Naomi popped into his mind, reminding him that he needed to take his own damn advice. She obviously didn't want his opinion, no matter how much he felt the need to give it.

"Couldn't agree more... speaking of problems. Do you really think the same guys who..." Nora swallowed, "kidnapped me and Ellie are gonna try to pull the same stunt this year? Like, really *really* believe it?"

Wes sighed, knowing what she was getting at. Nora had been roped into being a part of their current mission to infiltrate the Ashland Elite Scholarship Fundraiser, an annual party that was always kept a secret until only a few weeks before.

"Yeah, I think they're gonna go through with it. The bastards have been radio silent for the last year, which makes me believe they might have help in high places. I'd bet money that the traffickers are the reason why the fundraiser is Ashland County's best-kept secret."

Too bad for them. Not only did Wes love a challenge, he now had the master list of guests, donors, and eligible recipients, thanks to Naomi.

He winced inwardly. He'd hated lying by omission to Naomi to get the list. What he'd said hadn't been untrue. Ellie had met people at the party the year before and because she was drugged, she had no recollection of anyone.

Nora scoffed and propped her boots up on the desk before crossing her arms and leaning back. "More like best-kept scandal. Honestly, Superman, I'm not stoked about being a makeshift agent. I'll be Nora, *Nora the Explorer* in a freakin' James Bond movie. Although, Hawk *would* be a sexy AF Black Bond."

Wes didn't knock her boots down this time. A note in her

voice told him what he already knew. She was terrified. And who could blame her?

Last year, Ellie and her friend were kidnapped from the party. Her friend had been murdered, and during recon, a BlackStone team member, Draco, was shot and Nora was kidnapped too. Both Nora and Ellie were almost fucking *sold*.

"We have a month until the party this time. Last year, we were scrambling after the fact and had less than seventy-two hours to come to the rescue. No one should notice you since you don't have that purple hair anymore." He tugged at a faded black lock, like he used to do with his sister, and Nora swatted his hand while sticking out her tongue. "I miss the fun colors, by the way."

Nora's expression dimmed and she cleared her throat. "Yeah, well... ever since Draco..." She swallowed as she mentioned Wes's teammate, who was still in a coma after trying to save Nora. "I just haven't been in the mood for anything 'fun' lately."

Fuck, he hated seeing that look of guilt stain her face. Desperate to get his annoying 'kid sister' back, Wes knocked her shoes off the table again and grinned at her scowl. "On the plus side, *Agent* Nora, having a woman on the team makes a group of guys look way less suspect. You'll basically be there as Phoenix's arm candy if that makes you feel any better."

Nora smiled before pretending to gag. "Ga-*ross*. I've heard some... shall we say... *big* things about our good pal Phoenix from the strip club Jules represents. But let's also just say I've heard those compliments a *lot* from a *lot* of different women. The man seems to be there all night every night, so yeah... that'll be a big hard pass for me. Thanks."

Wes laughed until an idea hit him. He turned toward his computer screens again and navigated the BlackStone Security program he'd created, opening files and reworking code until he finally found the answer.

"Ah-HA! You used Phoenix's code to get in! Wait... how?"

Nora smiled her mischievous grin. "You gotta talk to your

dude, Superman. Phoenix is *always* on his phone and lousy as balls at hiding his screen when he enters the code to get into the compound."

"Fucking Phoenix." He took off his glasses and massaged his eyes. "That man's gonna be the death of me."

When he put his glasses back on, Nora was watching him thoughtfully.

"What's the beef with you two, anyway? Were you guys like this in MF7?"

He kept from flinching at a civilian mentioning their former paramilitary unit. Before they were the private security firm, his team at BlackStone was part of a project so classified, most of the US government didn't even know about it. Secrecy was the only way to make sure no one infiltrated or sabotaged their mission to rescue trafficked victims and takedown rings in hot zones throughout the world.

Instead, he rolled his eyes and turned back to the computer, pulling up the guest list Naomi had given him the week before. "Who knows? I think he's still got damage from that last mission with all of us. Somehow it was fucked from the start, and he blames me for the comms going down even though I *know* I triple-checked headsets, drones, and intel beforehand. They went down before the firestorm and I wasn't able to warn them that they were walking into a trap."

The 'last mission' the BlackStone men had together, nearly two years ago, was when they comprised the MF7. They'd been charged with saving trafficking victims, and their last mission in Yemen had failed miserably. No victims were saved, and they'd lost their team lead, Eagle.

Nora's brows furrowed. "So he's angsty about your walkie-talkies not working?"

Wes huffed out a breath. "That's one way to put it. It's a little more involved than that, but it works I guess."

Nora stuck her nose back in her phone before nonchalantly balancing her boots on his desk again. "Seems petty AF if ya asked me. Sounds like all of you guys were boned. I don't see why blaming one dude helps anyone."

Wes tightened his lips and didn't respond. He'd thought that a million times before himself. He sighed and shook his head before pointing to the list and various other programs on the screens.

"So you ready to do some digging and find out which assholes are dumb enough to try to pull the same stunt they did last year?"

"Uh..." Nora looked up from her phone and studied the large computer screens before smiling her evil little pixie smile. "Almost."

Wes followed her gaze to see a gray Nissan Murano pull up to the BlackStone Security gate.

"You called *Naomi*?"

The request for entry alerted on the screen, but Wes was too stunned to move. He'd been pissed when her name was brought up in the meeting and didn't agree with Hawk that she should be involved with their mission with the Ashland Elite. Wes hadn't any intention of actually asking Naomi for her help and had instead spent the remainder of the meeting brainstorming excuses as to why they couldn't use her.

Still frozen at his keyboard, his mind on the fritz and trying to figure out his next course of action, Nora chuckled and dropped her feet from the desk. She pushed his rolly chair out of the way to press the buttons that opened the gates and allowed Naomi inside the building before sitting back down.

"Hells yeah I called Naomi. Hawk said we needed to try to use her to go through the list."

"Nora, she works for one of the companies that helps throw this thing!"

Nora rolled her eyes. "I know you don't think she has anything to do with this crap. She was naïve enough to trust you with the list in the first place. I bet she'll want to help. Color me an optimist, but she doesn't seem the type to knowingly involve herself with a company that would harbor and support sex traffickers."

"Nora, I don't want her mixed up in all this shit. We can do this without her."

Nora frowned and wagged her finger at him. "Come on, Snake, you're sounding like Jason and Devil treating Ellie with kid gloves. Don't let your BDE turn into Big Dumbass Energy, too. Naomi's a grown-ass adult, dude. We'll set up the sitch and see if she wants to help."

"Nora, you don't understand. We didn't end on exactly the best note last week. I'm telling you, if I was hanging off a cliff with one hand, she'd stomp on my fingers. I doubt she'll want to help if I'm involved. I think I've made her smile maybe once."

"See! You guys are already in lurve! I knew creating those false alarm signals at Sasha Saves would do the trick." She covered her hands with her heart and sighed like a lovesick teen. "It feels amazing to use my techno powers for good."

Wes groaned before lifting his glasses and swiping his hands down his face. "I can't believe it's been you this whole time. I was seriously about to overhaul the whole system."

Nora scoffed and propped her hands on her hips in mock disappointment. "I'm a wee bit offended you didn't figure it out yourself, Superman. Did you really think I was too dumb to turn on a motherfluffin' switch? I mean, *come on*."

"Nope, didn't figure it out. I guess that makes us 0-1 since you pulled a tech hack over on me."

"Yasss! Victory!" Nora cheered before making a show of propping her legs up on the desk again and leaning back with her arms behind her head. "Don't worry Superman, someday you'll pull one over on me and you'll get to be the king."

"Hello?"

Naomi's soft voice called down the hall and Nora winked at him.

"Oh, and look at that, my good sir, your queen has arrived."

CHAPTER TEN

"In here, doll!"

Nora jumped out of her chair and headed to the door, but Wes was still too flustered to know what to do with himself. He and Naomi hadn't had a proper conversation in a week, the last time she chewed him out for being too nosy. Since then, she hadn't looked at him as anything more than something to scrape off her heel.

"Nay-*oh*-meee," Nora sang out the door and disappeared into the hallway, coming back linked arm in arm with the beautiful woman in question.

"Snake?" Naomi's head jolted back with a confused look on her face. "What are you doin' here?"

"Seriously? I work here, Naomi..." Wes scoffed, annoyed she would come into his home and still be rude. Normally her attitude was cute, but today he'd been just as thrown off as she was. The last place he wanted her to be was mixed in with all this. Everything BlackStone was caught up in was dangerous as fuck.

At least this time, she had the decency to look chagrined. Her fist scrunched up the hem of her sweater as she studied the concrete floor. "I know. Sorry, I don't know why I said that. I was just... surprised. I didn't know *you* were gonna be here."

Her shaky voice and fidgeting set off alarm bells. The last sentence could've ruined the apology, but the way she'd said it, accompanied by her obvious anxiety, made him wonder what else was behind her reaction.

Is she afraid of me?

As soon as he asked himself, he dismissed the thought. She was terrified of someone else, and somehow he triggered that in her. The need to set her at ease squeezed his heart in his chest, but if he was part of the problem, he couldn't be the solution. She also seemed like the type of person who might need to figure shit out on her own.

"Here you go, Naynay." Nora pulled out another rolly chair from the round wooden table in the middle of the room. It was the only other furniture in the roomful of concrete and electronics, and where all the BlackStone meetings were held.

"Not sure I'm a fan of that nickname, *Nono*." Naomi muttered under her breath.

Nora barked out a laugh. "I like it, but I'll try to think up another one, don't you worry."

She placed the chair between the one she'd been sitting in and Wes's, a move he would've attributed to Miss Stupid Cupid's diabolical plan except that it also situated Naomi in the best position to observe every screen.

Nora waved her hand in a voilà flourish and Naomi looked at her like she'd grown a second head before reluctantly taking a seat beside Wes. Naomi darted her glance over in Wes's direction, but as soon as he got a glimpse of those rich, fiery, chestnut eyes, she diverted them back to Nora.

"Sooo, what am I here for, exactly?"

Wes glared at Nora. "She doesn't even know why she's *here*, Nora?"

Little Miss Matchmaker rolled her eyes. "Okay, so here's the sitch. There're these big baddies who throw a party every year for fancy-pants assholes to allegedly give scholarships to a select few—"

"The Ashland Elite Scholarship Fundraiser?" Naomi's head tilted.

"One and the same, my dear. 'Kay, so these big baddies... they did a big baddie thing last year. I'll be real with you. They totally fucked up *all* of our lives in one way or another—"

"Nora—" Wes warned, unsure whether she should be spilling all their secrets to an employee of a company who participated in the party, but Naomi's concerned expression quickly morphed into horror as Nora continued on.

"They raped and murdered Ellie's best friend and kidnapped me, Ellie, and several other women. There's also a BlackStone agent who's still in a damn coma because of them."

"*What?*" Naomi's gasp sounded like she'd been punched in the stomach. "You're joking... right?"

"Definitely not joking." Concern touched Nora's voice, more subdued after dropping the bomb.

Naomi's mouth opened and shut several times before she shook her head. "H-how do y'all know all this?"

"We have tons of evidence from the government and our own recon. And... unfortunately, we have evidence that they're wanting to do it again."

"What? No... nononono. This is insane. The Ashland Elite party? My company helps plan this event. That means—" Her voice broke, and Wes's heart cracked at the moisture already filling her eyes. "Oh my god... I've been *helping* these monsters? This can't be true."

Wes's jaw unclenched as the small seed of doubt about her innocence completely vanished. From the way she'd so freely given him the list, the clue of all clues, he'd figured she was in the dark about who her company was in bed with, but her reaction confirmed he'd been right to trust her.

"It's true," he whispered, hating to confirm her horror. "And we have evidence that they're wanting to do it again."

"Oh my god! I swear I had no idea. Oh my god..." Naomi ducked her head and pulled at the hem of her sweater. He ventured out to tug her hand to keep her from ruining it, and his heart skipped a beat that she let him.

"We know. It's okay, we know."

She looked up to him gratefully before widening her eyes. "Wait, have y'all gone to the police? They need to know about this!"

"We have, but they haven't been terribly helpful," Nora supplied with a wince. "They're not the most reliable source of justice lately."

"They didn't *used* to be that way, you know." Naomi scowled and Wes resisted wiping the tear that escaped the corner of her eye. She hastily caught it with a shaky index finger, as if she was afraid to show her emotions.

Nora shrugged. "Maybe not, I wouldn't know. But we're working with them on it to the extent we can and we have a prosecutor who's got our back—"

"Within reason," Wes reminded her and Nora dipped her chin in acknowledgment.

Naomi expelled a deep breath and massaged her temples. "Shit. This... this is a lot of info, y'all. I'm not sure I know what to do with it. Wait a minute..." She whipped her head back up and eyed them cautiously. "Why are you tellin' me this?"

Nora glanced at Wes and widened her eyes, pointing to Naomi with her head, but Wes wouldn't take the bait. Nora had cast this line, so she'd have to be the one to reel Naomi in.

Finally, she rolled her eyes at him with a huff and turned back to Naomi. "Because we think that *you* can help us."

"Me?" Naomi's hand shot up to her chest and she looked at them both. "What can I do? I mean, I can *assure* you that Gail has no idea. She'd never get caught up in shit like this."

Wes carefully schooled his face. Hell, maybe the CEO of CTI was somehow blind to what happened behind the scenes, but he didn't think that was very likely. These types of things always had someone at the very top and Gail Haynesworth was high up enough not to get shit on, but in the perfect position to let it all roll downhill. But he certainly wasn't going to say *that* to Haynesworth's right-hand woman. Naomi seemed trustworthy, but she also seemed loyal to a fault, and she adored her boss.

"This list you gave me?" Wes indicated the screens and Naomi seemed to finally register the list on the screen. "We just need you to go over it with us. Help us connect names and faces. We need to know everything we can about the people who've attended in the past and who will attend this year. Anything at all that you can help us with could save lives."

Naomi's eyes widened with what seemed like fear. Understandable, since they were asking her to get involved with something that could be really fucking dangerous. It was why he didn't want her there, but fuck, what if she knew something that turned out to be the missing puzzle piece they'd been trying to put together for the past year?

"I don't want to scare you, but this is very important and we need you," he explained.

"That's it? All I gotta do is help identify people on the list?"

Wes and Nora nodded and Naomi bit her lip before continuing. "Is... is it safe? I-I don't want anything to happen to my daughter." Her brow furrowed and Wes gave in to his instincts and grabbed her hand and held it this time. Her tight grip back sent currents of electricity up his arm and into his chest.

"We'll do everything in our power to keep you and Thea safe. I promise. There's no way in hell I'd let anything happen to you two."

Naomi's intense firelight eyes bore into his a minute longer before she slowly pulled her hand from his grasp and turned to face Nora. Wes had almost forgotten they'd even had an audience.

"Okay, yeah, I'll do whatever I can to help. Ellie has been good to me, and... hell, I can't believe I've played a part in this for so long." Her voice cracked again, but she cleared her throat. "I'll do anything to make that right and anything to make sure no one needs our services at Sasha Saves."

Our.

Apparently, she was already feeling like she was a part of their team, or at least the Sasha Saves team. And from the way Nora and Ellie have talked about her, she fit right in. She was a natural at talking to survivors. Unfortunately, he only needed one guess as to how she knew the right things to say.

Not that Wes had personally experienced her compassionate nature. He loved her fiery side, but only got glimpses of her sweet and calm nature. And that was only ever directed at others. The glimpses alone were enough to take his breath away, though. He wished she felt comfortable enough to give him both sides, but he could tell she was holding back for some reason.

"Okay great, let's get started." Nora nodded toward the screen. "Superman, the floor is yours."

A thrill of excitement at finally finding answers shocked through him. This was one of the things he was good at, identifying the puppet masters controlling the arms and legs below.

Wes pulled up the list and one by one they painstakingly went through it, matching each attendee with online searches, newspaper articles, high school yearbooks and websites, and hell, even hacking into government servers. Wes pulled up the variety of information, Naomi studied it and provided any personal knowledge she knew, and Nora inputted the data in a master spreadsheet.

It wasn't the most exciting task Wes had ever performed at BlackStone, but having Naomi beside him kicked his adrenaline to the same level he sustained during missions. He had to try his best not to talk too fast or ask too many questions, or reiterate facts they already knew, but eventually they got through a good portion of the list.

"Okay, next on the list: Mitchell Strickland." Nora gagged after saying the bastard's name.

"Ugh," Naomi's eyes were on Strickland on the screen and her expression mirrored Nora's. "I can't *stand* that guy. He's so freakin' creepy."

"Our prosecutor contact, Assistant District Attorney Marco Aguilar received his invite from him." Wes supplied.

"I haven't been a fan since CTI was in that lawsuit." Naomi scrunched her nose in disgust. "He was one of the jerks who was on the other side. I'm one thousand percent sure he's a big reason the company was screwed over. Gail doesn't like him either, but somehow he has enough clout to make *us* throw his damn party every year."

Wes's ears perked up at that and he resisted meeting Nora's eye. "Strickland's the slimiest man in Ashland County, and the slipperiest. We haven't been able to find out much about him. All we know is that he has a brother that's somehow involved with the trafficking."

He didn't mention that the reason they know even that much is because of one of Strickland's partners, Andrew Wilton Ascot III. Ascot had a son who'd unwillingly played a part in Ellie's kidnapping a year ago. He'd redeemed himself though by throwing himself in front of a bullet to save a BlackStone agent. His dying words had been that Strickland had a brother.

It hadn't sounded like a riddle at the time, and it shouldn't have been. Family trees were usually easy to scrounge up. But it annoyed the hell out of Wes that he hadn't figured out who Strickland's brother was. By all intents and purposes, he was an only child.

"I don't know too much about him, either." She recited everything she knew and Nora studiously took notes. Unfortunately, Naomi had been correct. There wasn't much more she could add that they didn't already know.

They moved on down the list to a few more, filtering through the ones that seemed of no consequence—

"Wait!" Naomi's soft hand grabbed onto his forearm and he didn't move a muscle, afraid she'd realize she was touching him of her own volition. "That picture... it says his name is Benjamin Johnson on my list, but the picture you've pulled up..."

"Yeah?" Wes asked, his eyes narrowed.

"That ain't Benjamin Johnson, that's Nikolai Rusnak, Dmitri Rusnak's son. Last year he was the one who brought me a last-minute guest list..." She turned her head slowly toward Wes. "One with only two names. I don't remember the names, but I remember being ticked off I had to add just two more people to the guest list the day of."

Her words hung in the air like a cloud on the brink of a downpour.

"Do you have *that* list?" Wes ventured.

Naomi winced. "No. I got so irritated I remember throwing it away outta spite."

Nora glanced at Wes while she typed. "I don't know about you Superman, but I think that tidbit of information is worth facing Jason and Devil's wrath. We should ask Ellie if she remembers him at all."

Wes's lips tightened and he nodded his head once. Ellie and Sasha had been invited to go to the party by someone at a college fair at their high school. She hadn't been able to remember his name, but maybe seeing his face would trigger a memory. They'd just have to figure out how to ask her without Jason and Devil finding out first.

They continued down the list with relatively little new information, and when they finished, they all leaned back in their rolling chairs.

Wes felt accomplished that they'd finally gotten through the whole task, but Naomi was biting the inside of her lip with her eyes narrowed.

"What is it?" Wes asked.

She shook her head slowly. "I don't know. Somethin' just feels *off*." She tapped the pen they'd given her to write her own notes, since Wes only had two keyboards accessible for him and Nora. "I've been trying to trust my instincts more lately, and somethin' tells me we need to look more into the women we've got listed here. Some of their 'bright' futures seem a little dim."

"What do you mean?" Nora tilted her head at Naomi before following her pointed finger.

"Like that one. There've only been a few other potential scholarship winners like her, but accordin' to y'all's searchin', she did real well in high school, had plans for her future, friends, all that. And now you're tellin' me that she just up and left her family?" She shook her head with more conviction that time. "Isn't that strange? And as soon as she's gone, they moved from their mobile home and bought a new house. What's up with that? And there's a few more across the lists that aren't from here but have weird shit goin' on with them, too. I'm thinkin' we need to keep diggin' on those ladies."

Wes scanned the screens at their version of an Ashland County Elite Fundraiser yearbook with brief bios underneath each picture. As he scrolled down, he saw a few more young women not from Ashland who'd left their homes soon after their attendance at the party.

"Yeah... fuck, I think you're right." He took his glasses off and massaged his eyelids. They'd been at it for hours and his blue-light lenses were only helping so much. "Let's put a pin in it for now—"

Naomi slapped her hand against her hip with a wide-eyed expression. "Shit. Hold on." She tugged her phone from her pocket and cursed again once the screen lit up. "I-I have to go, y'all. Nora, I'll call you later."

She shot out of her seat and into the hall with the phone against her ear. "Hey, I-I was just gettin' ready to call you." The lilt in her voice punctuated her lie and Wes winced. If the guy had half a brain, her tell was obvious as hell.

"She needs to leave that bastard." Wes felt himself grumble aloud unintentionally. "Before it's too late."

"Just be patient. She's trying."

Wes whipped his gaze to his friend. "How do you know that? She's got to really love him since she's stayed with him. What if when she finally figures out he's wrong for her, her window of opportunity is gone?"

Still not looking at him, Nora's face hardened and her voice came out flat, almost as if she was somewhere else entirely.

"Women like Naomi hold strong to their convictions. There's something keeping her there, preventing her from taking that final step. But trust me, she won't need a door or a window of opportunity. When she's ready, nothing's gonna stop her from breaking free."

CHAPTER ELEVEN

Dean stared at the bouquet of flowers in the passenger seat before sighing and turning off his car. His long-ass day had gone down the shitter the moment he received that text message about Naomi. Hopefully, the flowers would make her feel as shitty as he did.

He slammed the door, just to make sure she'd heard him come home, and wondered what she'd do next. Would she greet him at the door like a loving wife to be? Should he confront her about all the suspicions he'd had running throughout his head all day? What would she do then? Keep up the charade? Or come clean? He wasn't sure which one he'd hate more.

Before heading in, he tossed the bouquet on top of his car and walked outside of the garage to feel the hood of hers.

Warm.

"Not good, sweets. Not good."

When he'd gotten the alert earlier about Naomi's newest friends, he couldn't believe it. BlackStone Securities was the fucking bane of his existence and the sole competitor with his company, AIE Securities. The fact that she would betray him in the worst way by degrading herself with that scum made him sick.

But he didn't want to confront her about it yet.

They'd been in a silent standoff since he'd lost his cool during their last miscommunication. He'd obviously groveled for too long and this was how he'd been repaid.

It all made sense, really. Mr. Dickins down the street had mentioned he saw Naomi and Thea ride home with a "tattooed man with glasses" who got picked up by some black guy. At the time, he didn't know what the fuck the ol' man was talking about, but the story was far-fetched enough that it'd stuck in his mind, especially since it answered a question he'd been wondering for a while. Was she fucking around on him?

He'd always thought that was the case. She was a prude little bitch when she wanted to be, never measuring up to that first night. The liquor might've helped, but she'd been so into him she hadn't even noticed he went without a rubber. Most chicks were on the pill, so he hadn't thought anything of it at the time.

But then came Thea. When Naomi wound up pregnant, he decided that was as good a time as any to become a changed man. He bought her flowers, took her on dates, and even swore off liquor and one-night stands. It'd been good for a while. She'd looked at him like he hung the fucking moon back then. He missed that look.

There was bickering, sure. She'd been a fiery thing at one point and he'd had to temper that side of her. But over time she lost the fight in her completely and became nothing like the fun, outgoing woman he'd fallen in love with. The arguments got nastier, and they'd been broken up over the last five years for longer than they'd been together. She hadn't even let him be there when she'd given birth. The fight after he'd found out Thea didn't have his last name had been a knock-down-drag-out. Naturally after that, his resolve to be the perfect boyfriend dried up, apparently just like her sex drive had.

He'd gotten wild again, screwing everything in sight and letting his temper get the best of him more than usual. It wasn't really his fault, though. The damned woman had a knack for bringing out old demons and acting like his old man. She always came back though, and after a while, they'd been off and on so many times he figured it was time to shit or get off the pot. Ever since he'd proposed he'd been a saint, but she'd grown too timid, unattractively weak and goddamn puritanical.

Offering up that date had almost reeled her back in. It pissed him off that something came up at work and he'd had to cancel. He would've definitely had her in bed after wining and dining her. She was a sucker for that lovey-dovey shit.

He could leave. There was always that option. But Naomi saw something in him a long time ago that he'd come to crave, and he'd always tried to be that man. This last stint of "on" he'd been on his best behavior.

A memory flashed into his mind of the woman at the bar last week when she traveled her hands down his chest all the way to his stiffening cock. He'd come so close to backsliding.

Well, almost my best behavior.

He'd fucked around on her all the other times, but last week was the first backslide since he proposed. It practically didn't count, though. All that damn space he'd been giving her since their last argument was adding on to an already long sex drought.

If he hadn't been so busy on assignment at work, he would've noticed more. But what was her excuse? Her refusal all pointed to her screwing someone else.

Best not to show his cards too soon. He needed to play it smart this time. Patience was something he'd been working on. If he'd had more of it when he worked at the Ashland County Sheriff's Office, he wouldn't have been *not so gently* pushed out.

But Naomi didn't need to know all that. It wasn't like that was necessarily *lying* to her. There was just a little more incentive to accept AIE Securities' offer after he'd been fired. He'd gone off to do bigger and better things, and he liked that she thought it was solely for the sake of their family.

That need to impress her was gone now that he knew she

was involved with BlackStone. He wouldn't be able to stomach catering to her anymore.

According to Mr. Dickins's descriptions, the men he saw with Naomi were Snake and Hawk. Dean didn't know which one she was fucking, but he sure as hell knew everything else about all of them. He'd studied them like he was going to get fuckin' tested on that shit.

Had she been using that dingy little store as her alibi when she was actually with the BlackStone Crew? He knew for a fact she was an actual volunteer there. He'd driven by every one of her shifts to confirm. But of course, the one time he decided to trust her, she proved how untrustworthy she truly was. She sure as shit wasn't there this morning, even though she'd sworn up and down over the phone she got in hours ago from volunteering.

Dean lit a cigarette and leaned against the warm hood of the Murano, an obvious tell that she'd lied and just gotten home. After the first drag settled his nerves, he pulled his phone from his pocket and thumbed through the messages to look at the one that had made him fly off the handle at work.

Unknown Caller: Your girl's at BlackStone. Doesn't look good for you.

He swiped his face before deleting the message. No need to investigate who the 'unknown' caller was. There was only one person it could be, and they were both working the same job. Although he wasn't sure what part the other guy played. Dean only knew they answered to the same giant-ass Russian fucker, Vlad.

The texter was right. Naomi's affiliation with BlackStone not only didn't look good, it'd be fucking humiliating if his team knew, potentially life-threatening if anyone else found out. Maybe he could convince them that Naomi was on the inside too, trying to infiltrate the BlackStone Securities team. That'd cast suspicion on her on their end, too, sending her right back to him. Except... the texter had said she'd turned over the guest list to one of the guys.

Fuckin' retard.

How stupid could she get? She knew how secret that dumbass party was supposed to be, and yet, she was risking throwing away all the goodwill he'd used to get CTI to hire her in the first place. At least she'd eventually made up for her lack of a college degree by getting buddy-buddy with the CEO, so she wasn't a total idiot.

Except now she was ruining everything.

The door inside the garage opened before dark auburn hair peeked out. Damn, it'd taken her long enough to notice he hadn't come in yet. The woman was infuriating as hell, but she sure as fuck was just as sexy. Unfortunately, he was quickly realizing he couldn't tolerate the first without getting to enjoy the second.

"Hey, you. I thought I heard your car. You, um... you comin' in?"

He lifted his cigarette. "Just takin' a moment for myself first. I'll be there in a minute, sweets."

She frowned but nodded. "Oh, uh, okay."

Her indifference burned his chest more than the nicotine in his lungs. "Got you flowers, ya know."

Big brown eyes widened with surprise before narrowing at him. "That's... nice." *Fuck, she ain't thankful for nothin'.* "What's the occasion?" Her face paled. "Oh god, did I forget something?"

He seriously thought about lying just to make her feel worse than he did at the moment. But there were multiple ways to do that, he just had to bide his time.

"Can't a man get flowers for his fiancée? Just because?"

"Oh, yeah, of course. Um... thank you. I'll put them in a vase right now."

He couldn't help his chest puffing up at her gratitude. God, didn't she see that was all it took? If she just said thanks every now and then for his hard work and faithfulness, he wouldn't have to get so firm with her all the damn time.

"Sounds good, sweets. I'll be there in a minute."

She gave him a small smile. "Alrighty, see ya inside."

Naomi ducked back in. He vaguely heard Thea screaming something about her stuffed bear and that damn movie. The kid was cute, but goddamn, was she obsessed.

Thankfully, Thea seemed smart enough to know not to bother him with annoying shit like that. She wasn't much of a talker anyway, and way more respectful around him than with her mom. It always pissed Naomi off that he was so much better at discipline.

There was an art to getting what you want, and going in guns blazing was only going to get him in trouble again. She still wasn't over their last fight, so as much as he loathed it, he had to keep biding his time before he could reveal that he knew all her dirty secrets. He couldn't wait to hear her begging him to take her back. She always did as soon as she realized how much she'd fucked up and how forgiving he really was. Then it'd be her turn on her knees.

The thought of her teary brown eyes full of regret as she begged for forgiveness was enough to make his dick twitch.

It was embarrassing at how easy it was to get hard for her, even after all she'd done to him.

He shook his head before taking one last drag of his cigarette and stubbing it out on her tire. Dean still needed to be patient, although it was only a matter of time before his blue balls were unbearable again. He wasn't going to let her off the hook so easily next time. There was no way he'd resort to random pussy again when he had one right in his own home. So, he had to play this right.

Naomi was on the brink of leaving last time and he couldn't let that happen. Besides the fact that she was his, who would protect her now that she was unknowingly playing double agent. She didn't understand how precarious her position at CTI was going to become if she kept it up. He had to figure out how to get her to stop discreetly to avoid embarrassment, or much, much worse.

After that, he was taking her and Thea away. Now that the other fucker knew she was helping BlackStone, it was only a matter of time before Vlad knew too. He had to protect what was his, and the payout from this job would help them get the hell out of Ashland. Maybe if he took her away from temptation, she'd finally wear her engagement ring again.

She'd thought she was being sneaky taking it off a while back, but he'd just been waiting to point that shit out, too. If he confronted her about everything all at the same time, she might even feel guilty enough to finally set a date for the wedding. Then she'd be his forever.

'Til death do us part, sweets.

CHAPTER TWELVE

"You ready for this?"

Nora's bottle green eyes watched her from behind round rose gold wire-frame glasses. On anyone else, they'd be reminiscent of a 1970s octogenarian. But normal fashion rules didn't apply to Nora. She looked cute as hell in them.

Naomi ignored her mental ramblings and nodded, refraining from telling her new friend that no, she was certainly not ready to console a sexual assault survivor in a hospital.

The truth was, she felt woefully unprepared for her first case as a volunteer victim advocate. She'd worked with victims at the clinic, but this was only her second time meeting one right after they'd suffered the trauma. Nora had tried to encourage her, insisting that no one was ever prepared. But hell, it'd only been two months since she'd needed Sasha Saves herself.

The only other time she'd come close to directly working with a victim was when one came for their help a month ago. The poor woman had literally stumbled into the store, but it'd been closing time and Naomi had to leave to go pick up Thea from the church night program. Naomi had panicked about how to help her, and instead of calling the on-call volunteer, she'd called Ellie to go with the woman to the hospital as support.

At that point, Dean had still been lenient. He'd gotten snippy with her after she'd helped Wes and Nora with the scholarship list a few weeks ago, but after she'd been able to calm him down by reassuring him she'd been working for the nonprofit, he'd apologized and immediately become remorseful. For a few days after that, he returned to his angelic facade.

But true to form, he'd slowly gotten more and more irritated with her. Everything she did was wrong in some way. She'd answer his calls, but not fast enough. She'd text him, but it didn't count if he'd had to prompt her. She'd leave volunteering early, but would still get the silent treatment or snide remarks if she came home a few minutes late. He was disturbingly calm every time Naomi 'accidentally' fell asleep with Thea every night while they watched a movie with her stuffed bear, Angus. He'd beaten her bloody the last time he'd tried to 'encourage' her to have sex. Perhaps the leftover guilt was why he hadn't insisted on it again.

But he hadn't blown up again. Not yet anyway. It was almost as if he was waiting for something. Hell, she didn't know which she hated more. The waiting game was almost as scary as when it was game over. Maybe he was just irritated with work and it was just her own paranoia and stress kicking in. The party she'd been both helping plan and sabotage was in two days. Playing double agent was enough to make anyone crazy.

As Nora and Naomi walked into the hospital, Naomi couldn't help the jitters trembling her hands. The past two months had flown by, but she was excited to finally be able to talk with victims face to face. Even though she was still stuck in her situation, for some reason it felt like by helping others, she was helping herself, too.

"'Kay, doll." Nora whipped around to face her and Naomi stopped short. "Just remember, above all else, listen. No judgments, 'kay? For all we know, this survivor has just been through the most traumatic moment of her life. Our job is to minimize the fallout the best we can and to help her feel like she's in charge of her own body again. We're basically the best friend she needs right now."

"Got it, got it." Naomi blew out a breath as they navigated the halls to the ER. "What if the victim—"

"Nope, nuh-uh, survivor only, *capisce?*" Nora's tone was firm, but not harsh, and Naomi slammed her lips shut. "She's here, taking control of her life. She's a fuckin' survivor..." She glanced at Naomi. "Just like you, doll."

Naomi's cheeks warmed. "Our situations are completely different."

Nora shrugged a shoulder. "Maybe. Maybe not. But like recognizes like. I have a feeling you'll find more in common with this woman than you think."

Naomi felt a scowl in response but swallowed back her rebuttal. Sure, she had an angry baby daddy at home who couldn't control his temper, but that was nowhere near the type of trauma this poor victim had gone through. The two situations didn't compare... right?

She sat in her thoughts while Nora approached a nurse. They were escorted into a room where a woman sat up on the examination table, much like Naomi had just two months ago at Sasha Saves. But that wasn't what made her halt in her tracks.

"*Sophie?*"

Naomi's friend lifted red-rimmed onyx eyes and gasped. She tugged a loose strand of fine black hair behind her ear and pulled at a loose thread on her cardigan lying beside her before crossing her arms over herself.

"N-Naomi? Wh—" She looked around the room as if it held the answers to her questions. "What're you doin' here?"

"I-I—" Naomi couldn't for the life of her figure out the right thing to say as she took in the light bruising down her friend's pale skin.

Thankfully, Nora stepped in, glancing between the two. "Hi Sophie, we're from Sasha Saves. We got the call that you were interested in talking to someone and having someone with you during the exam? I'm Nora and it seems like you've already met Naomi?" Nora paused, waiting for one of them to find their words.

"We went to college together—"

"—before Naomi dropped out. God, girl, I haven't seen you in forever." Sophie turned to Nora but nodded to indicate Naomi. "She met her dream guy and ghosted us to go live her perfect life."

Naomi opened her mouth to argue but snapped it shut, feeling like she'd been slapped. Sophie hadn't said it with derision or judgment, more... envy? It made Naomi feel sick to her stomach.

Sophie wasn't wrong about the ghosting part, but the rest of it...

When Naomi and Dean met at a college bar years ago, she'd been a sophomore and he'd been a police officer like her daddy. His wide smile and bright green-brown eyes drew her in like the final shot of whiskey right before last call. She'd felt like shit the next day, but she never realized how long the hangover from that night would last. A positive pregnancy test and a few months of 'trying to make it work' later, Dean's true nature finally revealed itself. That was when she began to realize his smile had a bite to it and his eyes reminded her more of dead leaves than a gorgeous autumn day.

Five totally *not* perfect years later, getting cut off from her momma for having a child out of wedlock, and having to drop out of college, she'd gotten her associate's degree and a job at a global charity that made her feel like she was doing something worthwhile.

But even with that, Dean liked to remind her she only got her foot in the door with that job because of him. She'd tried for years to make a life she could be proud of and to have a happy, loving home for her daughter. That hope would never fade, but she was still on the fence with her 'dream guy.'

As soon as she thought the words, a set of piercing blue eyes behind black rectangular frames and a smile that warmed her soul flashed across her mind.

Nora cleared her throat, clearing Naomi's thoughts with it. "Well, we're here to answer any questions you might have, listen to whatever you might want to tell us. Keep you company during your exam... We're here for you and whatever you need."

Sophie sighed and bowed her head. It seemed like she was taking in soothing breaths until they developed an unsustainable rhythm and sobs soon racked her body. "It wasn't supposed to be like this. He was supposed to be one of the good ones."

Naomi's heart cracked in half. What had happened to her friend while she'd been too caught up in her own relationship? Naomi couldn't even think if Sophie was with anyone, couldn't even remember the last time they'd spoken. What had happened to her over the years? The woman she remembered was a ball of swirling energy and defiance, loving life and kicking men to the curb when they didn't treat her right.

Naomi grabbed a chair from the corner of the small room and nearly tossed it toward Nora before climbing onto the bed beside her friend. She tucked Sophie into her arms and let her friend cry on her shoulder, trying not to hate herself for not being there when she'd needed her.

"Soph... what happened, girl?"

Sophie turned and wiped her face with the back of her hand. "God, I'm embarrassin'."

"No, you're not, doll." Nora reassured her. "Take your time, or say nothing at all. We're here for you whenever or however you need us."

Sophie sniffed at Nora's words, but straightened. "There's not much to tell, really. There's a guy I've been seein'. I thought he was one of the good ones, but I found out last night he's not. End of story."

Naomi and Nora sat in silence, taking cues from Sophie, hoping she'd talk more if she was ready. Sure enough, Sophie closed her eyes and cursed again.

"He's one of the ones who can't hear 'no' when he's had a couple whiskeys in him. When he didn't like that answer, he took matters into his own hands. I woke up this morning not remembering how I got in his bed but knowing sure as hell that I didn't get there just on one glass of wine. It took all day for me to get enough courage to get here." She covered her face and spoke through her fingers. "And what really sucks is that I know that type all too well. I dated one in college—"

"*Jeremy?*" Naomi couldn't stop herself from questioning her.

"*Naomi*," Nora hissed and shook her head minutely. They were supposed to be silent listeners until given the right cues and never interrupt, but she hadn't been able to keep her shock to herself.

Sophie groaned. "Yeah, fuckin' Jeremy. He got that way after we graduated. He never went as far as... *he* did last night. But I was so glad I got rid of him when he moved outta Ashland."

Naomi was floored. How had she not known what her friend was going through? Naomi searched her brain, only vaguely remembering seeing Jeremy and Sophie together. She'd thought they'd been happy. Was that how she and Dean looked from the outside? Had she really been so caught up in her disaster of a relationship that she'd forgotten all her other good ones?

Of course I did.

Naomi mentally chastised herself. Getting pregnant, in a new relationship, dropping out of college, and having a baby all in one year was a whirlwind for anyone, but it was no excuse to leave her friends by the wayside. Especially not to leave them to fend off predators by themselves.

"I'm sorry, I didn't know, Soph."

Sorry. She resisted the urge to grimace at her own apology. She knew better than anyone how empty it sounded in the face of reality.

Sophie waved her hand. "It's whatever now. The point is, the guy last night wasn't much different. I'm just mad it took a repeat of the past to make me realize it. He'd asked me out on a date. We went back to his place for drinks and I guess he thought that meant I was an automatic yes. I should've left as soon as he got handsy, but it felt good to be wanted again for a little while. Until he wanted more than I was willing to give him. I don't remember much after that... I think he might've done something to my glass of wine." She covered her face with her hands again and let out a muffled sob. "God, I'm such an *idiot*."

Anger crashed into Naomi and she braced herself for the impact right before she let it out. "You are *not* an idiot. The one who's in the wrong here is that asshole last night. *Not* you, Soph." Naomi leaped up off the examination table, adrenaline coursing through her. "Who is he? Are you gonna prosecute? This guy needs to go *down*."

"*Naomi—*"

"I-I wanted to do the rape kit... just in case, but..." Sophie's eyes were deep, dark pools of confusion, but Naomi could only see red. "I-I'm not sure I want to prosecute yet."

"That's okay, Sophie," Nora interjected. "The hospital keeps rape kits for up to a year, so you have plenty of time to decide what's best for you."

"No, screw waiting a year. How could you not be sure about reportin' him? This guy laid his hands on you, Soph!" She pointed to the light bruising dotting up and down Sophie's arms and Sophie tugged on the cardigan. "He drugged you and left *bruises*, Soph! He needs to pay!"

"I don't know, Nay, I just, I feel like maybe I didn't make it clear? Maybe I should've been more upfront? I can't ruin this guy's life."

"Ruin this guy's life? Sophie, he *forced* himself on you after *drugging* you." She was one excuse away from having steam blow out her nose. "Soph, you have to press charg—"

"Naomi?" Nora popped up out of her seat. "Sidebar, babe?" She tilted her head toward the door and Naomi bit the inside of her lip and nodded once. "We'll be right back, Sophie. Naomi and I are just gonna have a quick lil' chat."

As soon as they stepped out into the hallway, Naomi opened her mouth to light into Nora for interrupting them, but Nora held up a finger.

"Naomi, stop. You've got to chill. You can't be going around telling survivors how to live their lives—"

"Nora, she's gonna let that guy get off *scot-free*—"

"Maybe!" Nora raised her voice before lowering it again. "But maybe not." Nora backed away, creating space between them as Naomi concentrated on breathing in measured breaths. "This woman has just gone through what sounds like yet another traumatic event in her life. You can't go in there telling her what to do with the life she already feels like she's lost control of."

Naomi turned away from Nora, closing her eyes before massaging a temple, a soothing gesture that was *not* doing its job at the moment.

"But, Nora—"

"No Naomi, I know this is hard, but our job is to listen, explain her options, and let her know she's not alone and that we'll be with her every step of the way—" Nora tugged Naomi by the arm to face her. "No matter what direction she decides to take. *That's* our job."

"But this is my *friend*, Nora. Or was. Damnit, she has us to help her get through this if she wants to prosecute and this guy deserves to pay for the bruises he's made on her." Naomi threw her hand in the direction of the small examination room. "She's making a *huge* mistake."

Nora's lips tightened before she nodded and spoke in a low voice. "It's hard to watch... isn't it?"

Her quiet whisper barreled into Naomi like a freakin' freight train. Naomi's eyes widened and she stared off into space as she collapsed against the wall.

"Did I sound like that?" she finally asked, afraid to hear the answer.

"Honestly, babe? You still do." Nora placed a light hand on Naomi's shoulder and squeezed. "At some point, you might wanna think about why it's so much easier to downplay your own trauma when you're ready to crusade for your friend's. But right now, that friend needs you. We're gonna go in there, listen, and hold her hand through this sexual assault exam. We'll present all her options with all the possible outcomes. It's important that she knows she has agency over her life right now."

Naomi nodded before shaking her head slightly and exhaling on a slow breath. "Okay... yeah... I get it."

Nora patted her shoulder. "You ready for take two?"

Naomi snorted. "Yeah, I promise I'll try my best to keep it together this time."

She was greeted back with a small smile. "Our best is all we can do."

CHAPTER THIRTEEN

After Naomi and Nora spoke with Sophie, mostly letting Sophie talk, Sophie asked that only Naomi be present for the rape kit. Nora, of course, was treating the situation with way more understanding than Naomi could muster, but she left telling Naomi she'd be back soon after giving them some privacy.

Naomi was still upset about Sophie refusing to report her rapist. The idea that someone like that could go out in the world free of guilt and shame, and possibly do it to someone else, chafed Naomi's sense of justice raw.

But Naomi couldn't deny that she was just as guilty of letting someone go scot-free. Nora had warned her that she'd find more in common with the victim than she'd thought, but neither of them could've known how right Nora would be. Besides the fact that the victim was a friend of hers, Sophie's objections hit too close to home.

Naomi stood by, feeling helpless as her old friend was subjected to the process. Sophie turned in her clothes to the sexual assault nurse examiner, had her fingernails scraped, vaginal swabs done, blood, urine samples, pictures and her statement taken. By the time the exam was completed, Naomi could tell Sophie was desperate to leave, so they walked out to the car together as soon as they could.

"I know the SANE nurse gave me scrubs to wear..." Sophie pulled at the nondescript blue fabric. "But I still feel naked. Like I've been stripped of my dignity twice after that kind of exam."

Naomi closed her eyes briefly, blinking back tears. "I'm sorry, Sophie."

Such an empty, worthless platitude. Naomi wanted to say so much more, but she knew it'd come out wrong.

As soon as they stopped in front of Sophie's car, Sophie reached for Naomi's hand. "I know you want me to go to the police... I just can't. Not yet, Nay. Please understand." Sophie squeezed her hand and Naomi almost squeezed back three times, just like she did with Thea. She settled for one hard squeeze and smiled the best fake smile she could muster under the circumstances.

"I get it, girl. I do. I'm sorry I came on so strong."

"It's okay." Sophie snorted. "After the luck I've had with men, it felt kinda good to have someone fight for me instead of against me."

The words took root inside Naomi's mind, reminding her she'd thought the very same thing only a few weeks ago with Wes.

Unable to speak at first, Naomi only nodded before clearing her throat.

"You good to go home by yourself, or do you want me to stay with you longer?"

"Yeah, I think I need some time alone." Sophie must've seen Naomi's worry because she squeezed her hand again. "I'll be fine, though. Promise."

Naomi nodded, understanding that feeling too. "Okay, and you call me next time you're tempted to go out with an asshole, got it?"

Sophie snorted and held up her phone before opening her car door. "I've got your number now. You best believe I'll be hittin' you up to rant about more than just bad dates. But don't worry. Next time I go out with a guy, I'll think 'what would my friend, Nay, say?' If your bossy ass nixes him, then so will I."

"Girl, I know it's been a while, but how many times I gotta tell ya?" Naomi rolled her eyes as she backed away from the car. "I ain't bossy, I'm the boss."

Naomi winked and turned to walk back into the hospital. Once inside, she started to text Nora to find out where she'd gone off to but ran straight into a hard wall... and a soothing cedar and citrus scent, like peeling an orange in a homey cabin.

She took a deep breath of the soft fabric, trying to place it, right before she realized exactly who gave her that sense of comfort. Her eyes snapped wide and she pushed the man away.

"Snake! What're you doin' here?"

Wes nearly tripped backward, his eyes blinking quickly, like he'd been just as caught up in the moment as she'd been. He shook his head before clearing his throat. "Sorry—"

"Don't say that," she interrupted without thinking and immediately felt her cheeks heat.

That *word* always irritated her, but for some reason, hearing it come from his lips when he'd truly never done anything wrong made her want to scream. How many times had she heard an apology and been expected to magically forgive every sin? She didn't know how to react when there was actually nothing to forgive.

She grimaced, knowing she wouldn't be able to explain her odd reaction. "I mean... just... you don't have to say that. You're, uh, a troublemaker, and all, but other than that there's nothing to apologize for."

He narrowed his eyes at her with what looked like curiosity, and she just knew he was studying her again. She should've hated how well he already seemed to know her. But she didn't.

"Nora told me to come get you. I looked all over until a nurse said you'd walked the survivor outside to her car."

"Why didn't Nora come get me herself?"

He gestured the way ahead of them, waiting as she nodded and began to walk forward. His hand was featherlight on her back as he gently guided her. Flutters settled low in her belly at his protective touch, but when she remembered they were in public and anyone could see, reality hit her and she couldn't help the way her spine stiffened.

Wes must've mistook her fear for stubbornness. He huffed and dropped his hand, leaving an instant chill where it'd been. "I'm taking you to Nora, alright? I was visiting a friend and she tagged me out."

"Oh." She followed his lead through the halls as she racked her brain to figure out how to make their interaction less awkward after she'd started it off on the wrong foot. "You have a friend here?"

Wes nodded, his eyes crinkling at the edges with what might've been frustration or concern, she couldn't tell. "Yeah, remember my teammate that Nora mentioned? The one in the coma?"

Naomi sucked in a breath and paused in the hallway. "Oh god, I didn't even realize."

His hand gravitated to her elbow, continuing to steer her forward with a light touch. Other people might not even notice, but everything this man did blasted loudly on her radar. She allowed the contact this time, not wanting to miss his warmth again, keeping her response neutral so as not to scare him away.

Just as the thought crossed her mind, he dropped his hold. He hadn't done it harshly, but losing his warmth was abrupt all the same.

"He's been in a coma for a year. For a while it was like his body was taking care of itself after he'd been shot, but it's been a hell of a long time. Too long. We're all worried, but don't tell Nora. Knowing the truth might crush her and I think she's still hoping for the best."

At the crack in his voice, Naomi reacted on instinct and grabbed his tattooed hand. The ink on his knuckles peeked through her fingers and his palm was warm against hers. It was surprising to find something designed to look so intimidating could feel so comforting.

Wes's steps slowed, but he held on, squeezing a little tighter before continuing to navigate them through the hospital halls and up two floors. When they finally reached the room, Wes turned and stopped her from going inside with a raised hand. She opened her mouth to question him, but when he tapped on his ear, she closed it again and leaned in to listen to what was happening inside the room.

She strained to hear until Nora's laughter tinkled into the hallway.

"No way, she *definitely* wore it best. I don't care who you are, Khlo's body is bangin'. It's not her fault her sisters are fun-sized like me."

There was no response, and when Nora kept speaking as if someone answered, Naomi tilted her head and watched Wes's reaction to find sad eyes and a grim tightening of his lips.

"Okay, yes, maybe Kourt's my fave, but that's just because she does whatever the eff she wants."

Wes leaned into Naomi, his chest just an inhale away from hers as he whispered. "She does this all the time." His warm breath caressed her ear. That, plus the combination of them still holding hands, sent delicious shivers down her spine. "She's here nearly every day. Talking to him... like one day he'll talk back."

Naomi waited, listening a little longer before answering. "Maybe one day he will."

Wes pulled away and Naomi got lost in his piercing blue eyes, so full of sincerity and compassion.

"I hope you're right." He spoke at a more normal volume, as if meeting her gaze made him forget they were supposed to be quiet. She couldn't help but lean closer, drawn into the need to comfort him—

"You guys can come in, ya know. Drake and I can feel the sexual tension from here."

Nora's observation splashed over her and Naomi jumped back at the icy cold shock of panic in her veins.

"There's no tension! None," she called out before realizing she was still holding Wes's hand. The grip suddenly felt less innocent than it was, and she snatched her hand away before muttering to him. "Sorry, I don't know what came over me."

Ugh, don't apologize to him, just don't freakin' throw yourself at him anymore, damn.

Naomi pushed her hair back from her forehead as she tried to gather her wits. Finally, she leveled Wes with a look she reserved for chastising Thea.

"We shouldn't be all over each other in the hallway. It's inappropriate." At Wes's snort, she scoffed. "What's so funny?"

"Holding hands is far from being all over each other." A dark look clouded his face. "But either way, I'm sure your *fiancé* wouldn't have liked us as close as we were."

Naomi flinched. She hardly even thought of Dean that way anymore, hadn't worn the ring in months and even had to remind herself on multiple occasions of her relationship status when she drooled over Wes. Hearing him say it was damn painful.

"Come on," he passed by her and citrus-cedar washed over her as he turned to enter the room, again not giving her a chance to reply.

"My frandssss!" Nora raised her arms in a cheer. "Drake, we've got guests. Isn't that marvelous?"

Wes chuckled, likely at Nora's nineteen-fifties television accent, but didn't he see it, too? The pain written all over Nora's face was obvious to Naomi, as the poor woman held up the mask of false happiness like a shield.

Her posture was slouched, although she leaned against the bed as if to play off her exhaustion. Bottle green eyes were dull behind sparkling rose gold glasses as she watched Wes and Naomi enter the room, and her smile wasn't much more than an upward swipe on her face. No emotion, just a facade. Everyone always joked about how positive Nora was, but Naomi was starting to wonder if they saw her at all.

Like recognizes like.

Nora's somber voice echoed in her head, completely at odds with the one that chirped in out loud. "Have a seat, you guys. Drake and I were just in an intense debate about the Kardashians."

Drake, or Draco as she'd also heard the others call him, laid prostrate on the hospital bed, his eyes closed. The man was ginormous, and intimidating as hell, even in a coma. It was like the blond Viking was only resting before he was brought back to rain thunderbolts all over the world. Still, walking into the hospital room reminded her an awful lot of one of the sterile tombs, or Norse funerals she'd seen on the History Channel with Thea.

Naomi searched her mind for any suitable conversation segue before she remembered how disastrous her first experience with a victim had started out.

"Um... sorry about that downstairs. I wasn't expectin' the victim to be a friend of mine. Or for her to shoot down the chance to get back at the jerk who did that to her."

Nora waved her hand. "It's fine. You shoulda seen Ellie the first time a *survivor"* —she gave Naomi a pointed look— "said no to us. Our girl went ballistic and cried for days. Granted, that was before all her therapy to deal with her own shiz. She's definitely gotten better, and you will, too. But it's never easy."

After an eternity of Naomi just nodding, she finally realized she should ask about the literal comatose guy in the room. She was going to have to majorly work on her damn people skills now that she was training to be a volunteer victim advocate for Sasha Saves.

"Thanks, so um... This is Drake? How's he doin'?"

Nora had the grace not to point out Naomi's awkwardness, just lifting a shoulder. She got up and moved magazines from the chair in front of the window and glanced back at Naomi before pointing to the seat, indicating she could sit there. Naomi glanced to Wes before grabbing it to do just that.

"It's okay, I'm going to make a coffee run," he explained. "Do you guys want anything?"

Naomi and Nora both shook their heads before Wes nodded and left the room.

Once Naomi had settled herself across from Nora on the other side of Draco's bed, she waited for her new friend to speak.

"He's doing the same." Nora explained, finally answering Naomi's question. "Doctors say he could come out of it today, or tomorrow, or..." Nora trailed off and swallowed hard as she sat back down.

Naomi's heart ached for her new friend, for Wes and the rest of the BlackStone men, for the women Draco had been trying to save, for Draco himself. "I'm so sorry, Nora."

She cringed inwardly. *If I say that word one more time, I'm gonna lose it.*

"Do you think he can feel it? When I do this?" Nora took Draco's limp hand in her own small one and turned to Naomi, those big green eyes begging her to agree.

Tears pricked in Naomi's. She'd had hoped the same thing when she was fourteen, sitting next to her father's hospital bed. He'd never woken up to tell her.

"I-I don't know," she answered honestly. "But I'd like to think so. I don't think it does anyone any good to think he can't feel it, ya know?"

Nora nodded again and sighed. "Nurses do exercises with him, to try to limit any trouble he may have physically after waking up. I do them too, but I'm afraid that if he does open his eyes, exercises won't be enough to bring him back to who he was." She leaned on the hospital bed, still holding Draco's hand. "I always thought it was a miracle he made it out alive. But if *this* is alive..." She waved her hand, indicating his entire body, before shaking her head. "Sometimes I think I see his eyes move behind his lids when I say something crazy or his hand will respond when I squeeze it. The nurse says it's all in my head. Just hopeful thinkin'. I feel like I know everything about him, Naomi. But I don't. I don't know a godsdamned thing about this man except that he thought I was worth dying for. I just have this gut feeling that being trapped like this is his nightmare."

Naomi watched as Nora's thumb traced the top of his hand. "What makes you so sure?"

Nora snorted out a laugh. "Well, first of all, who in their right mind would want this? And second, I mean, look at him. He's huge. I just imagine him enjoying life outside in a flimsy ass tent like a loon who doesn't know electricity was invented over a century ago."

A chuckle escaped from Naomi's chest and she felt the first true smile, albeit small, that she'd had in weeks. Even when Nora was sad, she had a knack for making others happier. Naomi's grin waned as she thought about how exhausting and lonely it had to be, to always put up a front for others' benefit, never quite being able to feel what *she* needed to feel.

Unsure how to make the woman next to her feel comfortable enough to open up, Naomi moved on, hoping the answers would come to her at some point.

"What're those?" Naomi asked, pointing to the pile of magazines Nora had placed on the bedside table.

Nora turned to see where Naomi was pointing and laughed. "Oh, those?" It looked like she squeezed Draco's hand before she let it go to reach the magazine. "These are why I wonder if Drake's ever gonna wa—" She cleared her throat. She blew out a harsh breath. "Anywho, I read him these every day. Gotta make sure he's in the know whenever he comes back from his brain vacay."

Naomi took the magazine being handed to her and flipped through it. "*Cosmo*, Nora? Really? Isn't that a little risqué?"

A snort lifted Nora's shoulders up. "Oh my dear, sweet child. The fact that you think Cosmo is risqué is effin' adorable."

It was Naomi's turn to scoff. "Nora, I'm, what? Two years older than you?"

"Bah" —Nora dismissed her objection with a gesture— "everyone's littler, sweeter, and younger than me in my world. It's nicer that way. Otherwise it's the opposite."

"Okay, fair, but you seriously read women's magazines to him?" she teased. "You think this big man's gonna want to hear about 'Who Wore It Best?'"

Nora huffed before rolling her eyes dramatically and snatching the magazine back. "We'll have none of that negative energy in here, rude-y Trudy. 'Kay? There's valuable info to be learned. Like..." She flipped through the magazine. "Ah, yes. *'How to Give a Guy the Blow Job to Die For.'* Or how 'bout this?" She lifted the magazine toward Draco's comatose body and spoke to him. "This'll be handy for you someday, big guy, *'How to Tell Him He Doesn't Know Where Your G-Spot Is.'*"

She waited a beat before sighing, as if she really thought antagonizing him would wake him up. "*Fine*, be that way, ya jerk. Keep your thoughts to yourself." She turned back to Naomi. "There're also trusty horoscopes, 'Who Wore It Best,' hot celeb goss, and the shmexy story in the back. *That* part's my fave." She flipped the pages all the way to the end before clearing her throat.

"*Joanne winked.*" Nora's voice was low and husky, and Naomi hid her silent chuckles behind her hand. The woman was a riot. "'*Wanna take this to the bedroom, Scott?*'... Let's see... there's some makin' out, a little foreplay and—oh yes—get ready to cringe. '*Joanne reached into the bedside table to get a condom.*'"

Nora barked out a laugh and tossed the magazine onto Draco's still legs. "Those safety-first stories kill me every time. Like, safe sex is the sexiest sex, sure, blah, blah, blah, but it's a godsdamned three page short story for cryin' out loud. Like, *hellooo* can't we just assume that part with an asterisk at the beginning or something? I mean, what could be less sexy than the word *condom*?" She spat the word from her mouth. "Why can't it be something like 'shaft sheath' or 'cock cloak' or 'groin glove?'" She waved her hand with a flourish and a roll of her eyes like when Thea said 'duh'. "Obvi it would need to be an alliteration."

Naomi laughed outright even as she felt her face grow hot. She definitely wasn't used to Nora's brand of candor, but it was refreshing as all get out to be around someone who said what everyone was thinking.

"Anyway, that's on me and the big guy. What about you and your fella?"

"Uh, my... oh, my fi–um... Dean's fine. He's been workin' an alternating schedule and is on second shift today—"

"Cool, cool, cool. But what about you and Superman, huh?" She waggled her eyebrows. "I want the tea on Mr. Tall, Pale, and Handsome. He's been lookin' at you like you're birthday cake and he's on a diet. Spill, girl." Nora crossed her holey, straight-legged jeans and propped her elbow on her knee. She left her chin on her closed fist and smiled, blinking her eyes in expectation.

Naomi's already heated cheeks felt like they finally caught fire before she carefully schooled her face.

Fuck, am I that obvious?

She didn't want to snap at her friend, but she needed to nip this shit in the bud real quick. "I don't know what you're talking about, Nora. And I'd appreciate it if you didn't bring this up again, alright?"

Nora's eyebrows raised before smiling knowingly and relaxing from what was apparently her 'spill the tea' pose. "Alright then, Gandolf. Keep your secrets."

Naomi felt her brows furrow again before she huffed out a laugh when she finally sort of understood what Nora was referencing. "Girl, I swear, a conversation with you is like talkin' directly to Twitter."

"Excuse me, Nora?"

Naomi turned to find a tall man in scrubs with dark skin and black hair. His deep brown eyes seemed to only see Nora as he walked into the room with concern etched into his handsome features.

"Oh, hey, Matt." Nora's voice came out hoarse and Naomi swiveled back to see her pale face had somehow blanched further. "Uh, Naomi, this is Matt." As if he was registering Naomi for the first time, Matt lifted his hand in a halfhearted greeting with a small smile. "He's one of the nurses on Drake's rotation, so we've started to, uh... get to know each other. Um... what's up?"

Matt shifted on his feet before speaking to Naomi and then Nora. "It's really nice to meet you, Naomi, but I really need to speak with Nora... alone, if that's alright?"

"Oh, sure—"

"—No, stay!" Nora reached over Draco's body and grabbed on to her arm.

Matt shifted on his feet again, obviously uncomfortable. "Nora, I really wanted to speak to you alone... It's about Mr. Heklason."

"Whatever you have to say about him, you can say in front of Naomi."

Matt nodded, seeming to accept that was as good as he was going to get. "Okay... I would have preferred to do this in private, but..." He walked over to Nora and crouched down so he was eye level with her and took her hand. Naomi noticed her slight flinch, but it didn't seem like Matt did. "A doctor is waitin' to talk to Hawk since we don't have any family members on file, and I could get in trouble for tellin' you but I—" He looked at Draco and a look Naomi couldn't decipher crossed his face. "I know you care about him, so I wanted to talk to you first and take the sting out of what the doctor's gonna say."

"Just say it, Matt," Nora snapped and Naomi blinked at her tone.

"The doctor said that he's seriously considering discussing options... for Mr. Heklason's future."

"Really? I just spoke to a doctor recently and he didn't talk about that." Nora eyed him warily, and Naomi had to wonder where Nora's extreme mood change had come from.

"I know. But the likelihood of him wakin' up, Nora—"

She tugged her hand free. "I *told* you, he's responding to me when I talk to him. His eyes move and his hand squeezes back, and—"

"No, Nora." Matt shook his head and what looked like genuine sympathy washed over his face. "Babe, those are just reflexes. They don't think he's gonna come back. Not after this long."

After a moment of silence, Naomi noticed Nora's green eyes brimmed with tears as they bore into Draco's blanket. She closed them and seemed to literally swallow back her emotion, before opening them again with the moisture suddenly gone. "Thanks, Matt." Her voice was flat and distant. "I think you should go."

Matt's head dipped before he nodded. "I get it. Just... call me when you wanna talk. I'll always be here for you."

Nora's eyes never left the blanket in front of her. "Thanks."

Matt seemed to want to say more, but finally nodded once before leaving.

Naomi and Nora sat in silence together. Once again, Naomi didn't have a damn clue as to what she should say to console her. Of course, Nora took care of the awkwardness after clearing her throat.

"Naomi, I'm sorry, but do you mind giving me some privacy? I'd like to be by myself with Drake."

"Oh, of course, yeah sure." Naomi shot up to leave, saying her brief goodbye while trying not to stress over how she was supposed to get back to Sasha Saves.

I knew I should've ridden by myself.

She'd wanted to, but Nora had assured her that they would leave in time. As Naomi walked out of the hospital room, she looked back once to see Nora's forehead resting against Draco's leg.

For a moment, Naomi thought she saw it too, that quick movement behind his eyes, maybe a twitch of his hand. But Matt had said that the doctors were basically giving up hope. As usual, she was just seeing what she wished she could.

Was that really how she wanted to keep seeing the world? She was coming to realize that was definitely how she saw her relationship with Dean. Always wishing it would get better. Struggling to mesh her deep-seated need for Thea to have her father in her life with their reality. Hoping they'd last and provide a loving home for Thea on a wing and a prayer.

Naomi leaned against the wall outside of the hospital room and resisted looking at the time on her phone. Instead, she covered her face in her hands, once again trying to figure out what she should do with her own damn life. Why had it been so easy to figure out solutions with Sophie, but impossible to figure out her own?

What would my friend say?

Sophie's new mantra rang in her ears. Was it really that simple? Talk to herself like she would her friend?

She heard his steps and felt his presence before he leaned against the wall beside her, nudging her arm gently with his elbow.

"Hey... what're you doing out here?"

Naomi moved her hands from her face and brought herself to look at Wes. His concern was obvious and she couldn't keep looking at his expression or it would send those stupid butterflies fluttering in her belly again.

But as she moved her gaze down, she couldn't take her eyes off his intricate tattoos up his neck and down to those strong hands. Instead of fluttering, desire pooled in her lower belly as she thought about what those calluses there would feel like on the softest parts of her.

And there was another question she'd been craving the answer to. What would this man do with the vulnerable pieces of her soul? The ones she'd never felt comfortable giving away to anyone?

She closed her eyes against the hope that she'd finally found someone who would safeguard her heart. Dreams like that would only get her in trouble. Choosing Thea's father meant there was no use wishing to be rescued from a tower of her own making. Besides, this wasn't one of Thea's stories.

She'd learned the hard way that white knights only exist in fairy tales.

CHAPTER FOURTEEN

Wes's blood pulsed under his skin, growing hot at the desire burning in Naomi's smoldering eyes. But his heart slowed its arrhythmic beat as he watched her consciously blink back her need, replaced by a nervous energy.

"Hey there, trouble." Her chuckle was forced as she glanced at her phone. "Nora asked for some privacy... She's my ride back to Sasha Saves, so... I'm just waitin' for her to be ready."

"You know, you're the only one who's ever called me that? Be careful, though. I might start thinking you like me if you give me nicknames." He wanted to tease her more, but her weak grin in reply made him pause. "Shit, love, what's wrong?"

Her legs were shaking with nerves and she crossed her arms while pressing herself fully against the wall, as if doing so would keep her from running away from him. Or into him. But it was her furtive glance at her phone yet again that tipped him off.

His lips tightened as he realized the problem and confirmed his thoughts with his watch. "It's almost the end of your shift at Sasha Saves." Her gorgeous light ivory skin blanched and she nodded. Of course she knew that. She probably knew down to the minute what time it was whenever she had to go back to that asshole at home. "Do you want me to give you a ride?"

Her warm chestnut eyes darted up to his, searching his face before biting her lip. "I probably shouldn't," she whispered and ducked her head, her dark auburn hair spilled from her shoulder, covering her face.

Frustration zapped his nerves. Naomi sparked and burned with life when she was able to be herself, just like the campfire in her eyes. Her fiancé smothered that light, and Wes couldn't fucking stand watching it anymore or the thought of anyone taking away this brilliant woman's fire.

He'd developed a theory over the past couple of months, but he hadn't been able to test it just yet. Although they'd seen each other several times at Sasha Saves since the day they went over the guest list together, she'd managed to avoid him like the plague. But what he'd noticed during their brief times together was how alive she got whenever she decided to hate him for whatever reason. It hurt that he was the object of her anger, but it was refreshing to see the *real* Naomi, and he bet she thought so too.

Time to light the flame.

"Damn, he's got some hold on you, doesn't he?"

Those eyes narrowed at him and he could see the anger ignite inside her. Even though he wished to God it was a different emotion altogether, the fact that he could make her feel *something* besides responsibility or fear went straight to his cock.

"*No* one has a hold on me. I am my own person." She shoved her thumb into her chest.

That's it, baby, get mad.

Wes sipped his coffee, adopting the most nonchalant expression he could muster in the presence of the woman who drove him crazy.

"Alright then, prove it. Let me take you back to Sasha Saves. Think of me as a free Uber."

He analyzed her facial expressions, seeing her creative wheels turning, trying desperately to come up with some stupid-ass excuse. Finally, after a heavy sigh, she relented.

"Fine."

Wes couldn't hide his surprise, but Naomi breezed by him and strode toward the elevator at the end of the hall before pausing halfway and turning back to him. "Come on, Uber driver. I've got places to be. If you don't hurry, I won't leave you a tip."

Wes felt his lips curve up. "Oh, I wouldn't want to go without that. I think I'd do just about anything to see what a tip from Naomi Ward would be."

She pretended to be sucked into her phone, but he could tell she was fighting back a smile as he walked toward her.

He led her to his black Trackhawk and opened up the door for her. She seemed to be carefully avoiding looking at him and it made him want to irritate her more, do *something* to get a rise out of her so he could see that spark in her eyes again.

When he got behind the wheel, he set off for Sasha Saves. It wasn't very far, so sitting in silence wouldn't have been too awkward, except the air inside the cab was so thick it made it hard to think about anything else but how close she was to him. Her sweet scent, like a delicious dessert, was heady as he breathed in and he had a hard time maintaining focus while daydreaming about whether she tasted as good as she smelled.

Her phone vibrated and she cursed before digging it from her pocket. She cursed again before raising the phone to her ear.

"H-hey... Yeah... Yeah... I'm uh, I'm gonna be off to pick up T soon. Yeah, I've been at the store. Lots of customers today... Busy, busy."

There was more conversation, all of it punctuated by the little question marks she added in every statement, until finally she said goodbye in a low, timid voice that made him so sick he couldn't help but scoff.

"You're going to have to learn to lie better than that if you're going to stay with that asshole."

Her head whipped around to face him and he could tell even from his periphery that she was scowling at him.

"What's *that* supposed to mean?"

He propped his elbow on the inside of his window and leaned his cheek against his fist, trying to seem like talking to her about her asswipe of a fiancé wasn't killing him inside for reasons he didn't want to analyze too closely.

"You've got a tell, baby. Every time you lie, it sounds like you're asking a question."

Naomi sputtered, but by the way she gripped the hem of her sweater in a tight fist, he could tell that he'd unnerved her.

"I am *not* your baby. And you don't know what you're talkin' about."

"Maybe it'll surprise you, but I might actually know more than you think."

Naomi paused at that, seemingly trying to figure out what to say next. "Well, I'm sorry to hear that, but every situation is different. You don't know mine. What you think you saw is the worst it's ever been. He doesn't normally get that mean."

"Oh, hell, have I heard *that* one before. You know what that makes me think of?" Without waiting for her to respond, he answered. "Woo-hoo! He doesn't always beat you up when he's mad. Fan-*fucking*-tastic." He massaged his eyes under his glasses before looking at her again, hoping she could see how frustrated he was. "Hell, Naomi, your bar is so low for him, it might as well be on the goddamn floor." He gave her a pointed look. "You deserve to have standards higher than the fucking clouds. Don't settle for a coward who should be six feet under."

"I'm not settling!"

"Yes, you are." His words were simple and quiet, not even trying to argue with her anymore. Just stating facts. But he wondered if she could tell the undercurrent of fear in his statement, like he could tell the desperation in her lies.

She growled and looked at him. "*No,* I am not."

"Let me ask you something. Is it only when you lie to everyone else that your voice lilts up at the end, or do you also hear it in your head when you lie to yourself?"

"Snake—"

"*Wes*, please. And listen to me, if you're so *fine*, then why do you always flinch when your phone goes off? Or relax once you've read what I'm assuming is an innocuous text message? Why do you walk on eggshells every time you speak to or about him? Why do you have to call him every half hour or respond immediately to messages or you start getting fidgety—"

"I don't do that!"

"—and that's *just* what I've noticed concerning your damn phone. I won't even go into the rest of your tells... Naomi, please just tell me. Why are you with him if you're so afraid of him?"

There was a breath of a pause before she mumbled. "He's my *fiancé, Snake*—"

"He's your *warden*, Naomi. Damn, it's so easy to tell he's wrong for you. Don't you see what he does to you? I *hate* this scared, deferential side of you—"

"I don't care if you like me or not—"

"*No.* That's what I'm saying. That side is *not* you. Nothing like you, actually. I've seen the real you."

She scoffed and rolled her eyes. "How could you have possibly seen the real me? We've barely been around each other for two months, Snake."

"Stop spitting my nickname back at me like a curse. I know exactly why you won't say my real name—"

"Oh yeah? Why's that?"

"Because if you do, it's another rip in this fucked-up reality you've convinced yourself is your only option. Because if you do, you might actually have to confront your feelings, instead of hiding behind this wall you've built up."

Her eyes widened at him as she shook her head. "That's not true. I don't... I don't feel anything for you." *Lie.* "You think you've seen the real me, but you're just seeing this version you've created in your head."

"I've seen what I need to. The Naomi I know fights with me and I fucking love that fiery side. That Naomi loses track of time helping strangers, not worried to death over being a minute late. That Naomi would *die* before her daughter got hurt, not stay with someone who could hurt them both. *That* Naomi is intoxicating and I don't think I'd ever get enough of her."

The silence in the car was deafening, and he could hear her swallow. "You don't know me, Wes."

His name on her tongue sent electric desire straight down his spine, traveling to his shaft, but it mattered more that he might've cracked one of her thick walls. "I know enough, Naomi. I know the woman I like. The woman I wish I could spend more time with... I think you wish you could spend more time with that woman, too."

She bent her head low, avoiding having the rest of the conversation. But it didn't matter. He'd said what he needed to say and they were already at Sasha Saves. He rolled up beside her Nissan and parked his vehicle, waiting for her to talk.

His Jeep was off for a long minute before she spoke in a low voice.

"I-I wasn't always like this... pissed off and second-guessing everything. It took that last time to realize I've become someone I don't want to be. Someone I don't like. I had a vision for my life, of who I want to be and I-I'm tryin' to find that woman again. It's just takin' time."

Her tears crashed to her lap, making Wes feel like an asshole, but hell did he like seeing some kind of emotion on her. It was way better than the numb automaton that always arrived at Sasha Saves. Over the shift, she lowered those steel walls, only to raise them back up again before she left.

Wes grabbed her phone from her hand, entered his phone number and gave it back to her.

"Now you have my number. It's under "Sasha Saves - W," and I expect you to call me if you ever need me, okay?"

Her bottom lip trembled as she nodded, and before he could stop himself, he lifted her hand from her lap and held it between both of his. His heart stuttered when she squeezed instead of tugging away.

"I'm here for you, Naomi. If you ever need me. I know you can do what's right for you. I know the glimpses of the fiery, confident, smart, caring woman you are, is a fucking queen in her own right and I know you can be her again."

Naomi nodded and wiped a tear from her cheek. She missed one and without even thinking, Wes reached and caught it with his thumb. With a small shy smile, she slowly withdrew her hand.

"I hope you meet her someday. I think she'd like you."

Wes grinned, hoping she saw his genuine excitement at that idea. "I'm counting on it, love."

CHAPTER FIFTEEN

The next two days were a whirlwind, and some of the busiest and most rewarding in Naomi's life. She'd had no idea what more the BlackStone Crew would ask of her to help with the Ashland Elite Scholarship Party. Going over the guest lists from the past few years was easy enough and she wanted to help as much as possible, but she had Thea to worry about. Not to mention her father.

She thumbed over the empty skin where her engagement ring had been. She'd taken it off months ago, after one of their big blowups, and if Dean had noticed, he was keeping it to himself. But there was no telling how much longer that reprieve would be. She'd learned a while back, though, not to question his good moods. It made them seem that much shorter.

Naomi told her boss, Gail, that Dean needed her to stay home and watch Thea. Gail hadn't cared one bit that Naomi wasn't going to the party, even lamenting that she didn't have an excuse to get out of it, too.

What Gail didn't know was Naomi had been just outside the hotel as the BlackStone Crew successfully saved eight trafficking victims. Wes had asked Naomi to pick up Nora in order to meet the women at the hospital and Naomi had jumped at the chance.

She'd helped Nora talk to each one of the women as a victim advocate, or survivor advocate, as Nora had reminded her. They held hands with eight different women during the process of giving their statement. She supported the few who chose to get rape kits done and assisted Nora in finding the few who had families. None of the women were from Ashland, so they'd ended up having to search all over the southeast. Finally, Naomi and Nora helped set the kidnapped victims on the very beginning paths of rejoining the world as free survivors.

Unfortunately, that all meant that Naomi had lied more than she ever had in her life. She wasn't sure how convincing she'd managed to be when she told Dean an abridged version of her part in the raid at the hotel and why she'd come home late. He'd seemed oddly preoccupied himself, barely looking up from his phone at the time. She hadn't been relieved, though.

It was only a matter of time before shit hit the fan. It always did and since he still hadn't seen a therapist, there was no hope he'd suddenly changed his ways. But she didn't want to think about any of that anymore.

But it was the morning after the party and she didn't want to think about the nonsense in her life anymore. Wes had invited her to help fill in the gaps with anything the victims could provide, which unfortunately—or fortunately, depending on how you looked at it—wasn't much. An "after-action report" was what Wes called it.

At first she was worried that she wouldn't be able to go because of Thea, but her day care thankfully had room for her at the last minute. Since Dean was working first shift, she'd been able to tell him she was volunteering.

She enjoyed the camaraderie that came with being part of a team. That knowledge of having someone at her back, no matter what? It was a feeling she couldn't remember having since her daddy passed. She'd just sat through the meeting with all these people—virtual strangers—who knew and loved each other and felt the warmth radiating from them. She'd been lost in all their conversation, the mood in the room was relaxed and positive thanks to their successful mission, and she soaked up the sense of accomplishment and feeling like she wasn't alone in this shitty world anymore.

But even with the effervescent feeling of saving lives, Naomi was embarrassed to admit—even though it was just to herself—that all she could think about was how damn attractive Wes was in his natural environment.

Watching him help lead the meeting with passion for the victims and his teammates was incredible and nothing short of panty drenching. It was early the morning after the party and everyone was thankfully safe.

As the BlackStone Crew, Nora, Assistant District Attorney Marco Aguilar, Officer Henry Brown, Ellie, and Jules filed out of the room—or waddled out in Jules's about-to-pop pregnant state—Naomi waited beside Wes near his computers.

He was working on something, she didn't know what, but let him type away undisturbed until he paused.

"So, what'd you think?" he asked, lifting his hands to cradle the back of his head as he leaned back in his rolling chair.

Naomi shrugged and shook her head slightly. "It's wild what y'all do. I'm impressed and a little stunned, I guess? I can't believe you do this every day."

Wes grinned and she felt the heat of his smile down to her core. "Thankfully, we don't have to do this *every* day. There is downtime. I'll admit though... it is extremely rewarding when we get it right... especially since some days aren't as great as others. It's easier on everyone when it works out."

A shadow crossed over his face and Naomi wondered if it had something to do with the tension she'd felt between Wes and Phoenix, another teammate. Of course, she knew absolutely nothing about their relationship, but considering hers with Dean, Naomi was an expert in unresolved tension and sure as hell could identify it when she saw it.

Her gaze locked on Wes again, and she remained stock-still

as he watched her with piercing blue eyes that—despite her best efforts—had captured her soul. She may have been an expert in one kind of tension, but she was a complete beginner in knowing how to navigate the type she had with Wes.

She cleared her throat. "Well, it was amazing. Was what Phoenix said true? Did Devil really shoot Mitchell Strickland?"

Wes crossed his arms, his spell broken by her serious question, and nodded. "Yep. He'll likely be spending the rest of his days in jail with a colostomy bag, but he won't be abusing women any longer. I don't care how rich Strickland is. There's no way Marco's going to allow him to go free. Aguilar takes his position as an assistant district attorney really fucking serious."

"That's insane that someone with such a big name in our little town would be behind something so evil." She shivered. "It's nice that Ellie wanted him to stay alive to get justice for her friend, but men like that can rot in hell for all I care. My daddy died protecting and serving this town and he'd be rollin' over in his grave if he knew one of its members was traffickin' women."

Wes sucked in a breath. "I didn't know that about your dad. He was an officer?"

Naomi nodded before sobering. "Captain George Ward. He was shot in the line of duty when I was fourteen."

A look of an emotion she couldn't place made his brow furrow before concern further marred his features. "Fuck, I'm sorry, Naomi. Losing a parent like that is hard."

She braced herself for the inevitable cringe that always came with that word, but relaxed back into the conversation when it never came. "Thanks... I tell myself he went out the way he would've wanted to, a hero." She picked at a thread in the hem of her cream sweater dress, trying not to think at the dull ache that always accompanied thoughts of her father. "That helps sometimes. But not all the time."

Wes's ice-blue eyes softened before his lips quirked at the corner and he spoke in his calm baritone. "You're damn right he was a hero." He removed his glasses and massaged his eyes. "But hopefully he doesn't roll over in his grave too many times over all this shit."

"What's that mean?" she asked, feeling her eyebrows furl at the odd comment.

"I think there's more than Strickland who's involved in this. I actually think he was just a pawn and I'm afraid to find out who's behind the curtain, and who all paved the road to get him there."

"Seriously? Who else would be involved?"

"I don't know. But Ellie heard that Russian guy Vlad talk about how the investigator had done good work for *Alea Iacta Est*. All I know is that it's a Latin phrase that means 'The die has been cast.'"

"I remember you saying that in the meeting... and then Phoenix was rude as hell. What was that all about?"

He sucked his teeth. "Yep. That's me and Phoenix for you. I don't know what his deal is. Anyway, I need to look into it more, but I'm afraid Strickland might be a part of it, and if there's a whole group of Stricklands out there, that's fucking terrifying."

"What? Really?" she asked, feeling like a broken record. "Shit, this place has gone to hell in a handbasket. It makes me wanna pack up all my things, pick Thea up from day care at one of the town churches, and just drive away forever, never looking back on this godforsaken town."

His face had fallen into a grim smile as they spoke. "We're trying to make it safer. It'll be hell figuring out who's behind all this, but ADA Aguilar told me that the feds are willing to work with us—or at least me—to figure out who's behind everything. I think Strickland is the first domino. We've gotta figure him out. A year ago, a firm partner's son told us that he had a brother, but I've never been able to find evidence of that."

"Shoot, if you and your techno-wizardry can't figure out who his brother is, it's either not true or some pretty damn powerful people are burying it."

Wes smirked. "Naomi Ward, did you just compliment me?"

Her cheeks blushed at his appraising look, but she couldn't hide her smile back. "Maybe... but don't get used to it."

Wes laughed. "Wouldn't dream of it. Anyway, maybe now that Strickland will have some alone time in a jail cell, he'll consider working with us."

Naomi cringed. "Sounds a little far-fetched."

He lifted a shoulder before winking at her. "The best goals are."

She rolled her eyes. "Well, what happens after Strickland?"

"I think we go after the rest of the partners in his firm: Dmitri Rusnak and Andrew Wilton Ascot."

Naomi nodded, her mind trying to wrap around all the moving parts. But in the silence, Wes seemed to have no problem with watching her. Before long, she felt Wes's piercing blue eyes along her skin and she started to squirm for relief. Naomi looked around, suddenly realizing they were the only ones in the room, with the door closed. It was just the two of them alone with the words he said two days ago echoing in her head.

"I fucking love that fiery side... that Naomi is intoxicating and I don't think I'd ever get enough of her."

Had Dean ever said he loved her fiery side? The one that was so freeing to finally use again? Naomi couldn't even remember the last time she'd told Dean she loved him. It had to have been months... hell, maybe over a year for all she could remember. She'd long wondered if Dean even believed it himself when he said the words. They'd been staying afloat in their sinking ship of a relationship, hoping she could hang on until Thea turned eighteen. But the day Thea was out of the house, Naomi would be packing her bags with her.

Can I really wait that long?

She watched Wes as he typed on the computer. His over six-foot frame had to be at least an inch higher than Dean's, and Wes definitely towered over her five foot two, even sitting down. His glasses accentuated the faint laugh lines on the edges of his eyes, and although his jawline was sharp, his lips were always ready for a smile. So different than Dean's perpetually stone-faced demeanor.

"What're you thinking about over there?"

The low rumble of his voice caught her off guard and she realized he was eyeing her from his periphery. Her cheeks heated, but before she turned away or blurted out something snarky to save face, she asked him what she'd been dying to know for two months.

"What did you mean about the oxygen thing?"

His eyes were back on the hieroglyphics on his screen, but his brow furrowed at her question. "Not sure what you mean, Naomi. You might have to fill me in."

"You said, 'trust your instincts and make sure to put your oxygen mask on first.'"

Wes hit the ENTER on his keyboard before turning to her. He crossed his arms while leaning back like he owned the place. Hell, he could, for all she knew. The less she knew about him, the better. Keeping that buffer with Wes prevented the temptation to get to know him in other ways.

"Well." His eyes were soothing as they locked onto hers, like a trap in a cage she didn't want to break free from. "The first one I think is obvious."

She rolled her eyes. "Yeah, I got the 'trust your instincts' part. I've been tryin' to listen to my intuition more lately."

Wes's small smile widened. "I remember you saying that last time we were here actually, when you pointed out we needed to look into those other women with hardly any details on their future."

He took off his glasses again before massaging his eyes, and she wondered if looking at the screens made them tired, or if always facing the world head-on did it. Probably both.

"As for the oxygen mask thing... I don't know who my aunt learned it from, but it's something she used to tell my mom. 'Put your oxygen mask on first, Janet.' I heard that so much it kind of became ingrained in me I guess."

"But... what does it mean?"

"Have you ever been on a plane?"

Naomi nodded at the change in subject. "Yeah, once when I was younger and we visited some family up north."

"Well, you know how on flights they instruct you to put your oxygen mask on when shit hits the fan?" Naomi nodded. "One of the things they say is if you have a child next to you, put your oxygen mask on first before you help the child."

Naomi wrinkled her nose. "Yeah, I've never really liked that idea. Whoever made it up sure ain't a mother. I can't imagine makin' that kind of choice. If it ever came down to me or Thea, it's T all the way, hands down."

Wes dipped his forehead toward her. "Fair, but consider this. If something happens out of your control and you don't take care of yourself first, you might not be able to take care of Thea, either. If you want to be there for Thea, you've got to make yourself a priority and everything else will fall into place."

She frowned, not really sure what to make of that, unable to deny the logic, but not wanting to admit it. Her go-to defense mechanism reared its ugly, obstinate head, although she tried her best to tamp down her attitude.

"Why'd you tell me that? We hadn't even been in the same room for half an hour, but you'd already figured I'd need to hear it? How come?"

With a heavy look on his face, his eyes bored into her with compassion and... regret?

"Because I think you might be like my mom was, always putting us first, a lot of times at her expense. She thought putting herself above her children was selfish." Wes released a long exhale before bringing his rolling chair closer to her. His tattooed hands grabbed hers before resting his elbows on his dark-jeaned knees. For once, the immediate shock of fear that Dean would find out didn't slice through her, and she let herself be drawn into his eyes. Those icy blues that saw everything so clearly. "But more than once, Naomi, I've wished she'd realized that thinking about yourself isn't selfish and that self-preservation is self-love." He tugged her hands. "I-I guess that even though I didn't know you at the time, I needed you to know at least that."

His eyes met hers with a sincerity that literally drew her in, and she suddenly realized how close they were. Their chairs were nearly touching and her hands were cradled in his strong grip while her knees were locked between his. She'd watched every emotion written all over his face as he'd spoken to her: worry, hurt, frustration... desire. Each one drew her in like a moth to a flame and for once in her life, she wanted to take a risk.

Only... this man didn't feel like a risk. With every word, he felt more and more like a reward for all the screwed-up shit that had rained down on her life since she was fourteen. She deserved to do this one thing for her, just once.

"It's not selfish to think about yourself."

He closed his eyes before swallowing and tried to pull back. "I'm sorry, Naomi, I—"

Naomi tugged his hands to her chest, pulling him in, and crashed her lips onto his.

CHAPTER SIXTEEN

Naomi immediately felt Wes's body tense, and he stayed stock-still for an awful second, during which her mind went haywire. Maybe he didn't think of her that way. Maybe it was all her wishful thinking. Or maybe he was just as afraid as she was that the moment would disappear.

But she didn't have time to dwell on the answers. One moment she was questioning everything and the next she was scooped out of her chair.

He held her up with one arm before swiping his keyboard away with his free hand and sitting her on the desk. Standing between her legs, he caged her in with his hand on the side of her hip as his free one stretched to press a button behind her. She got lost in a cloud of citrus and cedar just before she vaguely registered a *click* coming from the closed door.

"It's locked. Now come here." He cupped her nape and drew her in, melding their lips together just as she sank her fingers into his thick hair.

If it were anyone else, the thought of being trapped would've terrified her. But she tasted freedom in his kiss, and the stress she'd been drowning under released in a deluge, leaving her light-headed with relief.

But she craved more and grew ravenous for his touch, opening her lips to let his tongue slip inside her mouth. Delicious need pulsed through her body and into her core, dampening her thong underneath her leggings and sweater dress.

He squeezed her ass and pressed her heat against the hardness growing in his jeans. Curling her body flush against his shaft, she sucked in a breath when she found the friction she needed to relieve the tension swelling in her clit.

His palms traveled down her hips and underneath her sweater dress until her groan made him pause.

"For the first time in my entire life, I wish like hell I wasn't wearing leggings."

He chuckled and splayed his large hands across her upper thighs. "Oh love. Do you really think clothes are going to keep me from making you come?" His thumbs grazed over her clit in a move that had her moaning into his mouth.

"I think I'm gonna enjoy feelin' you try." They weren't even skin to skin yet and his touch still sent a thrill up her spine.

"Fuck, Naomi, do you know how long I've wanted to touch you like this?" he whispered against her lips as he barely skimmed over her center, making her shiver.

"Too long," she whispered back before tucking the fingers of one hand into his waistband and unbuckling his belt with the other. He began to massage her clit, sending liquid heat to her pussy and her legs trembling.

"Goddamn, love. If you're this responsive with clothing in the way, I can't wait to feel you combust around my cock when I'm inside you."

She opened her mouth to agree when a faint vibration began to hum in her ears and her body stiffened with a completely different kind of tension. She tried to ignore the humming and the dread sinking into her stomach. But the vibration happened again... and again... until it finally dawned on her what was making the noise.

"*Shit!*" Naomi dropped her hands from Wes's jeans' button

and pushed him away like he burned her. His hands instantly flew up and off as he backed away. Something about that gesture sent a twin ache, loving that he was so attentive and respectful, and hating that the man she had to go home to was anything but.

She hopped off the desk and scrambled for her phone from inside her purse.

3 missed calls. Two voicemails. 7 text messages.

"Shit, damn, fuck, shoot." She mindlessly cursed under her breath. The erratic drumbeat of her heart in her ears gave her the sensation of having her head underneath a waterfall. She unlocked her phone to read the text messages first.

Dean: Got off early. Come home but leave Thea at day care so I can finally get you underneath me without her ruining it :)

Dean: When are you comin home sweets? Answer your phone

Dean: Answer your damn phone, bitch

Dean: Where the fuck are you? You better be busy as hell at that goddamn store or we're gonna have some fuckn problems

Dean: You made me have to look for you at that shitty ass place. And guess what? You werent there. Who are you fuckn??? WHORE

Dean: If you don't call me in the next hour we are fuckn done bitch. you might as well stay on your knees after you choke on that dick youre suckin. Maybe if you beg I'll be in a forgivin mood

Dean: I picked our daughter up. Dont bother comin home. She doesnt need a slut for a mother and you can forget being my wife. If your dirty cunt gets anywhere near my house I'll finish wut I started last time

The last text made her hands tremble and her vision blur. This man who could so casually threaten to murder her had her daughter. He'd never hurt Thea before, but he'd never threatened her own life before, either. Along with the fear making her adrenaline go haywire, her stomach also turned in knots with guilt. She'd heard his accusations before... but this was the first time there was truth to them.

She checked the time and realized he'd sent that particular text just a few minutes ago. She scrolled through and realized all but the Sasha Saves related text were only minutes apart. He hadn't even given her a chance to defend herself.

"I gotta go, Wes."

"What is it?" He gently grabbed her bicep, but she jerked it away, afraid his fingertips would brand her there for Dean to see.

"Thea's father is textin' me. I've gotta go *now*."

"Wait, let me see the messages."

She gave him her phone without thinking. Fighting past her blurry vision, she fumbled for the strap on her purse before slinging it over her shoulder.

"*Motherfucker*." Wes grabbed his midnight-blue hair with his free hand as he stared at the screen, then stared at her. "I can't let you go like this. No way in hell am I letting you be alone with that asshole when he's fucking threatening you with shit like this."

"I'm fine. I gotta go." She reached for her phone, but his firm hand cupped her shoulder, stopping her at arm's length.

"No way. Besides the fact you're too upset to drive, this is some scary shit."

It was only then that she realized her blurry vision was caused by the tears streaming down her face. She blinked hard, willing them to stop and tugged her shoulder free.

"I can't think about that. I'm sorry Wes, but this was a mistake." She ignored the lilt in her voice and her chest constricting at his stunned expression. Instead, she took the opportunity and grabbed her phone from his hand before rushing out of the BlackStone meeting room.

After a couple of steps, Wes followed at her heels.

"Wait, Naomi. Stop!" She burst through the door to the

garage and beelined to her car until his hand tugged her arm again. "Please. Stop. You don't mean that."

"Yes, I do!" She easily tugged free and held her hand up to halt him from getting closer. "This was a huge mistake, so I just need to get home—"

"No, *we* are not a mistake. Can't you feel that? I know I'm not the only one." He ran his hands through his dark hair. "Fuck, Naomi, getting to hold you felt like I could breathe easy for the first time in months. We are not a mistake. *This*" —he gestured between them— "is not a mistake. Going back to *him* is the mistake."

"You don't get it, Wes." She choked on the words as dread and guilt constricted her lungs.

"Well then, explain it to me!"

Unable to look at his pleading icy blue eyes anymore, she pivoted, aiming straight for her Nissan as she yelled over her shoulder.

"Throughout our entire relationship, Dean has accused me of cheatin' on him, he has... *hurt* me for those lies he believed, but for once—" She swallowed back the bile of the truth in her words. "For once, he was right. I have to go. I have to fix this."

"Naomi, no you don't! Don't go back to him, please."

She whirled on him and threw her hands up in frustration. "Why, Wes? So I'll stay with *you*, instead?"

Wes's mouth opened and shut quickly before he shook his head. "What? Fuck, I'd love for you to do that, but no. That's not what this is about. I don't want you to go back to him because I'm scared for you. You are too, I can hear it in your voice." He sidestepped around her and stopped in front of the driver's side of her car with his arms spread out, keeping her from getting inside. "Listen to me, Naomi, no matter what you've done, there's no reason for you to be literally shaking in fear of physical harm from this guy. *Please*. Don't go."

His voice broke on the last sentence, breaking something inside her too. Never had Dean cared enough to fight for her like this. He'd been the one to cause all the pain and she'd let it happen over the years because of some twisted view of the type of family Thea should have. The one she'd grown up with and craved for years since.

But Thea had never had that with Dean and maybe it was high time to stop trying to make something happen that just wasn't there.

This man in front of her was making her feel things Thea's father never had. Sure, desire, hunger, and need, but also strength, security, and... *treasured*. Dean never had more than a physical or manipulative hold on her.

Apparently, it took this man begging for her safety to make her realize all that. The ice blue in Wes's eyes pierced her resolve, breaking down convictions she'd held too tightly for way, *way* too fucking long.

She straightened before closing her eyes and making her decision. "I won't stay—"

"Thank *fuck*—"

"I won't stay. But he's gonna have Thea all by himself if I don't get there in time. If he gets her before I get home, I won't be able to leave. I'm not leavin' my baby with someone hell-bent on hurtin' me, even if it is her father."

"Fine, I'll go with you—"

Alarm shocked through her, making her nerves stand on end. "No, absolutely not, that'll make everything so much worse."

"Damn!" Wes pulled at his hair again, making it stand on end. "Fuck, okay... I-I'm going to follow you—" She opened her mouth to object, but he laid a gentle hand on her shoulder. "He won't see me. I promise. But I... I need to be near you, okay? I need to know you'll be alright."

Habit told her to rebel. That she needed to handle this on her own and keep prying eyes out of her business. But... instinct told her he was right. If she was facing her monster, she needed a knight.

"I-I have to go. Do what you gotta do, but I need to leave now, before it's too late."

He backed away as he frantically nodded as he followed her to the driver's side. "Okay... okay. But call me if you need me before I can get to you, okay?"

"Okay." She swallowed before opening the door and hopping into the seat. When she reached to close it, Wes took her face in his hands and kissed her on the forehead. Hot tears filled her eyes. She wasn't ready to leave this safety, this security. This *man*.

She'd just had him for a split second. What if that was all she'd ever get? Was a split second of freedom worth the rest of her life?

When his warm lips left her forehead, she withdrew and sat up in her seat, sighing.

"Goodbye, Wes."

She closed the door.

As soon as she looked out of her rearview mirror to back up, the garage door opened. Wes must've had some fancy way of opening it. She looked to him one last time, memorizing his face. It was stark white and worry was etched over his features. His arms were crossed, his back straight, and she blinked back her own stress.

"It's gonna be fine," she whispered to herself, ignoring the light lilt at the end.

CHAPTER SEVENTEEN

"Sweets."

Dean's voice was emotionless, but Naomi's back straightened to the point of pain as she closed the inside garage door. He lounged at the breakfast table in the kitchen directly in front of her. To anyone else, he looked relaxed, but the subtle rage in his eyes was easy for her to see.

"H-Hi Dean. Where's Thea?" She waited in the tiny laundry room for his answer, afraid to leave the safety of the door and potential escape.

"It's always about that damn kid." His fingers paused from their tapping on the table and formed into a fist.

"Dean... where is—"

"Still at day care!" Spit flew from his mouth and he wiped it with the back of his hand. "We have some things to work out. We can pick her up after."

"D-day care? Really?" She paused a moment before daring to yell. "Thea!"

"Don't fucking *question* me." His scream made her jump and tighten her grip on the handle, but the silence in the house brought her so much relief she almost collapsed.

She's safe. Oh, thank God.

"Honestly, sweets. She's the least of your concerns right now."

She needed to get out of the tiny laundry room. Flee to the day care, grab Thea, and never come back. But her legs were shaky with relief and refused to move, trapping her.

Just as she'd about gotten the strength to leave, Dean suddenly appeared right beside her, slamming his hand just above her head against her exit. His breath reeked of alcohol and his eyes were crazed.

Liquor... not beer ... liquor.... The man was a sleepy nuisance on grocery store beer, but a fucking nightmare on bourbon. *Not good. Not good. Not good.*

Shit.

This was going to be worse than she thought. Dean hardly ever drank. The last time she'd met him drunk in the kitchen, he'd been docile enough, almost sweet. But even then, she'd been scared to death. He didn't need alcohol to be mean as a snake, but it was almost a given that he'd strike if he had liquor in him.

"Where the fuck have you been, Naomi?" His voice had changed again to light and airy, as if he'd asked her how her day was or to pass the butter. That voice was the soft breeze stilling to a halt before the gusts of a storm tore everything apart. She swallowed and tried her best to hide her tells.

"I-I told you I was volunteering with Sasha Saves."

He tilted his head like a predator analyzing its attack strategy before forcing her to switch places with him. Now leaning against the door, he crossed his arms with a smile.

"Don't fuckin' lie to me, sweets. I know you weren't there." Watching her with his dead eyes, he used his thumb to scratch his five o'clock shadow before pointing at her with a wagging finger. "Hell, the cashier said she didn't even know who you were. You fooled me, Naomi, I'll give you that. All those times I saw you there, who knew you were such a connivin' little bitch?"

Naomi's heart stuttered as she realized Sasha Saves's secrecy policy to keep everyone safe was about to screw her over.

She tried to casually walk backward into the kitchen, putting the breakfast table between them. If she could entice him away from the laundry room, she'd be able to get what she needed and flee. Hell, at this point, she almost didn't even care if she didn't have time to follow through with her emergency plans.

I have to get the fuck outta here.

"I-I don't know what to tell you, Dean. I was there and then I realized you'd called and messaged and came home. B-But I think I should go get Thea. If we're both home she doesn't need to be at day care."

It was a lame excuse, but maybe he'd buy it and let her leave, not knowing it was for forever.

His short blond lashes outlined narrowed bloodshot eyes, giving him an almost demonic appearance. The reddened whites were proof he'd been drinking *a lot*. He couldn't have been home for too long, so he had to have been working on it to get to that level.

Not good.

"No. I think Thea's exactly where she needs to be. After we've talked, we've got things we need to take care of. You know, shit you've been holdin' back on."

As if she couldn't figure out on her own what he meant, his leering stare up and down her body made her squirm. There was a hungry look in his eyes that she'd been able to stave off for months, but it was looking like her time was up.

Not good. Not good.

"You know... whatever corner you were workin', you sure as hell dressed the part."

She looked down at her cream sweater and knee-high boots over brown leggings. The ones Wes's hands had stroked, making her feel things she'd never felt with the man in front of her. She met Dean's eyes and swallowed.

"I'll just change then and go get Thea. When I come back, we can do whatever you want, okay.... sweets?"

A dark chuckle rolled out of him as he grabbed his chair

from the table beside her. He collapsed into it just inside the laundry room, blocking her exit and everything she'd hidden for getaways.

"She's all you care about, isn't she? This whole time..." He chuckled before punctuating each word by banging his fist on the washing machine. "*This. Whole. Damn. Time.*" A livid glare seared into her before he spat at her feet, hitting her boot. He scrubbed his face again while shaking his head. "This whole... *fuckin'* time. It was only ever about Thea. Never about us... was it?"

The pain in his eyes almost made her feel sorry for him, but the clenched fist hovering over the fresh dent in the metal appliance reminded her what he was capable of. What was at stake.

"She's the most important person in our lives, Dean..." she reasoned carefully. Her purse was in the crook of her arm and she covertly positioned it behind her back to dig for her phone to call Wes. "Of course everything we both do is for her."

He waved his hand at her and scoffed. "That's not what I mean, bitch, and you fuckin' know it."

Naomi looked up to the heavens and blinked before swallowing. "I-I'm sorry Dean. We'll talk. Let's talk. Just let me go pick up Thea, 'kay?"

"No." He shook his head. "No. You've been holdin' out on me for months, Naomi. Maybe you have some other dick on the side, I don't know. But I'm gonna make sure I get what's mine before that brat comes home and lets you make another excuse. Hell, she can stay at that fuckin' day care for all I care."

Cold worry iced down her back. Dean was a lot of things. A lot of *terrible* things. But they'd only ever been directed at her. Never their daughter. She'd get on his nerves occasionally, but he'd never been *mean* or acted like he didn't want her. At least not out loud...

It had to be the booze, but in any case, this was new territory and she had no clue how to navigate it. All she knew was she wanted to finally abandon ship.

"Dean, we need to talk—"

He stood so fast it made his chair fall back. "Talk about what, *sweets*? Your lies? Where the *hell* you go all the time? For sure, ain't that stupid-ass store, but I wanna hear you say it!"

A shock sparked through her as his words registered in her mind. What exactly did he know? She thought she'd been careful, but she'd known deep down her lies would catch up with her eventually.

"Answer me!" He grabbed her arm and slung her against the wall near the laundry room door before getting so close that his red eyes were all she could see.

Using both hands, he squeezed the sides of her face, shaking her until she was dizzy. "I already know what you're gonna say, so fuckin' say it!" On the last word, he shoved her away and slapped his palms against the wall, so dangerously close that his hands tugged at flyaway strands of her hair. "Say it! Go ahead!"

She closed her eyes and took a deep breath. This might be the nail in her coffin, but she couldn't spend one more second of her life with this monster.

"Dean, I'm leavin' yo—"

The swift punches into her stomach were so quick, she didn't even have time to double over to protect herself from the second one. As she tried to capture her breath again, she resisted the urge to slap and scratch him.

Give in, just give in.

It was a mantra she told herself when things got heated. But no matter how many times she repeated it to herself, it took at least a few hits before she stopped fighting back, always realizing too slowly that he would stop if she just played dead.

But this time she had the eye on the prize, a game plan. If she fought back, it would only delay her freedom.

"You just had to be faithful, you ungrateful bitch, and I woulda done *anything* for you. But you had to go fuck with the *enemy*. You think they're gonna be able to protect you when you're found out?"

She closed her eyes, willing her ears to stop listening to his screaming nonsense. *Protect* her? Hell, the only person she needed protecting from was him.

He struck her again on her side, making her collapse to her knees. She clutched her stomach and curled into a ball on the floor to protect herself. Dean bent low and snatched her chin in his fingers, forcing her to stare into his dead winter eyes.

"Go ahead and leave, bitch. See how well you'll do without me. I don't know where you're thinkin' you'll go. You have no one who'll put up with your shit. Your own momma turned you out for gettin' pregnant. *No one wants you.*"

He gave her a cruel smile before shoving her head back down to the ground, causing her temple to bounce off the linoleum.

"You'll come crawlin' back. You always do." He walked over her and opened the door to the garage before appraising her with disgust.

"And if you don't come back, don't think I won't find you, sweets. Wherever you are, wherever you hide. I'll find you. God help you when I do." He spat on the floor beside her and slammed the door behind him. His Corolla fired up soon after and she listened in silence as he left, relaxing as he took her tense fear and panic with him.

She breathed deeply through the pain in her stomach, but she'd felt those blows before. He hadn't hit anything major.

The cold floor soothed her aching temple as she gained strength to get up. She had to get to Thea before Dean, but she seriously doubted he'd go pick her up in his state. Besides, there was no way in hell the church day care would give up her daughter to a man who smelled like the inside of a whiskey barrel. At least she hoped not. It was that last fear that made her pick herself up with a groan.

The door behind her swung open and she cowered at the shadow there, flinching at the pain in her stomach and in fear of receiving more blows. How long had she lain there? Was Dean back so quickly?

"Fuck! I knew we took too fucking long." At Wes's soothing baritone, Naomi relaxed. When his hands flowed over her, checking for injuries, the juxtaposition of his light touch versus Dean's made her choke back a dry sob. "Shit, did that hurt? I'm so sorry, Naomi."

That word. She didn't hate it when he said it. Maybe because he always meant it. Maybe because he was apologizing for things that weren't his atonement to bear. God, the difference between the two men in her life was stark and it made her wonder what the hell she'd been thinking all these years.

And now it's over.

The sob slowly turned into laughs and she lifted her eyes to see concern in Wes's blue eyes turn into confusion which only made her laugh even harder.

"Naomi... love... are you okay?"

"Snake, that asshole might come back—shit." Hawk, the guy who'd driven Wes home last time, filled the light in the doorway.

"Hawk, call Devil... I think she's in shock or something."

She wanted to reassure them, but hell, was she in shock? Maybe. But she didn't care.

"I don't know. I don't know. All I know is... I'm *free*, Wes." Her laughter grew manic and understanding mixed with the concern on his brow.

Slowly sitting up, she hissed at the throbbing in her side, but that ache was nowhere near the amount of relief she felt from the weight lifted off her chest.

He'd crossed her line. She was listening to her instincts and soaking in the new cleansing breaths of oxygen in her lungs. Done, she was fucking *done*.

It was going to be hard, she knew that. With Thea... old feelings... saying goodbye to a dream that'd never be a reality. But no matter what, she'd remember this feeling. The one when she'd *finally* broken free of her monster's chains. They were finally gone and she'd never felt lighter.

"I'm free, Wes," she gasped the words again, still unable to fully grasp them. "He tried to break me again. But this time... this time I'm gone and I'm never comin' back here. I'm gonna get Thea and we're gonna go..."

Like an anchor dropping on her chest in slow motion, she felt the words drift out of her mouth as the haze of relief lifted from her eyes.

Dean was right. She had nowhere else to go. After having a child out of wedlock, her momma cut ties with her, something she was sure as hell her daddy never would've allowed if he were alive. On top of that, she'd lost all contact with her friends from college.

Maybe she could call Sophie? No, that'd be so shitty to use her after only just reconnecting. And Sophie was dealing with her own shit. There was no way Naomi could bring their drama to her doorstep.

Sasha Saves had safe homes... but she knew for a fact they were all in use at the moment. Plus, Dean had his ways. He worked security, for God's sake. He'd be able to find her with no problem. The weight of her reality collapsed back on her, making her chest tighten.

"No... no, no, no, no. This can't be happening." Why hadn't she thought of all that before? Every avenue for survival flew through her mind quicker than she could understand. None of them worked. She hadn't thought this through. She hadn't—

"What, Naomi? What's wrong? Talk to me."

Wes's voice snapped her out of the terror now consuming her. She whipped her gaze back up at him, knowing she wasn't hiding her emotions anymore. Not that she could if she tried.

His jaw was set, like he was biting back a million questions, but she only had one thought on her mind.

"I don't have anywhere to go." The words wheezed from her, like her lungs were trying to hold on to their last chance for oxygen. She scoffed and massaged her temples, hoping the answer would appear. "I don't have... *anyone*. Safe homes are all booked. Dean could— Oh, God, Wes, I don't have anywhere to go! What have I done?" Hot tears burned her eyes, but she widened them to keep from breaking down completely.

"Stay at BlackStone."

Wes's words were like a floodgate to her tension, letting it flow out but unsure where it was going to go or if the release would ruin the world as she knew it.

"Wh-what do you mean?"

He darted his glance at Hawk, who nodded once. "Come home with me."

Naomi jerked back and groaned from the movement.

"Shit, I mean, no, it's not like that." He wiped at his face. "We have a guest room—or studio apartment. It's certainly big enough for you and Thea to stay in, at least for a little while until we find a place for you guys."

Naomi felt her eyes blink rapidly as she tried to follow what he was saying. "You mean... T and I come stay with y'all? Wait... is that the apartment Ellie is staying in?"

"Stayed," Hawk's deep voice answered. "She and Devil are moving her back to her dorm as we speak." He checked his watch and lifted his brows. "They might even be done by now."

Naomi swiveled her head from Hawk to Wes. "Really? Come stay with y'all? Just like that?"

"Yeah, I think you should. It's the safest place you both could be."

The idea was crazy but also... "That sounds perfect."

Wes's shy smile widened. "Yeah? Great... um... do you, uh, need help packing?"

Naomi shook her head. "No... uh, just help up please."

"Oh, right." He lent her a hand, being so ginger with her that it almost brought even more tears to her eyes.

God, I'm a mess.

"I'm gonna go pack a few things. If y'all could just... I don't know, make sure he doesn't come back without me knowin'?"

The two men scowled before nodding.

Wes turned to Hawk while pressing the button for the garage door, closing it. "You get the front door—"

"—and you take the back. We'll both keep an ear out for the garage door."

"Copy."

As they walked away, Naomi waited until she could hear their long strides farther in the house.

"I'll be just a sec," she called out before walking around the house, double-checking that she hadn't missed anything. She eventually grabbed dress-up clothes, Thea's teddy bear, Angus, and another small bag from Thea's closet before heading back into the laundry room.

She was embarrassed to admit that she and Thea had already packed go-bags full of everything they could need for a quick getaway. T had assumed the overnight bags were for sleepovers with friends. Naomi went with that explanation, hoping if she ever talked about it around Dean, it'd work in her favor. The duffels included essential paperwork, clothing, travel-sized necessities, toys, and some extra dash cash, all thanks to Sasha Saves's tips for victims...

No.

Survivors.

She smiled to herself before reaching the laundry room and digging into the extra hamper. To anyone else, it looked filled to the brim with unmatched socks. Bending to dig through the tall wicker hamper, she sucked in a pained breath. Pushing through her fresh injuries, she dodged the mismatched socks she'd planted in the hamper until she found the go-bags. Once she had their straps secured around her shoulder, she returned the socks that had spilled out.

The shelf above her head had the detergent she needed, but reaching up for it made her moan. Suddenly, cedar and citrus filled her nostrils as Wes reached from behind her.

"This what you need?" He grabbed the laundry detergent box and Naomi had no choice but to nod. When he set it down, she felt the heat from his cobalt gaze as she unlatched the top. She sifted her hand through the white powdery detergent until her fingers found the small plastic bag of rolled cash at the bottom of the container.

She tucked the Ziploc in a hidden pocket she'd sewn in her purse, just in case. Her first plan had been to have the money on her at all times, but carrying the large sum had made her nervous. Using the laundry room for her escape had been an excellent tip from a survivor. Lord knows Dean didn't know his bleach from his fabric softener.

After the cash was safely hidden, she crossed her arms and met Wes's eyes, daring him to say something. But when his only reply was a furrowed brow and silence, she did the job for him.

"Go ahead. Chastise me for stayin' with a man I had to plan to run away from. But know I'm already thinkin' it enough for the both of us."

"No, it's not that—"

"Then what? I know you're thinkin' somethin' so let's hear it."

"I just... I just wish my mom had had a plan."

A breath escaped her and all her anger dissipated with it. "Oh." She didn't know what Wes had grown up with, but if the shadows that darkened his face every time he spoke about his mother were any indication, then it had to have been bad. Damn her temper and her insistence on keeping him at arm's length. This man wasn't the enemy and it was high time she stopped treating him that way. "Let's go, um... let's go. I gotta get T from day care before Dean tries to."

Hawk met back up with them and when they reached outside, Naomi turned to them with her car keys in her hand as a thought crossed her mind.

"Um... do you mind followin' behind? Just in case?"

"Of course, love. You don't even have to ask."

Relief coursed through her even as her heart pounded in her chest. She stared at the empty house for a moment. It wasn't the last time she'd set foot inside, but she'd never stay under that roof with that monster again. Her hands shook from the mixed emotions swelling in her, unable to fully believe she was actually leaving him.

After five on and off tumultuous years of being a victim, she was finally taking her life into her own hands.

She was a survivor.

CHAPTER EIGHTEEN

It'd been eight days since Naomi and Thea began staying at BlackStone and Wes didn't know if he'd ever get used to it. When they'd first gotten there, it'd taken every ounce of his willpower not to hover over them, especially when she'd refused to let Wes help tend to her injuries. Thankfully, Devil reassured him that they were just surface wounds, and nothing vital was in jeopardy.

Since then, he'd secured Naomi's phone so Dean couldn't track her, but otherwise had carefully avoided her. He'd wanted her to get settled in her new safe haven, and hopefully let her come to him.

While he waited for her, he focused all his energy on the developments in the trafficking ring BlackStone was trying to tear down. After crashing the Ashland Elite Scholarship Fundraiser, all the shit in Ashland County had hit the proverbial fan.

Ellie had been kidnapped by an investigator with the Ashland County Sheriff's Office. Thank God, she'd saved herself and was healthy, safe, and sound now. The investigator wasn't so lucky and was murdered by the traffickers after having double-crossed them. He'd been corrupt as fuck, but his files had broken some major ground in the case, revealing damning evidence on many 'elite' citizens of Ashland County.

The authorities were particularly interested in the partners of Ascot, Rusnak, and Strickland, LLC, a law firm that Black-Stone always thought had its hand in the trafficking ring. When the BlackStone Crew crashed the party, they caught Mitchell Strickland with his pants down—literally—while eight women were being held hostage by two Russians who BlackStone suspected were henchmen.

Once Strickland was arrested, the dominos fell and it'd been extremely satisfying to watch each pompous bastard topple over. The feds were already looking for Andrew Ascot and Dmitri Rusnak for similar crimes.

Now the goal was to get Strickland to talk to them, followed by the rest of the trafficking scum in whatever *alea iacta est* meant and the organization behind the ring.

Wes opened the door to his BlackStone Securities studio apartment while tugging his black Henley over his head. With the fabric already covering his face, he paused at a feminine gasp.

Shit. The residential floor wasn't all men anymore. The fact that he'd forgotten about the woman he'd been obsessing over for months was a testament to how stuck in his thoughts he'd been.

He pulled down the Henley the rest of the way quickly to see that Naomi had been staring at his abs. The desire in her eyes made him stifle a groan, but he did his best to keep his cool.

"Wes!" Little footfalls echoed down the glazed concrete flooring coming from the living room common area. He kneeled down with his arms wide, barely readying himself in time for Thea to collapse into him.

"Floor is lava, Wes! Floor is lava! You can't put me down!"

He lifted her up high and spun her around before pretending to set her down. She giggled and lifted her legs up to keep from touching the ground. Her crown went lopsided as she yelled about the 'floor of lava' that was too hot for her to stand on. He repeated the movements as he tossed her around all the way to the dining room in the center of the residential floor.

"Again! Again!" Her squeals of joy went straight to his heart as he raised her one last time and stood her on top of the dining room table. "We-ess! I can't be on a table!"

"Well, where else am I going to put you? Everywhere else is lava."

She screeched with laughter before shouting with a toothy grin. "Throw me up high again! Again! Again!"

He smiled wide and began to pick her up again, but Naomi stopped him with a hand on his bicep.

"Thea, we talked about this. You gotta leave this poor man alone."

Wes felt his eyebrows furrow before he switched gears and waggled them, teasing Naomi. "No she doesn't. Playing with Princess T is one of the highlights of my day. Only second to seeing her mom, of course."

Naomi narrowed her eyes as Thea ignored her and reached for him. Her mother intercepted her, though, and gently picked her up from the table to set her down on the ground.

"Playing the floor is lava once a day is enough, baby. It's too early for all that right now and I'm sure Wes has work to do. You don't want to get him tired."

Wes settled his hands on his waist and raised a brow at her. "It takes a lot to get me tired, you know."

Heat passed over Naomi's eyes before she ducked her head. "T go back to watch TV, I'll be there in a minute—"

"But, Mommy. Phoe-nik won't let me watch my show." Thea's speech was perfect with a little southern twang like her mom's, but she still had trouble staying the 'x' in Phoenix's name, so she always said it very carefully. "Wes, will you tell him to move to let me watch Merida? Mommy won't do it." She glared up at her mom and Wes bit back a laugh at Naomi's widened eyes.

"No ma'am! Theresa Jane Ward, don't you dare look at me

with that tone of voice. Your grandmomma woulda tanned my hide if I'd talked to her that way."

The little imp looked the opposite of contrite as she tugged on the hem of Wes's shirt. "Help me, please."

Wes glanced at Naomi, who had a hand on one hip and was massaging a temple with her other. "Go for it. Girl's been wearin' me out already and it's only eight in the mornin'."

Wes chuckled and let Thea take him by the hand, leading him to the common room in her bare feet and signature green princess costume.

Her gorgeous, but exhausted, mom followed behind in a baggy sweater and leggings. Naomi's dark auburn hair was piled on top of her head with loose curly tendrils hanging out. He fucking loved it.

He caught Naomi's eye and winked before he nodded toward Thea.

"Must be tiring, huh?" he asked Naomi in an exaggerated voice. "Being bossed around by a *three*-year-old all the time."

Naomi's brow furrowed and she opened her mouth until Thea scoffed. Immediately, her face relaxed, seemingly figuring out his joke. The little princess dropped his hand before crossing her arms and pouting her adorable bottom lip. "I'm *four* Wes. And I *told* you. Mommy says I ain't bossy. I'm the boss."

"I know. I know. You *ain't* bossy. You're the boss. I apologize, Princess T. It'll never happen again." Wes couldn't keep a straight face and a chuckle rolled out of him. Thea smiled, showing all her teeth, before continuing her way to the living room.

"That was even funnier than I thought it'd be..." Wes wiped a laughing tear from his eye before looking at Naomi again. At the odd look on her face, he stopped following Thea and turned to her mother. "Naomi, what's wrong?"

After blinking several times, she cleared her throat. "Um... nothing. I just—you're really good with her, is all."

Wes smiled at her, his chest puffing with a light airy feeling, but he couldn't miss the opportunity to tease her. "That's two now, you know."

She tilted her head. "'Two' what?"

He shrugged with a wider grin. "Two compliments. Careful, my queen, or I might think you're actually beginning to like me."

Her immediate scowl almost made him feel bad for calling her out, but a twinkle of warmth in her campfire gold and brown eyes encouraged him.

Joking with her was the highlight of his day, and he opened his mouth to tease her about her lip trying to twitch into a smile when there was a shouted curse word from the other room. He tensed when the slaps of bare feet echoed back to them.

"Wes! Mommy! Phoe-nik said a bad word!"

"Phoenix..." He growled before beelining the rest of the way through the communal kitchen into the living room. Phoenix had the remote in one hand and the other holding his hat off above his head as he tugged his hair in frustration. His eyes were wide with dark circles underneath them and he was muttering under his breath. "What the fu—he—heck, man?" He caught himself before introducing two new words into Thea's vocabulary.

"Dude, I'm sorry. But look—"

He pointed to the screen and Wes followed his finger to see the headline.

DMITRI RUSNAK FOUND DEAD

"What the... turn it up."

For once, Phoenix did as he was told and the newswoman's concerned tone filled the large room.

"This just in. While authorities are still looking for Andrew Wilton Ascot III, Dmitri Rusnak, another man believed to be part of the human trafficking ring in Ashland County, has been found dead. Authorities have been looking for him for two days, only for a jogger to find his body in the river on her morning run—"

"Holy—"

"Hawk! Devil! Come out here!" Phoenix yelled loud enough for his voice to echo across the second-floor residence hall.

After only a second, both men burst from their rooms, half dressed. Ellie followed closely behind Devil while tying her robe.

"What's going on?" Hawk asked, immediately taking control of an unknown situation.

"Just look at this shit, dude," Phoenix answered.

Hawk and Devil watched as the reporter kept speaking about Rusnak, one of the partners of the Ascot, Rusnak, and Strickland firm that had a warrant out for his arrest.

"*—gunshot wound to the head.*"

The women gasped and Naomi turned to her daughter.

"Oh, god, um T? Go to our room, baby—"

"But Mommy I wanna watch—"

Naomi bent and wrapped her hands around Thea's shoulders. "Listen to me, T. Go watch the TV in our room, okay? Please?"

Thea must've understood the urgency in her mother's voice. She nodded and fixed her crown before she walked to their room on the other end of the hall. Once her little feet were out of earshot and the door closed, Wes spoke.

"You think it was a job?"

"Sure fuckin' sounds like one. *Goddamnit*," Phoenix answered, a look of rage on his face as he kicked the bottom of the black leather L-shaped couch.

"A job? Wh-what's that mean?" Naomi asked.

Wes blew out a breath. "It means the people we thought—or hoped—might be in charge of the trafficking ring... most definitely are not and this is far from over."

"Oh god." Naomi's eyes widened and Wes couldn't fight back the strong urge to comfort her. He cradled the back of her head with one hand and wrapped the other arm around her small body, bringing her into his chest. The vanilla and sugar scent from her hair teased his nostrils as he massaged the back of her head, loosening her wild auburn bun even further.

He kept his eyes on the screen as he spoke to Hawk in a low voice. "We need to get ahead of this."

He knew Naomi could take whatever they were talking about, but her ear was to his chest as she faced away from the TV. If she needed to block everything else out for a moment, he was going to let her do that, too.

"Looks like we're already behind." Hawk scrubbed his fade before cursing. "We don't know who, if anyone, is next."

"Rusnak was obviously a valuable asset. I wonder if Strickland and Ascot know anything?" Wes asked, mentioning the other partners of the godforsaken firm.

"We gotta find out, dude. This is bullshit. We can't have gone through all that work for nothing."

Wes narrowed his eyes at Phoenix. "It's never for nothing, Phoenix. We saved lives."

Naomi pulled away from his embrace but stayed close, her shoulder pressed to his. He was grateful for the closeness, that she was considering him safe enough to lean on.

Phoenix rolled his eyes. "Come on, I didn't mean it like that. I just meant, if people who know shit start getting picked off, we're gonna be up the creek without a goddamn paddle and I, for one, don't feel like having another mistake like Yemen on my hands. I don't know about you—"

"Fuck you, Phoenix. Of course I don't—"

"Enough." Hawk silenced them. "Okay, they haven't found Ascot yet, the bastard's probably in fucking hiding if he knows what's good for him."

"Mitchell Strickland's in the hospital though..." Ellie muttered before raising her voice. "Could someone go talk to him?"

There was a pause before Hawk nodded. "That's an idea... except—"

"Except Devil fuckin' shot the guy. I doubt he wants to be besties with us anytime soon."

Wes hated to admit it, but Phoenix had a point. He racked

his brain for a solution before Naomi spoke up. "H-he... he didn't see Wes though, right? Since Wes was controlling everything from BlackStone? Maybe he won't have the same, erm, reservations?"

Wes appraised her with an encouraging smile before nodding. "Yeah... that could work. We could call Marco to see if he has contacts who could get us an interview. Or hell, there's also Henry." Officer Henry Brown was a deputy with the Ashland County Sheriff's Office and had grown instrumental in their mission to dissolve this trafficking ring. Some of what he offered them was off-the-record help, but the risks he was taking were invaluable to the cause. "Maybe he can ask him if he'll talk to me? The worst he could say is no."

Hawk nodded. "Sounds like a plan. The sooner the better. We have to figure out what these motherfuckers know. We've finally got people on the inside... we can't let this opportunity go to waste."

"Got it, I'll call them," Phoenix offered and Wes narrowed his eyes before shrugging. The man never volunteered to do anything, but hell, if he was going to start now, why not?

"Good. Snake" —Hawk jutted his chin at him— "get whatever you might need for an interview. Dress on the DL. They won't let you into his room if they know you're packing, if you feel me."

"Noted." He nodded and—out of habit—turned about face to his room.

Naomi followed quickly behind him. When they made it to the hall on the other side of the kitchen, she pulled his arm, stopping him. "Wait... Wes, is this safe? Y-you'll be okay, right?"

Wes hated the fear in her eyes and he hated it even more that he was the cause, so he decided to lighten the mood. "Aw, Naomi, see there you go again. Letting me know you like me so much."

He could tell her first reaction was to scowl, but the worry on her face held steadfast. Dropping the act, he turned to her and cupped her shoulders with his hands, bending to see deep into those amber fire eyes.

"I'll be fine, Naomi, okay? First off, I'm not sure if they'll even let me—"

"Strickland says he'll talk! He'll meet with you and Marco but he wants to do it ASAP," Phoenix called from the other room, his voice echoing against the concrete industrial decor and Wes nodded once, his stomach turning in anticipation. It'd been a while since he was physically on assignment, but the adrenaline always felt like a jolt of excited energy.

Phoenix's message seemed to have the opposite effect on Naomi. Her eyes widened and she started to shake.

"Hey, hey, hey, Naomi, I'll be fine. I might be a computer nerd, but I've been in the field plenty of times." He cradled her face in his hands, his thumbs stroking just above her jawline, and he marveled at the fact that she was letting him touch her at all. The high from his assignment and her soft skin under his fingertips sent pulses of need to his cock. But he tamped it down. Her level of vulnerability only went to show how terrified she was. "I was trained for this, baby, and it's just an interview. That's it. I'll be a glorified reporter, okay?"

"Sometimes training doesn't give a shit about a bullet though."

At her whisper, he realized what she was afraid of and he cursed himself for not realizing his leaving was about more than just him. No doubt she was thinking about what had happened to her dad.

"Listen, I'll be strapped. They just won't know it. And I will come home, I promise you. Okay?"

Finally, she nodded and swallowed. She closed her eyes and took a long breath in and out before opening them again. He watched in disappointment as her proverbial steel walls raised back up. She backed away and nodded again.

"Well, um. Good luck."

He straightened, warring with himself as to whether he

should try to ease her worries anymore or if he should let her pretend away her fear. But something told him she wouldn't feel better until he came back.

"Snake, you ready?" Hawk asked, clapping him on the shoulder with his large hand, Phoenix behind him. "We need to get going, brother."

"Shit, I have to go, Naomi."

Wes watched helplessly as Naomi completely shut herself off and retreated into the fortress she'd no doubt erected long ago. She'd probably perfected her defenses over the past five years with that asshole of an ex-fiancé.

"Like I said, good luck." Her voice broke on the last as she turned away and walked to the apartment she and Thea had been staying in. The steel door closed behind her, creating a deafening separation that Wes felt cut deep into his soul.

CHAPTER NINETEEN

The hospital loomed in front of them as they sat waiting in Hawk's sedan.

"We've been going to this place too damn much lately." Hawk spoke low in his deep voice, but received no response. What with Draco being in a coma, the victims they'd saved, Ellie getting hurt a week prior... he'd only said what Wes and Phoenix had been thinking.

Wes blew out a breath before seeing ADA Marco Aguilar coming out of the hospital and waving toward them.

"That's my cue."

"Don't fuck it up," Phoenix muttered and Wes rolled his eyes. One day he and Phoenix were going to have to have a heart-to-heart, but now was certainly not the time.

"Don't plan to, asshole. Thanks for the pep talk." Wes got out of the car before Phoenix could respond or Hawk could reprimand them for acting like children. He'd been having to do it more and more lately, ever since Phoenix decided to be even more of a whiney little fuck.

Marco jutted his chin and straightened his lapels on his suit. "Ready for this?"

Wes nodded and fell into step next to him.

"When'd the government start working on the weekends?" Wes asked with a smirk, indicating Marco's suit.

Marco mirrored him and looked down. "Man, you assholes called me out of Mass."

"Oh, shit. Sorry, man."

Marco waved him off. "*Mi abuelita* will get over it. If the big guy upstairs is making this possible then I'm gonna do my job. I don't think you understand how fucking rare this is. I've never had a defendant willing to speak with us and waiving his right to an attorney pretrial. It's practically a miracle in its own right. Strickland'll be able to ask for one at any moment, but Henry says that for some damn reason the guy's ready to spill his guts."

Wes nodded. "What's the game plan? I think we should work in tandem. I don't want to ruin any possibility for a case. I know Rusnak's untimely demise probably—"

"Fucked my cases all to hell? Yeah, no kidding. Don't tell a judge I said this, but the guy deserved his reckoning. Who knows how high up he was in the chain of command, though."

"Not too high I'm guessing, since he got eighty-sixed."

Marco huffed out a humorless laugh. "True. Well, one thing I definitely want to go over is what Investigator Burgess had been working on for the past year. Apparently, there've been some women missing over the course of many years."

Wes almost stumbled, remembering what Naomi had noticed about who he'd inwardly started calling 'the women with no future.' "No shit?"

Marco shook his head before scanning the sterile hospital hallways. Wes had no idea where they were going, but apparently Henry had briefed Marco. "Yeah, I'm actually really glad the feds have agreed to work with BlackStone as a private contractor, otherwise I wouldn't be able to talk about any of this shit," he murmured. "But here's the thing, Investigator Burgess saw connections that I don't think anyone else bothered to, or wanted to see—"

"Or they were paid *not* to see," Wes pointed out.

"Possible. But what's crazy is he wasn't working on cases of missing women from just Ashland County, but all over the southeast. Many of the ones who were actually found were murdered, overdosed, stuff that could very well indicate they were mixed up in bad shit too. But there were a few he had question marks beside."

"What do you mean?"

"They're still missing and *someone*" —he gave Wes a pointed look— "needs to find them. It's out of my purview as a prosecutor for the county, but someone needs to fucking look into it and the feds are dragging their feet. They are recent missing persons and with the track record Burgess figured out, I'm afraid we might be running out of time."

"Shit, if the government's dragging their feet, then we'll look into it for sure..." They paused their conversation to let a nurse rush past them and halted their steps again when a doctor followed her down the hall. Anxiety prickled over his body and he began to widen his strides. "I think we need to go faster, man."

"Why? What's up?" Marco asked, but didn't hesitate to follow beside him. The guy was nothing like the attorneys Wes was used to working with. He was Wes's height and build and he kept up with Wes's jog, like he could do it all day.

"I don't know," he admitted, unable to explain his trepidation. "I just have a bad feeling. We need to move."

They picked up the pace, with Wes following Marco's lead since he still didn't know where they were going. After opting out of taking the elevator, they ran up the stairs. With each step, Wes's heart started pounding louder in his ears and he hoped to God he was being paranoid.

They broke out of the stairwell to chaos as officers and hospital staff crowded around a room at the end of the hallway.

"*Shit*, shit, shit, shit, fuck—" Wes let the curse words fly as he and Marco ran to the room. Loud beeping and shouts echoed down the hallway and Marco and Wes finally met the crowd when officers started pushing them away.

"Sir, you can't come—"

"Fuck that, Romano, don't 'sir' me," Marco snapped with all the authority of a prosecutor who didn't give a shit about propriety. "I was authorized to be here with my associate to speak with Mitchell Strickland. What the hell's going on?"

The officer, Officer Romano apparently, blanched and backed up a step. "Marco, man, I'm sorry. His vitals went crazy a few minutes ago. I heard someone say something about a heart attack. The doctors have been working on him ever since." He pointed his thumb behind him with a grimace. "It doesn't look good."

As if on cue, the frantic beeping took off in one long beep.

"Clear!"

A low whirring before a loud thump resounded from the room and he heard the doctor repeat herself. But the long drawn-out tone persisted in the silence. After what seemed like an eternity, the beeping stopped and the silence slammed into him before the doctor's voice rang out.

"Time of death. Nine thirteen."

Wes closed his eyes and sagged against the wall. He took his glasses off and massaged his eyes as Marco started yelling at the doctors and local cops he worked with every day.

"No one fucking touch that body, do you hear me?"

"Excuse me?" the doctor who'd called out the time of death scoffed. "Who the hell do you think you—"

"I'm the prosecutor who's going to make sure nothing *questionable* has happened while *you* were in charge of a prisoner who's supposed to be under interjurisdictional custody. Now back away from Strickland." The cold look on Marco's face sent daggers at the doctor. Credit to her, though, that she only gulped and nodded slightly. Lesser men would've no doubt pissed themselves. "One of you officers, get caution tape and the coroner here ASAP. I want an autopsy, but *no* one goes near that hospital bed until the feds come, got it?"

Low murmurs of agreement came from the Ashland County officers and they immediately backed up from the door as doctors held their hands up and walked out the door. Half of them probably didn't even know the extent of Marco's authority and that this was probably even above his paygrade. But Wes knew from the Army that if anyone spoke in the commanding tone that Marco had just used, nearly everyone would listen.

Marco was on the phone for less than a minute before he leaned against the wall beside Wes. Wes knew he needed to call Hawk. They needed to regroup and figure out their next step, but at this point, for just a second, he needed a breather to understand what just fucking happened.

"So you're thinking what I'm thinking?" Wes asked, not looking at Marco.

Marco blew out a deep exhale. "Jeffrey Epstein?" Mentioning the infamous name of the man who had been "suicided" in jail years before while awaiting various charges related to sex trafficking.

Even though it was the furthest thing from funny, Wes huffed out a laugh before answering.

"Yup. Mitchell Strickland just got fucking Epsteined."

CHAPTER TWENTY

"Eat your dinner and watch your show, baby." Naomi slid the grilled cheese with the edges cut off, with the dinosaur chicken nuggets on the side across the concrete countertop.

It hurt her inner chef to feed her child the fake orange cheese, but it was the only kid-friendly food in the refrigerator at that moment. Four of the BlackStone Crew lived on the second floor of the BlackStone facility and despite the fact that all four of them were jacked and fit, the fridge had been empty when she arrived except for beer and random snacks. She had no idea where they got their nutrition, but it certainly wasn't from their kitchen.

And poor Wes, bless his heart. He'd taken it upon himself to go grocery shopping to surprise Naomi with "every kid thing" he could find. Which unfortunately meant fake cheese, just-add-water boxed foods, and frozen items, all with cartoons on them.

She lifted one of the cereal boxes and sighed. The green little guy on the front was touting how many marshmallows were inside an allegedly nutritional breakfast.

"Yeah, I'm definitely giving him a list next time," she murmured to herself.

When they did need more groceries, she would either have

to ask Wes again or be very cautious about going out herself. She wasn't even going to work, instead putting down two weeks of vacation until she and Thea could get situated. Thanks to Dean, she was quickly running out of PTO.

Trying not to give that man another second of her worries, Naomi pushed the doom and gloom thoughts aside before returning the box to the counter. The colors on the cardboard were garish against the gray concrete countertop. In fact, the brightness was out of place in the whole damn facility.

Everything in the BlackStone Complex was concrete. The floors, the ceiling, countertops, walls. When they'd first arrived, she'd been afraid it would feel like a prison. But her fears had eased when she saw the well-decorated facades and accents on the walls and ceilings. Certainly not her style, but it was much nicer than what she'd expected from the warehouse the few times she'd visited.

Thea loved it all. But Thea loved anything new. Maybe that was why she hadn't asked about her dad. Not once.

Naomi expelled a deep breath and tapped her nails on the cement. "T, baby, I'm not askin' again. Come get your dinner. I'm not gonna bring it to you when the good Lord gave you two fine feet of your own."

"Yes, ma'am," Thea muttered in her mindless iPad-watching voice as she slid off her chair. The whole walk to the counter and back, her eyes were glued to the screen even though she'd seen the movie a million times. When she finally settled at the long dining table at the center of the kitchen in the floor's open concept, she mindlessly started to eat her grilled cheese. Probably not even aware of what she was eating.

Just as well. It was trash.

Male whispers came from the living room and Naomi went to Thea and tapped the large headphones hooked on her neck.

"Headphones, T. And not too loud."

Thea nodded, her eyes never leaving the screen as she clumsily placed the headphones on her head. Once on, Thea continued to eat the tiniest bites of her sandwich. It was a treat for her to watch a show while she ate. Naomi's rule was that she could watch the show, but when Thea finished eating, it was bath time and bedtime. So naturally, T was making her dinner last as long as possible with the smallest of bites.

With Thea preoccupied, Naomi focused on the conversation in the living room, far enough away for the whispers to be heard but not discernible.

The BlackStone crew had a meeting after Wes and Assistant District Attorney Marco Aguilar finally got back from the hospital, and Naomi could hear Wes speaking with Hawk in hushed tones in the living room.

As soon as she stepped into the threshold that marked the living room in the open concept design, their whispers quieted. She paused and eyed them both.

"What's goin' on, y'all? Is there somethin' I need to know?" They met her with silence and she felt a frisson of irritation. "I know I'm not one of y'all... but T and I are here for the foreseeable future. At least until I figure out what to do next. I don't want us here if it's dangerous. I also don't want to hide out without doin' my part. If I can help, I want to know. So, y'all don't have to tell me everything, but anything would be appreciated."

Wes and Hawk glanced at each other like two men who'd been working together for so long they could read each other's thoughts. Their faces were expressionless, but apparently still saying enough in their silent code. Finally, Hawk dipped his head and Wes turned his gaze to her before clearing his throat.

"Is Princess T around?" he asked and Naomi's heart skipped that he'd think of her.

Dang, Nay. Get a grip.

"She's got headphones and *Brave* on."

It was all she'd needed to say. Wes knew Thea's obsession with Merida. His smile reached the crinkle in his eyes. "Can't compete with that Mary-*dub*."

Naomi snorted at the way he copied Thea's emphasis on the Pixar princess's name, but quickly sobered. She didn't want to get distracted. Wes must've seen the seriousness in her eyes because his face cleared.

"Mitchell Strickland is dead."

"Oh god. What? From when Devil shot him?" Naomi's heart stuttered and she pressed her hand up to her chest.

Wes shook his head. "Ashland County officers were guarding the door, but we think someone helped him on his way to meet his maker, so to speak."

Naomi clumsily felt for the back of the couch with her hand before collapsing onto a cushion close to Wes. "Shit. Then do y'all think it's linked to Dmitri Rusnak?"

Hawk's lips tightened, but Wes continued. "Yeah... we do. We think whoever is actually behind this bullshit is picking off the players one by one. The only other person we know for sure is involved is Andrew Ascot, the third partner in the law firm with Rusnak and Strickland. The police have a warrant out for him but they haven't been able to find him."

Worst-case scenarios ran rampant through her brain. "But what if someone else finds him first?"

Wes dipped his chin again. "Yeah, that's what we were discussing at the meeting earlier. We think we're gonna have to... um... help the authorities out."

"Take this shit into our own hands. If you want something done right..."

At Hawk's statement, Naomi nodded before realization about what he was saying dawned. "But what about the police? Don't they need to be involved?" Even as she said it, doubt crept into her mind.

The same cops who'd help Dean in a heartbeat if I called them? The sheriff's office that hid an officer who was neck deep in the entire operation.

Even though the Ashland County Sheriff's Office had developed a lot of distrust over the years, she'd never wanted to give in to the rumors before. Despite Dean's treatment and threats to sic his cop buddies on her, it had always felt like a betrayal to her father to not trust the police.

But now one of the most influential inmates in Ashland history had been murdered right under their noses.

Or by one of them.

She blew out a breath. "This is a mess."

Hawk snorted. "Who you tellin'?"

Naomi closed her eyes, warring between the need to know everything and the peace of plausible deniability.

"I'd like to be kept updated... sort of. I don't need all the details, just need to know for me and Thea to be safe."

Wes nodded. "Of course. We'll share what we can. Right now... we've got something in the works, but don't stress, okay?"

A sardonic laugh escaped her at the absurdity of his statement. "I'll try my best."

A buzz in the room set Naomi's nerves on fire and she patted around her baggy sweater and leggings for her phone but couldn't find it.

"Hello?" Hawk's deep voice resounded in front of her, silencing the alarm bells in her mind. "Yeah, hold on..." Hawk held up his hand to both of them as a signal goodbye and left the living room, talking in hushed tones on his phone.

She closed her eyes and took a relaxing breath in and out of her nose.

It wasn't Dean. He's out of my life. I'm safe.

"You okay?" Wes asked, concern furrowing his brow.

"What? Oh yeah. I'm fine—"

"Don't do that."

Naomi stopped and widened her eyes. "Don't do what?"

"Lie. You're safe with me, Naomi. You don't have to lie with me."

She bit back a growl. "What makes you so sure I was gonna lie to you?"

Wes groaned before swiping his face under his glasses and

repositioning them. "How about this? Let's just pretend for one second that I get where you're coming from. And let's also pretend this is a safe, judgment-free space and I'm a good listener. So in that world, if I asked you if you were okay, what would you say?"

Naomi bit the inside of her lips together, fighting back the habitual need to lie to protect her secrets. Instead, she trusted her instincts. "I was afraid it was Dean."

Wes nodded. "Thought so."

"But I don't even know where my phone is..." The realization made her pause. "And I'm not sure I've been able to say that for the past five years. My, uh, Dean... He works security, too. With AIE—"

"AIE Securities?" Wes interrupted before widening his eyes and winced like he'd given himself away. "I might've, uh, run a background on him."

Naomi snorted. "Honestly, I'd expect nothing less. Anyway—as I'm sure you know—he used to be a cop. I-it's one of the reasons why I stayed so long. He's got a lot of friends on the force still. Anyway, he is kind of obsessed with makin' sure I'm 'available' at all times."

A grim anger seemed to radiate from him, but to his credit, he closed his eyes and when he opened them again, they were clear. She noticed his hands tighten and the impulse to flee or fight tried to shout at her to get up.

But Wes wouldn't hurt me.

The truth in the statement rocked her and she blinked back the sting in her eyes. She was close enough to see the calluses on his knuckles and without thinking, she reached to trace them. Instantly, he stilled as if she was a wild animal eating from his hand and he was afraid if he moved, she'd run away. Which wasn't that far off, if she was honest.

"Where'd you get these?" She'd seen injuries on knuckles before, but she knew without a doubt Wes hadn't gotten them from hitting a woman. "You been gettin' in fights, troublemaker?" She forced a laugh as she teased him, hoping he hadn't earned them actually hurting anyone.

He stretched his fingers under her hand and looked down at them before clearing his throat. "They're, uh, from boxing." Naomi felt her eyes narrow at his hesitancy before he continued. "Every crew member was military, special forces. We've all been taught expert fighting techniques. Boxing and mixed martial arts are the ones I've stuck with the best."

She relaxed at his explanation and nodded, following the divots and hardened peaks of each knuckle. "See, I knew you were trouble," she joked again, this time with a genuine smile of relief.

After a few more strokes, she felt Wes's heated eyes on her. She stopped and reluctantly moved her hand so slowly that Wes had plenty of time to grab a hold of it and keep it between his.

He'd done that before too, held her hand in both of his. It felt natural, and an unexpected feeling of safety came from the simple act, unfurling something deep in her belly that she had been afraid to explore before she'd left Dean.

She'd 'lost' her engagement ring months ago, and ever since Wes had guided her and Thea to her car, Dean's touch had felt like betrayal, not Wes's. It was one of the reasons why she'd been so persistently against Wes for so long. If she'd given in to how good it'd felt when he was around, she would've done much worse than what they had in the BlackStone war room.

One of Wes's hands left hers and stroked her cheek. "What're you thinking over there, love?"

She rolled her eyes but couldn't stop herself from smiling. "Just... I haven't felt this way in... a long time."

He tilted his head in question, but his eyes were intense and kind. "And what way's that?"

"Mommy! I'm done." Thea's singsongy voice echoed toward them, bringing them out of the moment.

"Sorry, I have to go—" Naomi shot up off the couch, but Wes stood with her and tugged her elbow.

"Tell me, Naomi. Don't run. What do you feel?"

Naomi thought through all the feelings roiling inside of her chest and chose the least risky one.

"Safe."

Wes's jaw ticced, but something told her he was mad *for* her, not at her.

"That's a shame, love. You should never feel anything but protected." He squeezed her hands and leaned in. His cedar-citrus scent cleansing and relaxing her nerves as he whispered into her ear. "Let me in and I'll make sure you know what it feels like to be cherished."

Then he kissed her cheek... and left.

CHAPTER TWENTY-ONE

"Who the fuck goes to a strip club at noon on a Sunday?" Wes mumbled into his microphone as he stood at the bar inside the strip club. Even with Original Sin's house music blaring into his ears, the covert headset was able to pick up his voice and transmit it so the others could hear with no problem. He hadn't really expected a response, but of course, Phoenix felt the need to put in his two cents.

"Jobless asshats with arrest warrants, obviously. Quit bitchin'. You and the whole goddamn world have been lookin' for this guy for a week and it took me and Henry bein' here last night to crack the damn case."

"Yeah, only because the idiot was still committed to getting his dick wet even while on the run," Wes muttered back.

"I mean, can you blame the guy? Any day might be his last fuck, who knows?" There was something dark in his tone that made Wes pause in his scanning of the club, but Phoenix's next sentence cured him of potentially worrying about the asshole. "Anyway, thanks to *me* we have the fucker and also thanks to *me* I convinced Henry not to tell his boss until this afternoon that he got the tip. I know you're not used to bein' out on missions, but suck it up. We don't need the Super Geek messin' this up for us."

"Phoenix, quit trying to get a rise out of Snake," Hawk reprimanded.

Wes refused to give Phoenix's childish behavior a response and resumed his perusal of the few patrons while trying not to look out of place in the nearly empty club. "How'd you do that anyway? Convince Henry?"

"I promised him I'd let him drive us back to BlackStone that night in my '67 Camaro. It took twice as long to get home because he insisted on takin' all the damn mountain backroads, and nearly fuckin' crashed into the BlackStone Security gate, waiting for it to open. Pretty sure he got high off the rush, but all I got was high blood pressure. So let's make sure my fuckin' heart attack was worth it, 'kay?"

"We should also be thankful that Charity has no problem blabbing to you," Devil grumbled about the dancer who'd apparently entertained Ascot the night Phoenix and Henry found him. "Not only did the guy go to a strip club on a Sunday, while on the run, he fucking *reserved* a private dance with her. If I didn't believe the guy was an idiot before, I sure as fuck do now. Unless this whole setup is an ambush."

Even though they'd prepared for that possibility, Devil's observation triggered the healthy dose of anxiety that always had Wes's mouth running during a mission. But now that he was physically on assignment, he had to remain undercover and keep his mouth shut.

"He's involved with human trafficking," Hawk answered into his own receiver, his voice much clearer without the added feedback. "I don't understand why going to a strip club on a Sunday is what surprises you."

Hawk's transmission was smooth over the microphone since he was positioned in the back parking lot. Fortunately, Original Sin was one of BlackStone Securities' clients, so Hawk was able to monitor the club from the back parking lot on the CCTV.

They'd decided Phoenix, Devil, and Wes were the best

choice in approaching Andrew Ascot, Wes's teammates were frequent flyers at the establishment—or at least Devil had been before he met Ellie. In any case, Phoenix was still a regular, so their presence wouldn't raise eyebrows despite the fact they were there in the middle of the "Lord's Day" in the Bible Belt.

Because Wes's normal role was controlling the situation behind a screen, it was his job to infiltrate the room. He had the lowest probability of being recognized by Ascot and whoever was protecting him. Just in case shit hit the fan, though, Hawk was Wes's getaway driver and Phoenix was Devil's.

Wes left the bar and ducked his head before moseying to a free chair situated near the confessional. He'd helped install the security camera system and navigated every angle in order to keep his face off the radar. They had the ability to take the system off-line altogether, but just in case they needed the footage, he'd kept it running. Maintaining a low profile kept his ass covered if the video ever got into the wrong hands.

He placed his prop beer on the table before sitting down. With a casual lean forward, he rested his elbows on the table and steepled his fingers to conceal at least half of his face. He'd worn a coat to conceal his weapons and tattoos, and contacts since glasses were such a defining feature. Thankfully, it was too dark to be able to tell the difference between the blue and black in his hair. Like his glasses, a ball cap might've made him too distinguishable.

Strip clubs weren't his thing, but he had to admit that Original Sin was much nicer than any he'd ever been to. The music was loud, the beer was flat, and it was too dark to easily find the glass right in front of his face, but he could see the appeal. Especially when a beautiful woman with silver hair and white wings on the stage in front of him did a split midair as she held on to a chrome pole.

"That's Charity there on the stage," Devil supplied. "We'll have to intercept her before she goes into the room."

"Shouldn't be a problem," Phoenix answered with a dark chuckle. "She's one of my favorites."

"They're all your favorites," Devil muttered.

"What can I say? I appreciate the human body in all its glory."

"The bodyguards are the ones I'm worried about." Wes darted his gaze in front of him to the left where Phoenix and Devil were lounging at their 'usual spot' then to the right where two huge, conspicuous AIE Securities bodyguards stood watch outside the door Ascot had booked.

It hadn't escaped Wes's notice that the company Naomi's ex-fiancé worked for was the same one that was guarding Ascot. He already knew her ex was bad news just from the way he treated someone he allegedly loved, but if he was also safeguarding sex traffickers... he shook out his shoulders to relax.

Thank God she's left him.

"I think I figured out the bodyguard situation, too." Phoenix offered. In Wes's periphery, Phoenix waved his hand and two wing-clad dancers approached their table. "These ladies can be hella persuasive with the right encouragement."

Wes watched the woman with the silver-haired wig twirl on the pole as the two dancers started touching Devil and Phoenix. Devil's hands immediately went up and waved her away before pointing to Phoenix. The woman only shrugged and changed course to the more than willing participant.

After a quick lap dance, Phoenix pulled them both close and gave them each a kiss on the cheek. When the women stood up again, one of them tucked something into her bra before they both left Phoenix's chair. No doubt, cash was Phoenix's idea of 'the right encouragement.'

The last beat of the song ended, and Charity made her way down the stairs off the stage. On the last step, she turned her coy smile to Phoenix and waved before exiting through a side door.

"Gotta go, my dudes. The lady calls." Phoenix hopped up only to be tugged back into his seat by Devil.

"Nope, I don't like that look. I'll take care of Charity."

"Come on, man—"

"Devil's got Charity, Phoenix," Hawk commanded. "Your idea of a distraction might be *too* distracting. You monitor the bodyguards."

Phoenix grumbled his frustration but Devil ignored him, casually heading toward the door Charity had entered.

The two women Phoenix had "encouraged" slowly stalked toward the bodyguards. They stopped by other tables along the way, as if Phoenix had told them to be discreet, and when they were close to Wes, he took out his phone to pretend to text, making sure to dim the light so it wouldn't illuminate his face to the cameras.

Just as the screen darkened again, a text message *dinged* through.

My Queen: Be safe today

Wes felt his pulse in his throat as emotion threatened to choke him. It'd been a long time since anyone but his teammates and his sister had cared enough to worry about him. He quickly typed out a message, noting in the part of his mind that was still focused that the women had passed his table without issue.

Of course. I wouldn't want to miss out on those cookies I heard you promising Princess T

He could imagine Naomi biting the inside of her lip, trying not to show off her gorgeous smile that was already so rare. He hated that she did that, tucked herself away to appear small. Whether it was out of shame, or to be less of a target physically, her habit made his stomach twist to the point of nausea.

Before he tucked his phone away, bubbles and a gray message came through.

My Queen: Well I'll make the same promise to you. I told her if she's good, I'll bake cookies from scratch tonight. So be good troublemaker.

His cock twitched in his pants and he paused over the letters before finally typing.

... Define 'good'

When there was a second of no bubbles, he made the decision to push. It was time for her to come out of the shadows she'd hidden in. His fingers flew over the screen to shoot off one last text as he grinned.

I'm trouble, remember? So tell me why I should be good... when I can make you feel good instead?

He tucked his phone in his pocket, knowing that text would get a rise out of her. If she took the bait, he'd make sure they'd finally finish what they'd started in the war room. The fire in her eyes that day had burned him up with need, and spending time with her since she started staying at BlackStone a week ago had only stoked the flame to an impossible degree.

"Your cue, Snake," Phoenix's voice brought him back to the mission. "The women have occupied the bodyguards. Devil's got Charity. Time for you to rise to the occasion for once, Super Geek."

Wes wouldn't let the jab get a rise out of him, instead risking a glance to find the two women Phoenix had paid off had enticed the bodyguards and were giving them lap dances at the front of the club, facing away from the door. Wes had never understood how men could become enthralled with a random pair of tits. Phoenix might make fun of him for it, but if there was no connection, Wes didn't want it.

He stood from the table and crept his way toward the private room Ascot had entered less than ten minutes ago, presumably to wait on Charity. Wes turned to see if the bodyguards were still occupied.

"Don't worry, Super Geek." Phoenix chuckled in Wes's earpiece. "Tweedledum and Tweedledee are face-first in tits right now. Can't guard much of anything if you're motorboating."

"Know from experience, Phoenix?"

Phoenix grumbled at Wes's comeback, but if he came up with a retort, Wes didn't hear it. Excitement was thrumming through his veins and the blood pumping muffled his hearing to listen to only what was important as he tucked himself inside the small room.

CHAPTER TWENTY-TWO

Once inside, Wes cataloged the room, noting the exit to the back hall in the corner, the small stage with a chrome pole, and a pleather couch with a man on his phone. Wes's hands hung loosely by his hips, ready to engage his Taser at any time. He had a gun too, on his ankle, but that was for emergencies. Andrew Ascot would never constitute a physical emergency.

Wes took the moment to study one of Ashland County's wealthiest. The harsh glow from the man's phone put his features in stark relief. Ascot's face had taken on that oddly smooth feline quality that the rich paid for to hide their age. He might've depended on Botox and plastic surgery to fool people, but it seemed he hadn't bothered with his thinning gray-blond hair or his portly figure.

This was a man who bought, sold, and *hurt* women. Who played a part in killing Ellie's best friend, and kidnapping Ellie, Nora and all those other women. A man who was now somehow inextricably intertwined with Naomi's ex-fiancé. Men who hurt innocents were scum and Wes wasn't sure what he'd do to Ascot if they didn't desperately need him to find the mastermind behind the human trafficking in Ashland County.

"Ah, finally. I was wondering if I'd have to order someone els

—" Andrew Ascot stood from his pleather seat and Wes took advantage of his momentum, immediately grabbing the man's fat wrist. Ascot shouted and Wes shoved him against the wall before the man's wild swing could make contact. With his other hand, Wes slammed the right side of Ascot's head against the sheetrock. His skull only made a shallow impression in the drywall, but Wes knew he'd been struck hard enough to likely cause disorientation.

Men like Ascot deserved everything they got. They used people up and left them broken in their wake. A simple concussion would never be enough. Wes's knuckles tingled to beat the pudgy flesh of this monster and unleash his own beast.

Ascot managed to yelp, but the music was so loud in the building, no one outside the small room would hear. These types of rooms were meant to silence the moans coming from inside. Although the confessional's current groans were being caused by a very different reason.

"Wh-what's the meaning of this? Who are you?" Ascot's voice was muffled against the dented wall.

"Let's do introductions afterward, shall we? I already know who you are, Ascot, and that's all that matters right now," Wes answered as he easily applied pressure against Ascot's neck.

"How did you get past my security?" he screamed and Wes shoved his head into the wall again, cutting off the yell.

"You brought dogs to a building full of pussy. Did you really expect them not to hump everything in sight? Shut the fuck up. Don't move."

Wes removed his hand from the man's wrist and Ascot instantly began to wriggle. Using his knuckle, Wes dug his pointer finger in the man's exposed temple and got close enough to smell the pungent alcohol on his breath, cloying aftershave, and the acrid scent of urine. Normally, the smell would've made him nauseated, but adrenaline flooded through him.

This was an opportunity to alleviate some of the anger that always boiled so silently under the surface. He closed his eyes, trying to rein himself in and remember the objective. When he opened his eyes again, he was focused.

"This right here" —Wes emphasized each word with a tap of his knuckle against Ascot's temple— "is called the sphenoid bone. It's one of the most vulnerable points on the human body, yet it protects the most important asset a man has." Wes applied more pressure. "And all I have to do is strike it *just* right... and man's most dangerous weapon is neutralized."

"Please, I-I don't know why you're here. I have money... whatever he's paying you, I-I can double it!"

He? Interesting... and fucking infuriating.

"I could give two shits about your money, Ascot." Wes kept his knuckle depressed into Ascot's skull and pulled handcuffs from a pocket on his utility belt under his coat. When he slapped Ascot's left wrist with a cuff, the man tried to push away from the wall, but Wes only huffed out a pleased laugh.

"I was hoping you'd fight back."

In his next inhale, Wes wrenched Ascot's arm back, popping the shoulder out of its socket and causing him to howl in pain. On Wes's exhale, he grabbed Ascot by his thinning hair and bent him forward while simultaneously driving his knee up into his face.

A roaring filled Wes's ears and his vision tunneled to the blood splatter on his knee. Something in his mind shifted.

"You hurt her! She was good and you hurt her!" His voice sounded odd and tinny to his ears as he got lost in his rage. He drove his knee up into the man's soft flesh again. And again... and again... and again.

He faintly registered someone yelling through the headset, but Wes ignored the irritating buzz as he threw the man to the wall.

The pressure inside him felt like it was being relieved through a small hole in a helium balloon. The hazy, red fog in his mind dissipated. Breathing hard, Wes stared with mild satisfaction at the unconscious heap on the floor. He stretched his knuckles. It hadn't been enough. It felt good, though.

The door behind him opened and Wes tensed his fists before he realized Phoenix was slipping in. His teammate cursed and rubbed his hand over his face.

"You crazy-ass motherfucker. You weren't supposed to kill him," he muttered with a defeated shake of his head. "You're *smiling*, you know that right? Christ, what the fuck's wrong with you, dude?"

Too much to admit.

Wes grunted at the observation and bent to check Ascot's neck. Although he knew he hadn't hit the bastard hard enough to kill him, he'd certainly done some major damage. Soft men are easier to take down. "He's alive."

Phoenix shook his head. "Yeah, well, even knocked out he's probably a thousand pounds of deadweight. You know the rules. You knocked him out, you carry his fat ass. We gotta get outta here, dude. Those asswipes out there are this close to bustin' their nut in their pants."

As soon as the words left his mouth, there was a knock on the door. "Mr. Ascot, sir. We need to leave."

"Shit, dude, okay, we gotta go." Phoenix whispered loud enough to be heard over the music and bent to help Wes.

"Sitrep?" Hawk used military jargon to ask if everything was alright.

Phoenix growled over the headset while glaring at Wes as he picked up Ascot's arms. "Our resident Dexter went psycho on the fucker. Knocked an easy target out cold. Devil, we might need your assist—"

The door behind them slammed open and the two burly AIE security guards stormed into the room.

"See!" Phoenix's yell distracted the guards, slowing them down. "I told you they're two-pump chumps."

One of the men growled a second before both attacked. Wes and Phoenix simultaneously dropped Ascot like a sack of potatoes. Normally, they'd do the minimum to just get away from the men, making sure not to hurt anyone too badly. But they were in a public place and needed to get the fuck out of there before they drew too much attention. Instead, Wes and Phoenix got into an offensive stance, ready to attack in order to take the linebackers out quickly and succinctly.

The thrill of the fight flowed through him like an electric current, and he channeled all his anger at the enemy in front of him, finally able to let loose.

"Make sure not to kill them, Dexter!"

That's fine. It's no fun when it's over, anyway.

Wes and Phoenix worked in tandem around Ascot's unconscious body, attacking their respective target with fluid strikes. The guards were good, obviously well trained, but he and Phoenix were better. Individually and as a team.

His blood sang with excitement during the familiar dance. He and Phoenix had been on the same team one way or another for eight and a half years. Their friendship was strained now, but their muscle memory and instinct didn't have that kind of petty drama.

He and Phoenix played off each other, exchanging kicks and strikes until finally Phoenix took a hit to the gut hard enough to make him pause. Wes sent an uppercut straight to Phoenix's guy's jaw, knocking him out cold. But the selfless act cost him.

Wes's open torso was perfect for the man's front kick to connect with Wes's ribs, sending him into the wall. The guy charged at Wes and he braced himself for impact only to see the guy's eyes widen as he seized up and collapsed rigidly to the side, jerking and contracting as 1.8 microcoulombs and fifty thousand volts of electricity flowed from Phoenix's Taser down the two barbs into the guy's neck.

"Let's go." Phoenix said as he laid the Taser on the sofa, no doubt to make sure to leave the Taser's barbs in the man's skin. If Phoenix took the Taser, the current would immediately cease, and if the man were a professional, he'd likely be able to get up like nothing happened.

Wes grunted and swallowed back the pain in his ribs before shuffling around the man jerking on the floor. He bent to pick up Ascot but hissed at the ache. After a fortifying breath, Wes exhaled through the pain and maneuvered Ascot across his shoulders in a fireman's carry.

"Jesus H. Christ dude, hurry up. We only have twenty-seven seconds left."

"Don't you think I know that?" Wes gritted out under the weight and his screaming torso. "I rigged the Taser to shock that long in the first place."

But Phoenix was already out the door. He had a point. As soon as the charge ceased on the Taser, the guy would be shaken up, but no worse for the wear.

Wes huffed as he followed Phoenix without looking back. Hopefully, the asshole on the floor was feeling every one of those 1.8 microcoulombs of incapacitating agony. After stupidly trying his invention on himself, Wes knew from experience it hurt like hell.

"Hey! Over here," Devil stage-whispered a few feet ahead of them as he pushed open the exit. Wes squinted at the bright sun and clear blue sky, but his vision quickly adjusted. Tires squealed as Hawk nearly drove up on the curb. Devil thankfully had Wes's back as he carried Ascot across his shoulders on the way down the stairs. Phoenix jogged down the stairs to open Hawk's trunk, scanning the parking lot as he did.

"Coast's clear, I think. You'll have to do your techno-magic on the cameras though, for sure."

Wes grunted and dropped Ascot into the open trunk, making sure to finish cuffing the bastard before they closed him in.

Without another word, Devil and Phoenix ran to Phoenix's Camaro while Wes rounded Hawk's sedan. As soon as Wes's ass hit the leather seat, Hawk peeled out behind Phoenix.

"So you knocked him out, huh?" Hawk's tone was neutral, but Wes heard the undercurrent of anger in his voice.

"Yes. But it ended up working out, didn't it? We got the target and—"

"—and our cover blown to pieces. You're going to have to fix that."

Wes swiped his face. "I know, man. I just—"

"You know the rules, brother. Fight it out in training or talk it out in therapy. The crew is a warrior. Devil's the fists. Jaybird's the heart and he's preoccupied with Jules about to pop at any moment. Draco's the legs and we've been cut at the knees with him in a coma. I'm the backbone and Phoenix is—"

"The dick?" Wes snorted. "For fuck's sake, don't tell me he's the soul or some shit."

"Fuck you, man. I'm a soldier, not a goddamn poet."

"It's a terrible analogy, Hawk."

"Whatever. The point is, we can't have our brain malfunctioning. I need you firing on all cylinders." Wes rested his elbow on the window ledge, trying to calm his knee as it jerked with adrenaline, and resisted rolling his eyes before Hawk continued. "You're hyped up on the fight. Your hands are bloody. What if Naomi sees you like this—"

"She won't," he growled out.

"You're damn right she won't. But it's more than that. She *can't* see this side of you and look at you the same way. Not after what she's been through. You should get that better than anyone. You'll terrify her if she sees this side. You know that, right?"

Wes's hands trembled and he tightened them into a fist, noting the small cuts on three of the knuckles, despite their calluses from training. He closed his eyes and mentally buried down the memories, the nightmares, the *rage*. Finally, he swallowed and answered his leader.

"I know."

CHAPTER TWENTY-THREE

"You fuckin' *lost* him?" Dean slammed his fist on the table, rattling the coffee mug on his desk. He'd been a supervisor at AIE Securities for two years and never in his life had he been more infuriated. Even as he thought it, perfectly formed lips telling him it was over flickered across his memory.

Well, I've never been angrier with my job, at least.

"We're sorry, sir," Davis answered. "It was BlackStone, though, we're sure of it. We had our eyes on the two assholes who are always in Original Sin, but we ain't never seen the other guy. Maybe they got a new recruit after Vlad put down that last one."

"He's a scary motherfucker, too." Benson pointed to his eyes and shook his head. "Tattoos of snakes and skulls and shit all over and eyes like ice, like he ain't got no soul in them."

Dean had already ground his teeth to nubs at the mention of BlackStone, but as he suffered through listening to his men fumble over their excuses, his teeth were nearly dust and his jaw ached. They were AIE Securities' most talented officers, which is why they'd been assigned Andrew Ascot's detail. And now they'd failed one of the biggest jobs AIE ever had.

He'd have to give Davis and Benson credit, though. They'd

been beaten to all hell by trained soldiers, and Davis had been attacked by a Taser that'd been rigged to perform way above civilian legal standards for thirty fucking seconds. It'd been deployed from such a short distance that the barbs had embedded under his skin and had to be surgically removed.

"Why the fuck were y'all at a strip club in the middle of a goddamn Sunday? Y'all'd've been better off on your own knees at an *actual* confessional rather than havin' a whore on hers."

Benson huffed. The bruise caused by the knockout uppercut he'd taken to the jaw had swollen to the size of a baseball and Dean could tell he was talking gingerly around the pain. "The ol' perv said he'd fire AIE if we didn't take him. We strongly advised him against it, sir. But nobody listens to the muscle, boss."

Dean closed his eyes and stretched his fingers as he thought. The last thing he wanted to do was report this to Vlad. He'd have to figure out a way around that. The giant Russian fucker could pop him like a zit with just his two fingers.

On top of everything, Naomi still hadn't come home and the rejection stung like a bitch. He even missed his kid, too. Naomi's obsession with the little girl and insistence on Thea always being around them bugged the hell out of him, but she was his own flesh and blood and the fact that Naomi had the audacity to take her from him straight-up pissed him off. Not to mention, Naomi turning on him was unexpected and the betrayal was a knife to the heart.

She had to have found another guy. That was the only explanation he could think of. Every other time they'd had a tiff, she'd stormed out all dramatic-like but eventually came crawling back. Besides him, she had no one else to turn to. Or at least that's what he'd *thought*.

He'd made sure those clingy college friends of hers knew their boundaries when Naomi had Thea. And her mom was a grade A self-righteous cunt who used religion as a weapon. The fact that Captain Ward, a legend in Ashland County, ever married that shrew, was a mystery to him. Naomi was better off without any of them. But somehow she'd turned to someone who wasn't even on his radar.

"What're we gonna do, boss?" Davis asked.

Dean hardened his fist until his knuckles cracked. "You say BlackStone took him?"

The two men who might get him killed nodded like bobbleheads.

AIE had been contracted to do a certain job by the big boss, but got offered double from Ascot. Dean had seen the writing on the wall with Ascot, but he figured they could take the money for a while until the big boss said time was up. If Ascot was out of their hands, though, there was only one way this could all go.

"Alright, you're dismissed."

The men's heads jerked in surprise before they looked at each other, then returned their gaze back at him. Fuck, they were the best in AIE, but they reminded him of damn cartoon characters sometimes.

"D-dismissed?" Benson asked. "That's it? We can go?"

Dean narrowed his eyes and Davis nodded once before using the back of his hand to slap Benson's chest. "That's our cue, man." He pointed to the door with his thumb.

"Oh right, sure. Th-thanks, boss." Benson's nervous stutter irritated him further, but at least the men finally shuffled out of his office. Once they were gone, Dean cradled his head in his hands before blowing out a frustrated breath.

After steadying his mind, he grabbed his phone and dialed. He hated talking on the phone, but it was best not to do this shit over text message.

"Yeah?" The man was shouting over the loud bass, his Southern accent already dripping with liquor. "Whatcha want, asshole?"

Dean gritted his teeth. They'd known each other for a while and had developed a mutual amount of equal parts disdain and respect. It was hard to be a double, sometimes triple, agent. The man on the other end probably was one of the few people Dean knew that could totally relate.

"I need info on BlackStone's facility."

"Ah, so you've heard, then." The music faded and Dean imagined him closing the door to one of the club's private rooms. Sometimes Dean wondered why the guy didn't just rent one out to live in. He was certainly there enough.

"Yeah, my men just told me."

"Shit, dude, yeah, she's practically shackin' up with Snake—"

Dean's heart stopped cold and he interrupted with a whisper. "What're you talkin' about?"

There was a pause. "Oh, so you *don't* know? Interestin'. Well, I'm sure you can puzzle out the pieces yourself, for now."

Dean felt the phone crack under the pressure in his hand. "Is Naomi at BlackStone?" How his voice came out so calm, he had no idea. Inside, he was a boiling vat of oil, ready to maim anyone who tipped him over the edge.

The pause told him everything he needed to know. He'd have to figure that situation out for himself, it seemed.

"I'm callin' about Ascot," he pivoted.

"Ah, right. Yeah, what's the angle with that? I know Vlad's got you on that job. I thought that was why we couldn't find him at first. But it was *your* men who got beat up today. So what the fuck's the deal?" Each word was more slurred than the next. Some guys just couldn't handle their liquor.

"Yeah, well, it seems one job's gone south, so I'm resortin' to the other. I doubt Ascot's gonna come outta that facility alive and we need to control that situation to get the cut."

"I dunno, man. We good guys don't kill people, you know. He might get let go."

Dean scoffed. "It's hilarious you still think you're one of the good guys."

"Hey now, I'm an opportunist, and opportunities *are* a good thing. Speakin' of which, what's in this for me?"

"Don't wanna do somethin' outta the goodness of your own black heart, huh?"

The laughter on the other line was loud and genuine. "Nope. I left that life a couple years ago, man. Tried it. Realized money was better. After what Vlad's promised me, I ain't never goin' back."

"Well, how 'bout this. If you help me, and this goes good, I'll tell Vlad the extent of your involvement."

"Hm... what if it goes bad?"

Once Dean told Vlad his plan, there was no way the Russian wouldn't lend a helping hand. When Vlad was involved, shit got fucking done. Fuck, he might even be scarier than the boss man himself. Dean wasn't worried about that, but the other guy obviously was.

"Well then, I'll tell Vlad the extent of your involvement... and maybe make you sound extra liable with a few lil' white lies."

"And if I don't help at all? I've got a pretty good gig goin' right now, my dude."

Dean chuckled. "We both know you're not gonna do that. You get high on the risks."

The man on the other end grumbled. "Fine, fucker. I'll do it, but this better not blow back on me. I've got it good right now."

"Can't promise anything, asshole. Except, if Naomi *is* at BlackStone, I'mma remedy that real quick."

The guy huffed out a gruff laugh. "Who knows? Maybe you can kill two birds with one stone. Later."

The call ended and Dean stared at the black screen. It was an idea. Good or bad, he wasn't sure yet. He'd have to investigate. Until then, he'd try another avenue first. If that failed, well, there was always a plan B.

Two birds. One bomb.

CHAPTER TWENTY-FOUR

Define good.

Naomi gulped at the innuendo and wrung her hands as she stared at the text Wes sent her hours earlier. He and the rest of the crew had been gone all day, and all she'd had on her agenda for the weekend was to watch *Brave* for the trillionth time, worry about her future, and dream about everything that godforsaken text hinted at.

She cursed and stirred the dough harder. Her recipe called for a handheld mixer, but for one thing, apparently bachelors didn't see the need for one. If she'd known that, she would've asked Wes to pick one up when he'd gone shopping for her. Second, it was helping her channel her stress and pent-up... aggression.

Finally, the dough was mixed so well she was doing more harm than good. She hated cookies that weren't soft and chewy and aerating the dough would do just the opposite.

She grabbed an ice cream scoop—*that* apparently was an essential item in a bachelor pad— and slammed scoop-sized cookies onto the tray until she got lost in the rhythm.

"What'd the cookie dough ever do to you?"

The ice cream scoop clattered onto the metal sheet and she

cursed under her breath before jutting a finger against Wes's deliciously firm chest.

"You can't just sneak up on a girl like that!" She returned to the cookies to try to play off how fast her heart was beating, but the only dough left was on the mixing spoon and sides of the bowl.

Wes's brow furrowed as he stepped closer. "I'm sorry, Naomi, I..."

Naomi watched his full lips move and she could've sworn she was listening, but Wes's actual explanation didn't register. Instead, she imagined him saying the words of his text message in his baritone. Heated desire crashed over her like a wave.

"I'm trouble... why would I be good, when I can make you feel good instead?"

"Mommy, is you okay?" Thea called from the dining table in her high-pitched voice, pulling Naomi from her trance.

"What, baby?" Naomi grabbed the baking sheet and shoved it into the oven, allowing three hundred and fifty degrees to blast against her face before she stood back up and closed the door. Hopefully, the oven's heat masked the blush she'd felt coming on. "Yeah, Mommy's okay. Why would you ask that?"

"'Cause your mouth was open and your eyes was big and you was starin' at Wes—"

"O-*kay* that's enough, I get your point." Naomi interrupted, in a higher pitch than usual. When she heard Wes chuckling, she scowled at him.

He held his hands up to the side and scoffed. "Hey, don't look at me, it's out of the mouth of babes. I'm just enjoying the show."

"Is it 'cause his blue hair's wet? Wes, Mommy says you have to scrunch your hair with a towel so the curls don't fizz."

Wes snorted. "I'll make sure to towel it off better next time so it doesn't get *fizzy*. I just couldn't wait to see your mom again."

Naomi rolled her eyes while her heart did that stupid pitter-patter and turned back to her daughter. "Thea, why don't you take Angus and watch your show in the livin' room? I'll bring your cookie when they're done."

"'Kay," she nodded and her bright red curls brushed over her shoulders as she and her teddy bear, Angus, slid from her dining chair. While awkwardly using Angus to stabilize her crown, Thea watched her iPad and walked to the living room all at the same time.

"Who says preschoolers can't multitask," Wes joked and Naomi snorted. When Thea had settled on the couch, Naomi returned her focus back to Wes and whispered.

"How'd... whatever happened today, go?"

She'd meant what she'd said a week ago, that she wanted to remain on a need-to-know basis. That meant she had no idea what Wes had been up to all day, but she was fine with knowing just the end result.

Wes nodded slowly and leaned against the stainless steel fridge and crossed his arms. "It was... successful in some ways. A setback in another." A shadow passed over his face before he seemingly shook it away. "But no need to worry. Everyone's safe."

Naomi nodded. She tamped down that natural curiosity that was bound to get her hurt. It wasn't in her nature, but in this circumstance, plausible deniability promised a much better outcome judicially speaking if things went south. If she went to jail and left Thea with Dean... she shuddered at the thought.

She wiped her hands over her face and ended by smoothing her dark auburn tresses. "Good. I'm glad everyone's safe."

There was a pause and she looked to Wes and his furrowed brow as he watched her.

"You sure you're okay?" he asked, snapping her from her reverie. "You seem..."

Turned-on? Horny? Needy?

"... stressed."

Yup, definitely that one.

She chuckled at her inner thoughts and hopped up to sit her butt on the counter. "There's just been a lot goin' on lately."

He nodded before he stood in front of her. More than anything she wanted to demand he follow through with the text message that she'd been obsessing over all day. But she settled for minutes of comfortable silence as he took her hands in his. He squeezed and she looked up from their connection and into his Arctic blue eyes.

They were so different from everything else about him. A story she wondered if she'd ever learn all the nuances. He was warm and kind, but his eyes made her think there was maybe something cold and dark hidden within. Granted, that was probably just her experience and paranoia more than anything else.

Wes stroked her palm with his thumb, somehow hitting all the nerves in her body that were in charge of desire. There was no telling what Naomi would let this man do to her if she gave into the pulse thrumming between her legs, but she had to get control of herself. Thea was in the next room, for goodness' sake.

Naomi blew out a breath and collapsed her back against the dark wood of the overhead cabinet. Her legs inadvertently spread a fraction, but she didn't change her position. Wes's eyes flashed to hers as he took a small step to stand between her thighs. It felt sneaky, like she was getting away with something, but being around Wes never felt *wrong*. Quite the opposite. Especially when his fingers started massaging the inside of her palm more insistently, making her bite back a moan.

"Why the hell does that feel so damn good?" The words whispered out of her as she closed her eyes and sank into the relaxation his touch provided.

He gave a knowing chuckle. "We've got a lot of pressure points and nerves in our hands. It feels good to find release."

The words hit Naomi and her eyes snapped open. Wes wasn't looking at her, but she caught his wicked smile and his skin pinkened from his pale cheeks all the way down his tattooed neck.

She opened her mouth to confront him about the innuendo, but as she did, the timer on the oven dinged.

"Shoot! I completely forgot."

She pushed him aside and hopped off the cabinet, turning to open the oven. The heat clouded her face and she stood back up, opening, searching and closing every sparse drawer. "Um... where are y'all's oven mitts?"

Wes cringed. "Honestly, I don't think we have them."

She huffed and turned off the oven, leaving the door open to let the heat out. "Well, how am I supposed to get them out? If they stay in there, they'll burn."

He frowned. "Okay, hold on." He reached behind him and tugged the collar of his white T-shirt, sliding it over his head and arms like he'd freakin' practiced the move that every red-blooded woman fantasized over.

"Wes, what're you doin'?" Her voice wavered and her eyes widened at his sculpted chest, painted with intricate tattoos that made her mouth water.

He ignored her as he wrapped the shirt around his hand multiple times and bumped her to the side with his hips.

It took her another second until she realized what he was doing and she watched in horror as he tugged the tray from the oven and held on to it long enough just to clatter it to the stovetop. He cursed and tossed the shirt onto the countertop as he wrung his hands.

"Did you just use a *T-shirt* to get out a three hundred and fifty degree metal pan? What the hell's wrong with you?"

"Mommy, don't say bad words."

Naomi swiveled her head around to see Thea eyeing her over the couch, her big round headphones laid around her neck.

"Watch your show, baby. Headphones up."

Thea sighed dramatically before turning and collapsing back into the couch.

"Of course she'd freakin' perk up for cookies and curse words." Naomi muttered.

Wes laughed, sucking on a finger. "Kids have a sixth and seventh sense for those things."

Naomi almost laughed with him until she noticed the redness already creeping over the pads of his fingers.

"Goodness gracious, come here." Grabbing his hands, she tugged him toward the sink and turned on the cool tap water, testing the temperature before soaking his fingertips. His palms were already an angry red, but as she inspected his injuries, she noticed his knuckles were split and bruised. Without thinking, her finger grazed over one of the small cuts and she shuddered from the memory of the last time she'd seen knuckles like that... the last time she'd *felt* knuckles like that.

No. This is Wes. He doesn't have a violent bone in his body.

"Dang, trouble, maybe you should try less to live up to your name and ease up on the boxin'. At least make sure these heal up before you go again."

"Yeah, um... you're right," he murmured and tucked his face away from her as he bent close to the water, like he suddenly felt the need to pay rapt attention to his injuries.

Weird. But it's not my business. Better to not ask questions.

"Your fingers don't look too bad, just red. This water should help. Maybe some petroleum jelly if y'all've got some—" She looked up to speak to him but paused as she realized how close he was to her.

Her eyes were level with his chiseled, bare, tattooed chest, and her own skin grew hotter with the need to touch him than it had from the oven behind her. His icy hot eyes bore into her, but hers darted to the sensual curve of his mouth. She licked her lips and Wes pulled his hands free before placing his hands on either side of her in front of the still running sink. Normally, his positioning would feel like she was trapped, but the overwhelming security she felt made her heart light. She leaned in as he grazed his nose along her jawline, and her breasts heaved with every panting breath.

"Naomi—" Wes groaned her name against her ear before moving his hands to her hips and tugging her into his hardening—

"Mommy, is the cookies ready? Wes... where is your shirt at? You can't go 'round the world with no clothes on."

Thea suddenly appeared in the kitchen as she used her sweet little voice to repeat words Naomi scolded her with all the time. The combination splashed cool water over Naomi's libido, way better than the rushing tap water beside them could provide.

Wes chuckled before kissing Naomi lightly just under her ear. She swallowed and moved her hands to his chest with every intention of pushing him away, but she couldn't bring herself to create space between them. He did it for her, though, as he cleared his throat and backed up.

He assessed the shirt he'd tossed on the counter, likely to see if there were any burns before sliding it back on. When his body was finally covered, he leaned forward at an awkward angle against the island countertop, drawing her attention to the thickness straining against his jeans' zipper. He snorted and she met his laughing eyes as he adjusted, hiding his hard-on behind the island cabinet.

"Mommy, is they ready?" Thea asked with an insistent pursing of her lips.

Naomi yelped, somehow forgetting *again* that little eyes and ears were present. She smoothed her dress and coughed.

"It's 'are', baby, but yeah, the cookies *are* ready. I just gotta drizzle the caramel..."

Wes's eyes were still full of need and Naomi quickly diverted her attention to the baked goods. She'd get caught up in the moment again if she let herself, and she wasn't sure how much longer she could go without throwing herself at the man. "Wes was just helpin' me." She turned back to T, who was now walking into the kitchen from the living room. "You only get one, alright? It's almost your bedtime. I don't want you bouncin' off the walls when I've got work tomorrow and you've gotta go to day care."

Wes grinned as Thea rounded the counter like a racehorse. "Ready for that cookie, huh?" He picked her up like her forty pounds were nothing and tossed her in the air, causing giggles to cascade throughout the concrete aesthetic. He quickly turned her to face the oven, settling the girl's slipping crown back onto her head. "I say you should at least be able to pick the one you want. So which one shall Princess T have, hm?"

Thea giggled and hugged his neck before her face grew serious over the most important decision a four-year-old could make.

"That one—"

Wes caught her hand before she could get too close to the pan and burn herself.

"This one?" he asked, pointing to two flat, crispy cookies that had morphed into one.

Guess I overmixed the dough after all.

"The princess gets what the princess wants." He looked at Naomi and winked. "Just like the queen."

CHAPTER TWENTY-FIVE

There he went with that hot, confident male energy, zapping her cold, dead heart back to life. And damn him for that wink. It went straight to her clit every time and she was tired of the workout she was getting from having to squeeze her legs closed all the time.

Wes placed Thea back on her feet and tried to pick up the molten hot treat with his bare hand. Naomi slapped it before *he* could touch the hot pan and laughed. "Geez, trouble, I thought you were too smart to burn yourself twice."

"If the prize is worth the pain, I'll get burned as many times as it takes to get what I want." His mischievous grin tugged a moan from her core.

Did he just imply that I'm a prize?

She snapped her mouth shut and swallowed, trying not to succumb to yet another innuendo that would certainly send her into a desperate, needy spiral. Instead, she went back to the drawers and pulled out the shittiest spatula she'd ever seen in her life.

"Y'all have a facility that probably cost over a million dollars, and yet—" She bent the flimsy spatula with one finger. "Y'all don't have anything in your kitchen. I'm disappointed, really. You have to work hard to have *this* stereotypical of a bachelor pad." She smiled as he scoffed in mock offense.

"Well, I guess you're just going to have to remedy our bachelor ways, aren't you? Yet another reason I'm glad you're here." The desire in his eyes went straight to her center and she placed a hand over her lower belly. She hadn't felt the need pulsing through her since... Well, since the last time she was alone with Wes, but before that, when had it been... Ever?

"I'll give you the black card tomorrow so you can pick stuff up on the way back from work."

"Oh, no Wes, really I can't accept anymore of y'all's hospitality..." Panic jolted down her spine and she trailed off as her mind tried to analyze whether this was a trap.

Surely he wasn't suggesting she spend their money so frivolously. What if he didn't like what she bought? Or what if she chose something too expensive? Was this some sort of test? Was he trying to see if he could trust her and she really shouldn't take the credit card—

"No, love. Don't do that," his voice was kind but firm as his hands caressed along her shoulder and up her neck to cup her jaw. "Don't worry about the money, okay? It's not a big deal and you don't have to buy anything with our card if you don't want to, but that'll be *your* decision. I'm asking you to do us this favor and cure us of our bachelor ways. This isn't a trick."

"How do you always know what I'm thinkin'?" she asked before she could stop herself. His eyes bore into hers, seemingly searching for something as he opened his mouth, only to close it again.

"I just get it, is all." He let her go and turned back to Thea. "Now back to the cookies, right Princess T?"

Thea's eyes were narrowed at them, no doubt trying to make sense in her four-year-old brain of what was happening. But when Wes mentioned dessert again, she perked up and nodded in agreement.

Naomi huffed a laugh and shook off her nerves before she

got out one of the simple white plates from the cabinet and began to transfer the treats from the pan to the plate, drizzling caramel over each one from the mason jar of caramel she'd made before baking the cookies.

"T, get your dinner plate from the table. I'll put yours there but don't touch it yet, it's still hot."

Thea did as she was told before going back to her seat at the table, likely to eat it in very small bites again, since bedtime was right after she finished her dessert.

Despite Naomi's warning, Wes went in and grabbed his pick. Before even getting his hand around the molten hot cookie, he dropped it, yelping no doubt at his still sensitive fingers. Naomi picked it up, swirled more caramel on top, and blew on it before taking a bite.

"Hey, that thing was like lava! How come you can pick it up?"

"I've been burnin' my hands since I was a kid and I've built up a tolerance to it." Naomi shrugged with a laugh. "My momma and grandmomma taught me how to cook. Since my daddy had a sweet tooth, bakin' stuck with me best."

"That makes sense." He nodded with a thoughtful look on his face.

She narrowed her eyes and scoffed. "Really? A woman in the kitchen joke?"

"No. Sheesh, always so quick to be hostile." The hurt look on his face made her chest tighten.

"Sorry, that was snippy... I think I need to work on that."

Thankfully, Wes was a damn saint and let her rude behavior roll right off him before he leveled his gaze at her. "It just makes sense because you smell like a sweets shop. It's intoxicating, actually."

Once again, she melted as the heat returned to his eyes.

Gah, he knows how to flip my attitude like a damn switch.

She leaned into him, drugged by the thought of his lips on hers, when all of a sudden he closed the gap between them and licked the warm caramel off the dessert in her hand.

"Ah! Off! I don't want your tongue lickin' all over my cookie!"

He howled with amusement and it took a second, but she realized what she said and groaned into a laugh of her own.

"I didn't mean it like that. Obviously."

"Oh, so you do want me to lick your cookie? Happy to oblige, love."

Her cheeks warmed and she covered her face with her hands with a groan. Wes chuckled as he reached for the last cookie from the hot metal and yelped again.

"What is wrong with you?" She snorted. "Why don't you learn?"

He lifted a shoulder. "Well, if I wasn't persistent in life, I'd miss out on a lot of things I ended up really, *really* liking." He gave her a pointed look and she darted her eyes toward the desserts like a coward.

She tested out the temperature of a couple of cookies on the plate before choosing the coolest one, twirling more caramel on it, and handing it to him.

"Here, try this one."

His eyes were on her lips and she smirked before tucking a finger in her mouth to lick off some of the chocolate.

"There's a thin line between persistence and insanity. Tryin' the same thing over and over expectin' a different result, and all that."

"True." He nodded at her before averting his eyes. "Insanity would explain a lot about me, actually." The sentence was muttered in a much darker tone than any of his flirting, and she didn't like the change. She scoured her mind to think of anything else to talk about.

"Well, except for the insanity part, tryin' your best to make things work is better than just givin' up, at least."

He tilted his head, his lips in a thin grim line. "But, that's not always true... is it? I think you know that now."

His words brought that darkness in her life back to the forefront of her mind and she felt her good mood shutter closed.

"Good point. Maybe I need to break free from that particular line of thinkin'. It nearly got me killed."

It took Wes stilling beside her to realize what she'd said. The admission had surprised her probably just as much as it had him. She could tell that both of them were waiting for the other to speak, to figure out how to navigate the truth of her poor choices and misguided determination. After a moment of silence for the life she'd had, she finally spoke.

"I-I don't think I've ever actually said those words... out loud." She swallowed and collapsed back against the counter.

Wes's arm curved around her back and he pulled her into his chest, closing the distance between them but giving her the emotional space to continue talking.

"I was with that man... Tryin' with him off and on for five years. I hoped and wished for Thea to have the life I did... before my daddy passed." She sighed. "He was my world, ya know? Momma's too. When he was gone, so was the woman I'd grown up lovin', and I got lost, too. So I always wanted the life my daddy gave me, for Thea."

"What about you? What kind of life do *you* want?"

Naomi blew out an exhale. "Well, I want a good home for Thea. I want her to have two parents who love her and adore each other—"

"No, what do *you* want? For *your* life?"

Naomi blinked, so thrown off by the question, she answered honestly. "I... I'm not sure I've ever really thought about it. Definitely not since Thea was born." She massaged her temple. "Honestly, 'out of wedlock' wasn't really in the plan, so baby girl threw me for a loop."

Wes nodded. "Same for my mom. I was a surprise... and an anchor." His lips tightened and she suspected there was much more that he wasn't ready to say yet.

"Well, I went to school for business, but had to drop out after havin' Thea. Momma cut me off. My sins were too great, I guess."

Wes growled, but she was over it. There was no love lost in that particular relationship. The mother she'd adored had loved her father more than anything. Now she only loved herself, even at the detriment of her own daughter and granddaughter, and Naomi would *never* understand that.

"As for what I want now... I like workin' for Gail. She's an incredible mentor. 'Pre-T' I wanted to be a CEO. I've always had ideas runnin' 'round in my head. But I guess they slowed to a stop when it wasn't just me I had to think about."

He nodded in a way that suggested he might truly know where she was coming from. "Family's important, but you have to remember the oxygen mask."

Naomi gave him a small smile.

"Mommy, I'm done."

Naomi broke out of Wes's hold. She wasn't with Thea's father anymore, had cut him loose a lot earlier than two and a half months ago when he'd beaten her so badly, but Thea was too young to understand. Naomi wasn't ready for the "Wes is Mommy's special friend" conversation.

"Take your plate to the sink and let's get you ready for bed, okay?"

Thea groaned while literally dragging her feet and her teddy bear to the sink. Wes chuckled with his arms crossed as they watched her theatrics. As soon as Thea got the plate into the sink, she looked up at them with her big hazel eyes before shoving Angus under her arm and grabbing Wes's hand in an awkward angle to accommodate the bear.

"I'll go to bed, but I want Wes to read me my story."

Naomi's eyes widened. "Oh, so this is a negotiation?"

Thea nodded, although Naomi was quite sure the girl didn't know what a 'negotiation' even was, but Wes just laughed.

"Fine by me, Princess T. But you gotta listen to your mom until then, okay? After you do everything she wants you to, I'll read whatever story you want. Deal?"

"Really? 'Kay!" Thea jumped up and down and grabbed

Naomi's hand too before the three of them and Angus headed to their room. Wes made a quiet noise of surprise and Naomi watched as he looked down at his hand clasped around Thea's with a curious expression on his face. After a beat, Thea looked up at him. "You're supposed to squeeze it back," she whispered.

Before Naomi could ask them what was going on, Wes smiled and opened the door to their new apartment.

Throughout Thea's bedtime routine, Wes joked around at the breakfast table in the small apartment's kitchenette and talked to them through the cracked bathroom door. When they were finished, Thea ran to the bed in her *Brave* pj's—the girl was *obsessed*—and jumped onto the bed. She patted either side of her, demanding Naomi sit on the left and Wes sit on the right during story time.

As Wes read, Naomi grew entranced by his soothing baritone and how much Thea adored him. She was sprawled all over Naomi while flush up against Wes, and it filled an ache in Naomi's heart that she hadn't realized was there.

No, I realized it... I just didn't want to acknowledge it.

Wes's voice trailed off, bringing Naomi back in the moment to realize Thea was out like a light. Wes held a finger to his lips and pointed to the door and Naomi agreed to his silent invitation with a single nod. They gently extricated themselves from underneath Thea's wild limbs before Naomi followed Wes out the door. She turned off the light and paused before closing the door.

Thea's red angelic curls spread out across the pillow, shining from the sliver of light coming from the hallway. Naomi's heart squeezed with love before she closed the door and followed Wes.

CHAPTER TWENTY-SIX

Her feet padded softly on the concrete floor, but the noise echoed against all the hard empty interior. The floor was a ghost town.

"Where is everybody?"

Wes checked an app on his phone. "Hawk's, uh… downstairs. But other than that, looks like it's just us. A lot of times after a mission, the crew kind of separates and does their own thing. Lets off some steam."

"A mission?" she asked, a spark of fear igniting. That familiar need to both know everything and nothing at the same time shot through her.

He nodded and watched her reaction. After a moment, he gave a quick nod and grabbed her hand for a quick squeeze. He did that a lot, she'd noticed. Held her hand. She was beginning to love it more and more every time.

"Yeah… we, uh, had a bead on Andrew Ascot."

"Y'all found him?" She felt her eyes bug out. "So… what happens next, exactly? Is he willin' to talk to y'all?"

"Um… he's not exactly ready to talk to us just yet. But we think he will be in the morning."

"Not ready? What's that mean?"

Wes's lips tightened. "I'm keeping you updated, Naomi, but there are some things that are best for you not to know."

A sting of pain jolted from her lip and she realized she was worrying it as they spoke. Her imagination was running wild, but all she could do was trust that Wes would do the right thing. After what they'd all been through, they had to be dying to know what the hell was going on in Ashland County like she was.

Her own company, Charitable Technologies International, had been involved with human traffickers, for God's sake. Had Gail known? Dean's security company was contracted with CTI, did *he* know anything? Had Naomi unknowingly helped when she planned the parties where women were taken?

Each question was worse than the one before it, and she was afraid of the answers. But if she were honest with herself, she was tired of sticking her head in the sand when it came to her life. Besides all that, she didn't want to be at the facility if Black-Stone was doing anything illegal or dangerous.

Morals were all well and good if you had control over your life, but unfortunately Naomi was at the whim of her hosts until she saved up and figured out another safe place for her and Thea to live. At the moment, she was good with trusting Wes to make the right decisions. He hadn't done anything to ruin that trust... *yet.*

No, I can't think that way. She physically shook out the paranoia with a roll of her shoulders and moved on in the conversation.

"So what do y'all do for fun 'round here besides save the world from trafficking?"

"As noble as the fight against human trafficking may be, secret jobs don't keep the lights on, so we do have other clients that *actually* pay us." Wes shrugged. "Aside from that, we do all sorts of things. I read, usually." She smiled at his idea of a rip-roarin' time and he rolled his eyes with a shy grin back. "Riveting I know. Anyway, Ellie and Devil are probably together. They've been inseparable since they started dating. Jaybird's obviously with his fiancé, Jules. Like I said, Hawk's downstairs right now, but as for fun? I'm honestly not sure what he does. He's not much of a sharer and keeps to himself. And Phoenix..." Wes huffed a derisive chuckle. "He's probably at a strip club."

Naomi felt herself jerk back. "A strip club? On a Sunday?"

Wes huffed before leaning against the kitchen counter. "Phoenix isn't really bound by religious morals. If the strip club is open, he's probably there or somewhere else with some woman he picked up at a bar."

Naomi hopped up to sit on the countertop before grabbing a cookie from the plate beside her. They might be on the crispier side, but they were still good, especially after she plopped a dollop of caramel on top. "I mean, no judgment... I guess. I was just surprised." She leaned back against the cabinet and yawned before taking a bite. "Whew, I'm worn out."

"Are you sleeping alright? I'm not trying to keep you up."

She waved her hand. "No. It's nice to have someone to talk to. I don't have too many friends, and Dean certainly wasn't much of a conversationalist." A shadow of anger passed over Wes's face and she immediately felt a twist in her gut for putting it there. "I don't mean to always bring up my situation—"

"No, it's okay. I want you to share with me."

"That's... I like that. Thank you. To answer your question, as for a good night's sleep... Let's just say I may have broken it off with him two weeks ago, but I've had Thea as a bedmate for much longer. Now I get to share a king-size bed, which is a *major* upgrade from a twin-size princess bed. I can't remember the last time I slept so good."

"Well, you can stay here as long as you like."

"I sure as hell ain't goin' back to that house. That's for damn sure." She took another bite of the cookie in her hand before holding another out to him. "Want one?"

A mischievous glint shimmered behind his glasses and he dove at the treat in her hand, taking a huge bite. She giggled, but kept the remnants in her hand while he ate.

"Gorgeous." His low voice made her core tighten.

"What?"

Her breath hitched as he traced her lips with his index finger.

"This. Your happiness." He finished the upward path with a swipe at the corner of her bottom lip. A dark chocolate smear tinted his pale finger before he licked it clean. "I think I could bask in your laugh every day and never need the sun again."

Her heart stuttered and desire flooded her center. Even though she cleared her throat before speaking, her voice came out breathy. "I've definitely done it more the past two weeks than I have in... years probably."

Wes crossed his arms and leaned back against the kitchen island directly in front of her. "Why do you think that is?"

She scoffed, thinking at first he was fishing for a compliment until she realized he was being sincere. Her brow furrowed as she really thought about his question.

"I guess... it's hard to enjoy life when there's a constant stressor. It's been nice to feel free. Like I've broken a chain I didn't realize was trapping me to the ground."

He nodded before adopting a wicked grin. "Sure it's not just 'cause of me?"

Naomi swatted playfully at his chest. "I *knew* you were fishin'!"

"Can't fault me for wanting to catch another smile, love."

She rolled her eyes and held out the rest of the chocolate chip and caramel treat for him to take. "Just shush your mouth and eat your damn cookie, troublemaker."

Another wink and his mouth enveloped the cookie, taking the tip of her index finger with it. Her chest seized, capturing her breath and sending her heart racing. He chewed and swallowed before lifting her hand to his lips and sucking the remaining chocolate and caramel from her finger, all the while looking straight into her eyes.

Her breath came in hard pants as Wes stepped into her parted legs, wrapping her arm around his neck. She hadn't realized it, but her other hand had gravitated to his chest and as he moved forward, she joined it with the other behind his head. His hands landed on her knees and her dress skirt was long enough to make sure she wouldn't flash anyone as he stretched her. Once he settled between her thighs, he rested his hands on either side of her hips, his body protecting her from the world behind him.

"I don't feel caged in with you. Never when you're around." Her voice was a whisper tinged with need, but she didn't care. "And even now, you've got me locked in, but I've never felt trapped. Like I couldn't say no."

His brows furrowed, but in a blink, his desire was back to heating them up. "The only place I want you to lose control is in the bedroom. And even then, your wish is my command."

Like I'm his queen.

The thought sent a tingle of excitement down her spine and straight to her pussy. When he'd first started calling her that, it'd felt silly. And when Thea started repeating it, she'd nearly had a heart attack every time she spoke at home. The fear that Dean would hear their daughter say another man was Naomi's king had been her worst nightmare for two months. But now that Dean was out of the picture, every time Wes said it, the more she dreamed it could be true.

Her eyes left his and gravitated down to his lips. They glistened thanks to the sweet he'd licked off, but a small dab of chocolate still painted the corner.

"You missed a spot."

"Is that so?" The ice in his eyes burrowed into her, making her shiver. "What're you gonna do about it, Naomi Ward?"

She bit her lip before making her decision. All at once, she used her arms and legs to hook around him and dove for his mouth. Their lips met and he moaned when she teased her tongue against his lip to get the last lick of chocolate. It was sweet and rich, but she forgot all about it when Wes stroked up her back to grip her nape. His other hand tugged her ass closer so her pussy was flush with his hardening length.

"You smell just like that cookie, you know," he whispered against her lips before leaning in. "Vanilla... sugar... delicious."

His nose traced her cheek and her chest brushed against his with each breath. She got lost in the kiss when his hands delved under her dress and traveled up her bare leg.

Her skin tingled as he whispered in her ear. "I need to know if you taste the same way."

One hand gripped her ass, and with the fingertips of the other, he grazed up her inner thigh until his thumb caressed the thin layer of fabric over her center. It had her trembling with need and she wondered if he could feel her desire through her panties.

Teeth teased her sensitive earlobe and she shivered when his tongue traced the shell. His thumb tucked under the thin fabric of her panties and stroked the seam of her center, spreading the moisture around before zeroing in on her clit. He circled just around it, making her moan against his neck.

"Goddamn, you're responsive." His hot breath tickled her ear and all the sensations at once set her body on fire. "If you like my fingers, love, how loud can I make you scream my name with my mouth on your clit?"

Her breath hitched as the hand that had been massaging her ass lifted her up, just enough to realize what he wanted. She helped raise herself off the countertop so that he could pull the waistband of her panties, tugging them down her thighs before setting them aside on the counter.

Excitement coursed through her at the wicked gleam in his eyes and she closed her own to try to calm her racing heartbeat. Something scraped the counter beside her, sounding like it was placed on the floor, but the thought slipped her mind right after Wes began to glide a hand along her inner thigh, rolling up the hem of her dress. With her eyes closed, the sensation of his warmth and the cold concrete countertop on her thighs made tiny explosions of goose bumps across her sensitive flesh.

She opened her eyes again to see Wes's devoted attention

solely on her. The gravity of what he was about to do, where they were about to do it, all mixed with the heat in his eyes, hit her like a static shock. She leaned back, trying to see if anyone was coming down the hallway as she pulled her dress back down. He halted, but didn't let her tug the fabric away from his grip entirely.

"Wes, stop, what if someone sees?" The kitchen was positioned in the middle of the second floor and had counters in a U-shape around an island in the middle. With her sitting on the countertop, they were out in the open. No one could see it if they were just passing by, but if anyone entered the kitchen, they'd be able to see her pussy in all her glory.

Wes's brow lifted as he watched her carefully. "Is that your only objection?"

She felt herself frown in confusion. He could've been worried about her feelings for Dean, but she'd thought she'd made it clear that she was done with him. Thea was asleep and the girl slept like the dead, but what about his teammates?

"Yeah, what other reason would there—"

"Then don't worry about it." He gave her a scorching kiss before placing his hands on hers, making her roll the hem up. "We're the only ones up here." Cool air met her sex and she shivered again, but more in anticipation than at the cold. "If one of the crew comes up, we'll change venue, but I plan to make a dessert out of you in this kitchen. Once I start tasting, you'll beg me to make you come. No matter who's watching."

He kneeled before her, his head level with her pussy and spread her wide with his hands on her inner thighs. She closed her eyes, overwhelmed with the idea of what he was about to do, but she was brought back to the moment when something sticky and warm slid down her inner thigh.

"Wes, what the—"

She looked down to see his finger in the caramel jar, swirling it around with a wicked grin on his face before pulling it out. Wordlessly, he painted her inner thigh with another swipe of warm caramel. The heat from the sweet mixed with the cool air kissing her thigh made her shiver.

"Your caramel tastes divine, love. I can't wait to taste the rest of you."

He kneeled forward, watching her as he gave her slow licks up her thigh that sent shocks straight to her clit. Her core tried to grab onto the promise of release and fluttered against the emptiness that was craving to be filled as Wes traveled his tongue all the way up her center. He began near her knees, trailing along the caramel path and sucking in hard against her skin to soak up the sweet.

The closer he got to her center, the more she wanted to tug him where she needed him. Her hands threaded into his hair, pulling slightly, testing his limits, but he only chuckled against her thigh and kept his slow pace.

She groaned and leaned her head back, but Wes bit her thigh hard enough to make her curse and look back at him. He was licking the caramel off his lips and held a finger up to her.

"Taste it."

She was short enough to be able to lean over and take his finger into her mouth. She sucked up the sticky sugar, loving how his eyes darkened with need. She swirled her tongue around his finger, making sure to get all of it. When he drew his finger out of her mouth, he pulled her close to kiss the caramel off. The angle was almost uncomfortable, but she didn't care as she gave into the messy kiss, tasting the last remnants of caramel. She moaned into his mouth right before he broke the kiss.

"Now for the real dessert."

Her jaw dropped as he made a long swipe of his tongue through her arousal. The direct contact with her clit at the end made her draw in a harsh breath and she clutched the edge of the countertop.

Risking one hand to hold the hem of her dress, she watched in awe as he drove his tongue into her center. When it ventured inside, she bit her bottom lip so hard she tasted blood. It stung, but it was either that or moan too loudly and wake Thea up. With the industrial aesthetic, the facility echoed like a fucking concert arena.

His fingertips dug into her thighs and hers got lost in his thick hair as she tugged the strands like reins to ride him. He pulled her close to the edge, supporting her with his shoulders to keep her from falling.

Her muscles began to tense as she climbed to her peak. His icy blue eyes froze her in place as his thumb found her throbbing clit while his tongue speared her opening. When he withdrew from her core, she whimpered, afraid he was going to leave her hanging, until he delved two fingers inside her and went back with his mouth focusing on her clit.

A random beeping sound chirped in the hallway. Naomi's hazy mind ignored the noise, but Wes stiffened beneath her and his tongue left her clit.

"What?" Her voice squeaked with her protest. "No, no, no." She'd been *so* damn close. "Don't stop. Please... keep goin'," she urged, pulling his blue-midnight hair closer.

He tugged the fabric of her dress from her hand and she let go of her grip on him. The loose material covered him and as it smoothed down her legs, it sent shudders over her sensitive skin.

Slow, heavy-booted footfalls echoed on the concrete and her eyes widened, finally understanding that someone was home. She tried to move away from Wes, but he twirled his tongue around her clit and she melted against the cabinet with a moan.

Her free hand tried to grip the counter's edge, but slipped on her panties. Reacting as quickly as her distracted mind could, she blindly opened up a random drawer before tossing them inside.

Should she have stopped him? Sure. Would old Naomi have stopped him? No, because old Naomi would never believe a man could make her feel this good.

So, for once, she wasn't going to feel any shame. Fuck her modesty and fuck her fear. Aside from the pleasure, it was a heady experience to have a man kneel before her. She didn't want either feeling to stop.

At least the dress mostly covered him. Hopefully. They could play it off if someone came into the kitchen, right? Maybe.

Maybe not, but Wes's attention felt so good she'd take the risk.

Wes used the hand on her ass to pull her in closer for his feast, effectively hiding him even farther under her dress. She breathed deeply through her moans, but when his tongue found her clit and started to stroke, she lost the battle and released a quiet whine.

"Hey there…" Phoenix's slurred introduction made Naomi jump, and Wes paused. *Shit.* "Didn't think you'd shtill be up."

In her pre-orgasmic haze, Naomi vaguely confirmed that with Phoenix lounging against the bar behind her, he had no clue she was getting eaten out right in front of him. Plus, Phoenix's red eyes were half closed, and if his speech was any indication, he had to be blackout drunk.

Wes must've realized Phoenix's level of inebriation too and slowly began to move his fingers inside her again. She gasped at the motion and accidentally inhaled the alcohol fumes wafting from Phoenix's body, making her a little queasy. But then Wes resumed sucking her clit and she forgot whatever the fuck it was she was thinking about.

"Sho why're you shtill up? Just got back myshelf. How ya likin' it here?"

Yeah, there was absolutely no chance in hell he'd remember this moment. She could tell the liquor had brought out a light accent, but beyond that, Naomi could barely understand the guy. As if Wes had the same thought, his fingers narrowed to her G-spot. The damn troublemaker was *trying* to make her come in front of his teammate.

"Uh… I, um…" She tried her best to be articulate, but Wes's tongue swirled her clit and she moaned the rest. "Love it, oh my god."

Phoenix chuckled. "Well damn. Glad you like it sho much. You practically live here now anywayyyysh."

"Yeah, uh-huh."

Wes caressed her inner nerves with featherlight touches, and his mouth pulsated against her bud in a steady rhythm. A low whimper escaped, and she pulled Wes in with her heels on his back, pinning his head between her inner thighs. They were so tight against his ears, he probably couldn't even hear. She hoped he didn't mind, because she certainly didn't care, not one damn bit so long as he could breathe enough to keep enjoying his dessert.

"Damn, you *really* love BlackStone. I wish I liked it that much. I think I'm fuckin' broke inside though."

A sardonic laugh punched out of him, bringing her back to the fact that there was someone watching her rocketing toward oblivion. Or not watching, actually. Phoenix's head now lay against the bar with his eyes fully closed.

"You ever feel tha' way? Like... you've *heard* too much... *shit*... And when you're alone... Ish damn loud in your head, ya know? Like those shcreams... Onsh ya hear 'em, dude, they shtay in ya, ya know? Up here." He tapped his temple. "Ain't never forgettin' that shit. Nope. Not even if you fuck so much pushy your whole damn dick fallsh off, amiright?"

"Yeah, sure..." *What the hell? Can he really not see what is going on here? Go the fuck away.* She silently begged the drunk ass cunt-blocker, although she had to admit it was definitely a thrill of its own to get away with an orgasm in front of someone. It made every slick brush of Wes's tongue that much more electric.

Naomi felt her body tense as it rose to a peak again. She held her breath, afraid she wouldn't make it there, and settled for the near-perfect pleasure of that moment right before cresting. If she didn't reach the top, that was okay. She'd enjoy the plateau just as much. It was already higher than she'd climbed in *years*.

"Anywayyyysh. I guess we're all shome kinda fucked up in one way 'nother, huh?" He slapped the bar top, making Naomi jump farther into Wes's now... hell, was his tongue *vibrating*? She didn't even know they could do that...

In her periphery, she saw Phoenix pointing at her with a side-ways smile. "Shee ya later, Naynay. Got a big day of interrogatin' pervs to rest up for. If I wake you up, don't worry, it's just shcreamin'. Once you hear it, you don't forget it. Anywayyysh..." he said again before leaving and calling over his shoulder. "Nighty night!"

As soon as he began to stagger down the hall, the pressure low inside her reached a fever pitch. With another flick of Wes's tongue, Naomi released the breath she'd been holding on a deep exhale. It ended with a long, low moan as she tumbled over the blissful cliff in heaving pants. Her legs trembled around his head and her body pulsed with release.

Finally, after coming all the way down, she went weak with relief. Wes gave her one last swipe, dragging another tremor from her body. He slid his fingers from her sensitive core while kissing and nipping down her inner thighs, and when he stood up, he straightened her dress back down.

Her chest was heaving like she'd run a marathon, but it didn't help that he swiped at her arousal still on his lips and licked each of his wet fingers one by one, the heat in his eyes driving her wild. She grabbed his shirt collar with both hands and brought him crashing to her lips. A mixture of her pleasure and caramel flavored his tongue and she moaned at the taste.

He wrapped his arms around her and squeezed her against him. The move pressed her center against his hard cock, making her gasp before he whispered against her lips.

"You taste just as sweet as I thought you would."

Before she could demand he take her to his room and finish what he started, he swiped a cookie and brought it to his nose to sniff in one big breath and exhale, his eyes never leaving hers as he took a bite.

"I don't think I'm ever going to be able to eat caramel the same again. It'll always remind me of your sweet cunt on my tongue." He licked the melted sugar off the cookie and grinned. "I've got to say, I'm not mad about it at all."

Her mouth fell open, but his eyes twinkled as he walked backward. "Sleep well, love. I want you to rest up. Next time I dine with my queen, I'll want more than just her dessert. I'll want the whole damn meal."

He winked before he rounded the corner and was out of her sight, leaving her there dumbfounded and totally at a loss for words. When she heard his apartment door open and shut on the other end of the hall, she thought about going after him. But a realization crept into her mind, making her pause...

That was the first time a man had ever done something for her and not demanded the same for him. She'd literally just had one of the biggest, strongest men she'd ever met, kneeling at her feet, worshiping and feasting on her like it was the best damn thing he'd ever tasted.

Thinking about Wes's promise, she reached for a caramel chocolate chip cookie and looked it over. She smirked and whispered to herself right before taking a crunchy bite.

"It feels good to be queen."

CHAPTER TWENTY-SEVEN

"Do you have to be so fuckin' loud?" Phoenix grumbled curses under his breath and Naomi just snorted.

"I'm makin' *y'all* breakfast. It's not *my* fault basic cookin' is loud and it's certainly not my problem that you gave yourself a damn hangover." She maybe, not so accidentally, allowed the sheet pan to clatter against the oven rungs after turning the thick-cut bacon over.

"Fuckin' A, dude. Goddamn."

"Language," Naomi tried to use her best 'mom voice' to reprimand him.

"Oops, shit, sorry. Forgot about the kid."

"She's not here. It's just fun messin' with you. I told Thea's teachers that we're back from 'vacation' and dropped her off this morning so I can get some work done. Wes said Dean's at his office today, so I figured I'd take her there late and pick her up early, just on the off chance Dean decides to pick his daughter up from school for once in his parenting career."

"Is that why Snake called Henry? To get him to check up on your ex?"

Naomi nodded. "Yup. Henry drove by AIE Securities and made sure his car was in the lot. We're in the clear."

Gail was out of town and had given Naomi the okay to work from home. Normally, Naomi would've gone with Gail on the work trip, leaving Thea with Dean. But obviously, that was out of the question now. She could've kept Thea, but Naomi hadn't worked without distraction in two weeks. Besides, it was good for Thea to get back into a routine. Maybe if they got back to normal, everything else would fall into place.

"She'd probably just be watchin' TV if she was here, anyway."

Naomi rolled her eyes, trying not to bristle at the comment. "You know what? I get enough of that from mean moms, alright? I don't need to get it from some unmarried, childless twentysomething drunk-at-ten-in-the-morning guy who asked *me* to fix him breakfast. Watch your 'tude, *dude*."

Phoenix cringed. "Shit, I didn't mean it like that. I don't know anything 'bout bein' a mom. As you can obviously tell from my perfect male body."

"Gah, if I roll my eyes at you one more time, I'mma be stuck that way and you're gonna have to finish this cookin'."

"Please don't," Phoenix groaned. "The bacon is callin' to me and I'll burn this fuckin' place down if I'm in charge of the oven."

Naomi smiled. "Don't worry, I'm hungry too, so I'll leave you be this time. It's just mommy bashers are everywhere these days, bullyin' perfectly great moms and it's ridiculous what people get self-righteous about. We already can't sneeze without crossin' our legs, maybe we should, I dunno, at least be nice to each other? The world's already mean enough, ya know?"

She pivoted to find Phoenix scratching under his slightly raised ball cap while his face scrunched up in question. "Why do y'all gotta sneeze with your legs crossed?"

Naomi snorted. "You'll find out when you're older."

"I'm older than you, though?" Phoenix countered in a question.

Naomi continued, shaking her head. "Mommy bashin' aside. I've seen the writin' on the wall. If I refused to let Thea near a screen, she'd be behind the rest of her classmates. These kids are smarter and quicker than we ever were—or will be—and they'll never be told 'you won't have a calculator on you at all times'. My baby might learn how to code something into a computer that cures cancer, or some shit. It's better for her to learn how to navigate the internet than Lincoln Logs in this day and age."

"Jesus H. Christ, you and Snake are made for each other."

Naomi laughed as she turned back to the stovetop. "I'm rollin' my eyes again, just so you know. I've probably got one more eye roll in me before I'm stuck that way. It'll be hard to keep cookin' like that and this bacon ain't near done in the oven. And no one likes overcooked eggs or lumpy grits."

A watery belch behind her made her whip around to see Phoenix's blanched face again. "God, why does that sound like heaven and hell in the same bite."

"I figured you were sassy 'cause you're feelin' last night a little."

Phoenix groaned. "A lot, actually. I don't remember the last time I got that gone. I guess Devil always kept me in check more than I knew."

"Yeah, he doesn't go anymore, right?"

"Nope." Phoenix rested his head in his palms, squishing his face before declaring his woes with all the airs of a soap opera actress. "All the good ones are gone, Naomi. Stolen from me. I keep tryna tell 'em, can't be puttin' pussy on the pedestal, my dude. But they don't listen. "First Jaybird... then Devil..."

"Don't be so dramatic. That's growin' up. We all gotta do it sometime. Besides, you've got Hawk and Wes still."

Phoenix scoffed. "Yeah, sure. I'll party with the machine and the robot. That'll be greaaaat fun."

"Hey," Naomi turned and snapped the tongs at him, far away so that if any bacon grease or eggs flew off, it wouldn't be anywhere close to hitting his whiney ass. "Wes is fun. Y'all gotta get all your issues out on the table." A memory wriggled in the back of her brain. Maybe it was something Phoenix had said the night before? She'd been preoccupied, so it was hard to recall.

"That ain't happenin', Naynay."

Naomi growled, all attempts at remembering the night before's conversation forgotten. "I *really* don't like that nickname. But you and Nora are stickin' to it, I guess."

"I like it," Phoenix joked. "Makes me wanna dance." He did a shimmy and immediately turned an off shade of green. "Ugh, is it gonna be ready soon? If not, I might go pray to the porcelain gods first."

"Should be done actually." Using Wes's tried-and-true T-shirt method, she pulled the hot baking sheet from the oven and laid the metal on the stovetop, careful to do it without hurting Phoenix's delicate ears. "Where's everyone else?"

Naomi crunched bacon into the grits and added cheddar cheese. Operating on autopilot, she piled grits, scrambled eggs, toast, and bacon on Phoenix's plate before serving him.

He tilted his head before taking the plate. "Thanks. I know I'm a sad sack of shit this mornin' but I coulda at least served myself."

Naomi felt her eyes widen a fraction and she huffed an awkward laugh, confronted again with how fucked up her relationship had been.

"Shit, sorry, just habit from home, I guess. It was, um... expected." She cleared her throat and added smaller portions onto her plate. "Should we tell everyone else it's ready or eat it all?" Her pasted grin was brittle enough to disintegrate, but thankfully Phoenix was too consumed with his food to notice as she turned to talk to him.

"Everyone else?" Phoenix took a bite and groaned with his eyes crossed. "Gawd this is good. I didn't know oven-baked bacon was even a thing. My mamaw always fried it over the stove."

"My grandmomma did too, but once I found out about the oven, there was no goin' back. I like how it gets crispier all over."

"It's damn good. That all you gonna eat? Don't want it to go to waste."

"Won't Hawk, Wes, and Devil want some too?"

Phoenix kept shoveling in as he answered. "Doubtful. After they're done 'interrogatin'' Ascot, they probably won't have the stomach for it."

Naomi's fork paused on the way to her mouth and the eggs fell off. "Wh-what's that mean? Wes said y'all were gonna persuade him to talk today?"

Phoenix snorted. "Sh'yeah, right, *persuade*, that's a fancy-ass name for it, but sure."

Naomi blinked a few times, watching Phoenix scarf down his food like a starving man. "What's the *right* name for it, then?"

"Um, *torture*? Shit, if your beloved *Wes* was in charge, the guy might not even be above ground right now, let alone in our basement." Phoenix continued to laugh before looking up. Whatever he saw in her face made him green again and curse under his breath. "Aw hell, he didn't tell you."

Naomi set her plate aside and spoke low. "Phoenix, I'mma ask this nicely. What *the fuck* is goin' on?" Her conversation with Wes flashed across her mind like headlights in the dark.

"...maybe you should ease up on the boxin'..."

"Yeah, uh... you're right."

He hadn't lied, *per se*, but omission was just as bad.

Phoenix swallowed hard, even though he'd stopped shoveling food down for the time being. "Uh... I-I dunno." He lifted his hat and turned it around on his head. "I-I'm still drunk, who the hell knows what I'm sayin'?" He forced a laugh, but Naomi glared at him until it died. "Shit, you're scary when you go all mom face, you know that, right?"

"Where are they, Phoenix?"

"Like... really, really scary. You just went zero to one hundred, real quick."

"I ain't fuckin' around, Phoenix." She was so pissed off, her accent came out thicker than even she was used to. "Take me to 'em right now, or so help me I'll tell everyone what you said last night."

A flood of panic and bewilderment filled his face and she could tell her bluff had worked. She couldn't remember what he'd said the night before, but obviously he was filling in blanks he didn't want anyone else knowing about. She mentally pinned that in the back of her mind to investigate.

He gulped and nodded. "Okay, sure... just, uh... just follow me."

As Phoenix led her through toward the staircase in the center of the converted warehouse, Naomi silently cursed her blind trust in Wes. She'd promised herself that she'd stay clueless. Plausible deniability and all that.

But she wouldn't let herself stay in the dark any longer. Her daddy had been the best investigator Ashland County had ever seen before he got promoted. Needless to say, Captain George Ward's genes held strong, and she couldn't go one more second without figuring out what the hell was going on.

They traveled the stairs, but when they got to the first floor, Phoenix led them out of the stairwell and into the war room where she and Wes had had their first kiss. It'd opened her eyes to her feelings for him and how much she needed to get out of her toxic relationship. But had she just traded one monster for another?

They entered the war room and Phoenix went to the opposite wall and pressed what looked like simple grooves in the metal.

"Fuckin' A, they're all gonna kill me," he murmured under his breath.

"Wes won't if I get to him first," Naomi grumbled back.

A hole in the floor opened up like magic. Seriously, one moment it was a seemingly impenetrable concrete floor, the next it was a damn hole that led to the basement.

"This way."

Phoenix descended the steep metal staircase and Naomi had

a moment of hesitation. She obviously had poor judgment in men. What if this was a trap? Immediately, she shoved the paranoid thought away. She had nothing to offer these men. At best, she was good at making breakfast and exposing party guests. At worst, she was a drain on their resources and a potential liability that could get them all killed.

She took a breath and followed Phoenix down into an empty hallway made of concrete and metal. They didn't have to walk far before he stood in an open doorway.

"Guys... we have a visitor."

CHAPTER TWENTY-EIGHT

"A visitor?" Wes asked, unable to keep the confusion from his voice as he straightened from testing Andrew Ascot's zip tie and cuffs. Ascot was out of shape on his best day and there was no way he was getting out of the confines, but it never hurt to make sure a prisoner was secure.

He turned to the open door to see shock and disgust in brown-hazel eyes, singed with fire.

Naomi's gaze took in the scene, darting her eyes from Hawk to Devil, then to him, and he felt her scorching disdain, hurt, and...

Fuck, is she afraid of me?

Just as soon as he was able to analyze the emotion, she turned to look at the mangled man in the center of the room. Wes had to admit, it looked bad. The man was bent at the waist in the metal chair in the middle of the room, unrecognizable except for the bloody suit with his initials at the pocket. Okay, it looked really fucking bad. But when her gaze tripped over the drain underneath Ascot, her eyes widened in disbelief.

"What is all this? What am I lookin' at, Wes? Because it looks a helluva lot like a fuckin' horror movie."

Wes was too stunned by her presence to answer. She thrust

her hand at the bloody pulp that used to be the proud Andrew Wilton Ascot III, seemingly searching for something there.

"Is he dead?" she finally asked, apparently unable to answer her own question.

"No." His voice sounded odd, even to his ears, almost detached in the echo of the metal bunker. Unable to connect with the reality that he might be losing Naomi right in front of his eyes.

"Is he gonna die?"

"No," Devil's deep voice answered when Wes's voice was again caught in his throat.

She snorted. "Glad to see you have a fuckin' medic on standby while you *torture* someone. Who did this?" She was met with silence and finally lost her shit.

He didn't know why he did it, but Wes looked to Phoenix for the first time. The fucker was pale with bags under his eyes and an unreadable expression on his face, but Wes knew he'd done this shit on purpose. He had to have. The man was always setting fires to watch the world burn. He was probably jealous of his and Naomi's relationship and decided to light a match.

"*Who did this?*" Naomi screamed into the room. But she was looking straight at Wes. She obviously already knew the answer. She just needed to hear it.

"I did." Wes stepped forward, his shoulders back and his face carefully blank. "It was me, Naomi. I-I lost it yesterday on a mission," he admitted before turning to Ascot. When he turned back to Naomi, he cringed at how she looked at the man. Like *he* was the victim, instead of the pervert who was helping buy and sell women. "I let my emotions get the best of me and—"

"You... let your *emotions* get the best of you? What the fuck does that mean, Wes? You let me believe your bloody knuckles were from *boxing*! But they're because you were beatin' a man to death?"

"Not to death—"

"Really?" Her sardonic chuckle slithered over his skin,

making his hair stand on end. "Is that the difference we're gonna argue about? Is it really so much better that you *nearly* beat a man to death and not *actually* beat a man to death?"

He wasn't going to dare answer that. He had a feeling she'd be disappointed in his answer.

"H-help me," Ascot groaned for the first time since Wes had fireman carried him out of the club. Devil assured them that Ascot wouldn't die, but Wes had clearly gone too far. They were on a crunch time to figure out who was behind the trafficking and Wes had lost control so badly that Ascot had taken entirely too long to wake back up.

Wes watched Naomi's face carefully as Ascot pleaded with her, resisting the urge to knock the bastard out again. The light ivory tint to her skin turned green.

"Oh my god, y'all have to let him go. He needs to go to the hospital—"

"Can't do that, Naomi," Hawk interrupted. "He looks weak now, but when he has power, he wields it to traffic young women. We need to figure out what he knows."

"Noth-nothing. I don't know anything."

"Oh, god, what if he really doesn't know anything, y'all?" Naomi asked, her voice watery with emotion.

"Naomi, I love that compassion you have, but you have to set it aside for men like him. He'll use it to manipulate you. You have to remember why the fuck he's here," Wes reasoned, hoping she'd understand. "You *saw* the women that were saved from that hotel on the buy that *he* helped organize. More lives than his are at stake. If he doesn't turn over what he knows, we have to find out the hard way."

Her angered expression faltered, and her brow furrowed when he was finished, as if she wasn't sure what to think.

"But... how do you know he was involved to that degree?"

"We don't," Hawk explained. "But we won't know unless we ask him."

"And he's not going to answer if we simply *ask*," Devil clarified.

"I don't... know anything... I just fuck them. Wh-when I get them... th-they want it. I s-swear."

That was obviously the wrong thing for him to say if he was trying to gain sympathy from Naomi. The concern that had taken over Naomi's face cleared away, like she'd traded her comedy mask for her tragedy one. Her face twisted in scorn and she crossed her arms under her breasts.

"They want it?" She stepped forward, the fire in her eyes no longer turning Wes's heart into ash. "The women you buy and sell... you're tellin' me they *want* you to fuck them?"

"Yes, I swear!" Ascot raised his face to answer, but Wes kicked him in the shin, not too hard but hard enough that he looked down again before scowling at Wes. Wes just bent forward to meet Ascot's eyes but not low enough that they were on the same level.

"Don't fucking look at her. Answer whatever she asks, but don't ever fucking look at her again. Got it?"

The anger in the man's eyes stayed, but he gulped as he averted his gaze at another one of Naomi's loaded questions.

"Did you know I met the women who were saved from that party?"

Ascot seemed to analyze the question before shaking his head no.

"I sat with them as they were poked and prodded, their modesty violated all over again during every rape kit." —she stalked forward, but when Ascot tried again to look at her, Wes cuffed him on the back of the head, not bothering holding back — "I called their mommas for them, the ones who had them at least. I cried with every one of those women as they gave their statements, and do you know what? Not a damn one of them said they wanted to be there. Not a *fucking* one of them said they liked being raped or kidnapped or drugged with the constant fear of being murdered or that they *wanted* to have their futures taken from them by nightmares and PTSD. Not a *fucking... one.* So forgive me if I don't believe a damn word comin' out your mouth."

Ascot swallowed hard, but Wes could see the sneer forming on his face before he finally replied, raising his head in defiance but still not meeting Naomi's eyes. "We only ever picked poor sluts lookin' for a way out. It's not like they had much of a future to start with—"

Naomi's slap was loud in the metal room and made Ascot's head whip to the side. His cheek was immediately bright red and he had tiny cuts from where she'd let her nails scratch as her hand left his flesh.

She pointed at him. "You almost had me. I've given my life to a man for the past five years who's used my emotions to manipulate me. And fuck, you almost had me, too." Her dark laugh echoed in the room as she crossed her arms again. "Thanks for remindin' me that some people deserve what they get without me feelin' sorry for them." She turned to the rest of the men in the room, carefully avoiding Wes's eyes. "Carry on, guys." Her gaze cut back to Ascot. "This man won't be gettin' any allies from me. I'm done with all this shit."

She turned on her heel and Wes looked at the open door for half a millisecond before darting his eyes toward Hawk. At his leader's single nod, Wes turned on his heel and raced toward Naomi through the short tunnel and up into the war room. When he finally made it, she was already about to walk out and Wes had to shout for her.

"Naomi! Wait up!"

Naomi paused before turning on her heel. "What do you want?"

Her tone had him jerking back. He'd forgotten how scathing her defenses could be.

"About what just happened—"

She held her hand up. "Save it. I'm not ready to talk about this shit with you yet."

Wes felt his brow furrow. "But... I thought you understood?"

"Understood what? That you fuckin' torture people in your day job? Is this such a common occurrence that you are genuinely surprised that I'm disgusted with you right now? Or that a lie by omission is still a lie. You let me believe your injuries were from boxin'. You had the opportunity to be honest with—"

"Naomi, you didn't want to know!" he yelled, reaching for his excuse and hoping it was enough. "Look, I'm sorry—"

The laugh that came from her was so dark, he had to almost do a double take to make sure it was her.

"You're *sorry*?" She ripped at her dark auburn hair. "Gah, do you even know how much I fuckin' hate that word? It's a pathetic way for someone to feel better about their guilt without doing a damn thing to change the hurt they've caused. Sorry, sorry, sorry, *sorry*. Fuck your apologies. Just don't *do* the things that you would need to apologize for, how 'bout that? And what are you even apologizin' for, hm? Beatin' a man up?"

"What? Fuck no, I'm not apologizing for getting answers from a monster to save innocents."

Something cracked on Naomi's exterior before she huffed. "Good, because honestly, I get that one. After two minutes with the guy, I hope y'all crack him like an egg to get to what's inside." Then her shields were back up as she narrowed her eyes again. "But please, tell me then what're you *sorry* for, hm?"

"For lying... I should've just told you—"

"You're damn right you should have! How can I trust you now? I *told* you I needed to know if Thea and I were in danger stayin' here. If you're bringin' high-powered people here to torture them, how can we possibly be safe here with y'all?"

"BlackStone's the safest place you could ever be—"

"But, what about you, huh? Can we be safe with *you*?"

Wes felt his mouth open and shut, completely thrown by the question. "Of course, you can. Why the hell would you think you couldn't be safe with me, Naomi?"

"You said you let your *emotions* get the best of you, and you nearly beat a man to death. What happens when I piss you off, Wes? Is this what I have to be afraid of? I already left one monster. I don't want to crawl into bed with another."

"Naomi, love…" Wes reached for her hand in both of his and he was surprised she let him hold it. "Fuck, you don't know my history, yet. And I'll tell you someday, but you have to believe me. I would never, ever hurt you or Thea. I-I'd die before hurting someone innocent, and besides that I… I… *care* about you guys too much to let anything ever happen to you again."

Her face softened, but shame ripped through his chest as a drop of moisture trailed down her cheek. He wiped it away with his thumb and continued to rub the soft skin there, pulling her in with her hand in his until they were flush together.

"I promise, Naomi… I will never let anything bad happen to you again. Not on my watch. I'm splitting in half just seeing this one tear. How could you think I'd want to cause another one?"

She sniffed and nodded, letting her cheek nuzzle his palm before finally squeezing his hands and stepping back.

"I… Thank you for sayin' that. But I need time. I need to think. This is a lot to take in and I have my baby to think about."

Wes nodded, hope lighting in his chest. "I understand. Take all the time you need. I'll be waiting. But please, Naomi, consider what we've been through together. Really ask yourself if I'm someone you should be afraid of. If you think I am, then I'll go. If I've lost that trust, I sure as hell don't deserve to be in your life. But you and Thea need to stay so you're safe." He stepped forward again, holding her cheek in his hand. "But if you trust me. If you care for me, then please come back to me. I'll be waiting."

She sighed heavily before low vibrations entered the metal halls. She took her phone from her back jeans pocket and cursed.

"Shit… it's Thea's day care. I'm sorry. I hate to leave like this."

"Of course, I get it... just... fuck it." He bent slowly, allowing her plenty of time to bolt if she needed to, but she stayed still until his mouth met hers. Her plush lips molded to his, salty from her tears, but before he could get carried away, he ended it chastely.

"I don't want to sway your decision, but I couldn't stand you leaving without your lips on mine first."

"Thank you..." The phone continued to vibrate and she stepped back. "I have to go." He nodded as she turned around, walking toward the center stairwell, with each step taking his heart with her.

He'd hoped she'd look back just before the metal door shut, reverberating in the halls and slamming into his chest.

She never did.

CHAPTER TWENTY-NINE

"This is Naomi," she answered the phone after it rang for the zillionth time. The stairwell had spotty service, so she'd waited until she'd gotten to the second floor to answer. Thea's school had never called before and Naomi's stomach clenched tighter with every step.

"Hi, sweets."

Naomi stopped dead in her tracks as Dean's rough voice replied over the phone. She hadn't heard it in weeks, thanks to Wes changing her number.

"D-Dean... wh-why are you callin' me from Thea's school? I-I thought you were at work." He'd never picked Thea up without being asked, not even when he'd threatened Naomi with the possibility.

"Got off early so I could surprise my little girl. I told you that, remember? I tried to get a hold of you, but for some reason, my phone hasn't been able to get through. Thankfully, Thea's nice teachers said I could call your *new* number from their line." Rancid charm oozed off his manipulative tongue, making her feel even more nauseous.

"There's a reason you don't have this number, Dean. I told you—"

"Granted, you've been forgetting a lot lately, haven't you?" His voice was light with an undercurrent of fury that only she would be able to detect. "Like the way you *forgot* to tell me that you were taking Thea on vacation? Her—again, very nice— teachers informed me of that when I called a couple of weeks ago to make sure you hadn't *forgotten* to send her to school without her coat. Good thing I decided to keep tabs on my girl after that."

"Keeping tabs? What? Oh my god, Dean, just... please. Let's keep everyone else out of this."

"Of course, I had to make sure my little girl is safe and sound after her *vacation*. It was easy enough to have one of my guys help out with surveillance. Anyway, I just wanted to let you know you don't have to come pick Thea up. I took care of it, so I'll see you at home."

Her pulse stuttered to a stop. "Dean? You can't take her. If you wanna talk, let's talk. L-leave Thea at school and we'll work things out."

"Oh, nah, sweets. I think that particular ship has sailed. Excuse me for a moment, I'll just be right in the hall." His words were muffled while he presumably spoke with Thea's teacher. A brief second later, he was back to his true, harsh voice, scratching her insides raw. "Listen up, Naomi. I've got Thea and I've also got a promise. Come home, and it'll be different. We'll be together, just like the family you always wanted."

Naomi growled. "I think *that* particular ship has sailed, *sweets*. You made sure of that the last time you hurt me."

"Thought you might say that, so here's the other plan. Come home... or you'll never see Thea again."

The air in Naomi's lungs stilled, making her feel like she was suffocating. "What?"

"I think you heard me, but I'll elaborate. I've hidden away pretty sizable sums in various private bank accounts over the years and I'm about to get an even bigger one. One that'll set us up for life. Us bein' me and Thea, or... all three of us. It's your call. But if you're not in the picture, I'm gone, sweets, and you'll never be able to find us. Not even with your fancy new friends."

"What friends?"

He chuckled. "Sure... Like I don't know you've been whorin' yourself out, suckin' on BlackStone cock in exchange for free room and board. I told you I knew you, Naomi," he tsked. "It's disappointin' really. Not a good example for our baby girl, and certainly not if you ever tried to bring the law into it. My friends on the force would back me up and the judge might not be so accommodatin' with custody rights after he finds out you kidnapped our baby to be with your new boyfriends."

Trapped. Trapped. Trapped. She felt fucking *trapped*. What could she do? Her mind tried to see other avenues, but he'd just placed a roadblock at all of her possible excuses and explanations.

"That's what I thought. See you at home, sweets. Don't think about gettin' those BlackStone fuckers involved. I've got resources you wouldn't believe, baby. You think you know who you've fucked over, but you have no clue. And believe me, if you resort to them, I'll know. They're not as good at keeping secrets as they think."

What the hell did that mean?

"Ah, yes, thank you... her bear too? Can't leave without Angus, right, Thea?" His saccharine sweet voice was back. "Alright, see you later, bye! Come on Thea, we're goin' home."

"But what about Mommy and Wes?"

"Wes..." The dark tone he took with Thea made Naomi's skin crawl. "I wanna hear more 'bout this *Wes*. Maybe you can tell me in the car. Mommy's gonna be on her way home soon. Wontcha sweets? I can't wait to discuss your new *friend*."

Naomi closed her eyes.

Trapped.

The echo in her mind made her feel like she was falling.

"Naomi," Dean prompted her, making her jump.

She swallowed, her mouth suddenly dry and raspy as she answered.

"See you at... home."

CHAPTER THIRTY

Wes itched to go after Naomi, but she'd asked him to give her space. Honoring that one wish was the least he could do after adding a new trauma to her life. The mix of disappointment and horror on her face wasn't something he'd soon forget, but he had a job to do. He wasn't going to let his emotions get away from him again.

Instead, he, Devil, Hawk, and Phoenix spent hours in the basement with Andrew Ascot. They'd tried every non-torture-related tactic and even the ones that were on the cusp but still had no viable information from Ascot.

"Maybe he actually *doesn't* know anything," Phoenix murmured, barely loud enough to hear over the heavy metal music drifting up from the locked basement door. "Also, Devil, my dude, I don't know how you listen to this shit. I get why the UN considers it torture."

They'd put on one of Devil's workout playlists and turned the volume up to deafening decibels, playing the tracks for Ascot while they "gave him time to think."

"ADA Aguilar said that there was enough evidence that Ascot was involved in the trafficking to sign an arrest warrant," Wes countered, trying his best not to snap at Phoenix's whining. He was still furious at his teammate for bringing Naomi to the interrogation room in the first place. Phoenix had done that shit on purpose, but Wes wasn't sure yet what that purpose was. "He knows something, we just have to figure out how to convince him to tell us."

"Yeah, well it sounds like y'all are about to level up." Phoenix slapped his thighs before standing up from his rolling chair around the round table in the war room. "And y'all know how I feel 'bout that, so tell me how it goes, alright?"

"Phoenix," Hawk growled. "We need you to stay on base."

"I will, I will. Cross my heart. I just can't—" He tipped his head in Ascot's direction. "I just can't. If anyone needs me, I'll be upstairs. Probably begging Naomi to make some more of that bacon she let get cold this morning."

Wes perked his head up. "What do you mean 'let get cold?'"

Phoenix shrugged. "I went upstairs after you and her had y'all's lil' lover's quarrel. When I got up there, she was runnin' around like a bat outta hell. Her plate was still full of food when she left." He patted his stomach. "Don't worry. I ate the rest. Can't let good home cookin' go to waste."

"Wait..." Wes waved his hand. "Back up. She's gone?"

"Yup." Phoenix nodded. "Looked like she had places to fuckin' be, too. I don't think she even noticed I was up there."

"*FUCK*, Phoenix, you asshole! Why are you just now telling me this?"

Phoenix frowned and waved his hands up, either too dumb to put two and two together or a genius at fucking Wes over. "*Dayum*, dude, chill out. I didn't know it was a big deal. You were busy."

"I'll be back." Wes stood from his rolling chair so fast it almost fell before he shoved it toward the table, not caring that it didn't stay under.

Wes started dialing the phone before he even got to the stairwell. He took it two at a time and had to call again to make sure the shitty service wasn't the reason why the call dropped.

The dial tone mocked him on the other line until it cued the voice mail.

"Hey, lov-Naomi, I, uh, I know I said I'd give you time. And I am, I swear. I just wanted to double-check something really quick. Call me when you get this. Please." He emphasized the last word for good measure, hoping he didn't sound so worried that he scared her, but concerned enough for her to know he was serious.

What was going on? She'd gotten a call from Thea's day care. Was everything okay with Thea?

Fuck, I should've asked on the voice mail.

Once he shouldered open the door to the second floor, he practically ran toward Naomi's room, halting about ten feet away.

"Please be here..." He was so close and desperately wanted to just chalk his intuition up to paranoia. All he had to do to find out was walk up to her door and knock. No big deal. But that awful feeling twisting his gut made him hesitate. The quiet *whirr* of the air conditioning and gentle hum of the refrigerator put the silence everywhere else in stark relief.

He finally closed the gap between his hope that she'd still be there and the reality that he could've just scared her off for good. Leaning into the metal door, he prayed to hear something, anything, behind it. After several minutes of absolutely nothing but the AC, the refrigerator, and his pounding heart, he rapped his knuckles against the metal door, only to have it open slightly.

"Naomi?" He pushed the door open and saw...

Nothing.

Naomi and Thea hadn't had much, but there wasn't a trace of them in the room. None of Thea's toys. No clothes on the floor. He walked in a daze toward the bathroom, but again, nothing. Not even a toothbrush. After a half-turn around in the room, scanning for any indicator of where she'd gone, he thumbed through his phone and found her name again.

"Come on... pick up. Pick up. Pick up. Pick *up*," Wes growled over the mocking dial tone.

"Dude, calm down."

Wes whipped around, finding Phoenix resting his shoulder against the doorjamb and felt an anger that had been brewing for over a year finally bubble up.

"Snake, you gotta chill the fuck out, man. Ain't no way you'll get her back with that crazy look in your eye right now. You're on the verge of psychopathic stalker mode."

"Shut the fuck up, Phoenix." Wes couldn't help the feeling that maybe he was already there. Nor could he help the overwhelming feeling that all this was partly Phoenix's fault. "Why did you take her down to the fucking interrogation room? You *knew* what would happen."

"Hey, man, I'm not the one who fuckin' lost it on a mission yesterday. If you'd just kept your cool, she wouldn't have had that reaction today."

"The voice mail box you are trying to reach is full. Goodbye."

Frustrated with Phoenix, with Ascot, but mostly with himself, Wes grumbled curses back at the robotic woman's voice before shoving his phone back into his pocket. He swiped his face, pushing up his glasses with the movement before groaning out a loud curse.

"Talk to me, dude. What the hell's wrong—"

Wes whirled around on Phoenix and pushed him in the chest. "She's *gone*, Phoenix! Gone! Because of *you*! You brought her down on purpose! Why?"

Phoenix's mock concern on his face melted, leaving a grim fury in its place. "Fuck you, Snake. You don't know what the hell you're talkin' about."

All of Wes's frustration surfaced until he asked the question he'd been wondering ever since the interrogation had started. "Why weren't you down there with us already, anyway? Was it because you were hungover? Or what? What'd you do? Wait for just the right time to go ahead and turn Naomi against me? Why do you hate me so much, Phoenix? Huh?"

Wes pushed him again, but Phoenix only took a step back. Why he was taking it, he didn't know. The lack of reaction was too much for Wes and his vision darkened. Red filtered in around the edges and he panted like he'd just been in a fight.

Phoenix just maintained his silence, both calming Wes down and enraging him more.

"What is it? You're always shit-talking me in meetings, never following my direction on a mission, insisting on blaming *me* for the disaster that was our last mission in MF7. What the fuck is wrong with you? We used to be friends, man... and now... Fuck, now you might as well be my enemy."

"You're not my enemy." But Phoenix's words came out flat, as if he didn't truly believe it himself.

"Then why did you bring her down there? You could've texted me to come up or warn me, why would you—"

"Maybe she needs to see what we do! Have you ever thought of that? Maybe she needs to see what we're capable of. It's better she knows now who she's gettin' in bed with than find out later!"

"Where is this coming from? We're trying to help shut down the trafficking ring. We're the good guys in this situation. Yeah, we might have to get our hands dirty, but at least we're not kidnapping and killing innocent people. What the fuck are you talking about?"

Phoenix scrubbed his head hard before slamming his hat back onto his scalp. "Everyone thinks they're the hero of their story. But since Yemen, hasn't it ever occurred to you that maybe we're the villains? Think about it, man. All those women we were supposed to save? Gone. Dead or God knows what else. What would've happened if we'd just left them alone? Would it have been better for them?"

Wes scoffed, trying to catch up with Phoenix's logic as a pit developed in his stomach at the answer to that question. "I don't know, but I do know that we did our best. Phoenix, we were ambushed by men we'd trained and thought were our friends. We couldn't have known—"

"One of us should've known! We were the 'best of the best,' and *none* of us figured out we were about to get stabbed in the back by men we trained? I just find that real fuckin' hard to believe. And you're the smartest of us. Did you *really* not know what was gonna happen? Or did you set us up?"

"Phoenix, what the fuck? Are you listening to yourself? Of course I didn't set us up!"

Phoenix's eyes narrowed. "What did you hear in Yemen?"

"What?"

"What... did you hear? I don't know about Eagle, but I know everyone else's headsets went static. Everyone's but mine... and yours. So tell me, Snake. What did you hear?"

"Phoenix, what the fuck, man, are we doing this now? I gotta find Naomi—"

"*What did you hear?*"

"Nothing! Everything was cutting in and out or static. I caught some feedback from enemy lines, but that was it. It was all in bastardized Arabic from what I could tell, and I was trying to get through to you guys to warn you of the parts I did hear." He waited, watching Phoenix's face as it got darker. "Why? What'd you hear?"

"*Everything.*" Phoenix's fists tightened and loosened at his sides. "You're not my enemy, but I don't think I can ever forgive you for that."

"Phoenix, I don't know—"

Wes's phone rang in his hand and he looked down to see *My Queen* on the screen. "Shit, Phoenix, I have to take this but we need to talk, okay—" He looked up from the screen, only to realize he was talking to empty space. Phoenix had already left.

He wanted to go after him, because what if Naomi was fine and he'd overreacted? What if it was all in Wes's head and he was losing the chance to have the first real conversation with his teammate in over a year? But he needed to hear Naomi's voice, needed to hear that she and Thea were okay.

He swiped the screen and answered. "Naomi?"

"Yes."

At her voice, relief came in waves and he collapsed onto her bed. "Thank God you called love, I was so wor—"

"Snake, I need you to stop callin' me." Naomi was definitely on the phone with him, but her voice was totally different. Despondent. Dead. Devoid of the laughter and light he'd come to know over the past few weeks. "We're done."

The two words were like barbs from a Taser gun, embedding in his skin and electrocuting him to the point of seizing up. He couldn't breathe, couldn't talk. He just sat there dumbly on Naomi's bed.

"After seein' you and... what you're capable of... I just... I can't trust that it won't happen again. What if you lose your temper and it's just me there?"

"Naomi, God, please, I would never hurt you. You don't know my past, but I swear on my life—"

"You lied to me, Snake. You lied, and you... you let your emotions lead you to beat a man to within an inch of his life. I can't be with you. I can't have left my... *fiancé*, to be with a monster."

His words caught in his throat. "Naomi, please." Every one of her words was a killing charge across the line, but he had to focus on what was best for Naomi and Thea. "I-I hate this decision, but... I respect it. I'm not trying to change your mind about me, but come back to BlackStone. Please. I'll leave, but it's not safe for you yet. If you're ready to move out, fine, but we didn't come up with a plan of action to keep Dean away—"

"I'm back with him."

The words hung in the air, threatening to collapse and suffocate him.

"*What?*" He growled the question, beginning in his chest and he was sure she could feel the anger coming through the phone. "Naomi, what the hell are you doing? You don't want to be with me? Fine. But for Thea's sake, don't go back to *him*."

"It'll be different this time. He's said he's gonna go to therapy.

We can be a *real* family."

The words twisted in his chest. Everything she was saying was something he'd always desperately wanted. Recently, he'd dreamed about it with her. But she wanted it with another man.

Of course, Dean was part of their 'real' family. I was just the place-holder in the abusive cycle... But what if he's right there listening? What if he's making her say those things?

"Please, Naomi... let's meet somewhere and talk about this. You should at least look me in the eyes as you tear my heart out."

There was a gasp and silence on the other end and Wes sighed.

"I care about you too much to see you go through this again. I'd need to see you, but at the very, very least, please just take a day and think everything over first."

"It's done. I-I'm in love with him." The last word dipped low and landed like an anvil on his chest.

She's not lying.

"Goodbye, Snake."

The call ended and Wes looked at his phone, completely dumbfounded by what he'd just heard, trying to make sense of it. Had she been deliberately pitching that last word to prove she wasn't lying? Or maybe she was trying to prove she was?

His phone vibrated in his hand again and he immediately looked at the screen, cursing at the text before he opened it.

Hawk: Break's over. Time to get back to work.

He desperately wanted to speak with Naomi, face to face, but she was refusing to see him and he still had a job to do. They needed to get answers out of Ascot before Wes tried to figure out his next steps with her.

Phoenix was an asshole about his temper, but what his team-mates and Naomi didn't understand was that Wes had never gotten violent with anyone who didn't deserve it. Ascot fucking deserved it, but Wes wasn't going to seriously injure an unarmed man.

But Ascot doesn't know that.

CHAPTER THIRTY-ONE

Wes stormed through the war room past Hawk and Devil to head for the basement trap door. Without looking at them, he opened up the app he'd set up on everyone's phone in order to operate and lock the door, and punched in the code.

"Phoenix?" Devil asked.

"Not coming."

For some reason, Phoenix always got to pussy out on shit like this. Hawk would let the man get away with murder.

The door hissed open and Wes slid down the ladder, with Hawk and Devil following closely behind. He hardly registered the blaring music echoing against metal walls and entered the second code on his phone to unlock the steel door, hiding the prisoner before wrenching it open.

"Turn it off! I can't take it anymore!" Andrew Ascot's face was red and his eyes were narrowed with frustration. Wes would've almost felt sorry for the guy after what they'd put him through, but Ellie's friend Sasha, and God knew who else, had died thanks to Ascot and his associates. Fear was the only way to get these kinda men to crack.

Wes kicked the front of the man's chair so that it tipped back violently and the metal slats landed on his handcuffed hands. Ascot howled in pain, almost in time with the music, until the throbbing beat silenced. Either Hawk or Devil must've thankfully turned that shit off.

"What the fuck do you know about the trafficking?"

"Nothing! I swear!"

Wes *tsked* harshly, but everything sounded much quieter now that the screaming music was gone. Using one of his steel-toed work boots, Wes toyed with a cut on Ascot's face before applying some pressure. "Why won't you tell us anything? You think your little friends are gonna come save you?"

Whimpers were muffled as Wes tore a small cut back open with the soul of his shoe. "I still don't know why you're so loyal to someone who's gonna kill you. Judging from your dead friends, what we would do to you is child's play. And yet you're going to go squeal to them like the pig you are, right to your death."

"Wh-what? H-he wouldn't kill me!"

Wes landed his boot between Ascot's legs on the edge of the chair seat. The man yelped and tried to protect the dick that'd gotten him into this mess.

Good. Fear of pain was always a much better motivator than the actual pain itself.

"You're right to be afraid. I could stomp your balls into your lower intestines right now. I might even be doing you a favor. If you don't have the urge anymore, maybe you won't be tempted to steal and rape women."

"He'll f-find me, you know. And once he does... you're all done for."

Wes tilted his head with a glance to his friends standing behind him, arms crossed and faces grim. He was able to identify the same curiosity that he felt at the faith Ascot had in whoever he was protecting. No one else would be able to see their expression under their calm exterior, but Hawk and Devil were his brothers. He knew their faces better than his own.

They'd thankfully let him take the reins, which provided its own sense of silent encouragement. Having his friends' trust gave him the confidence to believe he could remain under control.

With that in mind, Wes swung his leg up in the air and kicked it backward, making the heel slam into the chair seat, inches from Ascot's crotch. The man screamed as Wes's momentum brought the chair into an upright position before it teetered back and forth and settled on all four legs.

Wes dug his hand into Ascot's shoulder and met his eyes. Even though they were widened with fear, there was still a hint of defiant arrogance swimming in the rheumy blue-black depths.

That was why he'd refused to apologize for what he'd done to Ascot. Although losing his cool on a mission was worthy of an apology, Ascot sure as fuck wasn't. Wes put his teammates in danger by letting his emotions get the best of him. Now that he was in control again, they needed answers from the man who still somehow thought he pulled the strings.

"Tell me, Ascot, why do you think once he finds you that *we'll* be done for... and you won't be? Hm?"

Wes had a suspicion and he wanted to test the theory. The man had been in hiding for two weeks. Did he even know he was in danger on all fronts? Men like Ascot rarely fought the good fight, crumpling like a wet paper towel at the first sign of a threat. He had to believe either there was someone scarier than BlackStone or...

"Is it because you think he'll *protect* you?" A flicker of satisfaction flashed across Ascot's eyes. "Fuck, it is, isn't it?"

"What makes you so special?" Hawk asked in his deep voice. "Why would he protect you and not the others?"

Confusion wrinkled Ascot's sweaty brow. "The others? Wh-what do you mean?"

"Rusnak and Strickland," Wes answered with a shrug of his shoulder as he took a step back to stand in line with Hawk and Devil. "They weren't important enough to save. Why are you?"

Ascot shook his head violently. "No... Nonono. What do you mean? What's happened to them?"

Wes scoffed. "You really don't know, do you? How the fuck don't you know? Have you been hiding in a damn cave?"

"I-I've been without internet access in a shithole on the edge of town. Afraid to have people find out my whereabouts. M-my bodyguards haven't said anything. Wh-what's going on?"

Devil snorted. "You went through all those precautions, and got caught at a strip club? What an idiot."

Ascot's face reddened as he demanded again. "What's going on?"

Wes stomped his heel down hard on Ascot's foot and the man cursed a grunt. "I'll tell you because I want to. Not because you have the audacity to think you wield any power here while you're cuffed to a chair, got it?" At Ascot's slight nod, Wes continued. "Dmitri Rusnak and Mitchell Strickland are dead."

Ascot's eyes widened again. "Dead? *How?*"

Hawk answered. "Rusnak, bullet to the brain. Found in a river. Autopsy was performed on Strickland. Full results will be ready in a few weeks, but preliminary findings are that he suffered an ill-timed heart attack."

"But we both know how convenient that is." Wes offered with a nonchalant shrug, even while Ascot began to pant heavily.

"Strickland, too? If he'd go after his own brother..."

Wes's senses perked up and he resisted looking at his teammates as he spoke. "Who? Who is Mitchell Strickland's brother?"

Ascot muttered, his eyes wide in shock with a far-off look. "Half... very scandalous. Strickland's father couldn't have it in the press, so he paid the whore enough money to stay away. Now neither of them claim the other, but I never thought... I never thought he'd *kill* Strickland."

"*Who*, Ascot?" Wes asked. "Who wouldn't kill Strickland?"

Whatever trance he'd been faded away as he blinked rapidly

and shot a look of desperation at Wes. "I-I'll tell you everything. You just have to protect me from him."

"We can't promise to protect you from anybody if we don't know who it is." Hawk reasoned, but Wes felt the anticipation pulsing from his teammates.

Ascot's jowls trembled with another frantic head shake. "That's last. I'll tell you everything. But I won't tell you that until you secure me safe passage out of Ashland County. No, the *country*."

Wes waited as Hawk eyed their prisoner, no doubt weighing all the options. His forearms were crossed over his torso and his other elbow was propped up as he traced his lips in thought. There was no way they'd let him go, but Hawk was surely thinking of a solution.

"Deal." —Ascot blew out a heavy breath— "But if we feel like you're lying to us we'll come after you ourselves, got it?"

Ascot nodded so hard Wes was surprised the man's head didn't fall off.

All their questions came to the forefront of his mind and he sorted through them one by one, trying to find out which would be the most important.

"What is *alea iacta est*?" Wes asked, referencing something Ellie had said she'd heard one of the traffickers, Vlad, say when she'd been captured.

Ascot laughed. "Really? That's what you want to know? You have me at your disposal and that's all you want?"

Wes felt himself growling in frustration and Ascot gulped before answering. "I-it's a 'who' not a 'what'. Although I suppose, at its core, it's an organization dedicated to a state of mind. Men of my wealth and power who have certain *interests*. Strickland's brother provides us with those interests... but we're by no means the only organization he deals with."

"So, what? It's a group of hedonistic rich old white men?" Hawk ground through his teeth.

Ascot's cut lips tightened before he relented. "I wouldn't put it into those unsavory terms, but essentially that's the gist, I suppose."

"Who all's in the group?" Devil asked. "Is it just you three pervs?"

Ascot huffed but shook his head. "Dmitri, Mitchell, and I... we were the founding members. Others have trickled in over the years. It seems Assistant District Attorney Marco Aguilar was able to ascertain most of the list if the arrests of my friends right before I went into hiding were any indication."

"Was Investigator Burgess in the group?" Wes asked, mentioning the investigator who's double agent spying had brought to light the connection between the trafficking ring and Ashland County's elite members.

"No. He... he worked for Strickland's brother... in a roundabout way. Well, for Dmitri Rusnak, who was the right-hand man." He cursed under his breath before muttering. "I can't believe he'd dispose of him so... *cruelly*."

"You think Rusnak's death is cruel? After you've all kidnapped, drugged, raped, and murdered innocent women?" Wes's dark laugh of disgust snapped the man back in the moment. "Ascot, we're going to need a list of those names."

"I-I can't! Truly—"

Devil's strong fist laid into Ascot's cheek. "You will tell us *everything* or you will wish Strickland's brother had you in his sights, do you understand? *I* was the man who put Strickland in the hospital. I knew exactly where to shoot to cause lifelong damage. Don't think I won't do the same to you."

Ascot whimpered and nodded. Wes pulled out his phone and began to type.

"Start talking."

CHAPTER THIRTY-TWO

Ascot blathered as Wes took notes on his iPhone. They didn't know if the names Ascot was giving them were a pile of shit, but Wes would work his magic to see what he could find about each person.

When he was finished, Ascot fell back against his chair.

"Exhausted from telling the truth?" Devil asked, and Ascot glared at him before sighing.

"That's it... that's all I know."

But Ascot hadn't answered the question burning in Wes's mind ever since Marco told him that Investigator Burgess was looking into missing women. And then the few women Naomi had pointed out from the list...

"Where do you get the women?"

Ascot hung his head and blew out a breath. "It's been harder in the past couple of years. We used to have a consistent supplier. There was a group that helped us... erm... procure slu —" Devil growled, "—*women*... who'd come to them. They'd take them and distribute them. It was genius, really. No one was ever the wiser. But everyone in that supply chain is gone. We've been having to make do, hiding in the shadows and finding willing women at our fundraisers and events."

"'Willing?' That's what you call them?" Devil's pale skin was beet red with anger, his fists clenching and unclenching at his sides.

Wes couldn't blame him. Ascot's confessions were churning in his own gut like acid, bringing him to the brink of nausea when another question entered his mind. The timing of everything, how the traffickers had to resort to other means the past couple of years, what Phoenix had said…

"… hasn't it ever occurred to you that maybe we're the villains?"

"What's the name of the group?"

Ascot's eyes were focused on Devil's tightening hands. "Wh-what?"

"The name," Wes gritted out. "Of the group. What's the name of the group where you got the women?"

Ascot nodded. "Oh, yeah… uh… I've never, uh, been the religious type, but it's a weird Bible name."

"The Rahab Foundation?" Wes breathed the question, knowing in his soul he was right.

"Yeah, yeah, that's it. The Rahab Foundation."

"What?" Hawk sounded like he was in pain and disbelief. "That can't be the name."

The guy never showed weakness, but the implications of Ascot's confession were a nightmare too terrifying to accept. When Jules and Nora had raised questions about the organization over a year ago, the BlackStone Crew had even swept their concerns under the rug.

The Rahab Foundation was the nonprofit that rehomed all the trafficked women they'd saved over their seven years in MF7. If that organization was in on this scheme, what the fuck did that mean? The thought that every woman they'd 'saved' had been sold back into slavery couldn't be true… could it?

"So the Rahab Foundation took in trafficked women and did what? Sold them all back into sexual slavery?"

Ascot seemed uncomfortable with the question. *Good, maybe he's realizing just how fucked up that is.*

"Well, I'm not sure about all the specifics. AIE—"

"AIE?" Wes interrupted. One of the first rules of interrogation was not to interrupt the person being questioned, but not only was he exhausted, this whole process had caused him to become too emotionally invested and he was hanging on by a thread. "As in AIE Securities?"

The same private security company Naomi's ex-fiancé works at?

"No, *Alea Iacta Est*. Although *Alea Iacta Est* does fund AIE Securities. Most of the security firm is aboveboard, though. No, what I was going to say is that our organization was connected with the—Mitchell's brother, and he was connected with the Rahab Foundation—"

"Wait." Wes's breath froze in his lungs as he tried to keep up with the conversation despite his rapid pulse drowning out Ascot's voice. "AIE Securities is *funded* by *Alea Iacta Est*? I knew you personally employed them as your bodyguards, but I didn't realize the whole company worked for you, too."

Ascot had the nerve to laugh. "It's AIE Securities... as in *Alea Iacta Est*? It's on our website and everything. Didn't you do your research?"

Wes stepped back and tugged his hair on end, even though all he wanted to do was sink his fists into Ascot's pretentious face.

Naomi's ex works for AIE Securities. Naomi is back with her ex. Fuck. I have to warn her.

"Guys... I gotta go," Wes mumbled, and Hawk tilted his head before following him out of the room.

"Everything alright?"

Wes narrowed his eyes. "No, I-I don't have time to explain, but I've gotta go."

He bolted upstairs, through the war room, and into the garage. In the blink of an eye, he was on the way to Naomi's house. Trying to call her, but it went straight to voice mail each time.

"Fuck!" He tossed the phone in the passenger seat and

slammed his hand on the steering wheel before scrubbing his face and massaging his eyes under his glasses.

It'd never crossed his mind that Naomi could be in on the trafficking. She'd have to have been one fucking hell of an actress to pull that off. The alternative was that she was completely in the dark, about everything, and knowing her ex was a manipulative bastard only contributed to that theory. Knowing she was with a man that evil chilled Wes to the bone.

He sped through town to get to Naomi's house, trying to maintain his cool, but when his phone vibrated in the seat next to him, he practically leaped within the confines of his seat belt to see who was calling.

My Queen.

Naomi.

Without wasting a second further, he swiped his thumb across the screen to accept the call.

"Naomi, I need to talk to you. It's about—"

"Wes?" The fear in the small little voice on the other end cracked his control.

"Princess T, hey... uh, is your mom around?"

A hiccup on the other end had him crushing his foot against the gas.

"Wes... Mommy needs you."

A muffled scream sounded in the background and the call went dead.

CHAPTER THIRTY-THREE

"So glad to have you home, sweets."

Dean's calm smile as he shoveled another bite of steak into his mouth made Naomi want to vomit.

This is my life now. I just have to make it through. One day, one meal at a time. Maybe it'll be better this time if I go all in.

But a small smile that felt more like a wince was all she could muster. She'd never been any good at faking. Well, scratch that. She excelled at acting the part, she just failed at being comfortable faking. It was why she'd lost so many people over the course of her relationship with Dean. It was easier to avoid people than 'fake it 'til she made it.'

"Mommy, me and Angus like your dress. Don't we, Angus?" Thea nodded her teddy bear's head before taking a bite of her macaroni and cheese. The bear had his own little seat beside her at the dining table like Wes had set up for her back at Black-Stone. It would've been adorable if Naomi wasn't in physical pain from the stress coursing through her.

"Mommy *does* look nice, doesn't she, sweetheart?"

"Shower before dinner. I can't stand the smell of you and I won't have another man's cum inside you when I'm fuckin' you tonight."

She resisted the shudder of revulsion and cleared her throat before answering. Dean beamed over at her, like he hadn't physically shoved her into their shower, bruising her shoulder and knees against the tile as she ricocheted. Now that he'd figured out his leverage—letting her see Thea—the threats were already getting old and she'd only been there for less than twelve hours.

"Thank you, Thea. I wanted to make sure I looked nice for dinner."

"Wear somethin' good, or don't wear anything at all. Actually, that second idea doesn't sound half bad."

The only act of defiance she'd allowed herself was the shoes. They were the green ones that Thea had "bought" the first time Naomi had ever met Wes. Wearing them reminded her of him. But already her time at BlackStone felt like a life she'd never lived.

It was funny how the mind played tricks like that. Like her only way to survive her new normal was to pretend the old never existed. Like her mind knew that having hope would be too much for her to bear right now.

If it was all a dream, she could listen and obey in peace, without feeling the need to put up a fight. Plus, why would she expend that energy again? She'd tried her best to leave once, but she was realizing she was stuck with this monster forever.

Believing anything different would crush her.

Doubt and optimism tried to wriggle their way to the forefront of her mind, but it was no use. She'd been depleted. Her hope was gone, despondence taking its place. All she'd do was listen and obey. Listen and obey. Listen and obey... for the next fourteen years. After that—after Thea was off and gone—hopefully somewhere as far away from Ashland County and her father's reach as possible, Naomi would leave no matter what he did to her.

"Mommy, why are you so quiet?" Thea whispered in her patented stage whisper. "Do you miss Wes?"

Naomi's skin went ice cold, but she did her best to keep her face neutral. Eyes the color of dead leaves bored into her, waiting for her response. She raised her head like there was nothing out of the normal for Thea. At the very least, she didn't want the poor girl to feel embarrassed or feel bad if Dean acted out.

"I'm just feelin' a little quiet tonight, honey. There's nothin' to worry about. Wes was just Mommy's work friend at Sasha Saves."

A slight scowl of confusion marred Thea's face before she nodded. Naomi hated that look. Hated even more that she'd *caused* that look. Gaslighting her four-year-old felt wrong to her core, but at the same time, the alternative was Dean blowing up. The stark reality that Naomi was having to choose between traumas for her daughter made her eyes burn with unshed tears.

"I want to know more about Wes, Thea. You said he was where y'all were livin'. Where was that exactly?"

Before Naomi could interfere, Thea brightened up. "Oh, it looked like a big box on the outside but was real nice on the inside. Like a castle! And Mommy made cookies and dinner and bre-fast for Phoe-nik." She snickered before whispering, "Mommy says he has a hole in his stomach, so it's okay that he eats so much. And I got to play with Wes and I got to watch Mary-duh and I got to dress up like her and Mommy was the queen and Wes was the king and Mommy and Wes read me bedtime stories—"

"That's enough, Thea," Naomi hissed, immediately feeling guilty for chastising her daughter for telling a simple story. But poor thing didn't understand social cues or the fact that Dean's face had reddened to the point of concern. She certainly didn't register his hands fisted tight around his fork and knife.

"Go to your room, Thea." Listening to Dean's gravel voice was like walking barefoot and trying to figure out which rock would hurt and which one wouldn't. Spoiler alert, she didn't even want to make the trek in the first place.

"But Daddy, I ain't done eat—"

"*Go to your room!*"

"*Don't talk to her that way!*"

She heard the sound before she registered the sting of the slap to her face. When she opened her eyes Dean was standing up, lording over the wooden table with his chest breathing heavy.

Naomi darted her eyes toward Thea's as the green hazel grew shiny with unshed tears.

"I-I'm sorry, Mommy—"

"No, baby, don't worry about a thing, alright?" Naomi pasted a smile that she hoped was one of her most convincing acting displays yet. "Just go ahead and go to your room. Daddy and I have somethin' to talk about, okay? Make sure to shut your door, though, and don't open it for anything, no matter what you hear."

Thea nodded slowly, her eyes bouncing between Naomi's and Dean's as she slid from her dining chair. She hugged her teddy bear and started walking backward to her room, as if she was afraid to take her eyes off Naomi. Unfortunately, Thea's door was just inside the hall and only a few feet from them. All she'd have to do was crack it open to see the full show, but it was the best Naomi could think of to shield her.

Before she could even hear Thea's door shut, Naomi's dinner was strewn into her lap and Dean was hauling her out of her chair.

"Did you fuck him?" his growled breath tainted her sense of smell and she nearly gagged. "Did you?"

It took her a second too long to respond and he was shoving her against the wall.

Don't fight back. Think of Thea. Just take it. It'll be over soon.

The pain in the back of her head stunned her, and she realized he'd shoved her again, causing her head to recoil against the drywall.

"*Did you, whore?*" Spittle flew out of his mouth and onto her face. "*Answer me!*"

Should she? She hadn't slept with Wes, *yet*. But admitting to what they had done would be just as bad. Hell, he was already attacking her without any proof at all.

"Fucking answer me!"

He shoved her to the ground and the force of his push made her trip and fall to the hardwood. One of her shoes fell off and he kicked it at her, causing the narrow heel to hit her hand.

Get up.

Just get up.

I need to get up.

But why? What's the point?

Her mind was warring with itself and she was so dazed she wondered if she had a concussion.

He pulled her up by her bicep and shoved her against the sideboard table. The force of her body bending backward rocked the liquor bottles on the table so violently that they crashed on the ground. A drawer knob dug into her back and she squirmed to get out of his hold, but his other hand gripped her hip so tightly she hissed in pain.

"You think you can play me for a fool, bitch? I will *end* you."

Fear sliced into her. She couldn't go out this way, leaving Thea with this monster. And she couldn't fight him alone.

I need help.

"Mommy?"

Thea's sweet little angel voice entered the dining room and Naomi froze.

"Get the fuck out, Thea!" Dean screamed, sending a hot flash of anger throughout her body.

"Don't talk to her like that!"

Naomi ripped away from his hold and in a voice as calm as she could muster, she turned to her daughter standing in the doorway.

"Thea, baby. Close your door, okay? Mommy will be there soon." She was choking on her own spit in the back of her throat, desperate for Thea to listen to the need in her voice and hoping she wasn't lying. "Get Mommy's purse? Your iPad's in there. Watch a show."

An idea formed in her head and as much as she hated using her daughter, Naomi hoped Thea would be able to pull it off. She bent to Thea's ear until Dean growled.

"I'm giving our daughter a kiss, is that too much to ask?"

Dean narrowed his eyes but left her alone, his fists tight by his side as his whole body vibrated with fury. She turned back to Thea and gave her a kiss on the cheek before whispering in her ear.

"Go to your room, lock the door, and don't come out. Mommy's phone is in my purse. Call Wes, okay? Press the green button with a phone on it, and then find the name with the man in a crown, okay?" Once she'd moved to BlackStone, she'd altered Wes's fake name into a king emoji. It'd been her first admission of her feelings to herself and had the added pleasure of a silent *fuck you* to Dean, a rebellion she thanked God for at the moment. That act might save her now. "Tell him I need him. Okay?"

"That's enough, Naomi."

Naomi backed away, holding her daughter's round, pale cheeks in both hands and staring into those beautiful eyes, to make sure she'd heard.

But Thea reached out her small hand. "Mommy, come wif me. Please?" She begged with her eyes and Naomi swallowed, wishing she could, but needing Thea to get the hell out of the situation more.

Before she could answer, Dean stepped in front of her and *pushed* Thea. He'd used his big beefy hands and shoved Thea by her small shoulders, forcing their daughter to hit the wall just like she had.

Naomi fucking *snapped*.

CHAPTER THIRTY-FOUR

Her vision narrowed with rage, zeroing in on this monster who'd just had the audacity to hurt her child. She leaped onto Dean's back, scratching his face, kicking and punching him with everything she had. The pounding staccato rhythm of her beating heart drove her wild strikes, not giving either of them even a second to breathe. In the back of her mind, she barely registered that Thea had run off in tears, hopefully to get Naomi's purse.

Dean fell back, landing on her against the dining table. A sharp stabbing sting into her skin made her hiss in pain and recoil her grip. It gave her the freedom to take a breath, but also made her realize how tired she was.

When he turned and grabbed her by the front of her dress, she gathered her strength and clawed down his arms and face. His fingers wrapped tightly around her bicep before once again slinging her into the wall. She choked on the air as it was knocked from her lungs until Dean's hand gripped her neck, cutting off her inhale. Manic eyes narrowed into her gaze. His grip closed in and she felt history repeating itself as the room around her dimmed and spun.

"Get... *off*... me." The words were whispered and so hoarse she wasn't sure he heard until she was falling.

Lying on the ground, her hands shot up to her now bare throat to scratch at the air trying to force its way into her chest. She'd only just gotten her breath when sharp pricks to her scalp sent shooting pains down her spine as Dean grabbed her by the hair. He tugged her to the living room, forcing her to crawl backward and catch the furniture around her to help her balance. Despite her best efforts, she couldn't stand upright, and yelped with every trip and fall. She finally snapped her hands up to his and held on, trying to minimize the damage.

"We're gonna talk like fuckin' civilized adults. Hash this out once and for all." Dean gritted through his teeth. "No use in wastin' anyone else's time."

All of a sudden, she found herself at the foot of the couch in their living room.

"Get up, sit down."

Instead, she scrambled away, until she realized she'd backed herself into an empty corner of the room.

Stupid, stupid, stupid.

I'm trapped.

With no other ideas, she pulled off the one heel that had miraculously stayed on her foot and held it beside her. That way, if she needed to run, she could go barefoot.

He stalked toward her, his dead leafy eyes boring into her in a look she'd only seen one other time, two and a half months ago when she was sure he was trying to kill her.

When he reached her, he bent low, balancing on his heels with his elbows resting on his knees and his hands steepled in the middle.

"Why did you do this to us?"

Naomi's eyes widened at his question. The sadness in his voice as it cracked while he asked it almost made her feel guilty. Almost. Then she remembered the bastard had almost killed her now on two occasions and had just pushed her daughter.

"Why did..." Unable to stop herself, she huffed out a laugh

and his narrowed in response. "Why did *I* do this to *us*? Dean... you're the one who is hurtin' *me*, not the other way around."

Dean's jaw clenched. "No. Physical pain ain't nothin' compared to what you've done to me. I knew you'd leave me for another man. I fuckin' *knew* it, and yet here I am, still taking you back—"

"You *blackmailed* me back here! Do you really think this was my choice? To end up curled in a corner like a rat?"

She searched his face, trying to figure out if he truly believed the bullshit he was spewing. From what she could tell, he did. It was mind blowing that he'd been able to convince himself he was the victim in this situation.

"I didn't want to have to do it that way, Naomi, but you left me no choice! You weren't comin' home. You weren't takin' my calls. What was I supposed to do?"

"Um, respect me? Leave me alone? Move on? Not fuckin' attack me in the first place?"

He shook his head before threading his fingers through his dirty blond hair. "We were good together, sweets."

"Don't *call* me that."

Why am I arguin' with a man hell-bent on killin' me?

Something that might've been pain swirled in his eyes. "We were. You just don't remember it because you've insisted on creating this awful picture of me in your head. But look at yourself. You're whorin' around, tryin' to deny what we have... I just... I need to know. With all them lies, you've convinced yourself I'm a monster. Do you think you could ever love me again?"

She swallowed, not wanting to admit the truth. He'd beaten her, made her live in fear, and conditioned her to make herself small. But even with all that, there was something inside her that didn't want to hurt him, and honesty would either make him crack, crush him, or both.

Because the truth was that she'd never loved him. She had love for him, maybe, at one point in time, before he'd become the volatile monster he was now. But she'd never loved him.

Logic told her if she admitted that, she wouldn't come out of this alive. Another part of her knew, though, if she wasn't completely honest in that moment, he'd never leave her alone. And she was so goddamn sick of lying. It'd never gotten her anywhere but cornered.

"I loved the idea of Thea havin' a father like mine—"

"The fuckin' hero worship you have for that man is unhealthy, Naomi," Dean growled out and she resisted pointing out how unhealthy their own relationship was. "Is that all you think it was? You just wanted a good dad for Thea?"

"I've never loved you, Dean..." At the heartbroken look in his eyes, she grimaced at her own words. "I-I'm sorry."

He nodded slowly, swiping his hand down his face. "Right... Okay..." He stood from his crouched position and walked to the couch. Wait... not to the couch, to...

The safe.

It was underneath their side table for Dean to access easily if there ever was an intruder. Naomi stumbled to stand so she could flee, but didn't make it in time, too stunned when the metal barrel was suddenly pointed at her.

"Sit down, sweets."

No way in hell I'm doin' that.

She stood straighter, holding on to her shoe for dear life like it was a shield. After one slow, measured breath, she dug the balls of her feet into the hardwood and ran full speed to the right, giving Dean a wide berth. But with her five feet, two inches against his six-foot stride, there was no hope of outrunning him.

One minute she was upright, the next she had an over two hundred pound man tackling her to the ground. Before she could register what was happening, Dean was already dragging her to the corner of the room again. He pulled her to standing and dug the cold barrel of his gun underneath her jaw.

Jules's words from the day Naomi arrived at Sasha Saves rang in her head.

"A woman who's been strangled by her significant other is seven hundred and fifty percent more likely to be murdered by the same person... with a gun."

"I said... sit... *down*."

A loud slam shook the house and Naomi trembled, at first thinking he'd shot her. But then quick, heavy footsteps resounded in the hallway and the metal under her chin eased away.

"Let her go."

Wes's voice was steel and Dean's eyes held molten fire, threatening to burn to the ground everything that got in his way. He ground his teeth and turned around, pushing Naomi against the wall with his back. If he hadn't just threatened her with a bullet, she would've taken the gesture as protective.

Naomi peered around Dean to see Wes's blue-black hair tugged on end and his icy eyes cold enough to freeze her in her place. But not Dean. He raised his gun to put Wes in his sights, and to her horror, Wes wasn't armed. He'd brought fists to a gunfight.

"Thea, close your eyes," Wes commanded, but not unkindly.

Naomi darted her eyes to where Wes had glanced and saw the slatted closet door shut. When had she hidden there? Had she seen everything? The thought made her weaker than anything Dean had done to her yet.

"You must be the infamous *Wes*." Dean spat out the name.

Wes didn't say anything, his eyes were almost in a faraway state, like he'd gone somewhere else.

"Come on, what do you have to say?" Dean challenged, but Wes continued to just stare at him. His mind was working, Naomi could see that. Fists clenched and unclenched. Jaw muscles ticced... but what was he doing?

"Fine then" —Dean released the safety— "there's more than one bullet in here anyway—"

"No!" Naomi shouted and brought her heel to his head, blindly stabbing. Whatever she'd hit gave way and she swallowed back bile. Dean screamed, holding his neck with his hand while still somehow maintaining a grip on his gun. Blood spurted in her vision, leaving Naomi stunned, but still somehow able to realize the opportunity she had right in front of her.

As if they'd choreographed it, Naomi reached for the gun at the same time Wes leaped toward Dean, pushing him to the ground and striking him with his fists.

She shuffled backward, gun in hand, until she bumped into the couch.

More thumping behind her made her turn around to see Hawk and Devil entering the room from the foyer.

"Please... get Thea," Naomi yelled over the commotion, pointing at the closet and breathing a sigh of relief when Hawk nodded.

Devil came to her side and Naomi watched with a strange mix of horror, fascination, and gratitude as Wes fought for her. Dean was attempting to give back everything he got, but Wes was obviously the better fighter. After one particularly harsh strike to his bloody neck, Dean collapsed.

"Wes," she called, needing him to come to her. Hold her. Soothe away the adrenaline, pain, and fear coursing through her.

But the Wes in front of her was singularly focused. He'd gotten down on his knees and was punching a thrashing Dean. A demented, broken part of her loved it, finding a thrill in seeing the man who'd tormented her for years and made her baby girl cry finally meet his karmic retribution. But another part of her saw the consequences play out for Wes, too.

Naomi's eyes widened as Dean's face and body slackened beneath him.

"Fuck, he's gonna kill him," Devil murmured, taking a step forward, no longer holding her back, something she hadn't even realized he was doing.

Sirens in the distance snapped her out of her thoughts and before she could think, she ran up to Wes and jumped on his back. Whispering soothing words in his ear, he immediately went rigid underneath her. She held on, her arms clinging to his neck and her legs wrapped around his waist, hanging on for dear life as she talked him down.

"It's okay, Wes. It's okay. Come back to me."

She whispered the words over and over and over, hoping they'd reach through the haze to the calm, rational, caring man she'd come to know. She'd recognized the look on his face. Deep-seated anger boiled within him, threatening to take over reason. She'd had the same thoughts when she was defending Thea, and now they'd taken over him.

Wes fell back against his calves and wrapped his arms behind him awkwardly, holding on to her sides. She rose and fell with his breaths as he slowly stood. It wasn't until he'd taken a few steps away from Dean that she slid down. As soon as her feet were on the floor, though, he turned and wrapped her up in his arms, bringing her flush to his chest in his embrace.

He kissed her hard against the cheek, his breaths still coming in spurts and continued to back away until his back hit the wall.

"Fuck, I'm sorry, Naomi. I just... seeing him... with you? Fuck, I was gone. I wasn't here. I-it wasn't him. In my head, it wasn't him. But it was still *you*. I thought he was going to—"

"It's okay. I'm safe."

She didn't know what he'd meant, but it didn't matter at that moment. Dean couldn't get to her with Wes there and Wes had just proved to her that even at his worst moments, she was literally safe in his arms.

All of a sudden, the living room flooded with officers in uniforms and EMTs. A few went straight to Dean, where she realized Devil was already administering first aid.

"Why the fuck is he helpin' Dean?" she asked, all compassion for the man who attacked her daughter completely out the window. He'd made a grave mistake putting his hands on Thea. Now Naomi would come at him with everything she had to keep him away.

"Because if he dies, I'll probably get locked up." Wes's words came out matter of fact, but still sent a frisson of panic down her spine. He must've felt it because he squeezed even harder. "It's okay... you stopped me. They'll likely say it's in defense of others."

She pulled away to look into his eyes. "But Dean's got friends on the force... what if—"

"We do too, Naomi. Shh, don't worry about me. It'll be okay. Let's go get Thea and get you guys home."

Home.

For the first time in a long, *long* time, that word finally had meaning.

CHAPTER THIRTY-FIVE

"Tell me again what happened." Officer Henry Brown looked uncomfortable in his questioning, shifting on his feet. "Sorry, man," he whispered to Wes. "He's a former officer so we gotta make sure we play this one by the book."

Shit, maybe Naomi was right and her ex has more pull than we thought.

Wes nodded and did his best not to go into another fit of rage as he recounted what happened since Thea called him crying. It was hard to piece everything together as it was. All he'd known after hanging up was that he needed his teammates.

He'd put out an SOS alert on his phone to Hawk and Devil, knowing they'd be the fastest ones to Naomi's, and thankfully they'd pulled through for him. Wes didn't even want to think about what would've happened if they hadn't all gotten there in time.

Seeing that pistol underneath Naomi's chin had taken him back to a childhood he'd desperately tried to forget. One where he'd been helpless to do anything. That hadn't been the case tonight.

Naomi had given Wes an opening to intervene when she'd used her damn four inch heel to stab Dean in the neck. But once he'd gotten going, Wes gave in to a flashback and had nearly killed the man. It didn't help that Naomi had dug so deep with her heel that—according to the medics—the injury was likely going to have to undergo surgery to make sure she didn't hit anything too vital.

Paramedics checked Thea and Naomi over, too, and aside from minor injuries, gave them the all clear. Thea didn't have any wounds. Not physical anyway. Wes knew from experience that the pain of this memory would last a lifetime. Naomi's bumps and bruises were already starting to show. He'd watched her body language while she spoke to the medics and when she insisted she felt fine and was satisfied with an ice pack and extra-strength Tylenol, he believed her. It still made his soul ache to know she'd been hurt again.

Right before they'd been separated by officers and EMTs, Wes told Naomi not to worry about him and made sure she could leave with Hawk, Devil, and Thea after she gave her statement. But now that Naomi was gone and adrenaline had subsided, Wes recognized the shit show he'd thrown himself into.

Fuck... what if I don't get out of this?

As he retold his story, Wes swiped at his face, massaging his eyes. Thankfully, after pictures were taken, he'd been given the opportunity to wash his hands.

"Sounds like defense of others to me... *barely*." Henry gave Wes a pointed look. "Listen, man. Dean left on a shitty note with the station—"

"Really?" Wes was unable to keep the question out of his voice. "Naomi said he had lots of cop buddies?"

"Nah, man. Dude took bribes. When he got offered that cushy ass gig with AIE Securities, an internal investigation was already in the works against him."

"No shit?" Wes felt his eyes go wide in surprise as he ruffled his hair. "Naomi had no idea, I'm sure of it."

Henry shrugged. "He's still got some friends. She wasn't

wrong about that. But no one with near enough clout to make a difference." His eyes darkened, but then he shook his head. "This doesn't look too good for him."

Wes nodded, unsure of what else to say. Finally, he cleared his throat past the dryness there. "Can I go?"

Henry nodded. "Yeah, but stick by your phone 'kay? I gotta go interview Dean at the hospital. Then, since a former officer was involved, I'm gonna take the case to a judge to cover all my bases with warrants. Should be exactly what I said, but it's always good to be available if we need ya, ya know?"

"Yeah, yeah. Sure. Damn... thanks, Henry. I owe ya one. I'm headin' back to BlackStone to make sure Naomi and Thea are alright."

Henry nodded. "Just... be careful. When Dean gets outta the hospital, he might get a bond. No tellin' what he'll do once he makes it and gets outta jail."

"Thanks for the tip, Henry. Be safe." Wes raised his hand to say goodbye and tried not to focus on the bandaged wounds there from punching Dean.

The ride back to BlackStone was a blink and a blur. When he got to the facility, he parked his Trackhawk, ignored the aches already setting in after the fight, and took the steps two at a time to the residence wing.

"*Wes.*" His name was a prayer, and before he could fully register what was happening, he was enveloped in a warm embrace. Vanilla sugar calmed his senses and immediately set his muscles at ease as he returned the hug.

"Naomi." He wrapped his arms around her to hold her close as she clung to him, much like she had when she'd taken him out of his trance with Dean. The other hand cradled the back of her head, his fingers threading through the soft dark auburn tresses.

She leaned back and locked her fiery brown eyes, full of emotion, onto his.

"Thank you."

He was stunned by her whispered gratitude, and even more

surprised at her fierce kiss. Adrenaline that had taken over his body during the fight surged through him again, demanding a completely different dance. He picked up the rhythm and devoured her, sweeping his tongue against hers.

With her still wrapped around him, he walked them by the kitchen toward his room. Visions of the last time they were in that exact spot burst into his mind, and his length hardened against his pants zipper. Just like last time, he couldn't take his lips off her, craving her for dessert again.

"Thea?" His voice was heavy with need, even to his own ears.

"Asleep." She held on to his shoulders and nipped up his jawline. "Out like a light."

"Good."

Back first, he barreled into his room, turning the doorknob with the hand that wasn't helping lift her, pressing her core against his lower abs. Once they were inside, he led her to his bed, turning to collapse backward onto the mattress. The motion brought out the aches in his muscles from his fight with Dean, but he'd be damned before he broke the moment with Naomi.

He stroked up her dress, loving the feel of her soft thighs under his fingertips. Loving even more when he drove them farther up and grasped her ass hard in his grip.

She moaned into his mouth and ground her pussy against his shaft. The fabric of his jeans prevented them from connecting and he growled against her lips in frustration. She paused the kiss before nibbling his neck and shoving her hands underneath his shirt. Her nails scratched him just hard enough to make him hiss as the cotton rolled up.

"Off," she whispered, and Wes lifted into a sit-up to help her tear his shirt over his head. When it was gone, he couldn't stand not kissing her, so he wrapped his hand around the back of her neck.

"Shit," Naomi hissed in pain and Wes immediately let go. "No, no. It's okay, he just knocked me around a bit."

Fury boiled in his veins. He opened his mouth to speak and sat up on his forearms, but she surprised him by pushing him back down to the mattress.

"Listen, troublemaker. I see you gettin' that alpha male you-better-not-hurt-my-woman look, but I'm *fine*. Just a little sore."

He narrowed his eyes at her. "I don't want to hurt you."

"You won't." She bent to kiss him softly on his lips. "You never would. I know that now."

Before he could ask what she meant, her lips became more insistent and she ground her pussy into his cock. Need made him so hard it was painful. He nestled his hands in the crease of her hips and thighs, tugging her against him as he surged up, searching for relief.

"Too... many... clothes." She groaned and scooted back to unbutton his pants. He raised his hips so they could slide his jeans and boxers down, just enough to reveal his shaft.

The hem of her dress was rolled up, and he twirled his index finger around her lace thong before tugging hard. She yelped when the fabric popped off her, but in the next breath she had him in hand, stroking his cock up and down before her thumb spread precum around his swollen head.

She tightened her hand around his shaft and leaned down to kiss him once on his lips, ending with a whisper.

"Condom?"

"Nightstand."

She leaned the short distance to riffle through the drawer of the small table. When she came back to him, she sat her bare pussy on his cock and he moaned her name while her desire soaked him.

"Fuck, Naomi." He rolled underneath her, gliding his cock in her arousal.

The condom was in her hand, but she made no moves to sheath him. Her teeth captured her lip and the fire in her whiskey eyes begged him to keep going. He gripped her hips and moved in a delicious imitation of the way he was about to fuck her, ending every slick thrust to massage her clit.

Her hips rocked against him like a boat on an ocean, drenching his length. He got lost in the motion until he felt his cock breach her opening and they both stilled with him half inside her.

"Condom, now," he gritted between clenched teeth as he pulled out of her. She nodded and before she could obey, he pulled the wrapper from her hand, ripped it open, and thrust into his own hand to roll the condom on. In his next thrust, his hands aligned his cock with her entrance before plunging inside her.

He wanted to go slow and savor the feel of her warm pussy tightening around his cock. But need, desire, and adrenaline controlled his baser instincts more than the need to coordinate a romantic moment.

She kissed him again and he got lost in her plush lips against his as their tongues danced against the other. Slowly, he withdrew from the embrace and gently pushed her by the collarbone so he could look deep into those firelight eyes.

"Next time, love... I'm going to take my time. Candles, music, whatever you want. I'll treat you like you deserve. Like a queen. But right now—"

"Right now, I feel more like a prisoner who's finally broken free. You can have your way later. I've been caged for too long and I can't wait another second to taste freedom."

With that, she pulled his hands from her thighs and placed them on either side of his head in a position of surrender against the mattress. She intertwined their fingers, using him to balance as she rocked up and down his cock until she found a rhythm that made her breath heavy with panting moans. Her pussy throbbed around his shaft and Wes gritted his teeth to keep from taking over. Instead he watched, enthralled, as she took what she needed with a fierce determination that was hot as hell.

Her face was level with his, but her gorgeous eyes were

closed. Wes squeezed her hands once, trying to get her to relax and look at him. She squeezed back three times, jarring something from his memory until she lost her balance. The move shoved his cock so deep inside her, they both moaned the other's name. Still, her eyes were tightly closed, even etching a line in the middle of her brow.

"I need you here with me, Naomi. Open your eyes and let me touch you."

Bright fiery eyes fluttered open and she eased off his hands as her movements above him slowed with exhaustion. He stilled her hips and withdrew slowly, hissing a curse of ecstasy as her pussy trembled against his shaft on his way out. Banding his arm around her lower back, he lifted up and gingerly flipped their positions so that she was the one that lay on the bed and he was kneeling.

His pants were still around his thighs, so he backed off the bed to stand and let them slide down the rest of his legs. He stepped out and caressed his hands up Naomi's soft skin, rolling her dress all the way up as he explored.

Even though she moaned, she knocked his hands away. "Later. No time now," she whined and grabbed his cock, making him chuckle at her urgency.

He leaned over her, allowing her to guide his cock to nudge at her entrance. But before she could get farther, he grabbed her hand and stretched it across the mattress above her head and encased her with his body.

"Let me take care of you," he whispered against her lips before sinking into her and ending with a kiss. "I want you to feel what it's like to be treasured."

He drove deep inside her, loving how her hips met his thrusts, obviously having gained back some energy in this new position. Together they reached a pulsing tempo and Wes got lost in the give and take. She seemed to be just as entranced, her eyes unfocused as they looked up at him and her swollen lips parted.

That look made his cock jump, threatening to combust too soon. He pulled out again to stand, but dragged Naomi gingerly across the bed as he stepped off. The movement was so fluid, he didn't even give her enough time to whine before he was sheathed in her channel again. He hooked his arms underneath her legs, using his fingertips to dig into her bare hips to keep traction as he kept up his smooth strokes. With every plunge, he barely kept from coming as his entire length escaped her tight sheath just to fight for entry again.

"Touch yourself, love."

Her eyes widened and she gripped one of his wrists while the other hand traveled down the bunched-up fabric of her dress. When her fingertips found her clit, she bit her lip and released a breathy whimper before closing her eyes.

"Eyes open, Naomi." With that firm command, he pumped one long, hard stroke, making her suck back a groan and snap her eyes open.

Now with her sparkling eyes in the low ambient light of the room, she met his gaze, lids heavy with need. As she massaged the small bundle of nerves, it was all he could do to keep from spilling inside her at the sight. And when he felt her fingers stray to his shaft while she worked her clit, he bit back a curse.

"Wes... oh my God, I-I'm gonna come." Her voice was a higher pitch, almost like she was surprised at her own confession and Wes drove into her harder to release with her.

"Come for me, Naomi. I want to see your face when you get the pleasure you deserve."

She nodded once, seeming like she was trying her best to keep her eyes open and focused. But when a low moan escaped her, she succumbed to her ecstasy. She began to tremble just before her pussy gripped his cock, locking him into her core, and spurring his release. He shouted her name and dug his fingers into her thighs as he drew out their pleasure with deep, slow thrusts.

When his cock was spent, he collapsed over her, making sure

to catch himself on his forearms. She wrapped her arms around his back and squeezed him even closer. Still sheathed inside her, Wes palmed her ass and pulled her closer to drag her up the bed and rest her head on a pillow.

She reached up and kissed him, her pillowy lips melding against his for a quick peck before she spoke.

"So that *wasn't* treating me like a queen?" Her giggle made her pussy spasm around his cock and he resisted another moan. "I think I'll pass out if I receive your version of royal treatment."

He gave her another kiss and lifted up to look into her warm brown eyes with a grin.

"Oh, my queen. I've only just begun to serve you."

CHAPTER THIRTY-SIX

"I'll be back," he whispered against her lips before leaving a chaste kiss. He reluctantly peeled himself away to dispose of the second condom of the night, making sure to dampen a hand towel with warm water before he left the bathroom. When he came back, he paused when her head tilted in confusion.

"Oh, um... thanks." She tried to grab the towel, but Wes took her hand and kissed her knuckles.

"Let me take care of you."

With a slow nod, she leaned back and let him tend to her, the whole time visibly trying not to close her legs.

"I was just inside you, love. Why are you acting shy?"

She bit her lips and even in the dim light, he could tell she was blushing. "I, um... I've just, uh, never done this part before. It's usually me doin' it by myself. It feels intimate." He began to pull back the cloth, but she wrapped her hand around his wrist, keeping him still. "No, I love it. It's just new to me."

Her confession gave him a strange mix of disgust and pride. Disgust at the man who didn't treasure the beauty and strength in the woman in front of him when he had her, and pride that she was giving Wes the chance. There was no way he was going to squander it.

He cleaned her until her trembling told him his ministrations were becoming torture on her sensitive flesh. After he tossed the hand towel into the hamper, he grabbed some gym shorts and joined her in bed, not knowing how long she'd give him before she went back to her room to sleep with Thea.

He scooped his arm underneath her neck and pulled her chest to his side. His other arm wrapped around her waist, holding her so tight that other than their clothes, there wasn't room for even a breath of air between them.

Taking in Naomi's curvy body, he frowned at the flowing dress still covering most of it.

"Fuck, I can't believe I just did that."

"Did what?" she asked, apprehension filling her voice.

"This..." He indicated her body with a nod. "I had a beautiful woman in my bed and didn't even get the chance to admire her without her clothes on. If it weren't for the fact that I know I ripped your panties off, you could very well pass for being fully clothed right now."

Her response was in that delightful laugh he adored, but she sobered before she spoke and the words on her warm breath raised goose bumps on his skin.

"I might look fully clothed, but I feel stripped bare by you, Wes."

Although he wasn't entirely sure what she meant by her confession or what emotion fueled it, he didn't think regret laced her words until she spoke again.

"I saw you brutally beat up my ex tonight. That was... hard to see." Dread filled his chest and he opened his mouth to reply, only she beat him to it. "But I wouldn't be here if you hadn't."

He realized for the first time that he hadn't known what he was walking into when he'd arrived home. The way she'd reacted with Ascot was completely different than now and he wasn't sure what to make of it.

He dragged his mouth over her soft, dark auburn hair and smoothed it down before tracing her spine, afraid she was going to bolt on him. "You're not... mad at me? You don't think I'm a monster?"

"No." Warm moisture dropped onto his naked chest and he lifted his head to see a thin trail of tears tracking down her light ivory cheek. "You saved me and you saved Thea."

"Well, you had a hand in that. Or a shoe, I guess, if we're being technical."

"Ugh, too soon."

He grimaced. "Yeah, sorry. You're right."

"But it's not just that. I don't think you're a monster because... because you stopped."

"What do you mean, I 'stopped'?"

"As soon as I jumped on your back, you stopped mid-swing. It was like your body just knew I was there and then I had my Wes back. Even in the midst of a fight, you were able to keep it together to keep me out of danger. That, more than anything else, told me I'm safe with you."

Wes nodded, understanding where she was coming from. Being around people who didn't know whether they were hitting friend or foe was more than dangerous. It was deadly.

Fighting was a lot of things, sometimes violent and senseless, but sometimes necessary and purposeful. Knowing when to throw a punch was just as important as knowing when to pull one.

"The injuries you saw on Ascot, they were a mistake. I let my emotions get in the way, but I would never let them interfere with your safety. And I can promise you I'm working on it. I've gone to therapy for years. I thought I'd gotten better, but obviously being back in the field has made me realize I need a few— erm, a *lot*—more sessions."

"Can I ask you something?" Her fingernails tracing his pec made him shiver, and he barely resisted the urge to flip her on her back and have his way with her again. But when her finger paused, he remembered she was expecting an answer.

"Anything, my queen. I am your humble servant."

She snorted at his affected speech and he could almost feel her roll her eyes at him. Her fingers traveled up the tattooed snake on his chest, spiraling down its coils all the way to where it bit the inked version of the heart that beat so strongly for her.

"Can you tell me where your rage comes from?" Her whisper was light, but he heard it. It was the conversation he'd been avoiding since the day he met her at Sasha Saves. On some deep level, he'd known even then that at some point he was going to have to bare his soul to her.

Now that she was in his bed, away from that maniac of an ex, he wanted nothing more than to share his story with her. Hopefully, his past would solidify her decision to stay well and away from that lunatic.

"Okay, here goes." He blew out a breath. "My mom was the most beautiful, kindest woman in the whole world."

"Was?" The whisper against his bare chest made him shiver, but he couldn't stop. If she wanted this story, he was going to have to say it all in one fell swoop.

"She was short and round, the perfect size to run up to and wrap my hands around her waist and clasp them behind her back. Her voice was soft and gentle, never said an unkind word to anyone. Not even the man who deserved it most. She was pure, and whole, and good, and everything anyone would ever want in a parent. But my dad... was not.

"Everything my mother was, my dad was the opposite. Selfish, jealous, manipulative. No one knew what was going on behind closed doors, and as a kid, that just didn't make any sense to me. We weren't allowed to talk about what happened when my dad got mad, but I never understood how no one knew. It seemed obvious as fuck to me. Now I realize they might've been avoiding the truth just like we were."

"What was going on behind closed doors?"

"My dad. He'd... beat on my mom. When he had a job, he'd come home from work late, already drunk somehow, and let loose on her. Living like that was like walking on eggshells all the time."

"Yeah, except the eggshells are shards of broken glass."

His huff of laughter was cynical even to his own ears. "Exactly. Anyway, my sister and I would beg my mom to leave, but she never would. My aunt said she tried to leave him once before she had me, but she found out she was pregnant with me and believed it was too late. Mom was convinced a boy needed his father."

Naomi shivered against his chest, and he wondered if she understood too well.

"I was my mother's anchor and my father's weapon. Whenever she had the chance to swim to safety, he used me to tug her back down, drowning her with threats of stealing her child away. By the time my sister came along, my mother's will to fight was already gone.

"That last night, my father was in worse form than usual. He'd just gotten laid off *again*, and he was taking it out verbally on me and my sister before my mom got home from work. When she did, he picked a literal fight with her. She never fought back. In the end, she excelled at being silent and had learned to make herself small in every aspect of her life. Her cowering in the corner of our kitchen was the epitome of what that man had made her become.

"I don't know why that night broke me, but I snapped. He was going in on her, and I jumped in to defend her. But I was a ten-year-old kid against a man who'd been honing his 'craft' my entire life. He knocked me good, forcing me to the side. Fear and anger drove me after that. I kept trying to go back at him, but he swatted me away each time. Her screams were worse than I'd ever heard. He'd just kept shouting over her to be quiet all the while landing hits on her until... until she wasn't screaming anymore."

Wes closed his eyes against the memory, but all he could see was the man who was supposed to be his family's protector, staring at the broken heap that had once been Wes's mom.

Even decades later, he couldn't get away from the image. He saw that man in the mirror every day. His mom had always said he was the spitting image of his father. Stretching out his hand, he watched his inked skin roll with the veins underneath as he clenched a fist. At least the tattoos helped disguise the monster of his past.

"My sister called 911. After that, things went pretty fast. We went to my aunt's. My dad did the one good thing he's ever done in his life and turned himself in. He got sent to prison for the rest of his life, which turned out to be not even half the amount he'd tortured my mother for. He died of liver failure a few years in. Too good a death for a man like that."

"Is that why you don't go to Sasha Saves? Is... is that why you kept asking me why I wouldn't leave?"

Wes nodded. "Yeah, I think going to Sasha Saves that day, seeing your injuries, it woke some anger in me that I thought I'd taken care of. Obviously I haven't, but I'm going to reach out to the therapist my aunt got for me and my sister. I've had him forever. It'll be good to check back in."

Naomi nodded. "I'm sorry, Wes. I had no idea."

He scooted them up onto his pillows, giving himself a better angle before tipping her chin back. "It's a part of my past that I can't get back. I miss my mother. I don't think I could take it if a man like my father took your future, too."

Naomi shook her head, but not enough to break contact with his finger. "He won't. I'm done."

He narrowed his eyes at her. "Officers said they're going to charge Dean with felony domestic violence. He could get up to twenty years. Are you going to prosecute?"

She swallowed before nodding. "Yeah, it's time. I gave him too many chances as it is. I pretended that fairy tales existed, but it was a nightmare. He hurt Thea tonight and I lost my shit. I need for him to be held accountable so at the very least I can make sure he stays clear of me and my daughter."

Wes nodded, appeased by her answer, but only time would truly tell.

"I know you don't believe me. I'm sure you think I'll go back to him, like most survivors do. But I promise I'm done letting him chain me down. I've finally broken free, and I'm never letting that monster cage me again."

CHAPTER THIRTY-SEVEN

Naomi was fucking the enemy.

Despite the fact he'd thought it a thousand times already, Dean winced. For the disrespect and because the muscles in his neck were sore from clenching his jaw. Not to mention the goddamn hole stitched closed just above his carotid artery.

He was being kept for observation, resting up to go to jail and face God knows what. One thing was for sure, he'd have to do whatever he could to make sure he'd get a bond and get the hell out before they put him in a jumpsuit and set him free with the criminals inside. Jail was no place for an ex-cop.

Oddly, it was thanks to Naomi that he had some time to spare and get his affairs in order. His other injuries were mostly superficial, if painful as fuck, that Snake guy had a powerful punch. But if she hadn't stabbed him in the neck, he'd be behind bars already. He still couldn't believe she'd thrown everything he'd done for her back at him... with a goddamn high heel, no less.

It was obviously that damn tattooed emo Clark Kent getting in her head. She'd gotten all high and mighty since she left home, fooling herself into thinking she could find someone better.

Dean had tried his best to give her the benefit of the doubt, still not believing that she'd choose *Wes* over him. He'd done what he had to in order to get her out of there, promised her everything she'd always wanted, but she'd thrown it all back in his face.

Now he'd just received word that she was back in that godforsaken complex. She was too much of a scared coward to leave BlackStone anytime soon, since they'd argued again. As much as he hated to say it, that place was damn near impenetrable. He'd have to find a way to lure her out.

Good thing I've got someone on the inside.

He reached for his phone in the plastic bag on his hospital nightstand. They hadn't cuffed him, relying on the pansy-ass guard outside the room, and they didn't even bother to take his belongings. It was grade A rookie shit and if he'd still been a training officer, he'd have had their badges. Unfortunately, the station had gone for his badge first.

Dean riffled through the clear Ziploc to retrieve his phone and called one of the few numbers he had. As usual, the Russian answered on the first ring.

"*Da.*"

"Vlad, I have a proposition." After a beat of silence, uncertainty made Dean's stomach turn. "D-don't you wanna hear my idea?"

"No."

Dean growled into the phone. The Russian bastard thought he was so special just because he had the boss's ear.

"It's a good fuckin' idea, asshole. I've got a way to get rid of some of those security guys that have been on y'all's asses and pick off one of the final rich guys you've been lookin' for."

"You know where is Andrew Ascot?" The man's accent was deep and Dean couldn't tell if he was interested or accusing. "How do you know this thing?"

Uh-oh.

Vlad and his boss didn't necessarily know that Dean had been playing both sides. He'd thought his team at AIE Securities could accept the bodyguard job and take Ascot's money for as long as possible until they had to make good on the hit by the boss. Ascot had been kept radio silent and under lock and key, not allowed to leave the safe house or even get on the internet under the pretense of "safety precautions."

It was mainly to keep Ascot in the dark and prevent him from getting spooked, but it was also to make sure the Russian didn't get to complete the boss's hit before Dean got his payout. Or before Dean's deception was *found* out.

Dean had wanted his team to protect Ascot for as many of the rich snob's paychecks as possible. That way, if the boss ever gave an ultimatum requiring the prick's head ASAP 'or else', then his team could off him right there in the safe house. It'd been a solid plan to ensure maximum reward... up until the asshole was stolen right from under them. If Dean had known BlackStone was after Ascot, too, he'd have demanded triple.

"Uh, we, uh, we've been keepin' tabs on him for the boss's job. And I know where he's bein' held."

"*Da*. We do too. It is not hard to figure out in a small river where the big fish are hiding."

Dean huffed, annoyed that his leverage was dwindling. "Okay, if you know where he is, you know how impossible it is to get to him. How're y'all plannin' on takin' him out, hm?"

Vlad laughed. Fucking *laughed*. "And do you have a plan to do this thing?"

"Yes, I actually do. And I've already talked to the guy who can help. Y'all know him, but he thinks he's got it too good to fully take a side. But I think *I* can convince him."

There was a pause on the other end before the Russian giant grumbled. "I am listening, *durak*."

Thank fuck.

"I'll tell you if you let me take my money and go. My girl and I are gone after this job, ya hear me?"

Dean had to make sure all the parts were moving in the direction he needed before they left. Once BlackStone was taken out, there wouldn't be temptation for Naomi anymore. He could take his cut, get his family back, leave this fucked-up town, and never look back.

There was no way his contact would knowingly set everything up. The guy tended to like to play on the sidelines, but hopefully Vlad could take care of the rest. From what Dean understood, the boss wanted an in with the BlackStone Securities team anyway. Dean's idea would benefit everyone, Vlad just had to agree to the conditions.

What had to be Russian cursing filled the other line. "I will talk to boss."

"I have your word?"

"*Da*. You have my word I will talk to boss."

"Alright, here's the plan. First off, I need someone to pay my bond so I can get out of jail before they book me into gen pop tomorrow..."

CHAPTER THIRTY-EIGHT

"Ms. Ward? Can you come to my office?"

Ms. Ward?

Unease prickled the fine hair on the back of Naomi's neck as she stood from her desk. Her boss, Gail, rarely used that tone for their meetings. She was Gail's right-hand woman and they were certainly on a first name basis by this point. Something was wrong.

No, I'm just bein' dramatic. I've got way too much on my mind.

Thirty-six hours ago, she'd stabbed her ex-fiancé. Twenty-four hours ago, she'd gone to a bond hearing with Wes to request that Dean be given no bond. It should've been an easy request and according to the prosecutor, Assistant District Attorney Britta Thoms, if they'd had Judge Powell it would've been a slam dunk.

Dean was charged with domestic violence of a high and aggravated nature, a serious and violent felony that could catch Dean twenty years in prison. He could've been denied bond, meaning he'd have had to stay in jail until a trial. But no, the judge had granted him a measly twenty thousand dollar surety bond, of which he only had to pay ten percent, with barely any conditions other than no contact with the 'victim.'

Fuck, was she starting to hate that word. She was getting why Nora corrected her so much in the beginning.

All of it was bullshit. Complete and utter bullshit. She stood up in front of the judge with bruises healing all over her. Now they'd stain her body for possibly longer than Dean would even stay in jail. It was no wonder survivors never came forward when the justice system screwed them over.

ADA Thoms assured her the State would go hard in the case, but she also said that Naomi should still be emotionally and mentally prepared to go to war. Thankfully, the prosecutor had at least been able to help secure a temporary restraining order. If Dean attempted to contact her, he could get arrested just for a simple text. Considering the texts Dean had sent her in the past, it'd sounded great in theory.

But a piece of paper can't stop a bullet.

She shuddered as she busied herself, setting her desk straight in an attempt to calm her nerves before going to Gail's office.

At least she had Wes by her side now. Even if you never need him, having a white knight at your back is always better than fighting a battle by yourself.

"Naomi?"

"Comin'!" She'd officially stalled for long enough. Damn, why was she so edgy? Was it knowing that Dean was out of jail already? Was it just being on constant alert for the past five years? She didn't know, but she hoped it was all in her head.

Trust your instincts.

"Shit," she muttered under her breath before she entered the office and pasted a bright smile for Gail.

"Naomi, please sit."

Not a blonde hair was out of place in Gail's severely coiffed French twist bun. Her bow tie silk white blouse was steamed and she sat with her blunt, manicured red nails folded on her desk. But her normally warm smile was more brittle than Naomi's, stealing any reassurance Naomi could gain from her boss's appearance.

Naomi sat in the high-backed seat Gail used for clients and visitors across from her desk. She smoothed her black pencil skirt, even though she knew she'd ironed the life out of every possible crease.

After a moment of intolerable silence, Naomi cleared her throat. "What can I do for you, Gail?"

Her boss closed her eyes and swallowed. "Naomi, my dear, you've been with me for a while and I've appreciated your dedication to the job—"

"Yes ma'am. I love working here. You've taught me so—"

"—*However...*"

Naomi's chest deflated and Gail must've seen because she squirmed in her seat.

"However.. it seems as though you've been rather preoccupied as of late. Unfortunately, today is the first day you've been back in weeks—"

"Gail—"

"Ms. Haynesworth will do, thank you."

Naomi jerked back like she'd been slapped. Never in her years of being there had she called *Ms. Haynesworth* anything other than by her first name. Schooling her face, she made sure Gail wouldn't see how much her slight had affected her.

"Ms. Haynesworth... I know it was last minute, but I took company-allotted personal days—"

"Yes, well... those days shouldn't have been taken so closely together."

"But... you authorized them?" Naomi couldn't help but argue back. "I'm sorry, Ms. Haynesworth, I'm not sure where this conversation is comin' from."

"I understand your fiancé, someone CTI contracts for security, was just arrested for domestic violence?"

Naomi stilled, unsure of what direction she should navigate her next sentence. But every avenue felt an awful lot like crashing into a ditch.

"Yes ma'am. But... he's no longer my fiancé. Hasn't been for a while."

"That's unfortunate, Naomi. I'm sorry you're going through that, but we can't have homelife issues affect the company—"

"Gail, they were earned paid time off—"

"And CTI can't afford to have negative press tied to it."

Naomi stopped, registering exactly what she'd said. She didn't care how much she admired Gail Haynesworth. No way in hell would she let yet another person make her feel shame for what Dean had done to her. She'd done that enough on her own for way too damn long.

Steel resolve straightened her backbone and sharpened her voice, destroying her accent.

"Are you saying that because I have been physically assaulted by someone whom I trusted, and have since separated myself from, that I should be held accountable for his criminal actions against me?" She narrowed her eyes at her boss, who at least had the ability to look contrite. "I've heard of landlords and some jobs punishing the survivor for the sake of removing the drama, but are you really telling me that this *global* tech company is afraid of press about my little ol' relationship?"

Gail shifted in her chair, refusing to look Naomi in the eye and a thought entered her mind.

"What is this really about Gail?" After a moment of silence, Naomi tried again. "Could this possibly be about the pressure the company is receiving over being involved with several known human traffickers? And even helped fund an annual *party* for these men where the trafficking occurred?"

"A party about which *you* leaked important information in violation of a nondisclosure agreement you signed."

Understanding washed over her, burning inside like acid. She collapsed back against the high back, crossing her arms and shaking her head in pure disbelief.

"So it is about them." Her former boss and friend was still refusing to meet her eyes, instead writing something on what was no doubt Naomi's termination papers. "I never pegged you for a coward, Gail."

Gail finally lifted her head and narrowed her eyes. "There are many things at stake here. You're punching above your weight, Naomi."

She leaned forward, pressing her hands against the desk, zero fucks given at this point. "Is that so? Well, I think you're rolling with *pigs*, Gail. What're you doing? Why are you letting these men run over you? Especially since they're steadily getting picked off by whoever is pulling their strings?"

Gail tilted her head in suspicion and Naomi slammed her lips shut.

"What do you know? You're talking about things that haven't been, nor will ever be, given to the press. Who are you getting your information from?"

Naomi briefly thought about trying to get out what she could from Gail, but there was no way she'd leave this conversation better than she started. Shaking her head, she leaned back against the chair.

"Does it matter?"

Gail's lips tightened and she stabbed her pen at the bottom of the paper.

"I suppose it doesn't. Here. You've been provided a severance for your termination. Feel free to use me as a reference in your future endeavors. I won't let your recent job performance or this particular conversation taint my recommendation."

At that dismissal, Naomi took the paperwork and slowly stood up, her mind racing. Just as she was about to cross the threshold to the office, she paused and turned back to her ex-boss.

"You know... what I did helped save eight lives from human trafficking. I won't apologize for that, nor will I allow myself to feel guilty. But what hurts right now... what I *do* feel shitty about... is placing so much faith and respect in a woman I thought was a pioneer in her field. It's devastating to find out she's been a pawn all along."

Gail's eyes grew glossy before she swallowed away her emotion. Naomi wanted to feel good about hitting her target, but disappointment was all she could muster. She pivoted to leave, but Gail's voice caught her attention.

"Be careful out there, Naomi. There are much bigger threats in this game. Players whom I have absolutely no power to control. Ones who have the political backing to wipe not just my company, but my *life* off the map." She shook her head and Naomi's chest thundered at what she was saying. "It sounds like you know just enough to be dangerous to yourself as well as to others. Make sure you're on the side that wins."

Naomi narrowed her eyes. "Since when did justice become the losing side? Whatever side that saves lives and takes down trafficking *is* the side that wins."

"You've seen the world, Naomi. Don't be naïve. Lady Justice is greedy and blind. She doesn't see, nor does she care, whose hand stuffs her pockets." She gave her a small, sad smile. "True justice is a fairy tale, Naomi. But I hope, for all our sakes, that yours has a happy ending."

CHAPTER THIRTY-NINE

"You ready for this?"

Naomi snorted at Nora's question before answering. "You always ask me that, and the answer is always no. I don't think anyone is ever really *ready* to talk to a survivor. Everyone's just hopin' and prayin' the right words will fall outta their mouth at the right time."

"Look at you..." Nora twisted her hands up against her chest and gave a wistful sigh before swiping at a fake tear. "My lil' girl's all growed up."

"Good Lord, shut up." She rolled her eyes at the theatrics, but couldn't help her chuckle. The woman had a knack for making Naomi laugh away her nerves. "Let's go. I've had a shitty day and I'm in the mood to save someone."

Nora winced before giving her a smile. "I'm sorry about your job, Naomi. That sucks big donkey balls."

"Thanks girl, but you are so damn crass, I can't take it. Somehow you always know what I need, though."

Nora shrugged and stepped through the hospital double entrance vestibule with a smile. "Such is the fate of the side character BFF trope, Naynay. We just hang out on the sidelines waiting to cheer on the FMCs or die for their character growth."

"Nora, do you really feel that way?"

Nora stopped short at the question. When the automatic door entrance tried to close on her, she yelped to get out of the way. "What? Oh, um. No. It's just a joke." She waved her hand. "You know me. Can't be serious if my life depended on it."

Naomi scowled, thinking of the many, many times Nora had reined it in to comfort survivors. "Well, we both know *that's* not true."

Nora rolled her eyes. "Whatevs girl, don't worry 'bout it. We have someone who needs our help. So anyway, like I was sayin'. The caller said his daughter would be here, so he asked if we could get someone who was good with kids, maybe who could even bring her kid—"

"And I said I would absolutely not let Thea anywhere near a hospital. She's been through too damn much. But I'm here and I'll just have to do—wait... you said it was a man?"

Nora narrowed her eyes. "Girl, you know the stats. DV survivors are overwhelmingly women, but men can suffer from abusers, too."

Naomi waved her hand at Nora's reprimand. "I know, it's just I haven't worked with a male survivor yet, is all."

"Just treat him like anyone else. Except don't let him do that macho BS where he tries to say since he's the man he can't be abused by a woman. That's a sexist trope more tired than the BFF."

Naomi cut her eyes at Nora again, but they continued down the hallways to the ER, where they'd been told the survivor would be waiting.

When they got there, it was bustling with people and hard to get a nurse to pause for long enough to show them the way. Finally, when they found someone to help, she directed them to a curtained-off corner.

"Knock-knock," Nora announced. "Can we come in? We're from that clinic you asked for?"

There was a deep grumbled assent before Nora pulled back the curtain.

"Hi, my name is Nora, and this is—"

"*Dean*? What the fuck are you doin' here?"

Nora's head whipped from Naomi to her ex that lay on the hospital table. No doubt he'd connived his way into the ER with a fake name to add to his real injuries he'd received days earlier. The place was swarming and probably too busy to recognize him.

"Naomi..." His smug smile made her blood boil. "Good to see you again, sweets."

"Dean, I have a protective order against you. This is a violation. I could have you arrested." She hissed the last and noticed Nora was backing away, her fingers subtly pressing against her phone screen. Naomi stepped between the two to keep Dean's attention off the woman, who was no doubt calling for help.

"We need to talk, sweets. That place you're stayin' at ain't safe. That maniac you're fuckin' has enemies and you and Thea need to come on home. Drop this bullshit DV charge. You know I didn't mean it. If we get outta Ashland, it'll be better, I promise. It's all this stress we're under that's fuckin' us up, but I can get us outta Ashland, once and for all." He reached out his hand. "Come away with me, Naomi. We'll be that family you want so bad. It'll be different this time, I swear. Everything will be better if it's just you, me, and our baby girl."

She whipped her hand back, hoping that Nora's call had gone through so she could get away from this man as fast as possible.

"Wait..." He looked around. "Where *is* Thea? I requested you bring her."

Naomi scoffed. "You're un-fucking-believable, you know that? Of course I'm not gonna bring our four-year-old daughter to a hospital. Are you outta your damn mind?"

Dean's bruised face blanched, and she couldn't help but feel a weird sense of karmic retribution that he was now the one on the patient bed.

"Where is she, Naomi?"

Something in his voice made her pause and she narrowed her eyes at him. "She's not here, Dean. I'm not bringing her—"

"Where *is* she? I'm not fuckin' playin' around. Where the fuck is she—"

"With Wes," she spat out finally.

"You left her with *him?* At *BlackStone?*"

Dean's shout made her jump, but she relaxed a fraction when she noticed an officer make his way to their corner.

"Dean, what's wrong?"

"She's at BlackStone, isn't she? Fuckin' A. Fuck, fuck, *fuck*! You only had to do this *one thing*, Naomi, why didn't you just bring her?" He grabbed his phone and started jabbing his fingers at the screen. "Call your stupid boyfriend. Get her out of there *now*."

"Sir, you're gonna have to keep it do—"

"Why, Dean? What are you sayin'—"

"Call him *now*! I'm not fuckin' around."

Naomi snatched her phone from her purse and began the call just as Dean took his from his ear and started to curse.

Nora went back to her phone while Naomi dialed Wes. But after several rings, it went to voice mail. Nora frowned at her phone and shook her head, telling her whoever she'd called hadn't answered either.

Dean cursed again and threw his phone on his lap. He ripped his hands into his hair and stared at her with wide eyes.

"Did you get him? Anyone there?"

Naomi shook her head. "No, it's goin' to voice mail. What the hell's goin' on Dean? Is Thea in trouble? Nora, call the cops again."

"Naomi, God. You just had to bring her. That's all you had to do. Now..." Dean collapsed back against the bed, shaking his head as his eyes grew glossy and red-rimmed. The officer made his way toward Dean and Naomi vaguely registered that Nora stopped him to talk. Naomi couldn't get her eyes off Dean's though, as he began to plead and shout incoherently.

"Dean, what is goin' on? Is Thea in danger?" At his sudden silence, Naomi clutched her purse closer and cursed. "Nora, I've gotta g—"

"It's too late." Dean's voice came out robotic as he stared off. "You won't get there in time."

Naomi snarled. "In time for *what*, Dean? What do you mean 'it's too late?'"

Dean's eyes finally moved toward hers, although whether he actually saw her, she wasn't sure. "Everything's already in motion. It was all supposed to happen when you got here. You were supposed to bring her... You were supposed to..."

"Dean, I swear to God—what is goin' on? Fuck it, I'm leavin'."

"You're too late." He looked at his watch and winced before a tear leaked from his eyes. "She's gone."

CHAPTER FORTY

"Wes, what does this button do?"

Wes reached for Thea and plopped her into his lap before she could press the button on his desk in the war room at BlackStone.

"That tells me when someone I don't know is at the gate. I press it..." He depressed the black button and a camera angle of the empty closed gate came on the screen. "Then I can see if anyone's there and ask them, *Halt, who goes there?*" He used his best medieval sentry voice into the microphone and was rewarded with lyrical giggles.

"Wes, there ain't nobody there. See!" She pointed to the empty screen before pointing to another. "What do all those words mean?"

"Bah, you're right. Guess we'll have to keep waiting for someone to visit us." He pointed to the screen with the logins to answer her question. "That tells me who all's been in and out of here. See, that's your mom's name right there when she left for work this morning. From that list, I know everyone else is going about their day, and only you, me, and Phoenix are here."

He huffed at the time beside his last teammate's name. Typically he'd be out all night and just getting in during lunchtime. If the guy didn't have an STD by now, he must be invincible.

Wes shook his head before leaving Thea to play a game he'd downloaded for her on his phone. They'd just finished eating upstairs, and Wes needed to return to the task he'd been working on before lunch.

He was researching and cross-referencing the list of *Alea Iacta Est* members that Ascot gave him along with Investigator Burgess's notes, ADA Aguilar's case file, the guest lists that had missing women, and any information he could find on the Rahab Foundation. It was a bear of a task, but he was working through it as painstakingly as possible. The women they'd failed deserved at least that.

Ascot had apparently had a few more members he'd "forgotten" about until Wes was out of the room to go help Naomi. They'd originally thought it was a group of rich, old white men, but after everything they'd learned, he hadn't been too surprised to see Gail Haynesworth as one of the "members". She'd been added to the list of monsters in this whole nightmare. Wes knew Ascot had more information in him, but the pathetic asshole was refusing to give up the one name they needed most.

Careful not to jostle Thea, Wes shook out the tension he'd had ever since Naomi called him after her meeting with Haynesworth. His queen had been on the verge of tears, and he'd wanted to burn the whole damn CTI building to the ground. The only thing that'd kept him from losing his cool was Thea's oblivious smile at the time, and the anger and resolve that laced Naomi's voice. It seemed like getting fired wasn't going to keep her down, and she was refusing to let her happiness be a casualty in this battle.

His eyes drifted to another screen that displayed more possible victims. As far as innocent casualties went, all of his research that morning had shown him that over the years, there were at least three women who'd practically disappeared after attending the scholarship party. With what happened to Ellie and the most recent party, it was worrisome that he couldn't find anything out about the women. Locating their whereabouts was now one of BlackStone's top priorities.

And as for the Rahab Foundation... a year ago, Nora had told them that she couldn't find any information on it and Wes chalked it up to being an organization so hidden that she couldn't find it. The organization had been much like Sasha Saves, and he'd figured that Nora just didn't know how to search.

But now he knew Nora and that excuse didn't fly. The woman was nearly as proficient as him at finding out information about people. Maybe even better, although he'd never admit that to her. No doubt she'd think she'd earned another point in their silly game with each other.

With Nora's abilities in mind, Wes had scoured his usual and even unusual channels—aka government databases—and couldn't find any information on the organization. Now he was questioning everything.

If they weren't saving women from human trafficking, then what the fuck had they been doing for seven years?

"What does... *that* button do?"

He chuckled. Of course, Thea would be interested in the proverbial 'big red button'. "If something bad ever happens, I press that and it sends an alert to police, firemen, all of my teammates. It tells everyone we're in trouble."

"Police like my daddy was?" she asked with a worried look. "Will my daddy come if that button gets pressed?"

Wes gritted his teeth. "No. Your father isn't a police officer anymore. Cops are the good guys." *Or they're supposed to be.* "But you have nothing to worry about, princess."

A low mechanical whirring began next to him as the door to the basement lowered and moved back on its track.

Thea gasped and swiveled her head to the side, her bright red curls bouncing with the movement.

"Wes, what is that?" she whispered and Wes tensed around her until he saw the backward baseball cap.

"Bastard didn't want to eat— Oh, hey, there kid." Phoenix slid the full plate across the floor before continuing up the basement stepladder.

"It's just Phoenix," Wes answered, even though Thea obviously knew by now. "He was downstairs working on something."

"Phoe-nik, is there a kitchen downstairs?" Thea asked with a tilt of her head.

Phoenix cringed and looked to Wes for an answer.

"No princess, there's not a kitchen downstairs. Phoenix was just eating lunch down there, weren't you, Phoenix?"

Phoenix rolled his eyes, at what, Wes didn't know, but thankfully he played along.

"Yeah, just had a hankerin' to take my lunch to the basement. I'll go take this up right now," he answered without looking up as he keyed in the code Wes had set up on everyone's phone in order to shut and lock the hidden door in the floor.

"Wait, didn't you just get here?"

Phoenix narrowed his eyes. "Yeah, dude. I'm on Ascot's food duty."

"No, I mean—"

"Is that a cookie? Like my mommy makes?"

Thea squealed and jumped off Wes's lap, aiming for the plate on the ground. Thankfully, Wes pulled her back just as Phoenix snatched the plate up.

"This one ain't for you, kid."

Thea's green hazel eyes shimmered with tears. "But why can't I have one?"

"Damn, do they have a button or some sh-*thing*? That reaction was immediate as hell."

Wes laughed. "Don't worry, Princess T. I'm sure if you ask Phoenix nicely, he'll run up and go get you one."

"Dude, seriously?"

Wes glared at him while Thea tried to calm herself down. She hiccuped and nodded before turning on what Wes had come to realize was her "gimme" look. His niece and nephew had one, too, widening their eyes and sticking their bottom lip out. Every time they wanted something, instead of saying "Gimme that," they just gave the look. It worked every time for Wes and from the defeat on Phoenix's face, it seemed it worked on him too.

"Please, Phoe-nik. Can I have a cookie?"

Phoenix sighed before looking down at his phone and muttering under his breath. "Sure, kid. I'll be right back."

Thea squealed and hopped back into Wes's lap. Without a thought, he wrapped his arms around her. Naomi had told him how Dean had treated Thea that last time. The thought of anyone hurting her or making her cry made his teeth ache from clenching his jaw, and he wished he could go back and give the asshole a few more knocks to the head to teach him a lesson. But it wouldn't do any good. Men like that aren't cured by a taste of their own medicine.

A buzzing in front of him made Wes look to his phone in Thea's hands.

"Thea, is someone calling me?"

She stilled in his arms like she was afraid she was in trouble, but eventually turned to look at Wes with a toothy grin. "Yes sir, but can I finish first?"

Wes chuckled, shaking his head. "Sure thing, princess."

He hugged her once with one arm. She was fiery, like her mom. Was there any doubt why he'd almost told Naomi how he felt about her the night she escaped her ex? She'd squeezed his hand three times, just like Thea had before. He had an idea of what it meant, but hadn't wanted to confront her right then. That type of emotion could scare anyone away if it was admitted too soon.

But she had to know, right? He'd nearly gotten arrested that night for defending Naomi and Thea, and he'd do it again. With that thought, he realized he'd do anything for them.

A crash from below drew Wes's attention to the still open trap door.

"Fucking Phoenix," he muttered without thinking and the small gasp in front of him told him he'd been heard.

"Wes, you can't say bad words," the little girl admonished him like cursing was the worst thing anyone could ever do. It was refreshing. Hopefully her innocence would remain for as long as possible and her father's actions hadn't caused too much emotional damage.

"Sorry, princess." He tried to lean up to get to the button near the wall to close the trap door. The last thing Thea needed was to hear Ascot downstairs. Finding an interrogation prisoner might taint that angelic naivety quicker than even anything her dad had ever done.

He lifted her from his lap to set her down. "Let me just do something—"

Thea yelped and Wes sat right back down.

"What? What's wrong?"

Thea groaned and pulled her hand back like she was about to chuck his phone. Just as it was about to leave her small hands, Wes reached and caught it.

"What the hell, Thea? You can't throw my phone like that."

She crossed her arms and pouted. "Someone keeps callin' and makin' me lose my game."

"Thea, you can't just throw a tantrum—"

He'd swiped out of her game and looked at his notifications.

23 missed calls from 'My Queen'

"What the..." Wes's heart tightened and dropped to his stomach like lead. He opened up his voice mail and Naomi's scared voice came over the speaker.

"Wes! Oh my god, answer the phone! You have to get out of Black-Stone! Dean's scheduled some kind of attack—"

He immediately rolled his chair up to the desk and clicked through security camera footage. It took him a minute of searching, but he finally found the edge of a black van that sure as fuck wasn't supposed to be there. The driver had parked outside the walls of the weapons room next door and had somehow managed to position the vehicle in one of his camera's blind spots. Wes had to switch from one camera to another in order to make out what was happening.

A man carried something from the back of the van. At the camera's angle, Wes couldn't tell exactly what was happening, but it seemed like the man was stacking something against the outer wall. It was too hard to see clearly until finally he got a glimpse of the last box.

Sweat pricked across his brow. He'd bet every weapon on the other side of the war room wall that the man outside was stacking explosives against the facility walls.

As he watched, his mind raced, and Wes's hand flew to the alert button. The man wiped his palms down his pants and got into the driver's side of the van. Something that looked like a string or a cord maybe, connected to the tow hitch and instantly Wes fully understood what was happening. He tugged Thea close to him and stood to run.

But he was too late.

A boom and a child's scream filled his ears as he turned to shield Thea from flames and flying metal.

CHAPTER FORTY-ONE

Wes opened his eyes to blurry bright sunlight shining on his face and BlackStone Securities' war room up in flames. His skin was slick with sweat as he wiped his brow, empty of his glasses, and sat up on the hot cement floor. Acrid smoke burned his nostrils, telling him he needed to get the fuck out of there, but it was the high-pitched shrieks that brought him fully to his senses.

He hadn't passed out, but he was still disoriented. Although whether from the bomb, the head throbbing alert that automatically went off throughout the building during an emergency, or Thea's wailing, he wasn't sure.

"Thea, are you okay? Are you hurt?" His words came out quick and loud, but her screams didn't change.

They'd had barely enough time for Wes to hide them underneath the heavy round table in the center of the room and Thea was climbing onto him like a life raft in the ocean. He'd lost his glasses somewhere, and it was already so smoky that he could hardly see Thea in front of him. He got on his knees and ran his fingers quickly around the floor to find his glasses. They brushed over his frames, but when he brought them to his eyes, they were cracked beyond repair.

They'll have to work for now.

He turned to a less blurry Thea and tried his best to not sound panicked.

"Thea? Please answer me, princess. Are you okay?"

In answer, she threw herself around his neck and nearly choked him with her strong grip. He wrapped his arm around her back, tugging her close, hoping she felt a little safer. As he held her, he ran his fingers over her limbs and face to make sure she was okay to move. When he'd confirmed that her cries were from terror rather than pain, overwhelming gratitude shuddered through him and he sagged back on his calves.

"You're going to be okay, Thea. I'll get you out of here. You're safe with me, I promise."

Once the words left his lips, he shed his worry and allowed his training to take over, narrowing his focus to figure out the best escape route.

Thank God the war room was mostly cement and steel, but whatever had been used in the bomb had ignited the weapons room, too. Together it'd been strong enough to wrench open a huge hole in BlackStone's outer walls, giving him the odd sensation that they were already outside.

Fuck... the weapons room.

When they'd built the BlackStone facility, it'd made sense to have their weaponry, demolitions, and gun range all in one place. They'd also made it easy access to the war room and the garage so they could plan, suit up, and head out in one swift go.

No one ever thought about what would happen if it was all blown up. BlackStone was the safest place on earth.

Was.

Heat stung his skin, bringing him back to the emergency at hand. He slid with Thea all the way under the table for shelter while taking stock of the room. The gaping hole in the corner had taken out some of his screens and made them sitting ducks for any future explosions.

Draco had been their demo man, stocking up the room with basically every weapon and defense known to man. How had he stored them? Was anything volatile and vulnerable enough to ignite? He had to get Thea out of there before they found out.

In the space between his hiding spot and the door, cement and steel scattered in sharp pieces from the blast. Turning his head on a swivel, he mapped a way around the biggest obstacles to the war room doorway.

"Hold on to me, Thea. We're going to play 'floor is lava,' okay? Do *not* let go and don't touch the ground. Hear me?"

Unable to tell whether her shrieky reply was in response to him or not, he wrapped her around his torso like a baby sloth. Despite the fact that her screams echoed in his ears, he breathed easier, knowing that she had the lung capacity at all in the smoky room. Her fear would have cracked his heart to the point of paralysis, but his training took over and aided him to operate on autopilot.

Staying low on his hands and knees to avoid heat and smoke, he crawled through the maze of jagged, molten hot obstacles at an awkward angle to keep Thea safe from the fragments below them. Glass and lava hot metal pierced and burned his palms and he gritted his teeth against the pain.

The room was already gray and black with smoke, but he could make out the open doorway in front of them.

"Almost there, princess."

A deafening pop behind him made him jump, landing one hand onto a knife-sharp piece of glass. Ignoring the pain, he instantly crouched over Thea to protect her from whatever had detonated from the weapons room. His back stung like a sunburn from a new burst of flames behind them. Thankfully, his shirt still provided him a thin layer of protection against burns, but he knew that wouldn't last for long if he stayed put.

Thea's face tucked into his chest and her grip loosened.

"No, Thea, hang on! Lava, Thea. Remember? Don't touch the ground."

Small sniffles against his chest in response made him realize she'd finally stopped screaming, but it didn't provide the reprieve he needed.

Banding his arm around her waist and pressing her as close as possible so she had to breathe through his shirt, he lifted the hand with the glass shard and continued his trek. More fiery pops behind him spurred him on, and he bent even lower into a modified Army crawl across the broken remnants of their war room.

Cool air from the open door wafted in on him and he tried to breathe deep but it was still too smoky. A hacking cough forced its way from his lungs. Every inch in front of him felt like a mile. His limbs grew sluggish and he had to dig deep to access that part of him that kick-started his energy every time his emotions were involved.

Remember Thea. I need to get her safe. Get her safe. Just, get... her... safe.

Then go after the fuckers who did this to her.

The last thought gave him that rage he'd grown up on, lighting his own fire underneath him to cover those last few feet.

Suddenly, the cool air enveloped him and he closed his eyes with relief. His body nearly gave out, and he would've collapsed to the ground on top of Thea if strong arms didn't scoop him up underneath his armpits.

He and Thea were turned over, so that Thea was on top of his chest, still clutching him for dear life as they were dragged into the garage on the opposite side of the hallway. Wes looked up to see Phoenix's harried expression.

Finally, they stopped moving and Phoenix settled him and Thea against the wall near the garage door. Phoenix kneeled down, his eyes wide and hands brushing through his hair, his ball cap forgotten.

"What the fuck is goin' on?"

Wes tried to hear him over the emergency alert pounding in his head. He huffed out a cough and struggled to sit up, but was already feeling his energy come back now that oxygen was filling his lungs.

"Someone... attacked BlackStone," he coughed out his answer. "Can't stay here... war... weapons room... gone." He sucked in another healthy gasp of air and swallowed it down his dry throat. "I don't know if... there are more weapons... bombs. But the weapons room... it could blow. We have to go."

As he said it, he gathered his strength to get up, still holding on to Thea with his good hand. The other still had a thin glass shard embedded inside the palm, so he gingerly used it to pull his phone and keys from his pocket. Thank whoever the hell up there was watching them that he had both still intact.

"Right, let's go." Phoenix nodded. "Wait—*Shit*. Ascot."

Thea was back to crying in his ear and Wes blinked, pausing for a second to understand what his teammate was saying.

"No Phoenix, we can't..." He swallowed again and finally felt like his throat was coated enough to talk. "Down in the base-ment... door's closed. No one can possibly get in... without a code... it's a bunker... hidden. We'll get him... later. When whoever attacked has left—"

"No man, you know he's the target. They'll do whatever it takes to get him. We can't just leave him chained to a damn chair!"

Wes narrowed his eyes at Phoenix's point before cursing again. "Fine... if you can't get him... leave him... we'll figure it out."

Phoenix nodded and was gone in the next breath.

CHAPTER FORTY-TWO

Wes limped his way to his Trackhawk, ignoring how raw his knees felt from the tiny cuts and burns, and the glass splinter still in his hand. When he finally made it to his vehicle, he tried to peel Thea off him, but her muffled cries turned into ear-piercing screams again as she clung to him for dear life.

"Fuck it," he muttered before banding an arm around her and hopping behind the steering wheel. Once inside, he unlocked the garage, bracing himself for anyone who could be on the other side, only to relax when no one showed up.

A nearly full water bottle sat in a cup holder, and he twisted off the cap around Thea to leak water into her wailing mouth before taking refreshing sips himself.

"I know you're upset, princess," he said, now able to make full sentences with a hoarse voice. He wrapped Thea's fingers around the bottle. "But drink more of this for me, okay?"

Her small hand crinkled the thin plastic as she obeyed. Wes ordered the car Bluetooth to call Naomi. He didn't know where the rest of his teammates were, but from checking earlier, Phoenix was the only other teammate in BlackStone.

"Wes? Oh my god, are you—"

"Mommy!"

"Shh, shh, Thea, it's okay." He cradled her head and spoke softly into her hair. "We're okay," Wes replied to Naomi, loud enough for her to hear, but quiet enough not to alarm Thea.

He shifted his vehicle in drive and stepped on the gas, checking the rearview mirror as he blasted out of the garage. Fuck, he hated leaving Phoenix, but he had to get Thea to safety. The only place he could do that was far away from the facility. His tires squealed as he raced out. Thea tensed against his chest and he patted her back, trying to smooth her fears away, but the poor thing was definitely traumatized.

"There was a bomb at BlackStone Facilities—"

"*What?*"

"Phoenix is still back at the facility. He's the only one and he stayed back to get Ascot."

"Okay, but where are you?"

"I'm getting us out of here. No one else is here, but I sent an alert to law enforcement and the team," he explained.

Wes navigated the facility grounds, driving to the gate and typing his four-digit code into his phone to open the gate. As soon as he turned outside the gate, he heard faint sirens. Wes couldn't wait around, though. He didn't know what they were dealing with. Hopefully, Phoenix would be able to handle himself.

As soon as he thought it, a deafening boom seemed to make the ground under the Trackhawk quake.

"What the hell was that?" Naomi's frantic voice barely registered as he swiveled his head to the side to find BlackStone.

Or what used to be BlackStone.

Wes's heart throbbed and his breath caught in his lungs. Smoke billowed from the back of the building he'd once called home. Even from his distance outside the gate, he could see the corner of the building that housed the weapons room, gun range, and war room had crumbled to the ground, engulfed in flames from the blast.

Phoenix.

Wes slowed almost to a halt, desperately wanting to turn around to get his teammate. But Phoenix was a trained soldier, BlackStone was under attack by some unknown entity, and he had a four-year-old he needed to get to safety.

The sirens he'd heard whistled closer, making his decision. As much as it pained him, he had to leave Phoenix and hope first responders could help him.

"Phoenix is smart. He'll be fine." His voice was weak in his ears.

"Wes, answer me! What *was* that?"

"I'll explain. I promise. I've left the facility. Where are you?"

"I'm on my way to BlackStone."

Fear sharp as a knife cut down his spine. "No, stay the fuck away from here, Naomi. I'll meet you somewhere safe with Thea." He racked his brain for a location. "The QT gas station. The closest one near the facility. Meet us there."

BlackStone was on the outskirts of town, nearly in the middle of nowhere. Wes was able to navigate the empty, crooked roads at breakneck speed until he arrived at the QuikTrip gas station. Those locations had the best video surveillance, hands down. In a pinch, with a faceless enemy, this was the safest place for him and Thea until everything got sorted.

"We made it," he sighed, the words loud enough for Naomi to hear on the still open connection. "Thea and I are at the QT."

"Okay, we're almost there, too."

"We?"

"Me and Nora."

He paused before connecting dots. "How did you know we were in danger?"

Naomi huffed. "It's a long story. Let's just say Dean's back in jail and I don't think he'll be getting out so easy this time."

"How close are you—"

A horn honked and Naomi pulled into the parking space beside him. "We're here."

Wes checked all his mirrors and everything around him

before gingerly stepping out of the car with Thea. The terrified child was hiccuping and crying, but at least she wasn't screaming anymore.

Naomi tripped out of her Nissan and ran around the front of his Trackhawk, arms wide open. Wes readied himself to hand Thea off, expecting Naomi to take her from him, but to his surprise, she fell against them both. Her arms wrapped around them and Wes used his relatively uninjured hand to pull her close, whispering soothing words to calm Naomi's hysterics.

They were collecting an audience, but Wes's attention was drawn to Nora as she stepped outside of the passenger seat, a phone at eye level in her hand.

"I've got Hawk, Devil, and Jason on FaceTime. Everyone's on their way." She worried her teeth over the snake bite studs under her lip. "Phoenix isn't answering."

"Shit," Wes swore, not sure what the next play should be. The sirens that brought him comfort before wailed in his ears as a stream of fire trucks, ambulances, and police units raced past the station. Wes kissed Naomi on the crown of her head before passing Thea off and retrieving his phone. He dialed dispatch and waited as they transferred him to the officer who was on the way to the facility.

"This is Officer Brown." The man's heavy Southern accent came over the phone and Wes released a heavy sigh.

"Henry, man, I'm so glad you're the one on this."

"Yeah, dude, what happened? I got the call and nearly freaked the fuck out."

"BlackStone was bombed. I don't know the details. The weapons room and war room were hit. Phoenix is still there." He swallowed, hoping that was still true.

"Phoenix? Fuck. Fuck. Fuck. *Fuck*. Why the fuck is Phoenix there still? Did you fucking leave him? *Fuck!*"

Wes never in his wildest nightmares thought he'd leave a man behind and admitting that to Phoenix's best friend made him nauseous.

Wes lowered his voice as he spoke. "Is this your private line?"

"Yes. What the hell happened, dude?"

"We still had Ascot," Wes replied directly into the receiver. "We promised him we'd keep him alive, and Phoenix went to get him. The bomb opened straight up to the war room. He was at risk, but hopefully Phoenix got them out. There was... there was another explosion as I was leaving. I think the attackers fled."

Almost as soon as the words left his mouth, Wes realized he wasn't sure. It was mostly just a hope. He'd seen them drive away, no doubt setting off the bomb with the cord they'd used to trip the detonator. That's how Draco taught them to do it anyway. It was an easy way to set one off and drive to safety. But had they actually left? Or were they actually behind the second explosion, too?

"Fuckin' A, okay. I see the fence already, so I'll call you when I know somethin'."

Wes nodded, even though Henry couldn't see him. "Yeah, keep me posted. The rest of the team should be there soon."

Wes hung up and turned to Naomi. Tears filled her firelight eyes, but it wasn't sadness or fear there anymore. The warmth and gratitude radiating from her entire body eased the tightness in his chest and the way she clutched his hand made him wonder if she felt the same way for him as he did for her.

"Thank you, Wes. You saved my baby," she whispered. "I don't think I could ever repay you. I don't know what I'd do if I lost her..." she choked before swallowing. "Either of you."

"Come here." He pulled her into his arms, squeezing tight around both of the new loves in his life, and kissed their foreheads before pulling back.

Tears still trailed freely down Naomi's cheek, and he attempted to swipe them away before realizing he was bleeding. He quickly pressed his injured palm to the hem of his black shirt, hiding it from her view, not wanting to alarm her any more than she already was. Instead, he used the thumb on his good hand to dry the moisture from her cheek before bending to meet her teary gaze.

"I've only known you a few months, Naomi, and this definitely isn't the right time. But you two have quickly become my world. She's the light of your life, and you're mine. I'm not going anywhere, love."

Naomi grabbed his hand before giving him a watery smile, opening and closing her mouth like she was getting up the nerve to say something.

His phone rang and Wes winced, slightly annoyed that the moment had been interrupted, but more afraid of not answering it and missing literally vital information about Phoenix. He looked at the caller ID before he waved his phone at her. "Give me a minute."

She nodded before giving his hand three squeezes. He closed his eyes, surer than ever of what she felt for him, before he turned, placing the phone to his ear. "Henry? What's the status?"

There was a pause and Wes felt his brow furrow. "Henry?"

Finally, there was a choking sob on the other side of the phone. "He's gone, dude. Phoenix is gone."

CHAPTER FORTY-THREE

"She's asleep," Naomi whispered, pulling the cedar door shut behind her. It'd taken several hours of consoling and clinging to Naomi the entire drive from Ashland to BlackStone's hidden cabin on Mount Ash, but Thea had finally passed out.

Wes's face was a mix of emotions with his furrowed brow and soft smile. "Good. Hopefully, she'll sleep through the night."

Naomi leaned against the door, closing her eyes. "Hell, I hope I do, too. But I think she will. She's a heavy sleeper already. Plus, it's been a long ass day for everyone."

"No fucking kidding," Wes huffed, analyzing the bandage Devil had used on his hand. Having the glass splinter removed had to hurt like hell, but he never complained. Thankfully, his other injuries were superficial, although he was still clearly exhausted.

"Aren't we a pair," she half joked with a grimace, pointing to the wrap and then to the lightening bruises on her own arm. "I'm sure mine hurts much less than yours does."

His lips tightened into a grim line before he spoke. "The fact that you were ever injured at all hurts me more than my hand does, I can promise you that."

Her heart stuttered as she caught his striking blue gaze. "I know what you mean."

His eyes softened with an emotion she wasn't quite ready to admit to herself, so when he spoke again, she was both grateful for the reprieve and disappointed in her hesitance.

"Speaking of everyone, it looks like it's just us tonight. Hawk's still with the authorities. He said the facility's black box is still intact, so he'll be bringing it tomorrow morning."

"Black box?" Naomi asked.

"It's basically BlackStone's hard drive. We still don't know for certain why we were attacked. We think it was because of Ascot, especially since all evidence points to him being taken from BlackStone during the attack. But if it was for what we know in the trafficking case or for anything else, they miscalculated. I wired the place so I could have it nearby in my own apartment at all times."

"Shoot, that's good, I guess." She didn't fully understand what he meant, but the relief relaxing his shoulders guided her reaction.

"It's very good. That box has the security tapes downloaded on it and will help us figure out what happened to Phoenix. There's no sign he was hurt during the attack, but that means we have no idea where he is. It kills me that I can't do anything to help find him right now. I'm injured and basically useless without that camera footage."

"Hawk practically ordered you to rest up too. You'll do no one any good if you don't take care of yourself. Oxygen mask, remember?"

His grin was small, but it was still a smile, so she'd take it. She couldn't stand seeing him so defeated, and ever since they found out Phoenix was missing, he'd been destroying himself with guilt.

"Well, as soon as Hawk brings me that black box early tomorrow morning, I'll be back in action, injuries and exhaustion be damned. I have to ID who was behind the bombing and make sure Phoenix is okay. Hopefully, he got out before the second bomb."

A shadow crossed his face again and Naomi cringed at the pain there. There was no way she was going to let him feel bad for putting her daughter first and she refused to feel guilty for being grateful for that fact. She wrapped her arms under his and hugged him close to her, trying to embed those feelings past fabric and skin into his heart.

"It's not your fault, Wes. You had to get Thea outta there."

His sigh fluttered the hair on the crown of her head. "I know... I've just never left a man behind before. The guy's an asshole, but he's our asshole and our teammate, potentially in enemy territory. We're going to make finding him priority one as soon as I have that damn hard drive."

Wes pulled back and used his thumb and forefinger to massage his nose, but stopped himself from doing the same to his closed eyelids. His glasses broke during the explosion, so he probably didn't want to damage the only pair of contacts he'd squirreled away at the cabin.

Instead, Wes smoothed back his freshly washed midnight blue hair. The tattoos on the back of his hand rolled with the gesture. The artwork was so dense, she could hardly make out the skin underneath, but ink always did it for her. She swallowed and resisted the urge to beg him to touch her again. The need to feel his skin on hers was nearly overwhelming, but now wasn't the time to get horny. Right?

Right. Not the time. He nearly died today, saving Thea.

Of course, *that* reasoning didn't help get her mind off wanting him. Nothing like a hero crush.

But it's so much more than that.

Naomi mentally shook the truth away while outwardly nodding. "What about everyone else? Where are they?"

"Jason and Jules are staying back in Ashland. The hospital admitted Jules about an hour ago for observation. They think she's having contractions, but they're not sure if it's actually time to have the baby or stress. She's only days away from her due date anyhow, so they're keeping an eye on her and the baby. And Jason too, if I'm honest. The man sounded like a nervous wreck on the phone. With BlackStone blowing up, Phoenix missing, and his already helicopter tendencies, he probably won't let her leave the hospital until she's given birth."

Naomi snorted. "I get that. I was terrified when I had Thea, but even without that stress, Jason seems a little... erm... emotional. At least from what I've heard of him from Jules and Nora, and what I've seen at the BlackStone meetings."

"That's a way of putting it." Wes laughed and casually put his arm around her shoulder, leading her to his room.

The entire cabin was something out of *Southern Living*, and their room matched with bear and plaid decor and cedar walls. It was exactly what they all three needed after what they'd been through. Naomi had relaxed as soon as they'd stepped through the front door to the homey scent of citrus-cedar.

Like Wes.

A king-size bed with a forest green quilt took up the center of the room. Black bears traveled the hem, matching the curtains drawn over the window. Which was bulletproof, apparently, according to Wes's assurances. And the best part was Thea was able to be just next door.

She hadn't wanted to let her daughter out of her sight, but the poor girl was exhausted and Naomi was still keyed up. Instead of tossing and turning beside Thea, possibly waking her, she decided to stay up with Wes. Now she was wondering how soft his bed was, and how good it'd feel to lie in it beside him.

Wes pulled his phone from his pocket and typed until a flame erupted in the gas fireplace, completing the comfy ambiance. They both collapsed on either side of the bed together without a word. A comfortable silence rested between them as they both watched the flames lick at the ceramic logs. The orange glow was mesmerizing, and before Naomi knew it, she was leaning against Wes's arm, her eyes half closed with sleep.

It was perfect. She felt more at home in this cabin after a few hours than she had... anywhere, really.

"Devil and Ellie are at Sasha Saves," Wes continued. Despite his low murmur, Naomi's eyes flashed open at the gentle disturbance. She'd almost forgotten she'd asked about everyone else's whereabouts. "Devil didn't want Ellie anywhere near BlackStone, but Ellie refused to sit around and insisted they at least help at the clinic. The place is tricked out with the best security we could provide. Not that that means anything anymore."

She raised her head from his shoulder and held his uninjured hand, a reflex for comfort that she'd developed with Thea. "You can't beat yourself up. Whoever did this was obviously gunnin' for y'all. There's no way they weren't professionals. Especially, since Dean was involved." She shuddered.

"Shit, no. Stop that. We can't both feel guilty, love." He squeezed her hand and before she could think, she squeezed back three times.

It was a ritual only she and Thea had. She'd never wanted to hold Dean's hand, couldn't bear to reach out to the hands that hurt so easily. Come to think of it, she'd never seen Thea hold his hand either. But for both of them, it'd seemed, it came second nature with Wes.

He stilled before clearing his throat. "You have nothing to feel guilt over, Naomi. Just know that."

"Yeah, how 'bout neither of us do? At least right now. We can beat ourselves up tomorrow when Hawk gets here and we can actually do something to help. But let's give ourselves grace tonight."

Another gentle smile lifted up the corners of his lips. "I like that. We could all use a little more grace. Anyway, Nora is at the hospital, too. She's close to Sasha Saves, and she said that Jules might need backup. If Jason freaks out more than he already is, Nora didn't want to be too far away from the hospital."

And Drake.

The thought whispered across her mind, but she didn't want to out her friend. Nora hadn't said anything, but Naomi knew that the nurse's words weighed heavy on her.

Naomi leaned against the bed. "So it's just us, huh?"

"Just us."

The need to comfort and be comforted reflected in the faint worry lines beside his eyes, the cautious grin blooming on his face, and the way his hands flexed as if he was itching to hold her. She desperately wanted to have him do just that and leaned forward, but was stopped gently when Wes threaded his fingers through her hair and kissed the top of her head. Every time he did that, she soaked in the warm feeling that started in her heart and flowed throughout her body. She felt so safe, secure. So *loved.*

"Hey, I'm going to draw a bath," he whispered against her hair.

She felt her nose scrunch in confusion. "But you already took a shower?"

His chest rose and fell with his chuckle. "You're right, but it's not for me. So what do ya say?"

Naomi's small gasp at his gesture ended in a moan. "Good Lord, I hadn't even thought about that but now that you've said it I don't want anything else."

His low voice went straight to her core. "*Anything?*"

"I guess it depends on how good that bath is." She pulled back and gave him a wink. He laughed outright and pulled her in for a hard kiss against her lips that ended all too quickly.

"Challenge accepted, my *queen*." He hopped out of the bed to the en suite bath and closed the door. She crossed her arms, trying to keep herself from going after him and ravishing him, bath or not. Instead, she decided to go check on Thea one more time.

The cabin's layout was a huge open concept, with two floors, the top having what she assumed were other bedrooms overlooking the living room. She tiptoed across the wood floors to Thea's room next door. Naomi leaned in to listen, not hearing anything, before she cracked the door and peeked in.

Her daughter's red curls were strewn on the huge king-size pillow, and her thumb was in her mouth. Naomi ventured in and wrapped a curl around her finger, twirling it lightly. Naomi's heart ached in her chest.

Dean had almost hurt their daughter. Again. It didn't matter to Naomi if he went to therapy—something she was now sure he'd never intended to do—and came out a whole new person. Naomi was done. She was putting her oxygen mask on first. The man was toxic. Hell, more than toxic. He was fucking dangerous. There was no way she was subjecting herself or her daughter to that maniac ever again. She'd told Wes she was going to prosecute this time and she meant it. Dean had lied before and told her he was going to get help. Hopefully now a court wouldn't give him a choice.

Naomi pulled the door closed and made her way through the dim light back to Wes's bedroom. Just as she entered, Wes exited the bathroom in a cloud of steam, only wearing a pair of sweatpants. Her eyes ran the length of his muscles, damn near salivating at his tattooed pecs where a beautiful, colorful snake was twisted around his chest, taking a bite from his heart. Without thinking, she reached for it and traced it.

"Gorgeous."

"Funny." Wes smirked. "I was about to say the same about you."

Naomi rolled her eyes, but Wes wrapped his hand around the one still on his chest and pulled her against him. He leaned low, his voice coming out in a breath against her ear, causing shivers down her back and making her core clench.

"Are you ready to be treated like the queen you are?"

CHAPTER FORTY-FOUR

If Naomi's panties weren't already damp, that would've done the trick. She gave him a dazed nod as she squeezed her legs closed to prevent a flood.

"This way, milady." He pulled her inside by the hand and she fought the urge to squeeze it three times again.

They entered the room and the soothing scent of rich gardenias and green apples filled her nostrils and calmed her. A large white clawfoot tub sat catty-corner in the room. Lit candles covered every inch of the small tiered wooden tables lining the tub, leaving a small space for a bather to climb in.

Wes dipped the fingertips of his injured hand into the full, steamy tub, flicking bubbles off as he raised it again. He kissed her temple and let her go before indicating the tub with both hands.

"For you, my queen. Enjoy."

His eyes crinkled at the edges, free from their glasses. She missed the frames, but she couldn't resist lingering her gaze across his smile before he turned. Her heart stuttered and she grabbed his arm.

"Wait!" She swallowed. "Stay."

The surprise on his face was quickly replaced by a smolder that made her knees week.

Slowly, she let him go, and despite his mischievous grin, she was still afraid he'd leave. She stepped back and tugged on the hem of her shirt. Her eyes stayed on his piercing blue orbs before she followed through.

The ice there was completely at odds with the warmth and kindness that always surrounded him. It was only in his eyes that she could see the cold fear of losing control and his fight not to turn into the monster he believed he was. But she knew better. He wasn't a monster. He was her knight.

She pulled the shirt over her head, revealing her naked breasts, trying not to succumb to shyness, even though Wes had basically already seen the rest of her. When they'd had sex, they'd somehow managed to keep her clothes on and she regretted not taking the time to fully appreciate his body, too. Now she was getting completely naked, body *and* soul, for the first time in... well, ever.

Dean had plenty of shit to say about her small breasts, making fun of her for not even really needing a bra. But Wes's sharp inhale relieved her tension. She had curves, sure, but they were all in her hips and ass. The fact that he had an awed expression gave her the boost of encouragement she needed.

"I know you're already clean from your shower but... do you wanna get in too?"

He glanced to the water and back before giving her a wicked smirk. "I'd love to join, but if I sink into that tub with you, getting clean will be the last thing on my mind."

"Well then..." She dipped her hand into the warm water. Once it was soaked, she stood and bit her lip before closing the gap between the two of them. Using her wet finger, she traced the valley dividing his abs. Muscles tensed as she left a trail to his waistband. She ended her tease by curving her finger inside the fabric and giving a light tug. "Come dirty me up, troublemaker."

At her challenge, his stare grew heated while he watched her step back and hook her thumbs under her own waistband. He slowly began to mirror her movements, his focus holding steady on her hands as she slid her jeans and thong down her legs and stepped out of them both. Taking the moment they hadn't had the first time, she cataloged every inch of him, and she let him do the same.

The man was huge compared to her and looked menacing with his entire body almost completely covered with delicious tattoos of skulls and snakes. There were also patches of small scrapes and slight redness from the bombing and fire, evidence of how truly lucky she was that both Wes and Thea got out safely. All thanks to him.

Gratitude filled her chest and flowed through her veins, making her fingers tingle to touch him again. She licked her lips as her eyes trailed down his body to his already hard cock. Last time, she'd barely been able to conceal her surprise at his size. Back in college, Sophie told her it's always the nerdy, quiet ones who have the longest dicks.

Guess there's somethin' to that.

Her gaze traveled back up his chest to his face, expecting it to be full of smug male satisfaction at her stare, only to find reverent awe there instead.

"You're gorgeous," he breathed before dragging his eyes back to hers.

The heat of his gaze sent warmth to her center. She desperately wanted to pounce on him and show him with her body how she felt about him, but she also wanted to drag it out just a little longer.

He grabbed her hand before breaking eye contact as they both stepped into the hot water. Wes hissed while she moaned. Damn, it felt *divine.*

"How are women able to bathe in scalding hot water?" Wes asked before settling slowly into the big tub. It would be a tight fit together, but there was definitely room.

She giggled and lifted a shoulder. "Because our pain tolerance is much higher than y'all's, obviously." She positioned herself to sit on the opposite side of the tub, but Wes tugged her hand.

"Come here."

He already lay with his back against the tub and his legs spread. With a gentle twist, he wrapped his arm around her waist and tugged her flush to his chest. His thick cock grew impossibly longer underneath her butt as she settled in, making her core throb in response.

She soaked in the warm water and sighed before closing her eyes. "Mmm, this is nice."

He grunted his assent before reaching for the shampoo.

"Can I?" he asked, and Naomi turned to see heated anticipation written all over his face.

"Oh, um, sure. It won't hurt your hand?"

She nodded toward his injury, but he shook his head.

"It hardly even hurts anymore. Especially not when I've got something much better to think about."

"The prescription-strength ibuprofen helps, I bet. I know it's making me feel better right now."

"I'm glad you're not in pain anymore." The whispered phrase was heavy with meaning, but his kiss against her head was light. He twirled his finger, indicating she go for a quick dunk under the water to get her hair wet. When she rose back up, his hands were already massaging the shampoo onto her scalp.

"Good God, this is amazing."

He stilled his motions and his cock jumped behind her butt before he cleared his throat and continued his ministrations. "I've been wanting to spoil you like this for a long time. I'm glad the fantasy is living up to reality."

She laughed and soaked in the feeling of his fingers through her wet strands before she dunked again to rinse. When she raised back up, she looked to the side but couldn't find any conditioner. Only shampoo would have to do. Instead, she reached for the loofah on the side of the tub, but Wes got to it before she did.

"No, let me." His hushed whisper was cool against her skin compared to the steamy water, and she shivered despite the heat. She helped him pour body wash onto the loofah and he gently began to wash her with his uninjured hand. He started with her shoulder, but the soothing effect was immediate.

"Oh, god, Wes. This feels like heaven."

He chuckled against her ear before kissing the shell. "With what I have in mind, Heaven's just the beginning."

Her pussy clenched at the emptiness and she nearly turned around to say screw it, or screw him, really, but he held firm to her shoulder, keeping her in place.

"Nah-ah-ah, let me do this for you. I want us to savor each other this time."

He tapped her thigh and she lifted it out of the water for him to reach her legs. As he dragged the loofah across her skin, she closed her eyes, totally trusting him to take care of her. Soon, the loofah disappeared and she felt his fingers venture between her legs.

"Open for me, love."

She spread them and let his fingers explore her pussy. He pulled her closer with the arm banded around her and teased her entrance with his fingers. She could tell she was already slick with her desire.

"Fuck, you need this as bad as I do, don't you?"

She sucked in a sharp breath as his long finger entered her and his palm ground against her clit. She shuddered with a moan and lay back hard against his chest as he curled his finger to reach her G-spot.

"God, Wes, *yes*."

Having Wes behind her and his arm reaching around her, not only was she insanely turned on, she also reveled in how protected she felt in his embrace.

He pumped once before adding another finger and she writhed against him, working the slick skin of her ass over his cock, making him moan, too. After a few strokes of his fingers over her G-spot, he developed a rhythm. His lips danced over her neck, below her ear, until his injured hand left her waist to turn her head and kiss her. The angle should've been awkward, but the stretch added to the tension building in her center. He kissed her with the same passion as he did with everything, laying claim to her lips like no one else ever had. It was heady having all that intense focus all on her.

The constant pulse against the bundle of nerves inside her made her moan. She squirmed to help him as his palm adopted the same rhythm against her clit. Her lower stomach muscles tensed almost to the point of pain, but goddamn, that release would be worth it after the climb.

Wes's hand moved from her chin to one of her breasts, gingerly molding the small mound into a peak. His long, deft fingers moved to trace around her nipples, making the already stiffening tips stand up. Her body was so sensitive, just the barest caress of his finger over one nipple and then the other made her spine tingle and her toes curl.

"I feel you tightening around my fingers. I can't wait for your cunt to strangle my cock when I'm finally inside you again."

"Finally? It's been a few days." But even as she said it, she knew exactly what he meant.

"Days? Fuck, Naomi, every second I'm not buried inside you feels like an eternity."

That did it. She moaned and her body writhed in the water as she came on his fingers, shuddering and tensing with each wave of her orgasm, making literal waves around them. Wes's fingers never stopped teasing her inside, nor did he stop pinching her nipples as she tumbled into pleasure, until she finally relaxed against him.

He kissed her cheek and whispered into her ear.

"Want to make up for lost time?"

CHAPTER FORTY-FIVE

Having Naomi Ward come in his arms was a religious experience. He slowly removed his fingers after letting her ride out her orgasm. Every time she ground her ass against his cock, he had to grit his teeth against his own pleasure, making sure he didn't come too soon. He'd had a hard as fuck day and he couldn't think of a better way to celebrate not getting blown the fuck up than by making love to the woman of his dreams.

He kissed her neck again softly, pausing when she whispered.

"I want you to take me to bed."

Wes groaned against her neck and helped them both up from the tub. He let her get out first and when he exited the tub, he picked up one of the soft, fluffy towels on the counter. He gave it to Naomi before wrapping one around his waist and sitting on the wide lip of the tub. It was a surprisingly comfortable spot, except for the raging hard-on tenting the towel, especially as he watched Naomi dab the towel against her body, drying the water droplets trailing down.

"Come here." He grabbed her hand, not giving her much choice as he pulled her body to him. Her giggle cut off into a moan when he dove to lick one of the droplets, falling dangerously close to her trimmed patch of curls at the apex of her legs.

"I've never been jealous of water before." He chuckled against her lower belly before tonguing up her torso, his eyes on her fiery brown ones as he did. "How it gets to slide along your curves, never coming up for air."

She smiled and bent to kiss him. "You could do that too... if you wanted, ya know."

Suddenly, it wasn't enough for her to be standing in front of him. His towel fell to the floor as he scooped his hands behind her thighs so quickly, she yelped out a laugh. He placed her on top of his bare lap, helping her straddle his waist and leaving her legs to dangle back into the water with a splash.

He went straight for her lips while he wrapped her arms around his neck. Her pussy was slick with arousal while she pressed against the base of his cock and goddamn, it was driving him crazy. Their kiss was just as wet and passionate, full of lips, tongues, and teeth. He cradled the back of her head so he could suck her bottom lip into his and used his other hand to palm her ass, sliding her against his cock as it stood straight up against his belly button.

She reached past him and dunked her hand into the water before she sat back up and wrapped her hand around his length. She squeezed and used the water to pump him up and down.

"Fuck, Naomi," he groaned and moved his hands to her hips, continuing to grind the base of his cock into her heat.

A tingling sensation began at the bottom of his spine and his cock jumped, threatening to explode. He groaned and broke away from the kiss before he came *way* too goddamn quickly.

"Condom?" she asked, her voice almost a hesitation as if she was afraid to know his answer. "I-I have an IUD, but nothing's ever one hundred percent—"

He felt himself smile. Like protecting her and easing her worries wasn't all he ever thought about. "Would you hate me if I said I kind of came prepared?"

"Oh, thank God." Naomi laughed against his lips and met his forehead with hers. "I would expect nothing less. I just wasn't sure I had it in me to be responsible." Even as she said it, she ground against his cock and he had to clench his jaw to keep from encouraging her further.

Instead, he shook his head. "As much as I want to go bare with you, love, I'll always consider your safety and peace of mind first."

He searched for his pants, thankfully within reach from his perch, and Naomi leaned with him as he retrieved a condom from a pocket. Before he could put it on, Naomi dove in to kiss him again, and he got caught up in her mouth on his. She pumped his shaft again, pulling a groan from deep within him as his balls tightened with the need to come. He let her go on as long as he could take, but finally the pleasure was too damn much to hold back. Grabbing a fistful of wet hair, he tugged her away from his lips with every inch of his willpower.

"I want to sink inside your pussy more than I want my next breath right now. If we don't get that condom on, I'm going to drown my cock in your bare cunt and not apologize for it."

"Mmm... I do hate apologies," she whispered and shifted her hips. Before they tested his restraint any further, she took the packet from his hands and unwrapped it with a grin.

She watched with a look of excitement that went straight to his ego as she rolled the tip over his thick length. Once it was all the way on, she rested her hands on his shoulders and tried to lift herself up without any luck. Her feet didn't have any purchase while they dangled over the tub.

"I got you..." Even to his own ears, his voice was rough with desire and he felt her shiver against him. He palmed her ass with both hands and lifted her curvy body straight up in the air, using his biceps and back.

"Oh shit," her whisper sent all his blood rushing into his shaft as he positioned her over the tip of his cock.

He helped guide her down slowly. Inch by agonizingly teasing inch, he lowered her onto his cock until they both moaned. Her pussy gripped him like a vise and he had to breathe through the threat of an orgasm.

She seemed to be taking a settling breath too, and Wes waited for any body language that would show she was ready. But he couldn't resist touching her. He kissed each cheek, her forehead, and then her cute, perky nose, loving the fullness brimming in his chest. Finally, he claimed her lips, using his tongue to get her to open for him. As they kissed slowly, he positioned both hands on her hips and began to move her body at the same rhythm, grinding her clit against him and angling his cock to make sure he hit the nerves connected inside too.

"Damn, Wes, I'm so full..." she whispered it with a shudder, almost as if she didn't mean to say it and he couldn't help but smile against her lips. He quickened their pace, loving the way her body tensed and squeezed around him with another impending orgasm. She felt so fucking good riding his cock, but the way they were positioned was all for her. He couldn't wait to have her underneath him so he could push into her at the speed that would bring them both to the brink of sex-drunk insanity.

He began to feel the burn in his biceps as he helped her body ride him, but he knew she was close. Her breaths came in pants until finally she released his name on a low moan as she came a second time. Her pussy squeezed his cock, and he gritted his teeth to keep from coming too.

As soon as her pussy calmed around him, she repeated his name like a prayer, and he grinned at the emotion behind it. He stood up, keeping himself inside her as he took them to the king-size bed. As carefully as he could while still connected, he laid her out on top of the quilt and covered her body with his before pumping slowly in and out.

He pushed her hands above her head, intertwining his fingers with hers as he dove in to kiss her, mimicking with his tongue their steady pace.

He lifted from their kiss and squeezed her hands three times, analyzing her expression as she widened her eyes a fraction and relaxing them into an emotion he couldn't quite place.

"What does that mean, Naomi?" he asked, having a pretty good idea already. "You and Thea both do it."

Naomi gasped. "Thea does it for you, too?"

He nodded and noticed her eyes well up. His heart almost cracked with guilt for making her upset until she said the words that immediately patched it all together.

"It means... it means I love you."

Wes closed his eyes and released a breath, resting his forehead on hers as he paused his thrusts. "I thought so. And damn am I glad I was right." He squeezed her hands four times before kissing her. "I love you, too."

He increased his pace, but didn't go harder. There was no need to pound in and out of her. Hell, he already felt like he was reaching the end of her every time he completely sheathed his cock, and he didn't want to hurt her. She let out a guttural moan and started whispering his name again.

"Wes, yes, shit, yes. Please, just like that." She continued to whisper nonsensical encouragement back at him as he kept his good hand in both of hers and lowered his other to her knee. He raised it to bend so he could dip deep inside her and curve up to gently massage her cervix with his tip.

She moaned his name, telling him he was on the right track and he kept consistent pressure as he ground into her. With each push, he had to hold back the urge to spill before she came again. It wasn't until her nails dug into his shoulders and her pussy started fluttering around him that he began to let loose.

"Fuck, Wes, I'm gonna—" She never finished her thought as she came on a groan that sent his cock spasming inside her. His movements grew inconsistent as he moaned her name and on one final thrust, he spilled inside her.

He kissed her forehead, her cheeks, her nose, and her lips, repeating how they'd begun before hugging her close and flipping them. He knew he needed to get rid of the condom, to clean her up, but as soon as he tried to separate from her, she tightened her hold and laid her head on his chest. His hand found the back of her head and he kissed the crown, reveling in her sweet scent. Vanilla now mixed with green apple made his mouth water and somehow his already spent cock twitched. He groaned against her damp hair and she chuckled against his chest before stilling and looking up at him.

Her firelight eyes burned as her brow furrowed and she worried her lip.

He tilted his head against the pillow to analyze her. "That expression..." He brushed her cheek with the back of his hand and she turned into it. "What're you thinking, love?"

"I'm... I'm afraid you're not real. All this... it feels too good to be true." She pointed around the room, eventually landing on the wall connecting the bathroom before looking back at him. "And I don't know what I would've done without you these past few months. Would I have stayed with that monster?" She shuddered. "Hell, would I even be alive to ask that question? I mean... fairy tales aren't real, but here you go, making me feel like a princess and you're the white knight who's saved me."

He grinned and craned his neck for a kiss. His lips left hers too soon, but when he looked into her eyes again, the sincerity in his gaze promised a lifetime of moments just like this one.

"Except you never needed a white knight," he answered with a brush of his thumb against her cheek. "You're the queen in this story, and you've saved yourself over and over again." He kissed her one more time and whispered against her lips. "Now you just get to finally enjoy your happy ever after."

CHAPTER FORTY-SIX

"Fuck."

Soft hands caressed over Wes's shoulders and he leaned back into his chair and Naomi's embrace.

"What's wrong?" her voice whispered beside him as she bent to his ear. He lifted his hand to massage his eyes before he remembered he was wearing his contacts and diverted to his hair.

"This program is being difficult." He sighed and threw his hand up at the wide screen television he'd revamped to be his computer screen in the cabin. "I'm trying to open up the security for BlackStone yesterday, but it keeps fizzing out. I've tried almost every camera and they all show nothing out of the ordinary, but this one right here—" He pointed at the top right screen that showed a distorted and pixelated view of the outside of the BlackStone facility outside of the war room. "Is being a pain in the ass."

"Do you think you'll be able to fix it?" Hawk asked, his arms crossed off to the side as he paced. The man was a solid rock, but after the ordeal they'd all been through the day before, arriving back at the cabin without a wink of sleep, and with Phoenix and Ascot missing, their leader was off his game.

Naomi grunted before standing back up and rounding the couch to sit beside him. Thea's little voice repeating every word to Brave was a soft undercurrent in the living room that helped calm his nerves. He'd been preoccupied all morning with the programming, but Naomi had taken care of everyone by cooking breakfast for all of them. Thea was now happily in her own world, or Pixar's version of medieval Scotland, as it were, like she wasn't almost a casualty to a bomb yesterday.

"I've almost got..." He entered a few more keystrokes, ignoring the throbbing in his palm. "Got it! Yes!" Finally, the screen enlarged and settled onto a complete picture and Wes slapped his hands and immediately cursed at the pain. Naomi tensed beside him and threw her hand up to her heart.

"Shit, sorry, love."

"Wes, you can't say bad words." Thea spoke out, almost in a monotone.

"They hear everything, don't they?" Wes asked under his breath and Naomi chuckled.

"You have no idea." She turned to her daughter. "Thea, baby, go to your room, okay?"

The little girl sighed before picking her bear and her iPad up and taking them to her room.

"Close the door, T."

There was another insufferable sigh and the door closed. Wes smirked at the dramatics and huffed a laugh when Naomi rolled her eyes.

"What's that?" Hawk asked, completely ignoring them as he pointed over their heads at the screen.

Wes drew his attention back to the screen to see the picture still on the fritz, but at least they could see the large black van almost off the corner of the screen.

Wes resisted cursing under his breath and enlarged the picture further, only for a fire to explode on the screen. Naomi jumped back, as if the flames from the day before would reach out to grab her.

"*That* is what y'all went through? Oh my god, my baby..." Her voice trailed off and a tear leaked from her eye as she looked back at Thea's closed door.

Wes grabbed her thigh and squeezed three times, hoping it'd calm her jumpiness. She locked her arm in his and returned the gesture four times. He wanted to revel in the feeling, but someone exited the van on the screen, drawing his attention to the fuzzy picture to try to make it out.

"Is that..." Hawk asked.

"That Russian bastard, Vlad? I think so."

"Who's that?"

They didn't answer her, both in rapt horror as they watched the guy enter the hole created by the bomb in the building.

"He must've been in there right as Thea and I got out." His revelation had Naomi gasping and tightening her grip on him.

They watched in silence and rapt attention for several moments before someone else appeared on the screen. This time, all three of them cursed as Ascot came bumbling out of the wreckage with his hands cuffed behind his back.

"So they were after Ascot all along?" Naomi asked.

"Seems that way," Hawk answered as someone out of the frame pushed Ascot forward to the back of the van.

The frame went fuzzy again and Wes returned to his keyboard to see if he could fix it.

"How did Vlad get him out? He was handcuffed and taped to the chair. The only way they could've gotten him out is if they had a key and we were the only ones who have a copy."

Just as he said it, the screen cleared just enough to see another figure enter the screen, sending Wes's emotions haywire. No one said a word as Vlad followed behind Ascot... with someone at his side. No... not someone.

Phoenix.

"Son of a *bitch*." Wes slapped the table but kept his eyes on the screen.

Phoenix and Vlad stopped, seemingly having a conversation

before the camera footage warped again. Wes cursed and typed furiously until they could see Phoenix open the van's back doors and help Ascot inside. When he closed the door, he nodded and said something to Vlad again, before looking at the building and then going to the passenger side of the van. The picture was so poor it was hard to make out anything, but Wes could definitely see Vlad follow Phoenix to the passenger door and open it for him.

Before Phoenix got in, he looked up at the camera and his lips started moving.

"What's he saying?" Hawk asked as they all leaned in collectively.

"I think it's... I think he's saying, 'I'm sorry,'" Wes answered.

Phoenix shook his head, his lips now in a grim line, before half his body went off the screen to get into the van. Vlad's big figure closed the door and disappeared. After another moment, the van revved up and drove off.

Wes immediately went to look up the BlackStone facility's entry code access. When he saw the last name on the list, he shut his eyes and rubbed his face.

"It was Phoenix. It was all Phoenix, man. *Fuck*."

"What do you mean?" Hawk asked.

"See this—" Wes pointed to the screen. "Phoenix got home late last night, but his code was used to get in this morning just before the bomb. That's how they got in undetected. They used his damn code and then he left with them. He's been in on this shit the whole time."

Hawk shook his head slowly before scrubbing his fade and bringing it down to swipe his face. "That doesn't make any sense. He's our teammate and brother. There's no fucking way he'd be in on human trafficking. We spent years eradicating that evil *together*. He wouldn't do this."

Wes shook his head, almost unable to believe it himself, but it made sense.

"Fuck, Hawk, I would've thought so too, but think about it.

He didn't use his headpiece and was MIA when we went to save Ellie, Nora, and the other kidnapping victims last year. What was he doing in the meantime?"

"That's different—"

"And shit, when you guys were taking down the traffickers two weeks ago at the hotel, when you and Devil went with Phoenix to save those victims. Didn't he knock his guy out? Making it impossible for you guys to question him?"

"There was another one, too—"

"Maybe that one didn't know Phoenix, but the guy Phoenix took down did." Hawk was scrambling for answers, but Wes felt like he'd already solved the riddle and it made his stomach churn from the betrayal. "He's been getting drunk and going to the strip club nearly every night. No doubt he's depressed, but maybe that's because he's *guilty*. He knew where Ascot was going to be and when. He refused to interrogate him with us. Man, I'm telling you... this all fucking adds up."

Hawk tapped his finger against his lips in thought and his brow furrowed above his dark eyes. Finally, he shook his head.

"It might all add up, but none of it *makes sense*. Something's going on. I can't believe he'd betray us like this. Not after all the women we saved."

An anvil dropped in Wes's stomach as he remembered what he needed to tell Hawk. "Actually, man. I'm not sure we saved a damn soul."

Hawk's eyes widened and he stilled before he directed his strong gaze on Wes. After allowing Wes a moment to gather his confession, Hawk seemed not to want to wait any longer. "Speak."

Wes shook his head, defeat making his shoulders sag as he confronted his teammate, one of the most dedicated team members and leaders Wes had ever had.

"The Rahab Foundation. Ascot wasn't lying. It's a sham. I'm afraid every single one of those women we saved was put through that foundation and sent right back out into trafficking.

I've looked everywhere for them, but they were conveniently disbanded the same day we were attacked in Yemen. Everything about them was scrubbed from history after that—"

"Like we were." Hawk's deep voice was hard as the pieces obviously clicked together in his mind.

Their team at MF7 had been psychologically discharged after their disastrous attack in Yemen, and after that, MF7 wasn't classified, it was completely erased from government books. Like the seven years of their lives that they'd toiled and put on the line to save others was for nothing. Or worse.

"Every single one of the women was re-trafficked?" Hawk asked, stuttering back a fraction before his hand found purchase on the back of the couch. "All of them?"

Wes felt his lips thin. "I'm not sure. Too many, even if not all. I've been working with Marco on the information that Investigator Burgess collected over the last year. I've accounted for nearly all of the women, cross-referenced them with the lists I was able to find from my personal database concerning MF7. Only a handful were unaccounted for."

"What does a 'handful,' mean?"

Wes clicked through the screens and pulled up the very short list he'd compiled after all his research. "These names sounded familiar, but I wasn't sure why. I'd downloaded the MF7 database before we were discharged, so I checked the names against that. These three were 'attendees' at the fundraiser the year before we were discharged, and all three of them were women we'd previously saved from trafficking who had seemingly tried to get their life back."

"So some women were helped with the Rahab Foundation."

Wes grimaced and for the first time, he registered Naomi's hand on his thigh. He looked at the concern written all over her face before he answered. "None of the women were ultimately saved, I don't think. While some of the women saved by us were immediately trafficked again thanks to the foundation, others seem like they were given a second chance, only to be pulled

back in. That's my working theory, anyway. But these three—"
He pointed at the screen. "I can't account for them. They
might've actually been helped by the Rahab Foundation, but I
don't know what happened after this party, or whether they even
attended."

"So they could be safe... or they could be..." He didn't finish,
and his Adam's apple bobbed in his neck. Wes nodded to the
unspoken question and Hawk cleared his throat before jutting
his chin to the screen. "We need to figure out what happened to
them. That's our next priority. And this woman—" He pointed
to the screen. "What happened to her?"

Wes shook his head and blew out a harsh breath. "I honestly
don't know. She's the only one I have absolutely zero information on."

Hawk turned his head and something flashed in his eyes that
Wes couldn't identify before they closed again. His leader
seemed to stare off unseeing before taking a steadying breath.

"We need to understand what happened to these women. I
won't let another day go by without us putting one hundred and
ten percent behind finding them and making sure they don't
need our help. Got it?"

Wes nodded.

"Good." He scrubbed his fade again and turned away from
them.

"You okay, Hawk?" Wes asked, he'd never seen the man look
so rattled, but he could understand where he was coming from.
Wes had basically just told him their life's work had hurt count-
less people and there were still those out there possibly suffering.

He shook his head slowly. When he spoke, his voice was
thick with emotion. "I-I just need a minute. Can you call the
others? Give them the CliffsNotes version?"

Wes nodded. "Of course—"

Hawk left the room before Wes could finish his sentence and
he finally gave Naomi his full attention.

"This is insane, Wes..."

Wes nodded. "Yep, but we'll figure it out." He hadn't said what he'd been thinking, that maybe Phoenix had been in on the entire operation, Rahab Foundation, re-trafficking the women, Yemen, maybe even Eagle's death. That was too much to come to terms with after just figuring out everything else.

Naomi leaned against his shoulder and he soaked in the calmness her presence gave him. His previous life's purpose may have been tainted, turned and twisted into something awful that he couldn't—think about, but his purpose now? Thea and Naomi. Ever since he'd met them both, they'd captured his heart. He would do everything in his power to make sure his queen and her princess were safe in their kingdom. They hadn't needed a white knight, but their happy ever after was now his top priority.

"I love you," he whispered and kissed her head. Naomi lifted hers to face him with a small smile.

"I love you, too." Her brow crinkled with worry. "It's just Thea. We just got out of my relationship with her father. Then all that mess with him. She's been through so much..."

"I know it's soon," he began. "But... I'm in this. All in. I know having a kid changes perspective, but you don't have to worry about Thea with me. Everything we've done has always been on your speed, love. I'm not going anywhere until you kick me to the curb."

She laughed. "I don't see that ever happenin'."

He grinned back at her, letting the words soak in the air.

"Good." He leaned in and kissed her, loving the way she melted against him. He had so much to do, but being in this moment with her was exactly where he needed to be.

His back pocket vibrated and he groaned. Despite the fact that all he wanted to do was take Naomi and make love to her like they had the night before, bombs had been dropped, metaphorically and physically. Whoever was calling had to be important.

"One second and then these lips are mine," he whispered

before pulling at her bottom lip with his thumb. She blushed before he pulled his phone from his pocket and frowned.

"What is it?" Naomi asked, immediately seeming to sense the change.

"It's Nora..." He slid the green button over to answer. "Hey Nora, what's—"

"Superman! Oh thank God, no one's answering the phone—" Her words were coming at a mile a minute. "I'm at the hospital—"

"Is Jules okay?" Wes interrupted.

"Yes, she's fine, well, I mean. Babs is in labor but—"

"Jules is in labor?" he asked. "Does Ellie know?"

"Ugh, yes, I'm sure she does, but that's not why I'm calling—"

"Okay, why are you calling?"

"Will you freaking listen to me? It's Drake!"

"Draco?" Wes's stomach leadened as he used his teammate's call sign. "I know the doctor said it was..." He swallowed, remembering what the doctor told the team his suggestion was.

There was a choked sob on the other line and Wes felt his lips go numb as he asked the question he didn't want the answer to.

"Do we need to come... say goodbye?"

"No... no," Nora answered and seemed to take a steadying breath. "He's awake."

EPILOGUE

One month later

"But I'm not *tired,* Mommy. It's not fair you and Wes get to stay up and go dancin'."

Naomi resisted rolling her eyes, not wanting to teach her daughter a new bad habit. "Baby, Wes was just kiddin'." She whipped her head back to Wes and narrowed her eyes with a grin at his mischievous smile. "We're not gonna go dancin'. We're gonna stay inside and be borin' old adults, okay?"

"We *always* stay inside. But Wes and Hawk get to go outside all the times. It's not fair."

Naomi blew out a breath, not sure of exactly what to say, because her little girl was right. Ever since they realized their safe houses were compromised thanks to Phoenix's betrayal, the BlackStone men had taken significant security measures to protect their makeshift home for Wes, Naomi, and Thea to stay.

It was a luxury cabin in the middle of the woods on Mount Ash, an hour outside of town, and completely hidden to everyone but the BlackStone Crew. Which was the problem now that Phoenix had flipped. But it was still one of the safest places BlackStone already had on short notice, so modifying it was the best option.

Unfortunately, that meant that Naomi and Thea were essentially cooped up all day until Wes felt like it was safe enough for them to go outside.

"T, we'll get to go explorin' all over the mountain soon, I promise. I know you wanna go outside but just be patient a little while longer, okay? It's not safe yet."

Wes swore up and down that it wouldn't be too long now until she and Thea could explore the many acres of land the cabin sat on, even promising they could venture off Mount Ash soon. It was frustrating, but it was also the reality of their situation at the moment. She couldn't blame the guy for being over-protective. Hell, she was too.

Thea sighed and threw her head back onto her comically large, king-size pillow. "*Fine*. But I get one more story in y'all's bed for bein' good."

Naomi snorted. "T, we already read you a bedtime story and it's time for you to go to sleep now, okay? Remember how Ms. Erica said you need to get good sleep by yourself in your big-girl bed? I can't wait to tell Ms. Erica how good you've been at it."

And she really couldn't. Ms. Erica was Thea's new thera-pist. As soon as she safely could, she'd called every child thera-pist in Ashland County that Wes vetted to see if they'd do on-screen appointments. The woman was amazing. Hopefully, getting Thea in to talk with someone early would stave off any potential harm her father and the past year had done to her psyche.

"But I'm not *tired*," she grumbled into a very ironically timed yawn.

"Princesses need good sleep so they can rule their kingdoms, T." Wes leaned in conspiratorially, as if he were her royal adviser.

Thea pursed her lips and seemed to think about what he said. "Okay... then how 'bout I go to sleep if we watch one more movie."

Naomi laughed out loud. "That's enough negotiating tonight, my little CEO. I'm kissin' you good night and then I'm leavin' you to sleep like the big girl you are, okay?"

"*Fine*," she exclaimed yet again before crossing her arms and frowning. "But I won't like it."

Naomi kissed her defiant daughter's forehead before standing up to leave the room. It was basically Thea's now. It had been every night since they'd had to flee BlackStone.

"Good night, Thea."

"Good night, Mommy. Good night Wes."

"Good night, Princess T," Wes whispered before turning out the lights and letting Naomi leave the room first.

Naomi rested against the wall beside the closed door and massaged her temples.

"Dancin'? Really? You couldn't have said something less fun for a four-year-old?"

Wes chuckled and rested his hands on her hips, drawing her in close enough that she could smell his soothing citrus-cedar scent. It now reminded her of home.

He kissed her lips and she melted into his touch. "Well, I couldn't tell her what I *wanted* to do, now could I? Definitely couldn't lie. It was the best I could come up with on the spot."

She pulled on his shirt before tugging him toward their room. "Yes, thank God you didn't go with the truth."

They had the place to themselves. Everyone but Hawk had maintained their sleeping arrangements they'd had since the night BlackStone was bombed. Hawk had apparently gotten an apartment in town. At first she'd felt guilty that they'd run him off, but Wes had assured her that Hawk had always liked to keep to himself.

Hawk had Devil as a houseguest sometimes, but mostly Devil stayed with Ellie in her large dorm suite. Jules and Jason had their hands full with their brand-new baby girl, who was already proving sassier than her momma. And Nora stayed at Jules and Jason's, helping with the baby, and going back and forth from Sasha Saves to Draco's bedside at the hospital. The Black-Stone teammate had only just started to recover from his coma, but he was trying hard as hell to get back on his feet.

Even though they were alone, it was never very wise to get frisky out in the open with a four-year-old in the house. When they got to their room, Wes picked her up and carried her bridal style through the door. Naomi held on to her giggles, trying to make sure Thea didn't hear how much fun they were having, so she'd stay in bed.

Wes laid her out on the quilt and Naomi grabbed his shirt collar to pull him on top of her, kissing him with fervor. Wes broke away and stroked her dark auburn hair back before locking his icy blue eyes onto hers. All she wanted in the moment was to tell him how she felt.

"You've changed my life, you know."

He chuckled and gave her a peck. "You've changed mine too, you know."

"No. I mean..." she sighed, unsure if she'd ever be able to fully show this man how appreciative she was that he'd always been her champion. "I *love* my life right now. I love helping you find those missing women and I love working at Sasha Saves, even if it is remotely right now." She gave him a teasing, pointed look for his protectiveness.

"I mean, can you blame me on that one? I've got an ex-team-mate that's working with the enemy-at-large and you've got an ex that was just let out of jail on a GPS ankle monitor and God knows who was rich and powerful enough to convince the judge to let him go in the first place, let alone pay his bail. It's safer if you've got backup and we don't know who we can trust these days."

His eyes shadowed with pain as he spoke and Naomi's heart clenched. She knew Phoenix's betrayal had wounded him to his core.

"I don't blame you. I get it." She blew out a breath and rubbed his arms. He hooked his arms underneath her back and rolled them so she straddled him. She grabbed his hands and held them. "I love how safe I feel for the first time in my life. Just... thank you."

He tilted his head. "For what?"

"I don't know if I'd have had the courage to leave Dean, if I didn't have you. To *prosecute* Dean if I didn't have you as my rock to lean on."

The day Dean had organized the bombing and tricked Naomi and Nora, he'd been arrested for violating a protection order at first. Police were trying to compile a case to charge everyone involved with bombing BlackStone, but neither she nor none of the BlackStone Crew were holding their breath.

Jules had explained the process and it'd take a *while* before anything in the legal system actually came to fruition. But she wasn't changing her mind. Naomi was going to make sure he finally was held responsible for his actions, stayed the fuck away from her, and got the help he needed. Even if it was court mandated.

"I probably would've put up with everything he did to me if you hadn't come along. Maybe even until I couldn't anymore."

Wes's eyes searched hers. "You helped me, too."

"Really?"

"Yeah. I thought I was a monster before you. I've gone to therapy off and on for years. Afraid that what had happened to my mom had damaged me. I was scared that one day my switch would flip and everyone around me would be in danger. But I realized when you stopped me from going too far with Dean that I could stop. That I would never hurt you, no matter how angry I got."

She nodded. "I'm never in danger with you."

He smiled and she felt the warmth down to her core as he spoke. "Never."

She bit her lip, finally mustering up the courage to tell him exactly how she felt. "I know what I feel is crazy. We've only even known each other for a few months and I was with another man for part of that. But you said a month ago that you were 'all in' with me. Well... I'm all in with you too, Wes. And everything that means."

"Yeah?" he asked, and the boyish grin on his face made her heart light with emotion.

"Yeah." She leaned over to kiss him and got lost in his lips before she whispered. "I'm all in." She'd forgotten his hands were still in her grip until he squeezed them three times. She squeezed them back four.

I love you.

I love you, too.

MEANWHILE

The pounding on the door would've made a lesser man jump, but he had no time for fear. Instead, he rolled his shoulders and sat straighter, careful not to look at Vlad or show any weakness. Waiting a few seconds before responding.

It was a power play, but he'd come to learn power—or the illusion of it, at least—was all that was expected of a man in his position.

And he played to kill to make sure everyone knew he had it.

"Come in."

Two men entered the room. One with dirty blond hair, lightly tanned skin, and no idea how out of his league he was. He didn't give a shit about Dean Jones, though. The coward was lucky to have a man like him on his side, let alone a bankroll that got him out of jail. But it was always good to have people that *knew* people in his pocket. He could be persuasive when he wanted to be. The second man was living proof of that.

"Phoenix, you've been causing quite a stir since you arrived. I hear you wanted to see me."

"Sir." The man didn't answer further and his face was carefully blank, just like he'd been taught. You don't become the best of the best without a poker face. "It's been a long time."

"It has," he conceded, leaning back in his chair and assessing the former soldier. "You've been playing house with that security firm for long enough. I thought I'd pull you in."

Phoenix said nothing, not that he expected a response. Why had he asked for a meeting if he wasn't going to talk? What was his endgame here?

"Are you comfortable?"

A slight *tic* in Phoenix's unshaven jaw was his only tell. Still a weakness. He'd grown soft.

"Perfectly."

He grunted and moved on to the newest recruit. "And you, Jones. I trust your accommodations are better than the cell we liberated you from?"

"Um..." Dean Jones looked around the room as if the answer would spring out to bite him. "Y-yes, sir. Thank you for posting my bail."

"It was a pleasure, I'm sure. I always do love solidifying business relationships. But remember, you went behind my back when you hid Ascot from me. You're lucky I'm keeping you alive, let alone bailing you out of jail." He leaned up and placed his elbows on his desk, the mahogany one he loved so much. The one at his office made him itch at its poor quality. "The reason why I called you here is because, as both of you know, we've gotten rid of Ascot. He was our final loose end in that ridiculous society we worked with, and I abhor loose ends."

Neither man spoke, which irritated him, but he didn't let that show.

"Both of you have... *attachments* on the outside. I wanted you to know that you won't have to worry about them for much longer."

Phoenix's face remained frustratingly placid, but Jones's eyes widened.

"Sir? B-but my kid? And my fiancée—"

"From what I understand, she's in bed with one of the Black-Stone boys. Honestly, I'm surprised you're objecting to her getting her due. The disrespect she's shown you." He tsked, shaking his head. "She had to have known how whoring herself out to AIE Securities' number one competitor would make you look." Jones's mouth slammed shut. "Do you know how it makes you look, Jones?"

Jones's face turned bright red. "Yes, sir."

"Tell me, Jones."

The spineless man's fists tightened. "Like a goddamn fool."

"Precisely. Now Vlad, here, knows his orders. The *BlackStone* boys have gotten too comfortable in their arrogance. I don't want them to just be taken down a notch. I want them to be wiped off the map. I've given them too many chances thus far, and I've spared their lives already. Well... most of them."

Another *tic* in Phoenix's jaw and it made him nearly giddy with pleasure. It was always so much fun to get underneath a subordinate's skin.

"Anyway. That'll be all. Thank you very much for your cooperation." Before he went back to writing his order, he glanced at both men's expressions. One confused, the other stoic again. He tried not to show his disappointment, but when they finally turned to the door, he called out, unable to keep from poking the bear further. "See that he gets back to his quarters safely."

Phoenix's shoulders tensed, but the men kept walking. When the door had closed, he continued signing off on the order, ramping up protection on one of his charges. She was becoming more of a nuisance, but he knew she'd come in handy soon. He just had to bide his time. After a few more strokes of his pen, he registered the Russian's dark stare boring into his head from the giant's corner. "What is it, Vlad?"

"Why do you tell them your plan?"

He chuckled under his breath, but never looked up. It was important that even his right-hand man was never comfortable enough to feel like questioning his leadership was appropriate, but he was satisfied with the game he'd just played.

"Torture comes in many forms, Vlad. Mental and physical to

oneself is one. The promise of the same to others is another. It was time they were reminded of who is in charge."

"You do not think they know you are the boss?"

Anger welled within him at the question. The Russian was a brute, but he sure as fuck was no idiot and he saw way too much.

"Of course they know I'm in charge, you imbecile. But now they are aware that others will know it soon, too. It will ensure future compliance."

"*Da, ser.*"

Placated, he slowly went back to his paperwork before continuing. "You did well, with those rich assholes, Vlad, and securing Ascot."

"It is easy when you have someone on the inside."

"Indeed." He chuckled before sobering. "Although you will have to step up your game. From what we... *coerced* from Ascot and from what that idiot investigator found out, BlackStone knows more than we want them to. You'll have to make sure to take them down quickly, but discreetly. It sounds like they're going to start snooping around. See to it that they don't find who they're looking for."

"*Da, ser.* I understand."

～

Keep reading for a sneak peek of Healing Conviction!

ALSO BY GREER RIVERS

<u>Conviction Series</u>

Escaping Conviction

Fighting Conviction

Breaking Conviction

Healing Conviction - Releasing December 16, 2021

Title TBA - Releasing Spring 2022

<u>Ashland County Legal Short Stories</u>

A Tempting Motion: An enemies-to-lovers, office romance

Thank you for reading! Please consider leaving a review on Amazon, Goodreads, and Bookbub!

Just one word can make all the difference.

A Second Chance Romantic Suspense

Jason

I'm not letting her go after this.

I left the love of my life when she needed me most. I thought I was saving the world, but instead I lost everything.

Now I need *her*.

My sister is missing and I'm suspect #1. Without Jules as my defense attorney, I would be locked in a cell instead of trying to save my sister. Once I find Ellie, I'm never letting either of them out of my sight.

There's no way I'm making that mistake again.

Jules

He's just like every other client.

The man I thought was the love of my life, ghosted me when I needed him most. I'd like to say he was the one that got away. But no. He's the bullet I dodged.

Now he needs *me*.

His sister is missing and he's being charged with her kidnapping. He thinks we can mend what he broke. But I can't trust him.

There's no way I'm making that mistake again.

Read Escaping Conviction on Amazon or FREE on Kindle Unlimited!

A Brother's Best Friend, Age Gap Romantic Suspense

AN AMAZON TOP 100 BESTSELLER

#1 Best Seller Vigilante Justice

#1 Best Seller Love & Romance

#1 Best Seller Action & Adventure Romance Fiction

Devil

They call me Devil.

But I'm haunted by the deaths I've caused.

That's why I've hidden who I am.

A *failure*.

I control everything or I fight to block it out.

If I don't care, I don't lose.

But my defenses don't work on Ellie.

I saved her once. Now she's learning to save herself.

If only teaching her how didn't test my control.

She's my friend's sister.

Warm. Light. Innocent.

That's what I need to remember.

All I want is to fuel my angel's desire.

<u>Ellie</u>

He calls me angel.

But I'm no one's saving grace.

I hate what I am.

A *victim*.

I lost so much before Devil found me.

And I'm afraid of losing what's left.

But fear made me a coward.

He saved me then. Now he's teaching me to save myself.

If only he didn't make me lose control.

He's my brother's friend.

Cold. Dark. Forbidden.

That's what he wants me to think.

All I want is to feel Devil's burn.

Read Fighting Conviction on Amazon or FREE on Kindle Unlimited!

HEALING CONVICTION

Coming Winter 2021

PROLOGUE

Draco

Another right hook to his side knocked Draco's breath out of him. He'd never been so distracted in a fight. Paying attention to his attacker, this big Russian fucker, should've been his first priority. But he couldn't pull his focus away from the women being crushed on the ground mere feet away from him.

He was supposed to be protecting Nora. Instead, he was getting his ass handed to him because he'd been caught off guard, enthralled by the way her light purple hair looked silver in the moonlight. Then the giant's henchman came out of nowhere and attacked her. He'd shot that bastard in the head without another thought. Unfortunately he'd landed on top of Nora, and her petite figure didn't stand a chance against the dead weight on top of her.

Dodging another hit from the guy in front of him, Draco retaliated with an uppercut to the Russian's jaw.

"Nora, fucking... run."

Logically, he knew if she were able, she'd already have fled. But she had to be one hundred pounds soaking wet, and her five foot flat frame was struggling to get free.

Draco saw an opening while his opponent turned away from

him, and went for a one-two punch to his side. When he pulled back, he realized his mistake.

A sharp crack in the sky sent a blow to his side. The Russian may have left himself open for a hit, but Draco should've known the guy was too skilled a fighter to allow that kind of attack. It'd been a calculated move to whip the gun out from his holster and shoot.

The bullet hurt like hell, sending him to his knees, but Draco didn't think it'd hit anything vital, and the woman was still in danger.

"Nora... please... run."

He was desperate for her to listen, but she was still under that fat guy. Had Draco made a mistake killing him? He and his teammates at BlackStone Securities usually operated with tasers, but he'd seen the guy groping Nora, and he'd snapped, going for the kill instead of the stun-and-run.

The suited, blond guy the two Russians had been following around, stepped into Draco's view and Draco's heart raced more. Normally fighting off two guys was a practice round for him, but never after being shot.

Surprisingly, the rich guy tugged the guy pinning Nora, and slid him to the side. Nora grunted and finally was able to get up and relief coursed through him. Even though it was too late for him, she'd still be able to escape.

Just need a breath. Take a breath and get back into it. I can get out of this.

Except the Russian was still pointing his gun at his chest, and Draco was on his knees. There were few maneuvers that could get him out of that kind of tight spot. His hand drifted to his hip, forgetting for a moment that while he'd been distracted with Nora, the Russian was able to attack him swiftly enough that he'd lost his gun while they were grappling.

Nora's gasp drew his attention back to her.

"Nora... go. Run." His voice was hoarse and the words were a bitch to huff out. She stood frozen, and terror he'd never felt before, choked anything else he might've said. These men had to be part of the trafficking ring Draco and his crew were trying to bring down. What would happen to her if he couldn't protect her?

Why the fuck isn't she running?

The gorgeous green eyes he'd only seen over a video conference meeting were glossy under the lone street lamp in the parking lot. The gravel crunched under her high-heel combat boots as she stepped toward him, almost as if she was in a trance.

"Draco—"

"Nora, no!"

He shoved her away and she fell to the ground just as yet another bullet thumped into his chest. Horror flooded her pale face, made brighter by the silver in her purple curls. His arm stretched out, reaching to grab her, but he already knew he'd never be able to catch her hand.

This part always happened in slow-motion. He'd started questioning whether this was hell or not about a thousand replays ago. Was he being forced to forever relive the last moments of his memory in this sick version of purgatory? Was he being punished for failing to protect the woman who'd captivated him from the moment she'd made him laugh?

Draco had been trapped in this godforsaken loop. He'd brush her fingertips just as the Russian who'd shot him snatched her from the ground, stealing her away to God knows where. Then he'd fall, his face hitting painfully against the gravel, only to wake and relive the whole thing over again.

Even though he knew it was pointless, he still stretched his arm to hold onto her hand.

His arm ached as it came out of the socket, and the rest of his body collapsed. Sharp, small rocks cut into the palm of his left hand as he tried to catch himself, but the bullet wound on that side screamed in pain. The veins in his outstretched arm were about to burst at any moment with the tension.

Her already pale face was stark white with fear, sending another dagger-like pain to his chest. Whether she was terrified for herself, or him, he didn't know.

She was *this* close as she leaned into him, his fingers just a hair's breadth away. He knew it was going to be for nothing but he still couldn't resist giving everything he had to the moment.

Her nails grazed the pads of his fingers and all of a sudden he felt an unfamiliar surge of energy. It was unlike anything he'd experienced the many times he'd gone through this nightmare. A part of him laughed and told him he was falling for the illusion again. He should give up. The outcome would be the same anyway.

But the other part of him, the one that still had hope, the one that remembered smiling for the first time in ages because she'd called him handsome, the one that always stretched until his joints felt like they were going to pop. That part overrode all doubt and with a grunt from down deep in his soul, he gathered his final threads of energy and put his strength into enveloping her hand.

It hurt like hell, although he couldn't pinpoint where the pain was coming from, and fuck he didn't care not one goddamn bit when for the first time in any single memory, Nora's soft palm slid smoothly into his—

Abrasive, rhythmic beeping ached in his head, like a song that'd blared for too long and was somehow both background noise and jarring. Bright light beamed through his closed eyelids, so different from the lamps in the dark parking lot.

Heaviness weighed down his eyelids, but he continued to force them open.

He was in a hospital bed. The beeping was coming from a machine beside him. The bright lights blinding from the fluorescents above him.

And a small, dark-haired woman sitting in a chair beside him, was asleep on his blanketed legs.

He studied her for a moment, understanding creeping in as he took in her pixie-like features. She looked peaceful, but for the slight tension still in her brow, almost like even resting she couldn't relax. Her soft hand held his and his fingers twitched in hers before he squeezed. It took all his might, but his fingers still barely moved with the exertion. He kept trying though, needing to feel her hand in his, needing to grasp it and never let go.

Sweat prickled on his brow as every ounce of effort went into squeezing her hand, until he finally had a frustratingly weak grip. But her hand was still in his, and he'd fought an eternity to hold it.

The woman's eyes opened wide and she slowly raised up to a sitting position.

How long had he been out? He couldn't remember much since he'd been shot and they took her away. She was safe now though. That's all he'd cared about. Except, something was *off*.

Behind rose gold glasses, emerald green orbs stared back at him, slowly filling with moisture and her cute button nose sniffed. Nora opened her mouth to say something. Closed it. Opened. Closed. She seemed to settle for squeezing his hand and tucking her dark hair behind her ear with the other.

That's what it was. The dark shade highlighted the bags under her eyes and the worry in her face. Had she been by his bedside for long? Hours? Days? She looked like she hadn't slept in weeks.

This exhausted shell wasn't her. He hardly knew the woman, but he knew that much. The change in her hair seemed to alter her entire existence, and it gave him a cold chill down his spine to wonder what had made her make the drastic change. What had stolen her color?

His throat felt dry and his tongue was sandpaper against the roof of his mouth. He worked his mouth around words that were way too hard to get out. He couldn't get the old her out of his mind though, the silver-purple haired vixen with sky blue butterfly glasses and a smile. His addled mind couldn't help pointing out the obvious.

"Your hair's different."

~

Wanna read more? Pre-order Healing Conviction at pre-release day $2.99 price here!

ACKNOWLEDGMENTS

As always, I have a ton of shoutouts. My acknowledgements are crazy long and I make no apologies for that because I don't think we should ever apologize for being thankful. I was talking with someone just the other day about making sure I thank *everyone* I can for helping me release this baby into the wild. You obviously don't have to read this, but you can if you want to! Hell, you might even be in it. But the tl;dr version is: if I know you, I am thankful for you, more than you'll ever know.

First, and almost foremost (sorry, the hubs is always my #1), thank you READERS! The dream makers, the spicybooktokers, and the Boss Ass Bitches! I know your time is precious, so to have you spend it on something I wrote is a true damn honor. If you are also a booktoker/bookstagrammer/faithful reviewer, holy crap, let me just tell you that you make an author's world go 'round. Hanging out with y'all is why I do this and I love hearing from readers: good, bad, or ugly, although admittedly I'm always fingers-crossed for good. I'm truly so surprised every single time someone says something pretty about my words. I wouldn't be able to pursue this dream without y'all so thanks for making my dreams come true!

To Marisa at Cover Me Darling: Thank you so much for

putting up with me! I was a stressed out wreck and you held my hand while making a cover that was better than I could dream of!

Many thanks to Elle McLove, my editor at My Brother's Editor, and Rosa Sharon, the Fairy Proof Mother: Y'all are the freaking best and I'm so thankful to keep working with MBE. Elle, I'm so sorry... for the Oh Write punctuation that made my document have to have 9566 changes... I also apologize that I'll go to my grave not knowing whether it's rifle/riffle, wracked/rack, the Third/III, and further/farther... I truly appreciate your patience... even though I'm sure you want to beat me over the head with these needless ellipses in this paragraph. Lol, sorry girl, I had to poke fun at myself one more time. Rosa, it makes my damn life when you say you like something! As far as that very last comment goes, I'll tell you, you're onto something ;)

To BC's alpha and beta readers:

Lee J, Jessica, A.V., Kristen, Carrie, Ashleigh, Sierra, Whitney, Randi, Janet, Melissa, Jessica, Sara L., Amy.

This book would be an absolute disaster without y'all. Jessica, A.V., and Lee, we've been together since the beginning and I'm so grateful for each of you. Lee, as always your star sign shows in your comments and I love that you wear your heart on your sleeve, even when you read. A.V. I so appreciate your comments and that we're both on the same romantic suspense journey. I think just about every comment you've ever made I've followed through with and I'm super grateful you're helping make me a better writer. I'm so grateful for our friendship.

Thank you betas for telling me your pretty words and for those of you who shared your own personal stories. You have no idea how much that means to me that this book could help start those types of conversations. Changing a life for the better is all I could ever hope for with my books. I love you all and I'm so appreciative of my friendships we've developed.

Kristen and Whitney, y'all probably think this is all real

sappy and that's okay. Your sassy feedback and messages make my day and I'm so happy we're frandsssss!!

Carrie and Sierra, your constant support has truly made me choke up with tears at some points. Thank you for your encouragement, putting up with my delayed texting, and keeping me on my toes with writing.

Ashleigh, your specific feedback was exactly what I needed. Thank you so much for enduring me bugging you with questions and for being my friend.

Randi and Janet, thank you so much for checking in on me when I fell off the ends of the earth. You guys rock.

Melissa, Jessica, and Amy, thank you so much for taking the time to read and provide awesome feedback. I'm sorry I suck at emails and springing shit on you at the last minute.

Sara, you and I've been through it since the beginning too. I absolutely love that you give me the time to make it prettier before you get it because your feedback is *everything*. I'm so glad we're friends and that you're okay with me hermiting away in my writing cave half the time.

Moral of the story: I feel like I've made some great friends with all of you and that means everything.

Melissa, Sierra, and Carrie (again, lol): Thank you so much for your daily gifs and check-ins, always encouraging me, and being nice to me even when I'm being annoying and fishing for compliments. I cherish our friendships.

To my TikTok author friends: You have been encouraging as hell and also hilariously fun to get to know. Booktok is my people and I'm so glad I joined and met all you other thirsty bitches. This has been such an incredible journey and I am so very grateful to call y'all my friends! ORLANDO kicked ass and I CANNOT WAIT for NoLa!!!!! And hopefully Salem (fingers crossed).

To Lee J: You are the Cancer to my Scorpio and I swear every damn TikTok with us is exactly right. Thank you so much for loving me even though I'm your Simon Cowell alpha and even though we both fell off the face of the earth to write these books. I'm so proud to be your friend and I can't wait to see what happens next for us.

To Kayleigh: BISH. We have got to stop living on these damn deadlines. They are kicking our asses but I'm super grateful I can complain and rant and rave with you. I love that we're always on the opposite sides of the emotional roller coaster but we meet every time in the middle when we both just need someone to be mad with us. Only having one day for a real life visit was not enough, so we need to fix that pls. I'm excited for our shared Google Docs *eyes emoji* and Halloween.

To my OG BABs/Dinner Divas: Katie, Sydni, and Liz: YOU ARE THE BEST SECRET KEEPERS THAT EVER KEPT SECRETS. I seriously can't believe we made it like 9 months before someone found out. Y'all are seriously ride or dies and I'm so grateful for you. Thank you for throwing me book parties and drinking wine with me. I need it to happen forever please. I also love dancing with y'all at weddings. We should do more of those, *cough cough* *eye emoji* not looking at someone's significant other in particular of course.

Thank you, Katie, my bestie who always just gets me and knows when I'm gonna act like a crazy-person and cuts it off at the start. I love that we had the idea last year to always go out to eat every week. We've been busy as hell lately and slacked off, so let's be better about it so I can brag about how we see each other all the time in the next book, kay?

Thank you, Sydni, for being the bestie who gets real excited about the olives on my plate when someone accidentally talked about my book at dinner. I'm convinced you rock at literally everything and I'm so thankful that friendship is one of those things. When I was talking about weddings, I wasn't talking about anyone you know... *eyes emoji*... but if I *were* and when "it'll happen" happens, I promise to dance like a fool and we'll have the best time.

Thank you, Liz, for being the type of bestie who always

comes up with ideas and always invites me. The other day we were talking about how you're basically the driving force for our group *doing stuff*. I know that's probably a drag sometimes, but seriously, I love it so fucking much that you are always thinking about our friends and creative ways to hang out. I would probably never see y'all without you, and so I have you to thank for the strong group of ride or die bad bitches that I do. Y'all aren't allowed to leave me. I sent you a TikTok telling you, so you can't undo the friendship now. Sorry not sorry. P.S. I can't wait for autumn nights, mountain views, and good wine with y'all.

To my wonderful family, my momma, sisters, BIL, and precious baby angel face niece: if y'all ever read this, I'm sorry I've been MIA writing 110k word book in a month. In my defense, y'all know good and well I'm a "dilly dally" and you're deoxyribonucleicly obligated to still love me. May you always and forever be my oblivious supporters. I love y'all with all my heart but I mean it with all sincerity when I say please, for God's sake, do not read my books. If you are in these acknowledgements because you have indeed read a book or two, well, whoopsie, hope you enjoyed it, at least, lol. Keep your judgments, but I'll take your prayers. Lord knows I need them.

To Maria: I don't know what I'd do without you. The fact that you read my books is a testament to what a kickass therapist you are. I firmly believe that when everyone is born we should be assigned a therapist and I'm so grateful I lost my mind at the perfect time that I got to have you as mine.

To Athena, you crazy bitch.

And finally, to the hubs: You are my "Mighty Alpha," first reader, last reader, BUSINESS PARTNER, TikTok approver, cliff jump pusher/catcher, favorite encourager, IRL book boyfriend, best friend forever, and the love of my life. Thank you for "cobalt" and reading BC a million times. When you tell me pretty things, I listen, I swear. It fills me up and gives me the courage to do all the scary things in this writing world. I

CANNOT wait for January and BGP, and to just hang out while we take on the world together, even though I'll lowkey hate going to the gym at lunch. As always, I am so incredibly thankful for you believing in me 100% and encouraging me when it was crazy and not financially sound to do so. You've saved my life and you've changed it for the better. I wouldn't want to spend a moment of it without you and I'm super pumped to make that like almost 24/7 in a few months, God and TikTok willing. Thank you for making every day an HEA.

Love,

Greer Rivers

Greer Rivers is a former crime fighter in a suit, but now happily leaves that to her characters! A born and raised Carolinian, Greer says "y'all," the occasional "bless your heart" (when necessary), and feels comfortable using legal jargon in everyday life.

She lives in the mountains with her husband/ critique partner/ irl book boyfriend and their three fur babies. She's a sucker for reality TV, New Girl, and scary movies in the daytime. Greer admits she's a messy eater, ruiner of shirts, and does NOT share food or wine.

Greer adores strong, sassy heroines and steamy second chances. She hopes to give readers an escape from the craziness of life and a safe place to feel too much. She'd LOVE to hear from you anytime! Except the morning. She hates mornings.

www.ingramcontent.com/pod-product-compliance
Lightning Source LLC
Chambersburg PA
CBHW031741180726
48283CB00005B/1620